Praise for Racing the Moon

'Engaging'

Sunday Tribune

'A warm-hearted sensitive story'

Publishing News

'Elegant, engaging and confidently written — you won't
put it down'

Patricia Scanlan

'Enjoy the fun in an entertaining, fast-paced, often
hilarious debut'

The Irish Times, Dublin

Also by Terri Prone
Blood Brothers, Soul Sisters
Racing the Moon

About the author

Terri Prone has written several non-fiction bestsellers
and in 1994 published a collection of short stories,
Blood Brothers, Soul Sisters. Terri Prone is Managing
Director of Carr Communications, a PR firm; she
is married to consultant Tom Savage and has one
son, Anton.

Swinging On A Star

Terri Prone

CORONET BOOKS
Hodder & Stoughton

Copyright © 1999 by Terri Prone

The right of Terri Prone to be identified as the Author of the
Work has been asserted by her in
accordance with the Copyright, Designs and Patents Act 1988.

First published in 1999 by Marino Books
An imprint of Mercier Press
First published in Great Britain in 2000 by Hodder and Stoughton
First published in paperback in 2000 by Hodder and Stoughton
A division of Hodder Headline

A Coronet Paperback

10 9 8 7 6 5 4 3 2 1

A CIP catalogue record for this title is available from The
British Library.

ISBN 0 340 73824 3

Typeset by Palimpsest Book Production Limited,
Polmont, Stirlingshire
Printed and bound in Great Britain by
Clays Ltd, St Ives plc.

Hodder and Stoughton
A division of Hodder Headline
338 Euston Road
London NW1 3BH

For William B.,
without whose help,
life would be so simple

Contents

CHAPTER ONE

Screams, Lies and Misunderstandings

—————⫸●⫷—————

Nobody knows why I screamed for the first six months of my life, but the neighbours held it against me for life. When I was a toddler, the minute I was introduced to some adult around the area, she would say, 'Oh, this is the little girl we prayed for,' and everybody but me would laugh.

I didn't laugh because I could see they had hated me when I was smaller and they might hate me again if the wind changed. Awful things happened when the wind changed. My big sister was always warning me about it. I stuck out my tongue behind my father's back once and my sister said if the wind changed I would be left like that. I went to my room to test if I would be able to bear having my tongue out the whole time. After a while, the back part of my tongue got sore and the bit hanging outside got dry. Even when I took it back in again, it felt burned from being in the open air.

My sister was very pale and had long straight hair. She was an absolute angel. People always said that about her. That she was an absolute angel or just an angel. Her name was Gabrielle, so I thought the angel in the church statue of the Virgin Mary being told she was going to have the Baby Jesus was my sister with wings. The woman who lived at the end of the road heard me saying this and she told my mother I was a little fibber and my mother should watch me.

My mother thanked her very formally and walked home just fast enough, holding my hand, to make me run all the way, because my mother had long legs.

'Kindly go to your room,' she said when we got into the house.

When she was furious enough to say that awful word 'kindly', even my own room in the daytime was frightening, because the wind might change and I'd be left there for ever on my own.

I could hear my father's uneven footsteps some time later. I went to the window to look out at him. He waved at me, but I was afraid to wave back, for fear it would break the rules. Once before when I was sent to my room for cutting a worm into five pieces, happy thoughts invaded my mind after a while and I sang a song, which my mother said indicated how shallow and heartless I was, to be singing when I had killed a worm that did nothing but good for the world.

She would not listen to me saying that I was making a whole lot of new worms out of one old one, and that they had all wriggled happily away in different directions. So, on this occasion, I just looked at my father through the window and he was so surprised at me not waving at him, he took three steps backwards and waved at me again, to see had I misunderstood, but I stayed still, so he shook his head with a look that said he could get very cross with me, maybe even as cross as Mam.

Then there was a long time with no sound. After that I could hear him coming up the stairs. Each of our family made a different noise on the stairs. My sister always sounded regular, every footfall taking the same time as the last one, measured. My mother never walked up the stairs: she always ran. If she ran without saying anything, you were OK, but if she ran saying things at the same time, you knew you were in deep trouble. My father, on the other hand, had a funny missed beat in the way he came up the stairs. This was because he had broken his leg three times. The same leg getting broken so much resulted in it being shorter than the other one. I used to look at the shorter leg and think I was its special friend, because I was small compared to everybody else, just like it was. I figured the leg got fed up with growing and getting broken and having to grow again and just stopped.

When he came into the bedroom, my father did not look cross. He looked so sad and disappointed, I began to cry. When he took me on his knee and stroked my hair, I cried more. He said telling lies was the worst thing in the world. This was confusing, because a few days before, I had heard him saying that stealing was the worst thing in the world.

Maybe everything was the worst thing until the wind changed, I thought. Then whatever was the worst thing the time the wind changed would stay the worst thing forever. I said I knew that people who told lies went to hell for all eternity. He seemed unsure about this, so I explained to him that in hell you got burned in a circle because Fr Dave had told me that.

'In a circle?' Daddy asked and I said yes because that allowed it to go on all the time, you kept going back to the beginning.

'Oh, infinity,' he said and then told me never to mind about that, the issue was telling lies about black and white photographs of Gabrielle being in the church.

I told him I never said there were black and white photographs, and he said yes I did, and I began to cry again and he said there was no point in crying, that all the tears in the ocean wouldn't wash a lie off my soul. For a long time after that, I tried to find out from grown-up people how tears got from the sea into your eyes, but nobody seemed to know, so I gave up. I found grown-ups a lot like that. They gave you clues to secrets and then said you had imagined it.

My father said that each of us has a soul like our own little vest that nobody else can take and could never be mistaken for anybody else's, not for a minute. I didn't like vests because in the winter my mother made us wear woolly ones and they were hot and itchy. Also my Auntie Mae gave me vests for Christmas and I hated her for that. My father said these vests were where God kept score, which I thought was very mean of God, who could make anything up he wanted to, so why would he use vests when he could have given each of us a pad or a scroll? There were plenty of scrolls in holy pictures; it wasn't as if they were difficult to do.

'It's figurative,' my father said, so I knew God only used the vests for his rough work, like my father did when he was doing tots and used the backs of old pages torn from a used-up ledger.

'Have we each got a scroll, too?' I asked, but he said I wasn't to be distracting myself with scrolls and I was definitely to stop telling lies to attract attention to myself. I thought this was unfair; I never wanted attention to myself. The minute an adult had their attention drawn to me the first thing they said was about me screaming for the first six months. They always said it with their mouth pulled up in a smile but not their eyes.

'What are you doing, making faces?' my father said, which I could not answer because he seemed to have answered the question himself by saying I was making faces, but he persisted at me. So I told him I was thinking about the way people looked when they said I screamed for the six months. He said would I for God's sake concentrate on one thing at a time or I would end up in a loony bin dribbling. I asked him what a loony bin was and he closed his eyes and didn't say anything.

It was almost as if he was afraid words would escape by themselves, because he kept his mouth so tightly closed. All the air had to go in and out his nose and the hairs in his nose came down playing peep at me when he breathed out and went back up when he breathed in. I asked him if I was very good would I get hairs in my nose like his when I grew up and he put one big hand over his nose and the rest of his face which was turning a very deep red, and put his other arm around me and squashed me against his chest.

I always loved being against my father's chest because it made noises my mother's chest did not make. She said that was because he consumed coffin nails, but he said not to mind her, he just had the occasional fag. My sister gave me a completely different reason. She said it was wheezing, the noise, because of him smoking cigarettes. One of them had to be telling lies about it, but grown-ups who tell lies do not get into trouble for it.

After a long time, my father took me back downstairs and we had our tea. My mother said she would have been less annoyed if I had told the lie to anybody else.

'But that one,' she said. 'I mean, what better could we expect of someone who'd put their Christmas tree in the front window with balloons on it.'

My mother could give out so much that she would put herself back into good humour, so by the time tea was over she was in great form again. Mostly she was in good form, especially when she was sure of things.

My father and mother were sure of different kinds of things.

Dad was sure about big, worldwide things. Like if the Pope sold all his tiaras, there would be no poverty in the world. He quite often didn't believe what was on the news in the morning. We would all be at the breakfast table eating porridge when the news came on. My father made porridge overnight in the winter using a double-saucepan. I used to check every day when summer would be back because in summer you got to eat cornflakes instead. Porridge was a grey, yet moving, round slab of slime surrounded by lukewarm milk. If you hadn't learned the knack of closing off your nose and swallowing the minute the porridge slid off the spoon into your mouth, you would gag. If you gagged you got into trouble with both parents: one because of your bad manners, the other because you weren't respecting good food.

My mother said to a neighbour once that I was very quiet in the mornings. She did not realise that you cannot talk and at the same time concentrate on getting through porridge without gagging. It helps if you count the spoonfuls. You'd have at least ten and sometimes twelve. You would get hopeful at about spoonful number nine, but if you tried to talk at the same time, you'd get something wrong. I got so many things wrong anyway, I couldn't afford to start first thing in the morning.

I really got it wrong the time the man who knew both my parents came to the house one morning to deliver replacement china. Mam gave him a cup of tea with some fruitcake. She gave me some of the icing off the fruitcake.

When he was leaving, the man lifted me up so I could see into his face and said to me that one day he was going to come and get my mother to run away with him because she was a great woman. He was such a nice man, I didn't want to upset him by telling him not to do this, but later that day I mentioned it to my father because I thought he could stop my mother running away. He made me repeat what I had said, which was always a bad sign. Grown-ups hear you fine the first time. When they ask you to say something again they are just getting you into a better position for punishment.

'He said he was going to get Mam to run away with him because she was so great,' I said.

'Well, fuck that for a haircut,' my father said.

I thought for a moment he was going to hit me, but he went downstairs into the kitchen and there was shouting. I watched him and Mam very carefully for the next day, but neither of them got their hair cut. When I asked my sister what it meant she got red in the face and said I didn't need to know. I said I did so need to know, that she knew things and it was not fair that I didn't know things, but she said there was a time and a place. This was a phrase my mother used when she was being sure about things, and my sister, who was older than me, sounded quite like my mother when she said things like that. But whenever I said them, I got into trouble. I kept hoping they would make me sound sure of myself, but they never did.

My mother was sure of things like illness. Not that long after I stopped screaming, I started wheezing.

At first, they thought it would go away. When it settled in, Mam became the greatest expert on severe asthma. To such an extent that, at four, I thought 'feathers' was a dirty word. My mother behaved as if all feathers were out to get you. You couldn't have feather pillows or a down duvet. Before you went on holidays, you had to warn the hotel to be sure to have foam everything. You couldn't even own a budgie. You couldn't have a dog or a cat either, because fur was nearly as bad as feathers.

My sister wanted me to have a pet of some kind, because half the time I could not go out playing. Whenever she watched nature programmes on television, she would get ideas and call me to have a look. I never liked any of the things she saw. They never looked friendly. She said things with fur and feathers looked friendly, particularly as babies, but things with simple skin or scales didn't. Then she came across an ad in a magazine for an ant farm. It said it was all enclosed, with nutrients included, sealed inside clear lucite.

'Daisy could watch them work all day,' Gabrielle said, getting enthusiastic about this.

'Daisy could watch me work all day,' my mother said. 'And since I work all day to bloodywell keep insects *out* of the house, I don't see why we should spend good money to bring insects *into* the house. Let her read a book about ants.'

Gabrielle bought me this really old book about the life of the ant, but at the same time she got the idea that a turtle would be the best. A turtle seemed to fulfil all requirements. It didn't live in water or behind lucite, so I would be able to pet it. It had neither fur nor feathers and it hibernated half the year so it wouldn't be a burden on anyone. We would get a break from it in the winter.

She brought home a leaflet from a pet shop with pictures of box turtles. I didn't like the look of them. Truth be told, I was afraid of them, with their baldy wrinkly old heads and the way they looked sideways at you as if they knew every fib you ever told. Because I adored Gabrielle, I probably would have allowed her to wish a box turtle on me if my mother hadn't put the kybosh on it by discovering that turtles sometimes carried diseases. Really awful diseases I would get on my fingers by stroking the creatures. After that, Gabrielle gave up on pets and left me to my bald dolls.

All my dolls had been shaved by my mother because she was convinced their hair would harbour the house dust mite. He was the little guy who ran around looking for me to give me an asthma attack. I was convinced that if I stayed awake very late at night, I could catch him at it. One of my dolls was OK when she was shaved, because under her glued-on hair, the hard plastic of her head was shaped in a 1920's wavy hairdo. Whoever made that doll, my father said, had the foresight to work out that she might lose her hair and make sure she was presentable underneath. Pity the Almighty wasn't as thoughtful, he would say.

My other doll looked really peculiar, because she had this mechanism that allowed you to turn a knob and make her hair 'grow' out through holes in her scalp. You could put rollers in it and everything. After you styled her hair, you turned the knob the other way so the long hair got sucked back through the holes leaving her with just a bit.

'An inch left above ground,' my father would say about this doll.

After shaving, though, all she had was dozens of perfectly round holes in her head. The first time she fell in the bath, her whole head fizzed out bubbles as she sank to the bottom. Gabrielle had her out in a second and turned upside down. The water came back out of her like she was a watering can, but later her arms and legs would not move. My father said the water had probably rusted her insides and my mother said I should treat her as if she had rheumatism.

It wasn't that hard to get used to her arms and legs staying in the one position. Her eyes being fixed was more difficult. The eyelids used to close down with a click you could hear if you laid her on her back, and open up again – click – the minute you sat her back up, but now they would stay open even when you were trying to get her to sleep and if you shoved down the lids with your finger, you had to poke them open again when you woke her up. My father, whenever he would come across her lying on her back with her eyes open, would say she had insomnia.

'Insomnia and migraine are pretensions of the

under-employed,' my mother said. 'A good day's scrubbing would kill them.'

It was lovely, the way she said it. She put in this gesture at the end, as if she was sweeping these insomnia and migraine people into the wastebasket. I renamed the two dolls Migraine and Insomnia. I used to stand in my room and tell them they were underemployed and a good day's scrubbing would kill them. One day Gabrielle, hearing this, wanted to know why any of my dolls would have to do a good day's scrubbing.

'I'll explain later,' I told her, because that was what was always being said to me.

My father would actually try to explain things, like the time my mother said that people who tell you their dreams should be put down. I said put down where and my father said my mother meant they should be put to sleep. But that was no help of an explanation because if every time you went to tell someone your dreams you got sent to sleep, you would have more dreams and no time at all to tell them in.

Once I learned to read, I got sure of some things, but it was better not to say them out loud because of mispronunciations. Ballina, a town in the west of Ireland, I thought had a lovely name, the sort of name I would have liked for myself, but when I said it to my mother — 'Baleena' — she laughed and said it was 'Balinnah', which was not half as pleasant.

None of the people in the books I read lived in places or wore clothes or did things that were anything like what I knew. There was a silly man who had a servant, for example. Nobody I knew had servants. This man wore spats, which were things with buttons up the side on the outside of his shoes. In another book, there was a family called the Peppers who had high button boots. There was a little boy who cleaned chimneys by climbing up them, which would have got me half-killed by my mother.

There was never anybody in any book that had asthma. Probably nothing would have happened in stories if the characters were wheezing all the time. Cinderella wouldn't have been able to do the dusty housework her relatives made her do before the prince took her away from her stepmother. It was dead easy for Little Red Riding Hood to have a discussion with the wolf dressed up as her grandmother in the bed, but if she had asthma, and if a wolf was anything like the German shepherd dog on our road, his fur would have made her wheeze so she wouldn't have had the breath for all the comments about his nose and teeth.

When the wheezing got really bad, I would use

my inhaler. If I needed to use it more than twice, my mother wouldn't let me. She said it would kill me and that if I lay down on the floor on my back, things would ease. I would lie down near the window where I could see out. The hard wood of the floor hurt the back of my head, but my father said not to complain because my mother had taken up all the carpets because of my asthma. There were trees I could watch. Within their tree shape in the summer were all sorts of things like a map of Ireland and an old man's face with a beard.

Where we lived was near an airfield, so I would often see small planes coming in uncertainly as learners lined them up for landing. My dad bought me books so I could know which was a Cessna or a Piper and I got good at spotting which were old and which were new planes. The airfield was also the place where, during the summer, the plane that carried messages was kept. Usually, it trailed a long banner that said HB Ice Cream but sometimes it was for something different.

During an election, it carried the name of a man who wanted to be elected, but the spelling was wrong so the newspapers said he wasn't going to pay. I was afraid that would stop the plane, but a few weeks later, when the weather got hot, it was back up trailing the ice-cream message.

CHAPTER TWO

Audition and After

———◆———

Whenever I asked questions like, 'If the pilot of that plane turned right suddenly, could he get his tail caught in his propeller?' my parents would always tell me to look it up in a book. Which was very unfair, because it's only single words you can look up.

You can't look it up when your mother condemns a neighbour as the kind of person who uses margarine when baking a cake or when she says 'Pleased to meet you' is the mark of someone with no manners at all or when she says no girl under twelve should be allowed to grow her hair long no matter what the fashion is because it weakens the hair for the rest of her life.

There seemed to be guaranteed things other people

knew that I did not. They were as guaranteed as Tuesday following Monday, but I could never get the handle on them. My mother knew most of them. It wasn't just that she was certain when she said something like 'No human being should ever do something a machine can do.' She was pleased with being certain. I thought it would be fantastic to have those certainties and be that pleased. I was always on the hunt for them, asking the questions I thought would pin them down for me.

After a while when I had a question I didn't think my family could answer, I would ask other people. Like the priest who sometimes came to the house. Or the teacher when I went to school. Grown-ups, I found, are not happy being asked questions unless the questions belong in the thing they are talking about at the time. If you give them a saved-up question, they don't like it. They think you're trying to catch them out. Or that you're weird. Or sometimes that you're slow.

It took me a while to work all this out and to stop telling one grown-up what another grown-up had said. But gradually, I stopped getting into trouble. I just read and listened and didn't say much. Some people thought I was shy, but I wasn't. Some people thought I was stupid. At the beginning of secondary school, by comparison with Gabrielle, the teachers were sure I was stupid.

My sister was the star of the school because she was so clever and good at sport as well. If you have an older sister who is a star, her name gets like a surname: it applies to everybody coming from that family. You have to respond to it, even though you have a first name of your own, because the teachers don't really learn your own name. They stick with the name of your sister. My pet name at home – Daisy – did not go to school with me. The teachers never learned my real name – Dominique. I just answered to Gabrielle.

Mam got mad about this when she found out, because she hated comparisons between the two of us. She wouldn't let the teachers mention my sister in the same breath as me. The teacher who did the comparing said our IQ level was different. My mother said IQ was like hair colour. All sorts of things, including age, could change it.

'Dominique is not instinctive, she is systematic,' she said. 'Once she understands the system, she can learn anything. And will learn anything.'

Just when I thought I was coming to grips with school and not having so many misunderstandings where grown-ups thought I was lying to them when I wasn't, everything shifted again.

One day Mam gave me a page to learn off by heart but said that it wasn't for school, it was for an audition. She made me sit in my father's chair so the light from the kitchen window would be on my face. Then she told me I was eight years of age (I was actually eleven going on twelve, but very small for my age) and had just woken up from a car crash and wanted to get out of bed but my legs wouldn't work and that made me cry. Do it, my mother said, and I imagined my legs broken. Cry, my mother said, so I sucked all the sadness into one place, which made my throat hurt, and I began to cry.

My mother said that was OK and we took the bus to the TV station. Mam was brought to one place, and I got taken to a rehearsal room where there were lots of girls my age. They were in sort of clumps. Some of them were clumped by school uniform. The dark-greeny ones stayed together, and the wine-coloured ones were in a separate bunch. There were other clumps, too, and after a while I could tell that those clumps (they didn't have a unifying school uniform) were made up of girls attending a particular speech and drama school. There were maybe four or five speech and drama schools represented, and they kind of rehearsed out loud in a competitive way.

One girl asked her companions, very loudly, if they thought the audition would involve any fencing, and the girls from that school put their legs in odd positions and made as if they were sword-fighting. The girl was very dark, with jet black hair that was wrinkly. If it had been cut short, it might have been curly, but it went down nearly to her waist so all you could see were wrinkles. She looked like a princess in a fairytale book except that her hair started low on her forehead. If it had waited for another inch before starting, it would have been better. As it was, she had a slight monkey look to her.

To fill in the time, a few of the girls in the rehearsal room started saying stuff out loud, and I realised they had learned something in preparation for this audition that I had not. Maybe my mother had not known all the rules. I asked the monkey-princess girl if she had a copy of it. She smiled at me and thought about it.

'It's just lines,' she said.

I was going to say to her what my mother was always saying to me: 'That's not what I asked you.' But I knew, looking at her, that she knew what I wanted to know and if she had the lines, whatever that was, she would keep them away from me out of spite. She was standing there, smoothing the front of her skirt in a way I never saw a real girl doing before, waiting to see what I would do. So I just smiled back at her and didn't say anything. Shortly afterwards, she got called out – they were pulling the girls out one by one in a sequence that made me think they were taking all the girls from one drama class and then going on to all the girls from another drama class.

When the monkey-princess came back, she was pink in the face and thrilled with herself. I went over to a corner and picked up a magazine so she would not think I was listening, but I was. She went through everything she had done out loud. You think you're so smart, I thought, not giving me those lines, but now you've gone through them out loud so I nearly know them anyway.

I was one of the last to be taken out. When it was my turn, I was brought into a place so bright, it was as if all of summer had been concentrated in this one big room with a curtain all the way around it and a black ceiling with metal pipes criss-crossing it with huge lights hanging from the criss-cross bars. There was a bed and I was told to get into it, so I slipped off my shoes and got in. A man sat down beside the bed and smiled at me.

'I'll be feeding you your lines,' he said

I had no idea what that meant, but I smiled back at him. There were men on cameras that moved

smoothly around the floor like skaters in long skirts.
It was lovely and warm. One of the men shouted out
a lot of numbers and everything went quiet. The man
sitting beside the bed said something to me. I said
back to him what I had learned off. He nodded and
said something else. This time, I could not think of
the answer. I could feel my eyes filling up with tears
at the shame.

Then words that were nearly but not quite right
came into my head and I said them. A camera started
to slink in close behind him when I was trying to think
of the right words. I suddenly had this sureness that
cameras were like cats when you went 'pish-wish-wish'
to them – they liked to be in close, but they didn't like
you to be too direct in persuading them. So I looked
away from the man while the tears came during the
longest bit and sure enough out of the side of my
eyes I could see the camera slithering even closer.

After the last lines I got out, the man said nothing,
just looked at me, and because I did not know what
to do, I closed my eyes as if I were going to sleep. The
next thing was someone shouted a single word and the
man who had been sitting beside the bed helped me
on with my shoes.

'I think we'll be seeing you again,' he said. 'Mind
you, I've said nothing,' he added.

I did not understand this, either, but I imagined it might be one of those things you kept in a secret place in your mind and later, all would be revealed the way magicians did it.

I was taken back to the room where the other girls were. A few more were lined up, ready for their chance. Anyone would be able to spot the ones who hadn't yet done their audition and the ones who had. The ones who had were sort of ratty but relaxed. They were fighting with each other about things that had happened in school. The monkey-princess didn't get involved with any of that. She kept looking at me out of the side of her eyes. Eventually, I just turned and stared at her. She came over to me and offered me a sweet. I said thank you but no.

'You didn't know the script that well, did you?' she said very sympathetically.

The question was as hard as a thump. I shook my head, glad that my mother could not hear what the dark girl had said. I could feel my wheezes beginning to start.

'You probably didn't get it from them in time,' she said.

'When did you get it?' I asked.

She shrugged as if she didn't understand the

question, although I knew right well she did, but that she wanted me to feel guilty. There was no way she was going to tell me anything that would make this failure easier for me. I was staring at her again, but not deliberately this time. I was just trying to understand why this person I had never met would want me to know I had done badly.

The man who had been shouting in the studio opened the door of the rehearsal room and everything — every conversation, every argument, every movement — within the room stopped dead. He didn't even have to raise his voice to say that everybody could go home except — he looked down at his bit of paper — Dominique Dempsey and Richelle Governey. The monkey-princess put her hands up to the sides of her cheeks the way beauty contest winners do: fingers straight. That, and the others from her speech and drama class running around telling her she was great and that they always knew she was, proved she was Richelle Governey. I sat there, hoping they would all go away so I would not be noticed for staying. I think she thought I was upset, because she patted the front bit of my arm the way a grown-up that has no children would. Grown-ups that have no children do things differently. They sort of scruffle your hair. Grown-ups with children never scruffle your hair because they know they would have your mother to contend with.

Other girls were asking out loud who was Dominique Dempsey, was she in your group or your school? They worked out that it was me and they could hardly believe it, particularly the monkey-princess, but she was so busy getting girls from her group to take her belongings home with them so she would not have a million and one things to carry that she didn't pay that much attention to me. The room got emptied and the shouting man asked did we have someone with us?

I said my mother was out in the lobby and the monkey-princess said her elocution teacher was out there, too. The man said he would bring the series producer to talk to us. The monkey-princess went off to the ladies' room and came back with her wrinkly hair smoothed down. Richelle, I thought. I must call you Richelle, even in my own mind. She was back to giving me awful looks. We are the finalists, I thought, and she wishes I was dead.

The series producer was a big fair man in corduroy trousers. He sat on the edge of the table and Richelle and I automatically sat down in front of him.

'We've seen notable talent in action today,' he said. 'None of the auditions was poor.'

This is where Gabrielle would say yeah-yeah-yeah-cut-to-the-chase, I thought. Adults are always putting things in context and setting out to make losers feel better about losing, which is stupid. If you lose, you lose and children know that perfectly well.

'However, we have selected our Maria,' he said. 'Your mother is with our legal people at the moment, sorting out a contract.'

He nodded to me.

'Because you are a minor, there's a rake of laws we have to obey to prove we're not exploiting you. In order to keep the flow of work – we're always going to be under pressure – we'll have to have a body double for you. Someone very close to you in build. Richelle, I understand our legal people are talking to your father on the phone to offer a contract along those lines.'

She had her head lowered and was looking at him out from under her brows. Her eyes were swimming with tears, but he let on not to know and I looked away.

'The two of you will be working very closely together for the next six months, so I hope you'll get along.'

'Of course we'll get along,' she said, and threw her arms around me.

I was amazed. In my experience, girls your own age don't really throw their arms around you. I hugged her back, but only a bit, because I didn't want to get trapped in something that felt so peculiar. When she got back into her chair, the tears were gone, so I figured that was why she had done the hug. The series producer smiled at us in a distant way and went off.

The minute he was gone she stopped smiling.

'You're a cheat,' she hissed at me. 'You couldn't even remember all the lines when you were doing the test.'

'I know,' I said.

'I remembered every word, so I did,' she said and started to spurt crying.

I didn't know what to do. I would always try to mind anyone who was crying, but she seemed to be crying *at* me. It felt the same as if she was slapping me with her crying. If it had been normal crying, I would have tried to be like my dad. I'd have said she was probably mighty in the audition, but that you win some, you lose some and let's go home now and not be putting ourselves in bad humour.

She got mad at herself for crying and when my mother and her elocution teacher came for us was able, as she went out the door, to fix me with a look so poisonous it was like two streaks of lightning coming out of her eyes. Her teacher put her head back in about a minute later. She was a roundy easygoing kind of woman.

'Don't let that little viper get to you,' she said.

My mother looked at me, not having any idea what she was talking about.

'You did well, they picked you – end of story,' the roundy teacher said. 'That little madam has notions. Although you'd be surprised if she didn't, with that headbanger of a father. Forget about her and congratulations.'

My mother said much the same on the way home when I explained what happened. She had signed on my behalf a contract for a soap opera they were going to run five nights a week. Arrangements would have to be made about education and important issues, she said, making it perfectly clear that Richelle Governey was not an important issue, although my own feeling was that to Richelle Governey, she was the most important issue in the world.

When I arrived for the first day's work, there was a dressing room for me with a card stuck into a metal card holder on the door, giving my name. Underneath, in brackets, it gave Richelle Governey's name. Not only would we be sharing a dressing room, but every time she came to the door, she would see herself in brackets, in a constant comparison she could not win. I asked the shouting man, whose title turned out to be Floor Manager, if the card could not be made more friendly to her. That, as it turned out, was a stupid thing to do, because he rubbished my concerns to me, but then went off and told everybody else how nice I was, not wanting the body double to be upset about being in brackets. In Ireland, everything ever said about anybody gets back to the person within days. The result was that the first day Richelle and I were together in the room, she mimicked the floor manager telling the others about me trying to get the card changed.

'Little Miss Nice,' she hissed at me. 'Little Miss Brown Nose.'

I did not know what that meant, but it sounded bad.

'Little Miss Arse-licker,' she said. 'Making sure everybody knows I'm only muck.'

That evening, I made the worst mistake of all. I told Gabrielle about this Richelle who hated me. For a minute, I was afraid she would tell my parents, although I had made her promise in advance not to. She got so furious for me that I knew she would never be able to be natural if she met Richelle. Sometimes allies are worse than enemies and you wish you had never called them in. I decided that night never to tell any of the older people about Richelle, because she was very clever always being sunshiny and pleasant to me whenever there were people around, then the minute the door closed behind them, her smile wiping off so completely it was difficult to remember what it had looked like or that she could smile at all. Older people would not understand. The thing to do was to not say anything to her or about her, just smile at her. But because she was there, all day every day, it was like trying to smile into a black mirror filled with a growling hater.

Leaving the dressing room to go into the studio felt the way I imagined escaping from a dark clammy cave would feel. Once I was immersed in doing the work or listening to the other people in the programme, it numbed the dread I had when I was near her. I got a reputation, early on, for always being on time or early and for learning from the older actors, but mostly that was because I wanted to avoid being in the dressing room with the double. Not that she was always there. Some days she was not there at all. Those days were the best.

There was this old actor called Gareth De Black who was no use for stage any more because he could not learn lines, but the audience did not know this and regarded him as a classy actor. He was the grandfather of my character. That let them use his name to attract viewers early on, but once the series had been established, they were going to kill him in a car crash and me too, although I would live a week or so after him to say very touching things from the point of view of a dying eight-year-old.

That was why I had only a six-month contract. The rehearsals began immediately and went on during the summer holidays, with filming beginning in August. Six weeks after the first scenes were filmed, they were broadcast, and my life turned inside out. Not at home, but at school. The day I went in after the first broadcast, it was like when someone pins a notice on your back without you knowing, saying 'Kick me' or 'Stick out your tongue at me.' Everybody seemed to be looking twice at me. Some of the younger children pointed at me – I could have been a horse in the corridor, they thought I was so extraordinary. In Gabrielle's class, they all talked to her, and she began calling me 'Star of Stage, Screen and Radio'.

I wasn't a real star of anything, though. Just a bit famous. My mother, after the first week, began dropping me off early at school because she didn't want other parents coming over and telling her she must be proud of me. She said what nonsense and that my studies were much more important. Sometimes people would recognise me in the street and ask me about the show. The great thing I discovered through those early months is that most people who ask you questions do not want information from you, they just want you to make a little patch for them to stand on while they tell you things. I got very good at listening to them.

I did not tell anybody how awful the old actor Gareth De Black was. Especially his wife, who was there minding him the whole time. Even when he was looking for a cup of coffee, he would strike a pose like Parnell in the statue and throw his hand out, saying, 'Bitch, brrrring me a cup of coffee.' In the beginning, I saved up what he said and asked at home over the evening meal what was meant, but my father kept saying to my mother that I should not be in the company of that kind of person, so I gave up looking for explanations and I never told them that Gareth De Black sometimes wet himself and didn't seem to notice. His wife would get two of the stagehands to help her and they would take him away and bring him back in clean clothes.

He could not learn lines at all, but they had made him blind which was helpful, because he could look vaguely at anything in the room when he was supposed to be talking to you, and they would write his lines on the wall or one of the staff would hold up a poster with his lines on it. It was really awful how badly he read the lines, but nobody watching at home seemed to mind. It was as if he came on screen wrapped up in memories of what he had been, so people thought he was being thoughtful when he had a blank, or naturalistic when he would mispronounce things or fumble words. Anyway, he had a very posh way of saying words, and if you are posh, people sneer behind your back but they are impressed, still. You'll hear them saying the posh person must be very educated.

Coming up to the point where the car crash was going to happen, he was getting worse and worse. One day he was so bad that they had to cut most of his lines and give them to me, so I was sort of saying his thoughts to him out loud.

'Grandad, you must be thinking about the time they thought you were Michael Collins and pulled you off the dray you were driving to interrogate you?' I would say.

'I am,' he would say.

'Because you were a big, handsome man, then, Grandad. A big, handsome man.'

'I was,' he would say. 'I was.'

'Afraid of nothing,' I would say. 'Afraid of no man,' and he would repeat it.

In between the takes, I would watch his wife jollying him along.

'You can get anyone to do anything if you flatter them enough,' she told me one day. 'Flatter someone who has never climbed a hill in their life and they'll climb Mount Everest for you. You just have to pretend that it isn't flattery.'

Her theory was that everybody has an unfillable hole in them when it comes to flattery. I used to imitate her. Not with her husband. But I would tell other actors they were great, even when they weren't. That made me quite popular. They didn't like Mam that much, but they liked me. Mainly they didn't like Mam because she was always on the watch for anything that would make me wheeze, so the minute one of them lit up a cigarette, she was on them, they said, like The Wrath of God. After a while, they called my mother The Wrath of God, although I don't think she ever knew.

I did try to flatter Richelle Governey. She had to wear a blonde wig when she was sitting in shots for me. It was hot so she often got a headache as a result. In spite of that, when she was listening to Gareth De Black making a dog's dinner out of his lines, she would try to prompt him so he would get it right, but half the time, he would not hear her. I told her she was great to try, and for a moment or two, there would be a kind of a glow off her, but then she would go back, not just to hating me, but to hating everybody. She had bitter comments about everybody; you'd dread what she'd say about you behind your back. She said Gareth De Black's wife was much younger than he was because she had married him for his money, thinking he'd pop off and die but he was showing no signs of it, and she could get stuck with him for twenty more years if he came of long-lived stock.

There was a lot of publicity, but my mother was a Wrath of God on that, too. She put the word out that journalists were not to interview me, that she didn't want me having no normal life. Of course, I had no normal life anyway, but the secretaries belonging to the programme said that to the journalists and the journalists usually went away. Some of them wrote the stories anyway, based on pictures of me that got handed out by the Public Affairs Unit of the TV station, but my mother never showed me any of them, so I had no appreciation of how much this round-faced innocent grandchild of the TV dynasty had become imprinted on the public's mind. Mam spent a couple of hours a week processing fan mail.

Once, I heard her talking to my father about someone who had written a nasty letter wishing me bad luck.

'Fan mail is 99 per cent drivel and 1 per cent pure nastiness,' she told him, in exactly the same tone she used about migraine and insomnia.

I was very tempted to ask to see the letter, because I was sure the only person who would want to wish me bad luck would be Richelle. When I asked some of the other actors about nasty fan mail, though, several of them said that people seeing actors on TV get to feel they own them. Sometimes they want to marry the actors and if the actors won't, they stalk them. I thought stalking was when you put a stiff strong stick beside a plant that was a bit limp, tying the limp plant to the stick for support, but they said it was coming around to the actor's house at night and sending lots of letters. I was very glad I only had a six-month contract and was not the sort of famous actor that would happen to.

Because of spending so much time with really famous actors, I did not feel famous. Although feeling famous didn't seem to have much to do with how famous you really were.

Sometimes there would be an actor who was only in maybe three episodes, but would be convinced he was vital to the series. Sometimes, too, there would be actors who felt they were better known than they really were. Because almost all of them felt they *deserved* to be better known than they were, my fame, such as it was, did not interest them. Actors don't pay that much attention to people. Mainly they use people as mirrors to reflect back their own selves. So most of the actors went on thinking that I was eight or nine even when they were told several times I was older. They would rough up my hair and tell me I was a great kid even when I hadn't been particularly warm or winning, just ordinary.

Another thing they liked to do was give me tips and hints from their experience. Sometimes, when Gareth De Black was in good nick, even he would give me advice from his past. He said it was important to carry a white handkerchief, it being a very good way to attract the eye of the audience to take it out and blow your nose in it. A young actor who was regarded as a genius overheard the old actor saying that and went berserk, half at the old actor and half at me.

'What the hell is wrong with you?' he yelled at me. 'Why would you want dated oul' music hall tricks untalented oul' bollixes like him learned from their untalented oul' bollixes of grandfathers fecking around on the fringes of the fit-ups?'

'But you want people to look at you when you're acting,' I said.

He was going off in a sulk but he came back and sat down. He was very tall, so even though I was standing up, our eyes met. He whispered at me with such fierceness I hardly heard what he was saying.

'You want people to look at you. Not a hankie. Not a gesture. You. You. You. That is not done by a fucking trick. It is done by becoming still. Still. No motion. No flicking of your hands or your head. You just stand there and you make the decision that nobody in that audience has permission to look at anything but you, you draw their gaze as if you were a black hole pulling in the stars because that's what you are, an emotional black hole. It is an intellectual decision and a strength of the will, not a foothery fucking trick. You decide for an audience. You are their mind. You are not performing at their mind. You are their mind and if you decide to make their mind think you are beautiful or old or evil, that is what their mind will think, even if you have no lines to say. You think your truth at them. Think it. Truth. It is not the actor acting. It is the truth for as long as you decide it is the truth and you change their minds to that truth.'

I gazed at him wide-eyed. I had been practising

gazing wide-eyed for a while, because it had a great pay-off for Richelle, but this time it was genuine wide-eyed. The way he talked was so compelling it was like being afraid sunshine would go in behind a cloud and you wouldn't be able to remember what it had been like. He reached out, took hold of my jumper just below the collar and pulled me even further towards him with such force that when he let go of it, the wool stayed sticking out. I could see it without looking down. I was afraid to look down.

'And I know what you're doing, you creeping underage incubus,' he whispered. 'I know you for what you are, you parasite, you undersized bloodsucker. So steer clear of me in future, because if you come smarming at me, I'll break you in two.'

He pushed me with his closed fist in the chest so I had no choice but to sit down out of his way, then he walked off. I wanted to ask him was it not all right to flatter people if it made them feel better, if it gave them a sense of possibility they might otherwise not have? I wanted to scream at him that he was no gift to people himself with his bitter sidelong comments, that sometimes truth was not the virtue it was cracked up to be and that he had no right to call it smarming when more people were glad of meeting me in any one day than were glad of meeting him, which was true.

I wanted to tell him other actors said he'd be an alcoholic by the time he was twenty-five because he hated everybody and what was the good of genius if it corroded even its owner. Side by side with wanting to say all of these things to him was the realisation that not one of them would affect him.

I did not know, then, that his calling me an incubus sucking blood and smarming would stay with me as a self-defining truth all my life. It is an awful thing to carry around with you, all your life, a talking, berating version of somebody who has, in reality, forgotten you ever existed.

CHAPTER THREE

Being Allowed to Live

———————◆———————

My mother didn't tell me they had decided not to kill me. She must have been afraid I'd get excited over being allowed to live. Whenever I got excited, I wheezed. It was easier to let me go on thinking I was on a fast track to the cemetery.

The first time I heard I was going to survive was about five months after the soap began, when I was summoned to a script brainstormer. My mother, who had flu, sent Gabrielle along in her place. It would mean missing a couple of lectures at college, but Gabrielle said that would be no problem. Some of the young male actors knocked themselves out being nice to her in the big conference room where the brainstormer was to be held. She was asked was she OK for sandwiches and coffee about six times.

'Who's the head bottle-washer in the cords?' Gabrielle muttered to me out of the side of her mouth.

'The series producer. He's taking over direction of the key episodes at the end of the season where I nearly get killed. His name is Ambrose Feigherty.'

'The poor sod,' she said.

He came over to her and introduced himself. He never gave his name, I noticed. Just said, 'Call me Chip.' I wondered if Chip was an unexpected diminutive, the way Peggy is short for Margaret even though they don't sound at all alike.

'Call me Daphne,' Gabrielle told him in exactly the same confiding tone he had used. I nearly died.

'I thought your name was Gabrielle?' he asked.

'OK then, go with the Gabrielle,' she said, and he wandered off, looking puzzled.

'Chip,' she muttered to me. 'Frigging Chip. Can you imagine Mrs Feigherty calling her kid Chip?'

'Shhh,' I hissed, desperate that he would hear her. A couple of the scriptwriters near us were sniggering.

'Chip is like Chuck,' she whispered. 'American. Like Randy.'

'Hi, folks,' the series producer said, raising his

voice over the general conversation. 'Most of you know me. My friends call me Chip.'

'Your enemies called you Mary Magdalene,' Gabrielle said very quietly. 'I upchuck Chip.'

'As you know, we plan to end this first season on a high note,' Chip went on.

I found it difficult to concentrate on what he was saying because I was quietly testing out 'I upchuck Chip' as a tongue twister, saying it three times together quickly. It was better, I thought, than 'And still the sinking steamer sank.'

'So we will lose the grandfather and have a grievously injured granddaughter left at the end of the car crash. But we — we being the viewer — we won't necessarily know that one is dead and the other only injured. We'll leave that hanging.'

'Like who shot J. R., it will be that exciting,' someone said.

Chip looked sharply at them to see if they were being ironic, then went on.

'So the purpose of today's meeting is to harness the best creative thinking around this table and come up with the best way to do the crash. It will be one of the few scenes we'll shoot out of doors, off the set, so let's make it worth the expenditure.'

Because everything was shot in a few made-up settings

in the studio, there had never been a need to identify any car driven by a member of the drama family. It could have been a VW Beetle or a Jeep. One cast member offered his lemon of a car. suggesting it be filmed in such a way as to make inescapable what the brand was. Another said he didn't think Old Mikey would drive such a sporty car.

'Is Old Mikey driving the bloody thing? Oh, Jesus,' one of the actors said. 'Sorry, Mrs De Black.'

The old actor's wife laughed.

'Look at it this way,' she said. 'Once you kill him off, you never see him again. I get full title.'

'Here's how I see it,' Chip said, surfing past this. 'Tension building. Fast intercutting. Sense of over-whelming speed. Threat. We just know this is going to have a bad outcome — more intercutting, unbelievable impact, crushing, crumpling metal, splintering glass and the little girl thrown free while the car with the old man in it explodes.'

Gareth De Black's wife beamed at this. I supposed that the hassle she had with him made the prospect of seeing him exploded to bits — even in pretend form — something to look forward to. Everybody started to talk at once.

'No seat belt, serious implication,' a stolid man in navy said.

'Cameras'll have to be miles away or they'll get taken out by the flying flak.'

'Where the hell could you film that?'

'Why would the car go on fire?'

'What would the car have hit to make all this happen?'

The series producer patted the noise down, which allowed Gabrielle's tranquil comment to be heard.

'It may be worth registering at this point that The Wrath of God would not approve of Dominique being shot through a fragmented windscreen.'

There was a shocked silence for a second. Her own daughter referring to my mother by their secret nasty nickname? Then they laughed.

'Dummy,' one said.

'I won't take that personally,' she replied.

'No, I mean we'd use a dummy.'

'For what?'

'Sailing through the windscreen.'

'I'd do it. I wouldn't be afraid.'

Everybody turned to look at Richelle Governey, who was gazing at Chip while she offered to get airborne through broken glass for him.

'Never mind what the projectile is,' the special effects guy interrupted. 'What's the expulsive force?'

Richelle looked livid at being called a projectile. I didn't know what expulsive force meant.

'He's asking what's going to get the dummy airborne,' Gabrielle whispered. 'Like, are they going to shoot it from a cannon?'

'The crash will take care of that, surely,' someone said.

The special effects man looked withering. 'Oh, we're gonna crash one car once and a dummy sitting in the back seat – or this kid—' he gestured at Richelle '—is gonna take off on cue through the window and fly twenty feet ahead of the car.'

'Say if it's a truck they hit?'

'If it's a truck they hit, kiddo here has to do a vertical take-off in order to go splat on the windscreen of the truck.'

'She might go through it.'

'Through what?'

'The truck's windscreen.'

'Now, there's a thought,' the special effects guy said. 'Up, up and away, out one windscreen, in another, quick kiss for the trucker and bring up the credits, folks.'

'If she went through two windscreens, it would give her a reason for being confined to a wheelchair,' one of the writers said.

'Pardon me, you can't say confined to a wheel-chair.'

This last came from a woman I had never seen before. Evidently nobody had seen her before, because Chip apologised for not introducing her as coming from a disability advocacy group.

'Wheelchair users see their wheelchairs as freedom,' she said in a sort of pious way, the way people talk about counselling or achieving sobriety. 'They're the same as legs to the rest of us. We don't say we're confined to our legs, do we?'

There was one of those awful pauses where every-body politely hates the person who has just spoken. And hopes somebody else will remove them. Gabrielle scribbled on the pad in front of her, then slid it sideways so I could read it.

Call-me-Chip has his own little political correctness monitor!

I wrote beside her comment.

Give him a break.

She wrote back.

No. If he really cared about disability he'd find an actor who's permanently in a wheelchair.

I replied: *And make me unemployed?*

She smiled at me, then asked out loud how going through a windscreen, or even two, would put you in a wheelchair. The experience was surely more likely to make you bleed to death from multiple cuts?

'She's right,' a thirtyish thug to the left of the wheelchair woman said. He was introduced as an orthopaedic surgeon, there to advise on the injuries the victims should sustain. He had a thick neck on him like a movie heavy and an attitude to match.

'You're either going to get the kid to impact, head or back of the neck first, so hard it would fracture the C3 or 4 – the section of the spinal cord that would leave her a quadriplegic – or you're going to have to do it by crushing: getting her legs between the vehicles so what you end up with is eggshells in a polythene bag. She'd walk again, but pinning the bits together would take time.'

'The Wrath of God would want me to establish that for eggshell or C3 purposes, we're talking dummy, rather than Dominique,' Gabrielle said firmly.

'I wouldn't be afraid,' Richelle repeated.

Conor, the genius actor who had attacked me as a parasite, suddenly turned on her.

'Sweetheart, we've got the message. If self-immolation is called for, we do not pass go, we call you straight away. Anything close to Joan of Arc you have the franchise on.'

Neither Richelle nor I knew what self-immolation was, but she knew by his tone that he was mocking her, and in response she sulked, noticeably. The stolid guy in the navy spoke. 'If the little girl goes out the window—'

'Windscreen,' Gabrielle said.

'Does it matter?'

'Be kind of surprising, in a head-on collision, if one of the victims goes *pinng*, sideways out of a window.'

Please, Gabrielle, I thought, don't annoy these people. They will take it out on me. But the stolid man actually smiled at her and said she had a point.

'But anyway,' she prompted him.

'If she goes out the windscreen,' he conceded graciously, 'that means she had no seatbelt on—'

A chorus of tsk tsks and boos and cries of shame came from the actors present. Navy Blue looked taken aback by the histrionics.

'No skin off my nose,' he said shortly. 'But I gather this girl character is popular. A role model, even. Not having a seatbelt on is going to be taken as bad behaviour on her part.'

'She'll have to have a reason for undoing the safety belt,' Chip said.

'ESP,' one of the scriptwriters suggested, to instant irritation all round. 'I take it back,' he said. 'I eat it. I promise never to have another idea as long as I live. If I live.'

'Remember the way Princess Grace died?'

This was from Gareth De Black's wife. The younger people shook their heads.

'She was driving down a steep incline and had a stroke and her foot got stuck on the accelerator and her daughter was trying to steer it from the passenger seat and it went over a cliff or something.'

'Have Old Mikey have a stroke at the wheel. That'd be good.'

'But if he was having a stroke, his foot would relax, not jam against the pedal.'

'Have something fall on the pedal.'

'What the hell does anybody carry in the front seat of a car that's heavy? Not that many people put their ten-pound dumb-bells with them on the seat next to them like a handbag.'

'He could be wearing heavy boots.'

'Absolutely. Lot of senile grandparents wear steel-toed work boots these days. Cool and groovy,' Conor said.

Richelle was now saying nothing at all, just drawing. When she saw me looking, she put her forearm over her drawing.

She afraid you're going to steal it and sell it to the National Gallery? Gabrielle's note surprised me.

You don't miss much, I wrote by way of a response. She started to scribble again.

No, and the National Gallery's tongue is not hanging out for comic-book drawings of dead people bleeding like stuck pigs, either!

Richelle was watching the two of us, avid with curiosity. Gabrielle very noticeably put her forearm over our notes, the way Richelle had over her drawing.

Chip, meanwhile, had been writing the various suggestions on a flip chart. Now, he tore the sheet off and pinned it up on the wall. We all looked at it solemnly. He seemed to need us to.

'I'll tell you what I think we should really be aiming for,' he said. 'This crash should make some significant social comment.'

'Drive cars and you die,' Conor offered.

'Seriously.'

'Of course,' the young actor said, saluting. 'Not a dry arse in the house. No laughing at the back, you lot.'

'Maybe we should look at joyriding,' Chip said.

'Now? Great. I'd go for that,' Conor said, leaping to his feet.

'Conor, sit down and shut up or go away,' Chip ordered, all casual collectiveness gone.

'Thought you'd never ask,' Conor said. He reversed to the door bowing and kowtowing and exited.

'Feck,' Gabrielle said under her breath as the door closed behind him.

Easy knowing he never stabbed you with words, I thought.

'The Wrath of God wouldn't want Dominique to be joyriding,' Gabrielle said aloud.

Others rushed to explain that of course Chip meant the car with the little girl and her grandad would run into a joyrider's car. Or rather, be run into *by* a joyrider's car. It would give a wonderful opportunity to see a juvenile delinquent faced with the consequences of his act.

'That would provoke copycatting,' Navy Blue said. 'Kids who saw it would be stimulated to imitate it. The Commissioner would not countenance that.'

'And the Commissioner makes The Wrath of God look like a baa-lamb,' Gabrielle said. 'So our joyrider bites the dust. Hits the cutting-room floor. Shit, doesn't even get to the cutting-room. OK. How about a biker instead of a joyrider? One of those lovely fat guys with a ponytail at the back—'

'Difficult to have it at the front,' I said.

'On a Harley. Comes over the hill—'

'All bikers are already over the hill,' the props man said, as if he regularly had to fill orders for middle-aged bikers.

'—hits a pothole, loses control—'

'—only of the bike, we don't want biker filth around this nice domestic drama—'

'—comes flashing across the median into the path of Dominique and her grandad.'

'Flashing? On a motorbike?'

'I was once flashed at by a guy riding an ordinary bike.'

'You were? That guy had talent. Great sense of balance, anyway.'

'Feels on wheels.'

The policeman shook his head.

'G'wan,' Gabrielle said sadly. You're going to shoot my lovely exhibitionist biker in the ass, I just know.'

Navy Blue looked extremely regretful at being forced to do anything that would dismay Gabrielle in any way.

'It's just that I don't think even the heaviest biker would have the weight to stop a family car so suddenly that people would start popping out of windows.'

'Windscreens.'

'Exhaust pipes. Whatever. No. There wouldn't be

that much resistance in a biker. Even a well-built flashing biker.'

'With a pigtail out the back.'

'Anyway,' someone else said. 'The local authority would go bananas at you suggesting they were killing people with potholes.'

Richelle Governey was jumping up and down looking eager. When you are twelve or thirteen looking nine and you bounce up and down from a sitting position it just looks to everyone that you're dying to go to the loo. But Chip nodded to her, showing off, I thought, how democratic and patient he was.

'Aren't we forgetting your thing about a social comment, Chip?' she asked.

Gabrielle made a slurping noise beside me.

What a little arse-licker, she wrote on her pad. Then she put a little pointer after the second word and stuck 'obvious' above it. I took the pen and put an 'n' at the end of 'What a'.

'Could Old Mikey not develop Alzheimer's disease in the car?' Richelle glowed like a lamp and stopped jigging as she completed this offering.

Does Little Miss Creepo seriously think Alzheimer's comes on like a bad hair day? Gabrielle wrote.

'Where are we, anyway?' Gareth De Black's wife wanted to know.

'Conference Room 4, dearie,' the props man said. 'You've got a case of this instant, grow-your-own Alzheimer's? Forgetting where you are?'

'No, I mean where is this accident going to happen? Why are they out driving in the first place?'

'What's the motivation?' Gabrielle asked, worriedly, like a caricature of every Method actor.

'The motivation is they have to get killed,' I said, losing patience. 'The grandfather can have been a racing driver in his youth and show me what it was like to speed, then run into a post or an American tourist driving too fast or on the wrong side of the road or something. Do we need another car or thingie or will a lamppost or a bridge do, to run into?'

Someone said that every summer people got killed on coach tours. Coaches were really dangerous. Someone else pointed out that the fatalities connected with coaches usually happened halfway up an Alp or on an Autobahn. It was difficult to work up to Autobahn speed in Glendalough. So what, the coach-lover said, you could have the coach halfway up a mountain in Kerry, the grandfather come around this winding road in his car and whap.

'Jesus, that'd be great,' Gabrielle said. 'Wipe out twenty or more tourists in one blow.'

'Too many extras,' the production assistant said,

speaking for the first time. 'Too costly. A coach would also be too costly to wreck.'

Chip crossed out Tourist Coach on his sheet and hung it up. There were now four of these torn-out sheets stuck up around the room. They seemed to serve no purpose other than to give us all something to look at when we couldn't think of anything to say.

'They could hit a bollix,' Richelle said, bouncing again.

'No shortage of them.'

'Cost nothing.'

'Can I be the one who picks the particular bollix?'

'Whattya mean, a bollix?'

'One of those red and white things the guards put out for traffic,' Richelle said, losing confidence.

'Oh, a bollard. Too light.'

'Why'd we lose the truck? I had this final shot in mind: Dominique in a coma in the truck-driver's lap.'

'Too expensive,' the PA said again. 'The truck, I mean. Dominique isn't expensive.'

'Looks like we're down to hitting a bollix,' someone said. 'Cheapest option. No downsides.'

'Could we not drop the bollix on the car? A vandal on an overhead pedestrian bridge with a concrete block? Uh, uh. The Gardaí would disapprove of that, would they, Inspector? Put bad ideas into innocent heads, would it? OK. Forget the airborne bollix.'

Chip's summary now read:

Kid and Grandfather out for spin.

G/father stroke (?) Heart attack(?)

Foot on accelerator.

Kid tries to steer.

Car hits bridge.

'That would certainly make a quadriplegic out of her,' the orthopaedic surgeon said with relief. 'She comes out the windscreen, straight into the bridge, no problem.'

'A cripple for life?'

'A person with a disability,' the advocacy woman said. We had all forgotten she was there. 'You have to put the person first, before the disability,' she explained. 'And you can't call them a cripple.'

'But if they are?'

'Are what?'

'Crippled. If they are crippled, they are a cripple.'

'Crip for short.'

'No, they're not.'

Chip indicated that this linguistics issue was way down the line.

'You could have it filmed from above, so that you just see these tiny cars down below, and have one of them get in front of the other — there could even be a commentary, like it was being filmed by one of those traffic eye-in-the-sky helicopters—'

'O. J. Simpson meets Lorraine Keane? I don't think so.'

Gabrielle, looking thoughtful, was writing on the pad during all of this. Finished, she lifted her arm so I could see it.

I thought these people were supposed to be brilliant and creative?

I wrote just below her sentence.

Actors are dull except when there's bright lights on.

'Gabrielle, you've been making notes—' I blushed as if it was me who had been caught out. Of course, if making notes was wrong, I did share the guilt. 'And you're an outsider. Do you have any ideas to share with us before we wind up?'

Gabrielle looked at Chip for a long, silent moment. I could feel the heat of my blush dying down, so sure was I that she would not say something foolish.

'Thank you, Chip.'

He beamed. God, I thought, grown-ups can't be that easy to buy, can they? But then it struck me that it must have something to do with Gabrielle. If Richelle called Ambrose Chip, which she did all the time, it didn't make him feel great. When Gabrielle, sitting there so coolly comfortable, so easy with everyone, did the same thing, it obviously felt wonderful to him.

'If you can't afford a coach, you can't afford a car crash,' Gabrielle said. 'The viewers have all seen the great car chases in classic films. *Bullitt* and *The French Connection* and the James Bond movies – great cars, great chases, great crashes. On a small budget, you can only do something Mickey Mouse. What if you did a police officer's report with nothing but black on the screen, something that gave all the details, but unemotionally, so the viewer is saying, "But that happened to friends of mine, friends I watch every day." Something like that?'

There was a small silence.

'Dominique, do you have other sisters as bright as this one?' the prop man eventually asked.

I shook my head.

'That's a relief,' he said. 'I thought The Wrath of God might be breeding a whole new bunch of gorgeous superhumans out there in suburbia.'

When she was telling our parents about the day after we got home, she didn't tell them that bit. My father thought the whole thing the greatest waste of time and asked her was she not furious at having given up a good day's lectures. She told him he might be overrating the lectures on her first year course.

'It was quite interesting, actually,' she said, getting up off the edge of my mother's bed, where we had gathered. 'To discover there's a sort of natural law about car crashes. They're like orgasms. The more you plan them, the less likely they become.'

I didn't know what an orgasm was, but I did know that the minute she had said it she wanted to take it back.

'And another thing,' she said, before a silence could make statues out of us. 'I had a quick word with The Chip before I came away. To suggest that if their budget is tight (and it seems to be very tight) it might be a good idea to lose Little Miss Creepo, the walking, talking Ebola virus. He said they'd been thinking about it anyway. The need for her isn't as great as they expected. Also, he thinks she's a hyperactive nutcase who probably disembowels thrushes in her spare time. Plus she scares Dominique to death.'

At this, my father got mad and wanted to know what exactly this young woman did that scared me. Gabrielle said it didn't matter now, she'd be gone next season although they'd call her in as a casual if and when they needed her. One way or the other, I'd be seeing much less of her.

I felt dreadful not being completely 100 per cent filled up to the top with gratitude to Gabrielle, but there was a voice in the corner of my head that kept saying, 'I hope the series producer doesn't let Richelle know it was my sister who got her fired.'

'Daisy, we all meet people during our schooldays that cast a pall over everything we do, people who at the time seem omnipotent,' my father said gently. 'And you know something? A few years after we leave school we can't even remember their names. They have no power over us at all.'

My mother nodded.

'Richelle Governey is like nappy rash,' she said. 'No baby remembers it once they've grown up.'

Gabrielle clutched her own bottom, letting on she was the exception, that she was getting a stab of pain as a result of old nappy rash. I nodded and didn't say anything. From where they were standing, what they said was true. I knew in some part of me, maybe my soul, that Richelle could not be got rid of that easily. If I told them, though, they would just reassure me on and on, like when someone continues to pat you on the back long after you've got the message of the first pat.

I would have liked to have known at the time what an orgasm was and why my parents were so taken aback that Gabrielle seemed to know how to make one or do one. But the extra information I might gain probably wouldn't be worth the hassle the question seemed likely to cause, so I stayed silent.

When I asked her about it later, she said it wouldn't kill me not to know for a couple of years. So I looked it up instead.

CHAPTER FOUR

An Interesting Headache

———⟫•⟪———

Putting me in a wheelchair for a year was a great move. Viewers always think a wheelchair person is sad but noble. Brave, even. Someone with a broken toe has an awful time, because people laugh at the injury and then they think they look awkward moving around on crutches. They forget completely that at least if you are in a wheelchair you can take a cup of coffee from one room to another, but if you are on crutches, you are much more helpless.

TV soaps have a lot of wheelchairs. They don't have much in the way of facial scars or stuff like that. The make-up artist pointed that out to me, one day she was getting me ready for a scene. She had very well-defined eyebrows with no hairs in them which constantly intrigued me.

'See these?' she said, pointing, over my head, to her own boomerang-shaped eyebrows in the mirror in front of me. I nodded.

'Tattoos,' she said, powdering me. 'Goddam chip pan went up in flames and I stupidly put the lid on it and whoof. It exploded and burned the eyebrows off me. They never grew back. You don't see nasty stuff like that in a soap, though.'

That season I was filmed all the time in a wheelchair and a lot of the time it was easier to stay in it to do homework any time there was a hold-up in filming. I hardly ever saw Richelle Governey any more. Whenever they brought her in, it was when I was not on the set anyway, so the big bruise of dread began to fade a little.

The wheelchair distinguishes for me the year I was thirteen, but after that, the years all melt together. Featureless. Perhaps because I was always either learning lines or doing homework, I remember very little of my own teen years, which is weird, because I remember every milestone in the young life of the character I played. There was such debate about every one of them. As the series progressed, some of the scriptwriters and directors went on to do other things. (Call-me-Chip worked with Spielberg and occasionally gave interviews to Irish newspapers that would give you the impression he really ran Spielberg. Probably nobody in Hollywood ever knew his real name was Ambrose.)

Because the people who agonised over my character's developmental crises all moved on, I had to remember the details to tell their successors. It was like I was an anthropologist and a psychiatrist and a GP and a schoolteacher all at once, studying just one schoolgirl who was a few years younger than me. Keeping records. Making judgements. No, she would never do this, yes she could be tempted to do that.

I was so busy running quality control on my character, I didn't get a chance to be at my own life during those years. So, later, when someone would ask me about the first time I tasted this or drank that, what I retrieved with ease was the detail from my TV character's growing up, not my own.

Mostly, my adolescence is just a blur until the day Gabrielle announced she was going to marry this music student named Oliver. I must have been about seventeen at the time, and was very impressed by her decisiveness. She had only gone out with him three times when she came home and told us they were going to be married. Of course, my parents would have preferred if she was much less decisive, but they knew when Gabrielle made up her mind, that was it. They made the best of it and tried to come to terms with Oliver.

Oliver was not following a great family tradition when he chose music as a career. Contrast, not pattern. They marched before him, his agreeable brothers, to top marks in different disciplines and accomplished careers in unrelated fields. There was a lawyer, a doctor, a vet, a mathematician – and then Oliver. Achievers without ambition, the McDermott boys, swimming in a warm soup of easy expectations.

When, at four, Oliver began picking out tunes on any piano within reach, his father's proposal of lessons carried neither a hope that he had a prodigy on his hands, nor a sense of investment. It was, rather, as if the issue were one of safety. Get that young fella taught to do the piano thing right or he could do himself harm.

Very shortly, the lessons developed a talent in Oliver that evoked a mutuality of loaded glances between music examiners. But back home, there was no more hushed reverence for Oliver the Musician than for Michael the Vet. The McDermotts were broad spectrum people, in every way, including hospitality. The latter was best exemplified by Mrs

McDermott's instinctively plural invitation when she encountered friends of her sons in corners of their vast rambling house.

'Would you like coffee? Tea? A steak?' she would ask.

From the first time she met Oliver, Gabrielle expected to do a lot of mopping-up after him. She would be the ganger on his team, but it would be worth it. He was so easy to be with, and he had such casual, comfortable affection. He had the McDermott attitude to life. By its nature, it was so unselfconscious that none of them realised they had it. If you told them, they almost tried to feel the shape of it, the way you'd finger the top of your head if a doctor told you your fontanelle hadn't closed: golly, I had an attitude all these years and never knew.

If one of them did well at something, he came home and told the rest of them exactly how well he had done. An outsider might think they were lacking in modesty, but what they really lacked was a need for approval by others. I once told Gabrielle that Oliver's whole family were like a new version of that old psychological model, I'm OK, you're OK. The McDermott version was I'm OK (if you force me to think about it) and you're your own responsibility.

I often thought that when Oliver came to tea in our

house, he came for the laughs, rather than the food. He never bothered to be impressive to either Mam or Dad. He teased my mother and argued lazily with my father, which drove them both mad. My mother could not cope with teasing, and my father needed to be argued with passionately.

His unkemptness bothered my parents too. His hair never seemed to have been freshly washed, his hands were always grubby, and he was known to turn up at our house wearing the same clothes he had worn the previous day, which my mother regarded as a crime against nature.

What she didn't know was that on one occasion, when he seemed to have a fresh T-shirt on (albeit one very like the one he had worn the previous day, but with a higher neckline), not only was he in precisely the same clothing, but it had gone through a disastrous night, too. He had gone off drinking with the lads and as the barman was yelling, 'Please, gentlemen, finish up, now please', the man next to Oliver staggered and unintentionally deposited the contents of his pint glass down the front of Oliver's T-shirt. The thrower took it more amiss than did Oliver, because it robbed the thrower of most of his final drink of the night. The following morning, when Oliver was leaving the lads' flat, one of them blearily noted that he looked neater than the previous night's spill would have led anyone to expect.

'Fair dues to you,' the friend said to Oliver. 'Carry a spare T-shirt and all.'

At which point Oliver smiled his permanently amused smile and did a pivoting, sexy female model drop-off-the-shoulders job on his tweedy jacket, revealing the beer stain flowing, congealed like a filthy freeze-frame, down his back rather than down his front.

When – acting as Mam's emissary – I pointed out the great contrast between this quintessential slob and Gabrielle's pristine self, she responded, deadpan, that she was taking on a role like a missionary bringing new standards to the heathen. It would take a few years of good example before Oliver could be expected to convert, but at least during those few years she would be able to keep the cockroaches off him, which would be a good thing for the health of the nation generally. She would not want him to be a focus of epidemic disease, she said solemnly. When I passed this on to my parents, neither of them laughed as I expected them to.

My father did that shrug parents do when they don't want to crush you with their intellectual superiority, because triumphalism is bad form when the vanquished know it's time to cash in their chips. Like those statues of the Virgin Mary you see in hospitals where she's standing on a snake with an expression on her that says 'Snake? What snake?' The poor frigger is there with his forked tongue flying in total surrender and she letting on she wouldn't lower herself to do anything but serendipitously step-dance on him.

It was unlike my father to give up as easily as he did that evening. He seemed to completely lose interest in the subject of Oliver as public health hazard.

'I think I'll go to bed a bit early,' he said.

My mother looked at him as if she'd been struck by a passing cannonball, since he was always the last to go to bed. Dad came from a family where going to bed before midnight was equivalent to declaring a state of emergency. I thought she would diagnose something, but she just looked astonished. Maybe, I thought, she knows all about me and asthma, but because my father has no illness she has nothing to say about him.

The night my father went to bed early was the first time both my parents were in bed before Gabrielle and I were. We could hear the two of them talking, so we knew he hadn't been asleep, which again was odd. But odd hasn't got much significance until it gets framed in black. Once framed in black, odd becomes a series of tragically missed opportunities. That was certainly how Mam felt, telling us later that she had asked him, when she was going to bed, how the headache was, and he had said, lying on his back, 'Interesting.'

He was always given to understatement. The time I left the plug in the bathroom sink while the tap was running and made a fifteen-minute phone call, he described the area, after the inundation, as 'a bit damp'. So his 'interesting' headache must have been horrendous – as my mother realised four hours later, when he woke her and asked her to get an ambulance to take him to hospital. Because it was the middle of the night, the ambulance didn't have its screamer on, so I knew nothing about the terse, practised men who carried him down the stairs, only once tearing a deep-voiced wordless cry of agony from him on the way. My mother drove behind the ambulance, afterwards cursing herself for not choosing to go as a passenger in it.

'But I was thinking of driving him home afterwards,' she would explain to people later, trying to ease the raw pain of having missed his last wakeful moments, having failed to hold his hand when the pain ate away his consciousness and his well-stocked mind and his saddened tolerance and left an untroubled inflated version of him lying in an intensive care bed, breathing with mechanical regularity and sleeping the illusory sleep of the brain-dead.

The haemorrhage killed him before they could get him into theatre, the neurosurgeon told us. It was a nurse who surmised that he had probably not been a man to make a fuss about pains and aches. The patients who survived brain haemorrhages, she said, tended to be 'bad' patients: people who hit the alarm bells and complained loudly, rather than observing that they had an 'interesting' headache.

For my mother, the guilt of having failed to appreciate and solve the death threat reduced everything else to minutiae. We two sisters could cope with that stuff. So we listened to the person deputed to ask us about our father's heart and his corneas, and we signed the papers allowing them to take his corneas and put them in someone else. No, we wouldn't want to know anything about where they went. No, we wouldn't wait for them to turn off the machine. We knew they had to keep him alive as long as possible, so we would take our leave now and let them at it. Our parting with him would come later, when all the machines had been switched off and they had done what they had to do.

It was made easier by the strangeness of the figure in the bed. Nothing of him was familiar, not even his hands, puffed by organ failure. When we came back a few hours later, they had all the tubes gone and we could recognise him. The frightening thing was that my mother was less recognisable. Like a starched shirt hosed to limpness, she walked less erectly, seemed less sure of what, up to then, had always been inarguable and imperative. We thought at first it was a form of shock, but to me it was like an actress who always plays the mother suddenly shifting to take on the ingénue role. I kept waiting for her to go back to herself, but she never did. Never bright confident morning again.

We had not thought our father was the leader in their relationship, but in his death the truth was outed.

The day after the funeral, there was a picture on the front of the paper, showing me, hair pulled back severely, coat collar up, arm around my mother at the graveside. 'Comfort for a Loved One', said the caption.

'Bullshit, of course, that caption,' Oliver said. 'Who's supposed to be comforting who?'

My sister, putting a mug of tea in front of him, turned to examine the photograph. 'Daisy's comforting Ma,' she said.

'No, she isn't. She has her arm around her, but

that's – that's like cats grooming each other. You just do it if you're beside someone who's crying. Daisy's just standing there looking – authentic.'

'Authentic?'

'Yeah. All dry-eyed and dignified and kind of "I can see the future and it sucks." '

'Authentic, though,' Gabrielle said again, bothered by the implied insult: sincerity is everything. If you can fake that, you're made.

He was right, though. I was authentic at the funeral. I knew precisely how to behave. The model being cinema, rather than real life. Just as violence is unrealistically over-represented in episodes of TV drama series, so funerals are over-represented in plays and screenplays. Half the movies ever made begin with a funeral. Funeral processions in films do not behave the way people do in real life. They don't get shiny red faces, runny noses and black collars dusted with dandruff. In real life, grief makes the point, scrawbing its message on the faces of the bereaved. In films, the bereaved make the point, performing their way to the next scene. In real life, funerals are chaotic jostlings, stinking of boiled wool and candlegrease. In films, funerals are ordered chiaroscuro tableaux of hatted, well-groomed people whose heels never sink into sucking graveyard muck.

The picture in the paper attracted the attention of the man from the advertising agency charged with raising the profile of the soap opera which was now more than five years on the air. Twenty-two years old, dressed like a male model, mobile phone permanently at his ear, Nigel by name, he made himself known to me and insisted I have dinner with him.

Over dinner, he told me the photograph made me look vulnerable. He said good-looking women had to be vulnerable. It was no good being beautiful if you looked cocky about it, because other women would hate you, particularly the kind of woman who watches soap operas. It was OK to be gorgeous if you looked as if you constantly lost your keys.

'Does this apply only to women?'

'Oh, yes. Men like other men to succeed. Women hate other women to succeed.'

Because it was so much on my mind that day, I pulled the photocopy out of my bag. 'My mam isn't up to handling my fan mail any more, so I'm doing it,' I said. 'That came a week after the funeral.'

'In your fan mail?'

'Fan mail is 99 per cent drivel and 1 per cent pure nastiness,' I said, and did my mother's migraine and insomnia wave. Not that she could, these days, sum-mon up even a fraction of the lordly dismissiveness I remembered.

Nigel's eyes explored the picture with a sort of slurping, sucking sympathy and horror. 'Whoever did this can draw,' he pointed out.

He had a knack of stating the obvious which moved the obvious up a notch. The picture of me had been tinkered with so that on my face and hands were deep sagging wounds from which dripped big singular drops of blood. It reminded me of a picture my grandmother kept over the mantelpiece in her bedroom. It was a huge framed print of Jesus with an odd name printed on it. Sterrer Pinx. I never found out whether that was the painter or the printer.

Jesus looked long-suffering in it, rather than agon-ised. He looked the way you'd expect him to look if someone had delayed him and made him miss a bus. He had one of his very pretty pale hands pointing to his heart, which was out in front of his chest, decorated with a crown of thorns. The artist must have felt that if he didn't have Jesus pointing to the outrage, the viewers would miss it, given that Jesus himself didn't look that worked up about it. But where Sterrer Pinx really scored was with the wounds. On the back of the hands were these long, oval wounds, not ragged or new in appearance. They had the look of wounds-for-display over the long haul, and whoever had doctored the photograph of me portrayed wounds in much the same way.

'This will have to be reported to the man,' Nigel said.

'What man?'

'The Man,' he elaborated unhelpfully, tweaking little quote marks in the air. The waiter took this as a summons. Nigel ordered more wine, then explained that he meant the cops.

'We probably shouldn't even have touched it,' he said, lifting his hands guiltily in the air. (The waiter was getting seriously irritated by all these apparent signals.)

I said that I wouldn't waste my time taking it to the authorities, and tore it up while he watched. He watched me pile the scraps into the ashtray in the middle of the table.

'I suppose it comes with the territory,' he said, gravely.

When he pulled the car into the kerb outside our house, he kissed me and said he would give me a call. I mentally notched one in the air: men in TV programmes said they would give girls a call almost as often as they said 'Let's go.' He might have taken me to the door, except that, just as we drove up, Oliver emerged from our house, and Nigel seemed to feel that he should drive off very quickly.

'Heavy date, Daisy?' Oliver said, watching the ugly little car disappear.

'Not a date at all. That's a guy doing an ad campaign.'

'Hence the car.'

'Awful, isn't it? Carrerra or something, it said on the back.'

'That was a Porsche. Don't tell him a Porsche is an awful car – he'll never get over it.'

'I could meet him every day for a year and we'd never get around to my opinion,' I said.

All Nigel wanted was questioning about himself. By answering my questions, he discovered what he was. Creation by interrogation. If God created us, that should be an end to it. Thanks, Big Fella, have a happy eternity watching us little human ants getting and spending, defoliating and developing, coupling and uncoupling. Instead, we go needy on Him. We decide one life is not enough. We want seconds. A serving of the Hereafter, please.

Until Nigel met me, he was the promising creative on the second floor. His campaign for the soap repositioned it, they would say later. His slogan, under a haunting picture of me, was 'Much more than meets the eye.' It made viewers decide there was more significance to the soap than there really was. It became a programme only the cool could fully appreciate. Banality at the artistic cutting edge.

Nigel within a year was headhunted at twice the salary, attending an awards banquet with the directors of his current agency knowing that he would, on the morrow, tell them he was off to join the enemy. There as his guest that night, I would now and again flash him a teasing threat to tell all and wreck the evening. He was so on edge he could neither eat nor drink, and his small acceptance speech was straight out of an Esperanto chat room.

Since he had no idea what he had said or intended to say, nor any insight into how far apart the twain had been, he spent the evening like a thin grown-up version of the kids in the old porridge ads: an almost physical, aura-like glow suffused him. Every time he touched me, a charge like static electricity ran between us.

That was the first night I was in his apartment. One of the most expensive in Dublin, it was on the sixteenth floor of a tower built in the old docklands, floor-to-ceiling windows on three sides looking out over the city, over the river, over the bay. I sat on a cream leather couch, the city presenting itself to me in the golden brightness of spotlit landmarks. The Four Courts. The Custom House. Liberty Hall, with its pleated cap. I didn't tell Nigel my first reaction to his apartment was relief that it wouldn't start me wheezing. Not only was there no carpet, but for the most part, the hard white shiny floor didn't even have a rug on it. Beneath the minimalist black artist's table, there was a rug that looked like the skin of a zebra, but I could keep away from it.

He had a Bosé speaker system and, as a treat for me, a new recording in which Oliver had a brief solo. This must be the way a trout feels on a hot hazy summer day, I thought. Shimmying without effort in the cool depths, surrounded by the amplified perfection of the familiar, but knowing that to break the meniscus of the surface was to be assaulted by zipping, tiny-snarled buzzing busy flies. Nigel was all of those busy flies. He could not sit still.

He made coffee with a machine that spat and steamed and brought it to the low table in cups of glass and chrome. He transformed my quiet absorption of my city with a tourist guidebook's insistence on my not missing anything. Natives of a city always know what is significant. Outsiders never do, and Nigel was an outsider from the sticks trying to make like he'd never seen a tractor.

Come over here, he would order, lest I miss where one street emptied into another and where the building at the corner was an under-appreciated masterpiece. I would be settling back into the cream leather when a second landmark would attract him and he would insist on me moving over to a second window to see it. Ultimately, it was easier to stay standing, tracing in the sky low over the city the great fragile right angles of the cranes that would, next day, resume their rigid circling above each building site.

Nigel went to turn off lights in the galley. I could hear his returning footsteps on the stone carpet. Knew, when they stopped short, where he was, what he was doing. Standing, he was leaning against the counter of the kitchen, his undone bow tie hanging from under his collar in two crumpled black ribbons against, the multiplicity of pleats in the dress shirt. He was watching me, silhouetted against the city lights, the line of Prussian blue evening dress so stark, it amounted to a boast: see how perfect is this teenage slenderness. After a moment, I thought, he will say something. Let's see if I can predict it. Something like, 'You are so very beautiful.'

It took more than a moment, so I looked it out of him.

'You're very beautiful, you know.'

Not a good one, I thought. Selected from the mental index of the half-remembered. Half-remembered because they deserve only half-remembrance. I looked at him steadily.

'Very beautiful,' he said, echoing and admiring his earlier line and pushing himself away from the cream-painted wall. As he walked towards me, he pulled the bow tie remnant away from under his collar and threw it on a chair. I watched and evaluated the gesture (four out of ten) and tried to force myself to be fully present.

'Your presence is required at a deflowering,' I said aloud.

Not that he heard me. By then he was holding me, his mouth closing off my sentence and his hand sliding the narrow strap off my shoulder. For a moment, I flinched, surrounded by the open views of the city, glassed out. If I can see them, a child's thought came, they can see me. But there were no other sixteen-storey dwellings with watchers at their windows to see the second strap go and the dress slither unwatched to the floor. I stood, high-heeled but much shorter than him, watching the faint reflections in the windows as he unclasped the wisp of French lace black bra, sketching the freed breasts with his hand in a half-caress suddenly swamped by his need to mouth and tongue them; both hands on my back, going lower to drive me against the hardness of him, the pleasure of it dragging a grinding response from me so crudely knowing in its need it almost brought him to his knees.

Then the couch was at my back and the reflections more difficult to watch because we were cream-skinned against cream or perhaps because I could no longer watch or think but only react to root his hardness home, past pain, pressure and the movement of two in one, centring every sense in the building of the tight promise, the murderous expectation and then the release of it into waves of something better than pleasure, better than anything, better and repeated, better and receding, reducing, reminding, reminding now of the pain, only of the pain and with the pain the disarray, the sounds of it, the smells of it, the need to get away from it and him and wonder had it been real at all, knowing the answer would never come except in this new language.

In reflection, we were ridiculous, me still in high-heeled shoes, him grounded in a crumpled, leg-catching debris of clothes and underclothes, the shirt long as a dress, the trousers still around his ankles because he had never taken his shoes off. He lay on me as if the bones had been melted in him, spasmed by aftershocks, stuck to me, skin to skin by drying sweat, me stuck to the couch beneath me. I rolled him off me with a sound like peeling plastic, patted him into an agreed semi-coma, and was in the bathroom with the door locked within seconds.

In the mirror, I was dishevelled, mascara puddling under one eye, make-up absorbed so my face looked dirty. When I opened the bathroom door, on the floor outside was my dress, neatly folded, its straps drawn out like a hamburger joint's M, my underwear sitting on top. Taking in my orphan clothes, I wondered was this standard – leaving the girl's clothes outside the bathroom door for her.

Dressed again, I might have been setting out on the evening's revelry all over again. He, on the other hand, having pulled himself back into his trousers and tucked the ends of the shirt into the waistband, looked like he had gone three rounds with Mike Tyson. He could not even pretend to dissuade me when I rang for a taxi, but hung about, speechless other than for occasional embarrassing votes of thanks, looking like a leftover.

CHAPTER FIVE

Weddings and Partings

———◆◆◆———

Oliver came slightly unstuck two nights before his wedding. Playing a nocturne in the Concert Hall, about twenty minutes into the piece, he went into a kind of trance.

For three or four minutes, Oliver continued to play in the composer's style, although what he played was not to be found on the sheets of music in front of him. An improvisation of fucking genius, the conductor later said. But not what he was supposed to be playing. After three minutes, he apparently snapped out of it and went back to playing the music as written. The concert ended with neither concert-goers nor critics much the wiser.

The conductor was provoked by the episode into a multilingual screaming attack.

'How dare you Finger-Sptzenfefuhl, you schlub?' demanded the conductor after the concert. 'Zol vahksen tzibbelis fun pipek! You – you mucksavage, you toy vid a whole fucking orchestre.'

'I'd have toyed with one drummer just as happily,' Oliver pointed out. 'But all that was handy was a whole orchestra.'

'Sitting – stool-sitting – blunderfecking nobody knows which way you fart,' the conductor said. Which the oboist later confided to Oliver was a pretty accurate description of how the rest of the musicians had felt during Oliver's musical walkabout, although allowances had to be made for a man due to be married.

On the day itself, it was me who came unstuck. As Gabrielle's lone bridesmaid, I was startled by the number of photographers at the church when we arrived. Did we hire all of them?' I asked from where I was sorting out the train.

Gabrielle turned around to me. 'They are here for you,' she said, smiling. 'Because you and Oliver are famous, I get them for free.'

Tears boiled into my eyes and I tried to apologise. Gabrielle put her gloved right hand to my face and stopped the tears before they could fall. Then, white-misted through the veil, she smiled and showed the fingertips of the thin cotton gloves, darkened with the damp.

'Something borrowed, Daisy,' she said very softly. 'I had forgotten to borrow something.'

Then the driver opened the door with a flourish, and the bride came out of that car like a film star into a firestorm of flashbulbs.

It was so perfect, so happy a wedding day, that I thought, again and again, there would never be another like it. The bridal pair exuded prescience of a long ribbon of loving laughing days streaming away into the distance, over the hill of the years.

After the honeymoon, Oliver began to get a lot of work. Gabrielle cleaned him up, but did not cut his hair, so he had a very distinctive look to him which made him easy to remember. People called him a young André Previn.

When Gabrielle became pregnant, she had all-day morning sickness so horrific I had to spend weeks based in their house looking after her. Nigel was convinced that this was a sisterly ploy to remove me from his embraces.

'Unconscious, perhaps,' he said. 'Psychotic things are not always within our control.'

'Psychosomatic.'

'Whatever.'

I told Gabrielle Nigel thought she was only imagining the need to throw up, and she said she was sorry to have such a twisted psyche.

'Does he think you wheeze for the same reason?' she asked, before disappearing into the bathroom and putting the taps on full blast to drown the noises of her personal agony.

'You'll cause a water shortage,' I said when she came out, greeny-white in the face.

'There's enough on Nigel's brain to make up any deficit.'

'He says maybe you're doing it subliminally.'

'Subliminally?'

'I think he means subconsciously.'

'I hope Nigel never has to do a campaign about pregnancy. Unless the campaign teaches pregnant women to throw up subliminally. I'd love to be able to do that.'

'I wish I could get out of the TV series subliminally,' I said to thin air as Gabrielle made another run for the bathroom.

Wanting to get out of it had started as a mild longing and – over time – had become a raging need. The fear of celebrating a decade as one TV character gradually overcame the fear of being without that character. She might be four years younger than I was in reality but in many ways her life was an easier fit than my own. Every week there was a crisis in her life, and every week it got resolved. Consistency and continuity were the keys. She couldn't wear a brooch in one shot and not in another.

'She would never say that,' I would tell the latest scriptwriter, certain of my character's narrow vocabulary, verbal and emotional. There were no U-turns in her moral development, no discrepancies in her thinking. Everything matched. In my own life, I might simultaneously believe two mutually opposed points, but in her life there were no contradictions. Three standard pages were always handed to the new season's scriptwriters. Those pages told them her favourite food, drink, book, song, fabric, sport, perfume, wine, boyfriend-type and TV programme.

Most of the time, the producers, directors and writers were all united in the way they – and I – approached the character. It was only when there was a new person on the crew that things went bumpy for a while. A few of the old hands put bets on, the time Call-me-Chip's successor suggested she develop a long-lost sister or half-sister, that I would a) say it wouldn't fit with her character, b) say the actress the director wants would not be right. They didn't tell me they had put bets on it, so they couldn't blame me for the fact that they only won half the money.

I didn't say a half-sister, newly discovered, would not fit with my character. I said (logically) that it wouldn't fit with the established character of my 'mother' in the series, but they were right about the actress. They had a bit of video showing her, and she looked older than me, not younger, although she was actually five months my junior. She had very blonde hair and very black eyebrows.

'I know this one,' I said to the editor who was deputed to show me the footage. 'Why do I know her?'

He seemed puzzled by the question.

'She's on the set every now and then,' he said, his expression saying are you *on* something that you don't see her when she's in?

A hot, crumbling, weighted feeling happened in my insides. I asked to see the videotape again. Richelle Governey. Although she was only a few years older, they were the years that make the difference. The years, in her case, that made *all* the difference. Her appearance had gone from childhood to harsh, knowing adulthood without stopping in the middle for open-faced adolescence. Her slenderness had become brittle thinness, and the fact that she had dyed her very black hair ash-blonde gave a tartiness to what I remembered as almost classical beauty. Now that I watched her, I realised there was another difference. Something had been done to her forehead, so that her hair started higher up than it used to. It removed the monkey-princess look.

'I was being thick,' I said to the editor. 'You're right. I do know who she is.'

It seemed sad that she should lose another chance because of me, but when I mentioned this to my favourite director, he said not to worry, the new series producer fancied her so much she'd pop up somewhere, sometime. Wherever he went, she'd go with him. She never really did pop up much, though, except in bit parts. The series producer accepted that he couldn't make a half-sister out of her, so as a consolation prize, he gave her a couple of lines as a neighbour in our soap. It was a great relief to me to meet her only in character. In character, I was certain about everything and was able to carry off the scene without as much as a flicker – as was she.

In real life, I had no such fixed points, but vacillated, seeking certainties and reaching for a role. Not only was I unsure of how to play myself, but I also had a sense of unreality about the people surrounding me.

In Nigel's apartment on a Sunday morning, I would half-recline, my legs criss-crossing his on the couch, sipping café latte from a tall styrofoam container brought from the coffee shop along with the newspapers. This was probably what I should be doing to be in character, but Nigel was too jumpy to be good at the leg-crossing routine. Pretending to read, I would slither looks at him and decide that he was quite good as a yuppie advertising wiz. Rewrites were not called for, although he seemed occasionally to lack the detail a long-stay character requires.

I never told him that I wanted to get out of the series, because, the more I thought about it, the more I realised I would have to get out of the country for a bit, not just out of the programme. I should get myself written out of the series, then head for France to improve my French. People would have forgotten me by the time I got back. I could grow my hair. I could dye my hair.

'Why're you smiling?' Nigel asked suspiciously, when he caught me enjoying the thought of becoming a platinum blonde.

'Was I?' I asked, wide-eyed.

Wide-eyed still came in handy, at least with him. It gave just long enough an interval for his thought process to charge off in some alternative directions.

Funny, I thought, that the height of my ambition, if and when I escape the soap, is just to be inconsistent. To find the real me through random, rather than regimented, days.

Raising it with the production people proved to be easier than I expected. They got quite excited about the possibility of doing me in. Suicide was one possibility. A fire was another. Gabrielle did not want me killed, perhaps because she was made protective of all the world by her new motherhood.

'Certainly not a fire,' she said, burping Stephen with vigour. 'You're not Rochester's mad wife.'

'I'm not Sylvia Plath either.'

'You can't commit suicide with natural gas.'

'Really?'

'Well, maybe if you were very determined.'

'She's dating Nigel,' Oliver said, taking the baby. 'Of course she'd be determined.'

'What's wrong with Nigel?' I called after him.

Neither Gabrielle nor himself ever behaved as if Nigel had a future with me, no matter how many years the relationship lasted.

'Nigel is like a starter home,' Gabrielle said. 'Anyway, why do you have to be killed?'

'They can never revive me if I get killed. More dramatic, anyway.'

'Have you really decided you're going to France?'

'Yes.'

'Why don't you get your character to do the same?'

'I'll put that to them.'

The TV people toyed with the idea of packing my character, Sandi, off to France as an au pair. When I told my mother what I was planning, it evoked a brief flicker of her old self. The family I went to must have an asthma-friendly home, for starters. When I had selected one, in the light of advice given by an expert agency, she did consider going out on an inspection tour, but I think then began to wonder how effective she could be as the Feathers FBI working through a translator (me) whose school French was inadequate enough to serve as the justification for the whole venture.

'I don't have attacks that bad any more,' I consoled her, seeing her shoulder-shrugging relinquishing of the issue as loss of interest. When I was checking through my cases prior to departure, however, I found extra Ventolin inhalers and tablets stashed in the oddest places within them. I also found a sealed letter with 'Do not open until after departure' on the envelope, which of course ensured I would open it right there and then.

It was a letter from Nigel. A Dear John letter. A missive to say, 'Will miss you terribly, so am cutting off the relationship completely right now.' Since there was no intention, on my part, of staying in touch with him while I was away, in one sense the letter met my needs exactly. It nevertheless infuriated me to such an extent that I shared it with Gabrielle. She thought it was a scream.

'Who'd have thought Nigel the No-Hoper would have the wit to get his retaliation in first?' she giggled.

'Goes up in my estimation,' was Oliver's reaction.

'Goes up in your estimation? Makes him go right down in my estimation,' I said.

'You were going to face him nobly the night before you left, telling him he must put you behind him?' Gabrielle asked.

'No, she had her Dear John already written,' Oliver said.

'I did not.'

But they knew I wasn't planning to even send a letter. I was just hoping time and circumstances would solve the problem.

'And you're getting high-minded about this poor wanker giving Gabrielle a letter to stuff in your carpetbag?'

'It was you, Gabrielle?'

'It was I,' she said, clutching her brow in mimicry of the heroine in a melodrama. 'Who the hell did you think it was?'

'The two of you are wasters and worms,' I said. 'You think it's easy to end a relationship that's gone on for several years?'

'No, but what's rattling your fillings isn't ending the relationship,' Oliver said gleefully. 'It's being the one who got dumped, as opposed to the dumper. That's what's really knotting your knickers.'

Because it was true, I got twice as mad.

'He was my first love,' I yelled.

'If this was an audition, you don't get the part,' Gabrielle said, comfortably. 'You're OTT.'

'He wasn't your first love, anyway,' Oliver said. 'You didn't love him, he didn't love you. He may have been your first screw, but that's different.'

'Even a first screw has a place in one's memories,' Gabrielle said, still in melodrama mode.

'Not in mine,' Oliver said, after trying to remember.

This maddened Gabrielle and she flailed at him.

'Daisy, Nigel's a nice guy — and that's no foundation for nuthin',' Oliver said. 'He has a lot of dosh, a great car and according to you a cool apartment.'

'Shut up, for Chrissake, Oliver, you're making him sound more attractive by the minute,' Gabrielle muttered.

'All I'm saying is he was OK for your first, but there's no shortage.'

'What Oliver is trying to say, Daisy dear, is Get a Life.'

'Gettez Vous Une Vie, even,' Oliver added.

'Sans Nigel,' Gabrielle added.

'But avec lots of sex and that French yellow stuff.'

This floored the two of us. It sounded perverse and filthy.

'Pernod,' he clarified. 'Have lots of that.'

The TV station eventually decided au pairing was the best option for my character. Oliver said Gabrielle should have got a fee for the suggestion.

Thus it was that, one Monday morning, I had to act out a scene of parting from my family for the soap, and three days later, I did the same scene for real with Gabrielle and Mam. Oliver was away on a tour. Nigel and I had agreed to stop thinking of ourselves as a couple.

The final scene in the soap was a lot more moving than my real-life parting. It ended with a shot of this little person striding out as if she were pretending to be grown up. You knew she was going to be lonely, vulnerable, lost and brave. Although I was much older, in every way, than the character, I still worried for her, this girl I had half-lived in for so many years.

For myself, I had no worries. I had a sister who would talk to me by phone, with whom I could share every thought. I was going to a place where my face meant nothing. I was free of all entanglements. I was on my way to Paris. And, if I followed Oliver's instructions, lots of Pernod.

CHAPTER SIX

Paris and Pernod

━━━◆◇◆━━━

In Paris, I suffered homesickness so bad, it shrivelled, tore and flittered me. The children I was minding were good children, but might as well have been behind thick panels of transparent plastic. I hardly heard them. They were pretty pets belonging to someone else, cared for by me. If they threw tantrums or ran around for an hour screeching the same two syllables at the top of their voices, it reached me not at all.

Their mother thought I was the most patient carer ever, coming to this decision after several months of arriving home unexpectedly to see if she would catch me shaking them until their heads fell off. She also interrogated them to jolt them into recalling that I had shoved their fingers into electric sockets to frizz their hair. By comparison with whatever kind of au pairs they had before me, I was up there close to Florence Nightingale.

Being away from home and having no script to work from bemused me. Au pairing felt as if I was improvising a new part and doing it in a foreign language. The slight sense of sleepwalking this gave to the experience dusts my memories softly with sepia. I love the recollection of my time there more than I loved the reality as it was happening to me.

By the third month I no longer mentally translated everything I heard and developed the urge to 'pass' as a Parisienne; to distance myself from the gauche hordes of tourists. I changed my hair to a cut so simple that when it rained, the water smoothed it into a dark frame for my face. Because I was so much more active than I had ever been at home, I lost weight, going from a size twelve to a ten. The bones appeared in my face. Black and simple replaced pastel and pretty in the clothes I bought. In the place of the high-heeled shoes I had wanted, now that I was officially 'grown up', I wore cheap flat ballet-slipper shoes as I dutifully walked Paris to learn it completely.

That was how I was dressed, the foggy November day I ran into trouble in the Place de la Concorde. That morning, I woke up with an audible wheeze, explained, once I opened the curtains, by thick fog. At home, because we lived near the coast, fog was announced by the foghorns of ships ploughing through the Irish Sea. In Paris, fog arrived unannounced — except by my whining lungs.

Through the window, Paris might have been the London of old movies. By midday, however, much of it seemed to have lifted, and, since it was my day off, I decided to go for a walk in the hope of clearing my lungs, three or four puffs of my inhaler having failed to do the job.

At first, on that day, I walked in expectation of improvement. Then, in hope of improvement. Eventually, although I continued to put one foot in front of the other, I walked in despair of improvement. A steady trickle of perspiration ran between my breasts although I had only the lightest of windcheaters on. It was cold enough for most people to be wearing jackets. The world narrowed to the footpath in front of me and the effort of pulling air in. It was like trying to blow up a balloon being held halfway down its length by strong hands. There was never enough, yet still the need to let the precious ration go in the hope of more next time.

I could no longer muster the oxygen to seek right

of way among the other people on the footpath or to apologise to those pedestrians I bumped into. Without knowing where I was or where I was going, I stepped off the path on to cobblestones laid in fan shapes. Wave after wave of them. I lifted my head to get my bearings and the effort required by such a tiny movement made me realise how far I had walked into disaster and how far I was from help of any kind. There was a small imitation building – one of the pavilions of the Place de la Concorde – perhaps ten yards from me. I got to it, half-turned, holding the pillar on one side of the pavilion's locked door, and slid down, down, into a sitting position on its steps, my hand filthied from the slide.

Sitting made the breathing worse, as it always does. I groped in my windcheater for my inhaler. Never mind all the warnings about heart failure through its excessive use. I was on the way out anyway, from suffocation.

Got the inhaler to my mouth. Pressed the silver bit to make it deliver. Nothing. Did it again. A tiny whiffle of propellant gas, half-heard over the hissing, howling noise of my own breathing. Pulled it loose. Shook it. No payload. Never noticed it was low. The silver bit fell onto the cobbles in front of me. I could hardly see it, for now the black waves were coming up behind my eyes and the thunder of my own heartbeat in my ears was overwhelming.

Knees intruded in my line of vision. A hand picked up the empty silver canister. Man on hunkers. He would ask me all the stupid questions and I would die in the effort of answering.

'Piss off,' I thought and said.

The plastic bit of the inhaler was taken out of my hand and my hand was clasped around something cold.

'Drink it,' a voice said. 'Caffeine will help a bit. Drink it.'

I tried.

'I'll be back in a minute. Keep sipping it.'

I held the bottle. Heavy glass bottle. Heavy cold bottle. Waisted and ribbed. Coke. I could no longer remember the reason I should drink it, but I tried to swallow some of the liquid. Watched the bottle drag my hand down like a lead weight. Made a huge effort through the fireworks going off at the back of my eyes to hold on to it. The fireworks, a lucid thought said, are probably those haemorrhages they find in a corpse that was strangled. Happening in my eyes.

My head was pulled back and the mouthpiece of an inhaler forced between my clenching teeth.

'Breathe in.'

I sucked in the spurt of gas and clutched for the inhaler.

'Sit still. Ten breaths. Through your nose.'

By the ninth, I was whimpering for another puff.

'OK. On a count of three. One. Two. Three.'

I breathed deeper than I thought I could, and the gas flowered and fumed in me, making every later breath deeper, quieter, easier. My heart, swollen like a bloodied bag, was beating inside the cage of my ribs, knocking echoes into my throat and temples. I let myself slide backwards until my head was resting against the paint of the door behind me, my legs splayed on the cobbles. In the ecstasy of new oxygen, I listened to the noise of my own breathing die down, relished the matched slowing of my pulse. Into the vacuum thus created came the noises from all around, becoming much more present to me. There were footsteps and, a little further away, the engines and horns of cars. A continuous noise difficult to identify until I opened my eyes and realised that it was the fountain at the centre of the open space.

A hand expertly found the pulse point in my wrist. 'Doing fine. You're doing fine.'

I struggled to sit up, and the same hand pushed me back. 'Give yourself time, give yourself time.'

I half-lay, considering this. 'You a doctor?' I asked, my eyes still closed.

'No.'

'Asthmatic?'

No. But I've worked with athletes.'

I thought about this while I summoned up some energy, then yanked myself into an upright sitting position and opened my eyes. The owner of the voice was hunkered down in front of me, Ventolin in one hand, Coke bottle in the other. I took the bottle from him and drank the last of it.

'Was that true about caffeine?'

'Being good for asthmatics? Yeah. Gets adrenalin pumping. I wouldn't, if I were you.'

'Wouldn't what?'

'Stand up.'

'OK.'

I closed my eyes again, and could hear rather than see him laughing.

'What's so funny?'

'You becoming so easy to persuade. Having started by telling me to piss off.'

I opened my eyes again.

'Sorry. Didn't know I'd said it out loud.'

He shrugged, stood up and took the empty bottle to a garbage container a few feet away.

'How'd you get a new Ventolin?' I asked, reaching for it when he walked back.

He slid it into his pocket and like a drug addict in sight of a fix, I almost screamed at him. But I needed his arm to get upright and stay upright, so I saved the scream.

'Took your empty one to a *pharmacie* over there and explained.'

'And they gave you one?'

'I did pay for it.'

I started to root in my pockets for change. 'I wasn't suggesting you stole it,' I said. 'I'm just wondering why they were willing to break the rules for you.'

He wasn't listening to me. His attention had shifted to watching out for and flagging a taxi. One of them accelerated out of the main traffic, screaming to a halt beside him.

'You don't have to travel with me—' I protested, when he got in beside me.

For the first time, I realised he was a big man. His movement was so swift, he seemed light, insubstantial. Sitting beside me in the taxi, he seemed more solid. Dark-haired, dark-eyed. Watchful like a guard dog.

'Save your breath,' he said. 'Tell the driver your address.'

What surprised me most about our arrival at the

house where I was working was the fluency of his
French, when he explained the delivery he was making.
My hosts were charmed by it. English people, in their
experience, rarely spoke French like natives, but he
did. He left his name – David Carpenter – with
them. What annoyed me all over again was that he
also left the Ventolin with them, almost deputising
them as monitors, explaining that I had probably
ingested enough of it for one day.

He telephoned the next morning to see how I was.
The French couple found this captivating and could
not understand why I did not feel the same way. My
French was not good enough to describe to them quite
how gruesome I must have looked when he stopped to
help me. Nor could I work out how to explain that
when you meet someone in such circumstances, you
may be grateful for them doing so efficient a Good
Samaritan performance, but you hope never to see
them again as long as you live.

I told them I would appreciate it if they told him
I was much improved and would always be grateful.
If he rang again, the key thing they should find out
was his address, so I could send him the money for
the Ventolin and forget the embarrassment of being
seen swollen, sweaty and speechless in a public place.
However, he did not ring the following day. Instead,

an arrangement of flowers arrived from Elysée Fleurs with a card expressing the hope that I was feeling better. I got the address from the flower shop and and acknowledged both with a note so brief, it read like a haiku. He sent another note. I ignored it. A third.

'I wouldn't mind,' I said to Gabrielle on the phone. 'But none of the notes are witty.'

'Daisy, don't forget your background is kind of unusual,' Gabrielle told me. 'Our parents wrote funny poems to each other in pencil on the formica top of the kitchen table. You were moving among smart-talking actors from the beginning of your teens. You've been spoiled. Most people are not witty all the time.'

'Oliver is,' I said.

'Yes, he is witty at a keyboard,' Gabrielle agreed. 'But he's not verbally witty. People who think he's good company believe it because he's a good-humoured lump of blotting paper absorbing whatever slop they spoon out. I'd never have married him for coruscating wit.'

'Go 'way out of that,' I said in my mother's voice. 'You'd have married him if he was a wall-eyed child molester.'

The mimicry was a coded key to belonging, even at long distance, in the complex of linked legends and language, references, healed wounds and sheathed weapons that is a family. I was with another family, but had no ownership of the vinculum that bonded them together. I was a transient, an outsider pretending to be an insider.

'Gabrielle?'

'Mmm?'

'Do you ever feel you are playing the part of you?'

'Daisy, I really would love to hit you with a deeply experienced truth, but when you have a demanding baby, a mother in the throes of moving and selling up, and a husband doing masterclasses in Israel, you have no doubt what part you're playing. When your head is just above shit-level, you don't have time for speculation about existentialism. But it's really good to know some member of the family is pitching in on the existentialist front. Even while fending off strange Brits *sous les ponts de Paris*.'

'Not fending off, exactly,' I said.

'Get off. Think I can't spot a fender a mile off?'

'Kilometre.'

'Oh, Jesus, I'd better learn bloody metric or my kids will grow up as failures.'

'So what's your news, anyway?'

'Oliver has a mobile phone that works in different

countries. May not be important or earth-shattering to you, kid, but when you're married to a man who's in Glasgow one day and Israel the next, it's nice to be able to talk to him.'

'In Israel?'

'Not Israel. Not yet. He left it at home this time. I'm programming it with the most frequently dialled numbers. Such is married life. Be warned. Be wary of stimulating the hero of the Ventolin to amorous commitment.'

'You mean, have my way with him and throw him away like a worn-out glove?'

'Screw him till you're dizzy and drop him like a stone.'

'What about quality time?'

'That's what you have with kids.'

'Not when they have colic.'

'On the other hand—'

'Yes, Gabrielle?'

'Wouldn't kill you to be civil to him once. He did sort of save your life.'

'You will remember not to tell Mam? I don't want her worrying about my wheezing.'

'Would I?'

'Very easily, by accident, if you don't watch yourself. Remember when you told her and dad about car crashes being like orgasms?'

'The more you plan them, the less likely they are to happen? Will I ever forget it?'

A few days later, David Carpenter sent me an invitation to dinner. It very formally indicated that it was fair to assume (he used the phrase, I swear) that in the nature of things (that was in it, too) I was probably better by now, so he thought we might renew our acquaintanceship.

'This is probably not a good idea,' I said to him as we entered the restaurant.

'Why not?'

'Men don't ask women out unless they want to take it further, and I'm not into that.'

'Into what?'

'Into *further*,' I said, furious at having to attach heavy implications to a floating flippancy.

As we ate, I asked him what he meant when he said he worked with athletes.

'I used to, I should have said. Presently, I am completing an MBA,' he said.

'In Paris?'

'You thought they all happened at Harvard?'

I did my mother's sigh, where you breathed in, very slowly, through your nose, mouth closed, and then let the air back out through your mouth, indicating that the other person is too tedious for words. It usually provokes the other person into justifying their position, but David Carpenter was unprovoked.

'Why would an Englishman do an MBA in Paris?' I asked.

'Who said I'm English?'

'You talk English.'

'I talk French, too, but you didn't think I was French.'

'Well, what the hell are you?'

'Irish.'

'You are?'

He looked at me with an expression that said he had already answered this question.

'Why do you sound English?'

'I was raised mostly in England.'

'Conversation with you is like fecking stones into the Grand Canyon,' I said. 'You're not filling in an income tax form, you know. You won't actually go to jail if you let out a teeny bit of info.'

'What more did you want to know?'

'For Chrissake, why were you raised mostly in England?'

He had been born in Mayo, but his father, a bank manager, was chosen to head up a branch in Britain – and David lived there with his family until after he had left school and went to work with a group of athletes. Later, he had worked with athletes in France and eventually stopped that work to finish his MBA. He gave the details in a brisk, dutiful way, not trying to make himself likeable — or even interesting.

'Do you ever wonder what you might have become if your father hadn't moved to Britain when he did?'

He shook his head.

'Never?'

'I don't wonder about things. And before you ask your next question, I don't know why I don't wonder. I just don't. You can take charge of wondering for the two of us.'

I was silenced by the collective. Not by its presumption, but by its casual rightness.

'I'd like to go home now,' I said

'You have a choice,' he said. 'We have coffee here, or you make coffee when I get you home.'

'I will not make you coffee.'

'Then you can spare the ten minutes to have it here.'

The waiter appeared, and David ordered.

'So you've been out of Ireland for——?'

'Eleven years. Why?'

The arrival of the coffee prevented me having to say, 'That's why you don't know me from TV.' I was used to French people not knowing who I was. An Irishman in the same position was unusual and welcome. There was none of the question and counter-question I was used to doing with Irish men, where each side staked out its ground, advertised its wares. Incurious acceptance meant there were gaps in the conversation that discomfited neither of us. Going unrecognised was one of the two best things about being in Paris. The other was the removal of Richelle Governey. Now that there was never a chance of her turning up at my workplace, I began to believe my dad might have been right. In time, I would lose the heavy dread and perhaps even forget her name.

David Carpenter and I walked home that night mostly in silence. Our two shadows, separated, as we passed each lamppost, by empty bright air, started out as squat, sharp-edged, then stretched, taller and taller the further we went from that light, until their mile-high heads disappeared in the puddle of brightness provided by the next lamppost. There was a rhythm to our steps and a syncopated, longer beat to our moves from lamppost to lamppost.

'I wish I could whistle,' I said.

'What would you whistle, if you could whistle?'

'How many chugs would a woodchug chug . . .'

'. . . if a woodchug could chug wood.'

'A march, if I knew a march. The only march

I know is "Colonel Bogey" and that wouldn't be right.'

'A Sousa march,' he proposed.

My shadow's tall skinny shoulders shrugged: What's Sousa? His shadow put up its tall thin right arm, index finger — in shadow — at least eighteen inches long. Not so much directing silence as selecting the note to start from. The shadow conducted the opening of the march he whistled, then the arm dropped to his side again and we walked into another puddle of light, in half-parody step with each other, in warm companionship with the music he was creating.

This, I thought, would be romantic if it were in film. But it is just me and an ageing MBA student. We turned the corner into the avenue where my employers lived. The music broke off for a second.

'Would you ever stop thinking,' he said impatiently, and went back to whistling.

I must, I thought, stop trying to put things in context, stop trying to fit my life into a frame of reference from some other time, some other place. As if I was playing the part of me. Or was learning real life by correspondence course.

At the foot of the six steps up to my employers' home, he finished the march very meticulously. Once he was sure I was inside the first glass door, he walked back down the street whistling a brisker march and keeping time to it. I sneaked open the door to hear the tune and he turned at the corner to wave at me. Still standing there, I started to wonder what I would do if he telephoned again, and had to give myself a shake. Sometimes, just here and now is enough, I told myself. Sometimes there is a moment of perfect happiness you can recognise at the time – if you just stop thinking.

'This guy is less dull the more you get to know him,' I told Gabrielle.

'The more I get to know him?'

'Don't pounce, Gabrielle. You were never made to be a mouser.'

'I'm trying to be a ratter.'

'Don't waste your energy. He's certainly not a rat. Bit dull, maybe.'

'Dull is the most awful trait.'

'No, it isn't. Meanness is the most awful trait.'

'That's true. I'll tell you what I'm worried about – what I'm really and truly worried about. Will I?'

'Go ahead. All this euphemistic duplicity is getting me down.'

'Daisy. You see potential in people and you – you infuse them with the confidence that they can do anything. I just worry that you're seeing more in this man than is actually there. I'd be afraid that in the glow of your interest, he might grow temporarily and you'll fall in love with what you have created and then he'll – he'll – develop a slow puncture and all the puff you've put into him will leak out of him and you'll be left married to this flattened lump of – dull.'

'Gabrielle?'

'Yes.'

'Awful shame you never learned to be direct about things. The way you fudge ... anyway, where did the marriage bells come in? I met this guy only six weeks ago.'

'Oh, Daisy. We're the marrying kind. You know that.'

Oliver's voice, in the background, said he knew that, to his cost. Lovingly, she told him to shag off.

'Listen, I'm going to shag off, this is costing me every franc I earned last week.'

'Daisy, honestly, now, what do you see in him?'

'He's satisfied with himself.'

'Jesus, that's worse than dull. Self-satisfied, as well!'

'Good night, Gabrielle.'

'You're not offended?'

'Sure isn't it only for my own good?'

'Oh, shag off, Daisy.'

'I keep trying to. Not good at picking boyfriends, not good at shagging off. Think you could find me a remedial teacher?'

'Goodnight.'

'Bon soir, ma soeur adorable.'

The fact that I told David Carpenter my sister thought him dull says something about our location at the time. I was climbing the spiral staircase in one leg of the Arc de Triomphe five steps behind him. Five steps, because I was counting each and every step. He made no comment, just asked, over his shoulder, if Gabrielle was my only sister.

'Yes,' I said. 'Can we stop for a minute?'

'There's an alcove around the next corner.'

The two of us sat on the smooth stone in the alcove, watching people who had been behind us on the staircase pass us by. Bunches of kids on a school trip outraced each other. Fat men sweated grimly. Older women looked at me with frank hatred for getting the alcove first.

People tended to look in a much more friendly way at him, I noticed, even though he walked with his head down most of the time, and, when preoccupied, had a hawk-like predator's face. Strangers even spoke to him more than would normally happen. When they did, he was always affable with them, although he had a knack of turning to them so that I was excluded from the always brief conversation. Each person seemed to belong in a separate cell of his attention.

He stood up without putting his hand out for support or balance.

'Gabrielle your older sister, too?'

I nodded. He looked smug. A sudden spurt of fury came out of me.

'Who the hell do you think you are, with your nod nod as if you were bloody measuring me for something?' I asked his departing back.

He laughed.

'Well, answer me.'

'I'm doing due diligence.'

'What the hell is due diligence?'

'Due diligence is checking out the books of a company before you buy into it.'

'The goddam nerve of you. The nerve of you.'

'Everybody does it all the time.'

'As if people were companies? My sister thinks you're too bloody certain and self-satisfied and maybe she's right.'

We emerged onto the top of the monument, Paris spreading out like a wheel with us as the hub. Orderly and elegant. He knew every avenue, every boulevard. There was La Défense. Over here was the Eiffel Tower. Down that way was where we had met.

The footpath of each of the avenues was furred with trees, the dark green lines interrupted by bright umbrellas indicating where cafés were located.

'There are more small cars here than in Dublin,' I said.

He raised his eyebrows.

'Much fewer Mercs,' I said.

'Really?'

'Every second person at home has a Merc, a BMW or a Porsche. You'd better get home while the boom's still on.'

'Dublin's home to you.'

'And you?'

'Home's wherever I am at the time.'

For some reason, this sounded lonely, rather than cosmopolitan. It was drizzling, so we started back down the stairs. Paid our respects to the Unknown Soldier.

'Last of a dying breed,' I said.

'Who?'

'Unknown soldiers.'

'Dog tags implanted in teeth.'

'And DNA tracking.'

I was about to run across the street to the opposite

pavement but allowed myself to be directed down the steps of an underground walkway. A busker with a big Celtic harp was playing some Baroque guitar piece. David Carpenter put money into the velvet-lined instrument case. Quietly.

'D'you always give a donation?'

'Only if they're good.'

Because I wanted to ask him how he knew they were good (although I restrained myself), I knew I was beginning to find him too interesting. So I told him I was seeing him too often. He wanted to know what scale I used to decide this. It was the last responce I had expected, and I had no idea how to cope with it. Like a child, I found myself saying there was no scale, it was just because.

He asked me how many fewer meetings I would like us to have. I said probably once a month was enough. He agreed to this with such casual amity I wanted to hit him.

Then he kept to it much more religiously than I would have wanted. Occasionally, in the three weeks between meetings, he might drop me a short note about a show that was opening, and if I did not contact him to say he shouldn't bother, he would buy tickets for it and pick me up at such a time on such a date. I never contacted him to prevent the

ticket-buying and the shows were always fun. On a
couple of occasions we went to Monday night poetry
readings at Shakespeare & Co. In the warmer months,
we often sat in the open, drinking coffee or Pernod.

'I really hate this stuff,' I told him, pouring the
water into the glass to make the drink murky and
milky. 'Tastes like aniseed balls.'

'Why do you drink it?'

'I feel I should.'

'You should?'

'When in Rome.'

'You wouldn't feel sure you were in Paris if you
weren't drinking Pernod?'

'I wouldn't feel I measured up. I'd feel I was playing
a role without the right props.'

As the year wore on, I met and dated a few other
men. I would tell David Carpenter about the funnier
dates, including the evenings with a man who turned
out to be married and who held the view that one
married a wife for one set of reasons which did not
preclude a social life with other beautiful women.

'What are the reasons for marrying a wife?' David
asked when I told him about this encounter.

'His or mine?'

'Yours.'

'I couldn't have reasons for marrying a wife.'

'Well, for marrying a husband, then.'

'I don't have any. I'd be happier living with some-one – knowing I could walk away if things didn't work. Feeling I could breathe.'

'What were his reasons?'

'Babies, I suppose,' I said. 'He'd feel if you were into procreation, you should be married.'

He thought about this for a moment.

'Makes sense,' he said, to my slight disappoint-ment.

'What? Just for babies?'

'Why not?'

'What about sex, love, intellectual growth, com-panionship, shared interests?'

'You can have all those without getting married. In fact, you can have them without moving beyond friendship.'

I could not locate a safe way to say what I thought I believed. It slithered away from me, my certainty, and came back into focus dressed up as a pleasing anachronism my parents would have liked.

'But then, I probably have a low sex drive,' he said casually.

Since we had never had a sexual encounter, I won-dered if this was in the nature of an explanation.

'I've always been turned on more by physical

closeness — the great comfort of closeness — than by the prospect of sex, so I suppose I do not invest sex with the all-fired significance others do.'

'Others like who?' I asked, eating raw spinach salad and trying to convince myself I liked it.

'Our parents invested happy-ever-after in it. They saved up all of their urges until the priest said, "Have at it, you're legal." Some of our contemporaries either invest competitiveness in sex — how many times in one night — or see it as therapy.'

He paid the bill. His French always surprised me, it was so fluent, so elegant. As he held the door of the restaurant open for me, I said, 'Say something in French, just to me.'

'*Allez vite, les flics,*' he said obligingly. As corroboration, a police siren screamed in the back streets.

'I meant something personal,' I laughed.

'I know you did,' he said flatly. Refusing to be drawn.

'D'you rehearse making people pointlessly uncomfortable or does it come naturally to you?'

He didn't answer. We were walking now along the river, past the spot where, in the summer, a swimming pool was fenced off within the Seine. Our chins were tucked into the collars of our coats to draw up the warmth from our own bodies. We walked in silence until we arrived, faces glowing from within but cold-skinned, at the front door of my employers' house. He bent to kiss me.

'I'm going back to Ireland soon,' I said.

'How soon?'

'Six weeks or so.'

'Why?'

'Done this.'

He stood, my face held between his big warm hands, absently tidying my eyebrows with his fingers.

'I'll be going back later in the year myself.'

'How much later?'

His shrug indicated this had not been established. 'But I'll see you there,' he added.

'Won't be the same as here.'

His two hands squeezed my face just tightly enough to make my mouth purse like a feeding goldfish.

'Don't make more of here than was here,' he said.

I dragged his hands away from my face and started up the steps. What was most wounding about the blow was that it seemed to give him the initiative. I wanted to yell at him that I was just as casual as he was, but casual is one of those claims difficult to make when you're wrongfooted.

'Why don't you go to hell?' I suggested.

'If that's what you want,' he said, and walked away.

I was resolute in not watching him, resolute, too, in the quiet way I closed the door behind me and greeted the family. Nobody would know that I was furious. There seemed to be a satisfaction due as a result of this minor performance triumph, so I stayed awake for a long time waiting for it to arrive.

CHAPTER SEVEN

Testing, Testing

——◆◆◆——

There was a stir of approval at the party when Robert Allen said it.

'I would hope, at the end of my days, to be able to say with truth, "I was faithful to that woman."'

He nodded across the room at his wife. Too far away to hear him, she did the collusive facial tic that means 'you and I are a team. I would rather be over there with you than here where I am, but needs must.'

'Not that women are going to be falling over themselves to tempt me,' he added, laughing and running his hand over his balding head. 'Not exactly God's gift—'

Several of the women rushed to tell him how

attractive bald could be, as if his self-esteem was in immediate danger of meltdown. It seemed pointless. As far as I could tell, Robert Allen's self-esteem was not in danger. Short, overweight and bald, he nonetheless carried himself with the assurance of a handsome six-footer.

The party conversation moved on to the theory that a good marriage cannot be broken up by the intervention of a third party.

'The Other Woman gets blamed, but if you examine the situation, the marriage was always on the rocks long before the Other Woman hoved to.'

Coercive consensus built, silencing those who thought marriages could be broken up from the outside.

'If you were given the task of improving the image of the Other Woman, how would you do it?' I asked one of the women, who was famous as a PR strategist.

'Which other woman?'

'Any other woman. The Other Woman as a concept.'

'Why would you want to?' Robert Allen asked.

His wife abandoned the group she was with, sidling over to sit on the padded arm of his chair.

'Oh, I could see why you would want to. The

Other Woman has had a very bum deal. Nobody approves of her. She may get her man, but she's always disapproved of.'

'Helen, you're right,' Gabrielle said, returning, soothing baby Stephen who had been crying. 'One step above the prostitute, that's where the image of the Other Woman is.'

'Except in France.'

'Oh, France,' someone said dismissively.

'But isn't that the image the Other Woman should have?'

'Why? For picking up someone who's fallen out of an unhappy marriage?'

'For having a relationship with someone who's still married.'

Several voices talked at once.

'For not caring about the children involved.'

'If there are children involved.'

'Well, of course.'

'The Other Woman doesn't have any of the responsibilities.'

'Like what?'

'It's the wife who washes his dirty underwear.'

'Why does this discussion always come down to dirty underwear?'

'Anyway, that's done by machines. Wives only sort.'

'They also sort who only—'

'In marriage, you see all aspects of a man, but when you're just the Other Woman, you see the best, you see the social side.'

'Or the professional side, when someone's really on top of their job.'

'As opposed to seeing them at home where they may be useless.'

'Useless at what?'

'Everything. Anything.'

'And have halitosis.'

'The Other Woman wouldn't fail to notice halitosis.'

'Or fart.' This last came from Robert Allen, whose wife laughed down at him from her perch on the chair arm.

'That presupposes,' she told him, 'a man saves up his farts to do at home.'

'Well, he might make an extra effort not to do it in the presence of the Other Woman,' someone suggested.

'But it shows how the marriage was rubbish before the other woman arrives.'

'Or that the marriage is so solid it can sustain the odd escape of . . . of . . . methane,' Helen Allen said, mischievously.

'That's right,' Robert said, warming to this. 'It says a lot for a wife if she's the sort of woman you can fart in the same room as.'

'It could say she's the sort of woman you have no respect for,' someone on the outskirts of the group said.

'Does one measure respect in farts unspoken?'

'Unspoken?'

'Would you prefer unsung?'

'Or unignited. You can set fire to them, you know. Methane is flammable.'

'The Other Woman doesn't see a man slumped in front of the TV, doesn't see him being rude to the kids, doesn't see him postponing fixing things—'

'Portrait of a troubled marriage coming out here?'

'As if I would ever be rude to my obnoxious offspring.'

'No, but you know what I mean?'

'She means,' Helen Allen said helpfully, 'it's not just farts.'

'It's farts, plus,' Robert added.

'Now, there's something the divorce lawyers haven't copped on to: saving up farts as a form of marital abuse.'

'The Eskimos say that each man loves the smell of his own farts.'

'Oh, please.'

The couple in the chair exchanged an expressionless glance which nonetheless carried a series of messages. You would never say that, love, went one of the messages. Still and all, the man who did say it has a few scoops in him, went the response. Wouldn't want to make him uncomfortable, though, by a reproving reaction.

'You're all talking as if the wife was better, more long-suffering,' I said quietly. 'As if the Other Woman had it easier.'

Faces turned to me, surprised at the new voice.

'Often, the Other Woman is much more long-suffering than the wife. She has to take whatever shit gets dished out by the wife or friends of the wife when they find out, she has to fit around his schedule—'

'Always be glamorous and dolled up, because she has no excuse of kids,' Gabrielle said from the hard dining-room chair Oliver had brought for her to sit on. She was pregnant again.

'Every Other Woman I've ever met,' Oliver offered mischievously, 'has been aching to slump in front of the TV watching sport with her man.'

'What's stopping her?'

'They're braver and more loyal, too,' I said.

Helen Allen looked at me with real interest this time, nodding at me to go on.

'If you think about it, who died along with Mussolini and Hitler? Their mistresses. Not their wives.'

'Eva Braun was his wife.'

'She didn't know she would be when she committed herself to dying with him.'

'D'you remember the pictures of Mussolini and his mistress strung up on meat hooks upside down?'

'One of the English kings had a mistress who bore him about eighteen kids and was more his wife than his wife was,' Helen Allen said.

'So?'

'So if you have a situation – no, look at it this way—'

'What Helen means,' Robert said delightedly, 'is that she has no clue why she introduced this nameless hussy who was mistress of the king.'

Helen Allen struggled for a moment to retrieve the rationale behind her introduction of the royal mistress, then laughed and hugged her husband.

'My point is that if you introduced an Other Woman to Robert, for example . . .'

Robert Allen looked eagerly around him. 'Where? Where?'

'She would have no effect. A marriage like you two have is impregnable.'

Helen Allen freed her arm from around her husband's shoulders and did the vampire keep-off sign. 'Kiss of death,' she said, patently uncomfortable at being held up as part of a perfect marriage. 'Kiss of death. Minute you say that, there's a pothole around the next corner. Dug right through to China.'

I noticed Gabrielle sliding a hand behind her own back to help with the ache of her now-evident second pregnancy. Robert Allen's gaze met mine in a flickered acknowledgement that he too had seen the movement. He got to his feet, careful not to dislodge his wife from the arm of the chair.

'Helen, you on for returning to our den of dirty clothes?'

His wife stood into his embrace, smiling at him with both affection and irony.

'Long as they're your dirty clothes, sweetheart, I'll return to them any time.'

'We won't ask about his farts,' someone said, to a chorus of shushing.

One of the guests went to get the overcoats. People reached to pull their coats out of the pile. Others called out descriptions – the one with the torn label and the scarf in the sleeve.

'And another thing,' Oliver said, helping a bulky man into an anorak that gave him the look of someone recently inflated. 'I don't rate the Eskimos, anyway.'

'You're dead right. Offering their wives to any passing stranger.'

'What about wives allowing themselves to be offered?'

'Your igloo or mine?'

'Plus they all die young from eating whale fat.'

'Wouldn't you hope to die young if you were in a farting culture in an igloo?'

'With your wife in the guest igloo farting with a total stranger.'

Oliver opened the front door and couples surged out through it, thanking the hostess, colliding in kisses, getting in each other's way.

'Did you never hear of women and children first?'

'Whose children?'

'The Eskimo's children.'

'The eighteen kids yer wan the prolific mistress had.'

'Don't you be using filthy words.'

'Sshh – the neighbours.'

'Frig the neighbours. They're lucky to live near a genius. They can cope with the noise of his friends.'

'If they were Eskimos, they'd have to lend him their wives.'

Car doors banged, engines started up. As the Allens' car came level with the front door, Robert rolled down his window.

'Magic evening, Gabrielle,' he said, mouthing the syllables to compensate for the quietness of his voice. Helen leaned across him and did a thumbs-up sign as the window rolled back up and the car began to move.

'Nice couple,' I said.

'Aren't they, though?' my sister said. 'Hope, when we're a hundred and three, Oliver, you'll be able to say, like Robert, you were faithful to one woman.'

Oliver, his arm around her thickening waist, said he would be glad to be able to say anything understandable when he was that old.

No, I thought, you're missing the point, Gabrielle. He said he *hoped* to be able to say, at the end of his days, that he had been faithful to her. Hoped. Interesting, that passivity. Makes it a contingency, not a promise.

I will contact you, Robert Allen, I thought. I will contact you.

CHAPTER EIGHT

At the Podium

———➤◆❮———

In fact, he contacted me, at the suggestion of his wife.

'I need a speaker for a retreat, and Helen says I should ask you.'

'A retreat?'

He laughed.

'Sorry. Jargon. We take our staff away for a weekend in a hotel once a year to kick around ideas about where the company's going and we call it a retreat. We invite guest speakers. This year, because we're going through a big transition phase, we need the speakers to address the issue of change.'

'What do I know about change?'

'You've done it.'

'Gone from acting to child-minding.'

'That's what you chose, is it not?'

'Yes, but it's not going to give your manacled slaves a collective orgasm about ambitions fulfilled.'

'Whattya mean, my manacled slaves?'

'Sorry. Your highly motivated staff. Who not only have to work like hell for minimal pay but have to go on retreats during their spare time to learn to be flexible so if Massa wants to shift them from weaving to road-sweeping, they'll doff their little forelocks and say, "Yessuh".'

'You can't doff a forelock.'

'Yeah, you can. At some point in the past, you doffed that forelock of yours permanently.'

He roared laughing, and I could hear him telling someone in his office that this woman he wanted for the conference was insulting his baldness and calling him a slave-driver.

'So, will you do it?'

'I charge £2,000 a go.'

'As the actress said to the bishop.'

'Or 2K, if you prefer it that way.'

'Sure.'

'Now I know I should have said £5,000.'

He listed a number of much more famous people he could have hired for £5,000. I told him he was shredding my self-esteem.

'I'd say your self-esteem is invincible,' he said.

'Just shows you,' I said, in a voice gone slightly distant, carrying a hint of melancholy. Then I rang off, saying I looked forward to receiving briefing notes from him.

I was sure, then, I could make him fall in love with me. That I would do it, not because of attraction to him — there was none — but in a reflex testing of powers. The instinct was so strong, so unquestionable, I assumed it to be common to all young women, this exigent internal predator deciding, in regard to this or that married man: 'I could take you.'

I could not be alone, I thought, in possessing the silent unacknowledged truth that my youth made any woman even ten years older than me vulnerable. It had to be rooted in race memory, this certitude that one could take a man from another woman, and that even if one liked his wife, one would still take him. Because it was possible. A muscle to be tried out.

It was there to be spotted, all around me. This teenager, sulky-silent with the parents of her friends, making one of the fathers watch dry-mouthed as she walked away, her back sweet-slender in silhouette. That dutiful twenty-year-old, the daughter everybody wished for, docile and shaped by the demands of others, yet somewhere in the pale eyes a cat's need to leap, to claw, to play with deadly, atavistic intent and to abandon when life leached out of the plaything.

There was a helpless preparedness, too, in the men, as raucous as the red oestrus display of a rutting primate. So ready, these men, that the young women picking them off did not even have to speak their language or pretend to find them interesting. Some chemical interaction lent mystery to every surly shrug, made the one-word put-downs — 'Whatever' — individual and engaging, turned the mass-produced habits reprehensible in one's own children into delightful expressions of uniqueness in the beloved.

You did not have to woo these solid citizens, these good family men. Once the first filament was thrown over them, it gave a shimmering significance to every message about you. So if you were away, they imagined rescuing you from handbag-snatching biker Latins. If you were ill, they noted the languor in your gesture and found puzzling their own sense that you should be carried and rug-cocooned like a latter-day Elizabeth Barrett Browning.

If you drank too much or they suspected you were 'on' something, that, too, was an added draw, evil rendered into virtue by the alchemy of denied attraction in a boundless illogic which, for the wife involved, was the most maddening aspect of the whole thing.

'He fell in love with a Curehead,' I heard a woman say on a radio programme. 'A filthy, white-faced girl with black around her eyes and black clothes. The same age as his daughter. If his daughter had ever dressed like that he'd have had her washed and straightened up immediately, but in this girl, it's like the awfulness of it was the attraction. The rest of us were somehow old-fashioned and hicky because we were clean and wore bright colours.'

Having decided to have an affair with Robert Allen, I was able to pick up and decode signals never received before. If I did not contact him before the date of the speech, he would — I knew — ring me at my sister's to confirm. I had the right day and place. I knew, too, he would enjoy having to perform this extra task.

On the night of the retreat, when I arrived, Robert was warm, welcoming and self-mocking.

'Aren't you nervous about what I'll say?' I asked him.

'Should I be?'

'If I make a balls of it, they'll blame you. You picked me. It'll be your failure.'

'Grand,' he said, the two of us now in the corridor leading to the conference room, his hand lightly, impersonally, at my back.

'How well do you cope with failure?'

He stopped dead, head on one side, looking into the middle distance. I stopped too. Waited. 'I don't know. I've never had a failure.'

'You're kidding.'

He laughed, shaking his head.

'It's probably not politically correct to say it, but it's the truth. I've never had a failure. I've had injuries in sport, but they weren't failures.'

He cast around for a moment, embarrassed by his own confession of consistent success.

'I am bald and fat, though. Would that do?'

'You tell me. Do you regard those as failures?'

We were moving again, he nodding to acquaintances.

'Bald is an injustice, rather than a failure. I wish I wasn't.'

'But not enough to get a transplant?'

He dipped his head to show the extent of its hairlessness. 'Wouldn't have the time — can you imagine how long it would take to put transplants all over that acreage? On the other hand, this,' he said, indicating his tuxedo-encased paunch, 'probably is a failure.'

We had arrived at the conference-room door, him on my right. For a few seconds, we stood, me with my left hand around the pull-bar of one side of the double-sided door, drawing a few deep breaths. Then my right hand, speedy as a sigh, palm-patted the heaviness he had acknowledged.

'On the contrary,' I said. 'That's the sexiest thing about you—' and was past him, into brighter lights of the big room with its logo'd podium.

I started the talk with anecdotes from the soap-opera experience, including reference to the problem posed when the actor playing a beloved character wants to leave the series, but the producers want the character to continue.

'As long as the plot keeps moving,' I told them, 'a TV audience can cope with a replacement actor. Can make the change. The new actor doesn't even have to physically match the earlier actor in appearance: the character can go from being red-haired and five foot six, to being blond and six foot tall, without audience mutiny. Of course, nobody has yet challenged an audience by replacing a male actor who has loads of hair with one who is – is – is—' Apparently lost for words, I gestured helplessly at Robert, and the audience laughed and applauded. As did he.

I have you, I thought. I have but to make a half-reference to you and it's like touching the glass globe of one of those electrical storm lamps: brittle links of light spark between us.

'Didn't I tell you she'd be wonderful?' Helen asked her husband afterwards.

'Oh, you had to persuade him to invite me to talk?' I teased. 'You met with resistance, Helen, did you?'

Fingers to the glass globe, I was thinking. See the broken angles spark together, united for a fractioned second, even as he stands, arm around his wife.

Helen, that hand at your waist seems the secret language of your unity, but this time it is half-Judas kiss, half-concealment of the faithlessness I will cause to flower and fruit into unfaithfulness. Today, I will talk to you, Helen, not to him, knowing he attends upon our conversation, glowing at the affection between us, pleased we self-evidently like each other. I will move with you so we two precede him and he will contrast the slenderness of me with the stockier solidity of you.

When it comes time to step into the waiting car, I will have an afterthought that will catch me in awkward honesty, forcing me to say to Robert that this speech has probably opened up possibilities for me I had never considered, and it's all thanks to Helen. You will laugh easily in self-dismissal, Helen, and for just a split second Robert will be unsatisfied with that response to my openness, and so will find some reason, in the coming week, to contact me to 'make it right'.

Four days after the speech, the call came from him. An invitation to lunch.

'I don't think you had any idea of the impact you had on my slaves,' he told me. 'I've had a number of approaches from people wanting more. Particularly about dressing to conceal flaws.'

At the restaurant, where he was evidently a regular, I accepted his recommendation on what to eat so readily that it bothered him.

'Fact that I like it doesn't mean you'll necessarily like it.'

'But you've never had a failure.'

He settled into laughing recognition of his own comment, then talked about his growing business, its overseas outposts and future directions. There was uncomplicated zest to everything he did. A happy man, not showing off or pretending. An unobtrusive host, pouring the wine and introducing business acquaintances.

'Without Helen,' one of them told me, 'this man would be nowhere. Nowhere.'

'Too bloody right,' Robert said.

As the man walked away, Robert watched him, smiling.

'Seems to me that roughly half the guys in Helen's year in university were in love with her. Think they could have married her — maybe should have married her. Have their jury still out on me.'

It was almost as if, because she had taken ten years out to be with the children when they were small, I might underestimate her if I didn't know she had held her own, in college, with this (current) senior counsel or that junior minister. It was easy to provoke him to praise Helen.

I realised, for the first time, that a man praising his wife to another woman doubts his own praise as soon as it is bestowed. Because the praise renders the absent woman unreal. The man struggles to prevent her being faded by the bright gaze of the woman he is with. The woman he is with calls her 'your wife' as she mentions what is admirable in the wife, her praise as counter-productively generous as the gesture from a lead actor of 'please applaud my colleagues' when the audience cares only for the star. The man applauds his wife and simultaneously finds her wanting. Applauds her louder to compensate and hates the husband stereotype it makes of him.

Listening and prompting, I was conscious of the heightening electric current between us. There was a physical tightening of the tension, like a fisherman sensing the spring of a line.

'I shouldn't invade your privacy, getting you to

talk about your wife so much,' I said at one point. 'Although I'm sure she's used to being latched on to as a role model. She's so sure. Not shaken loose, constantly, by doubts.'

My voice tailed off in deference to the waiter's arrival, and I listened to the descriptions of the items on the sweet trolley, conscious, all the time, of Robert Allen's gaze. If a cartoon speech bubble had been suspended over him, it would have read, 'Gosh, my wife is old enough to be a role model. And this girl is so vulnerable: shaken loose by doubts.'

As if erasing the speech bubble, I brisked the pace of the conversation so that he briefed me on staff reaction to the talk. He told me that I should do more of such talks.

'The national attention span is too short,' I said. 'Eighteen months from now, nobody will instantly associate the soap with me. Even now, most of the people in the street who register any kind of recognition of my face think I'm a distant acquaintance of theirs. They don't remember they saw me on TV.'

'But the points you make out of the drama are valid.'

'I'm not sure I want to be like that bunch of thesps in Britain who go around teaching people to be better in business by reference to Hamlet.'

Robert Allen touched my hand. I started as if he had poked me with an electric cattle prod. He withdrew his hand in exaggerated guilt, pretending to look furtively around to see if anyone had seen my reaction.

'I'd love to be around when someone gooses you, if that's your reaction to a casual touch.'

'I'm sorry. I was miles away. Thinking. There's a role in business — based on what you're saying — a role in business for someone who can look at someone the way a designer for a play looks at the roles, and dress them appropriately. But not for me. I'm not going to tell people to wear blue to match their eyes and up and down stripes to make them look thinner.'

'I must say, when I went into business, I thought nobody would ever bother about clothes again — I figured we'd all live in jeans for the rest of our lives and be judged on what we were.'

I sat back in my chair and laughed at him. 'Steve Jobs meets Sixties hippie? That what you are?'

'Wannabe sportsman, more like,' he smiled. 'The athletes I admire — you don't even notice what they wear. Understated performers who could deliver if you put them in sacking shorts and T-shirt. David Carpenter. That kind.'

Second cattle prod, I thought, taken aback by my

own almost physical reaction to the name. As was he. His expression said 'Helloo? What's going on here?' I laughed.

'Sorry, it's just I don't know the David Carpenter you're talking about, because I know nothing about sport, but I do know a quite different David Carpenter, and for a moment I was confused. Tell me about your David Carpenter.'

'No, you tell me about *your* David Carpenter. If the mention of his name electrifies you, he's probably much more interesting than a soccer player would be.'

Carpenter was a man I had met in Paris when I was au pairing, I explained. Nice chap. Superb French. Finishing an MBA. Hadn't been in contact with him now for about a year. He was probably back in Ireland.

'He is. Back in Ireland. Same David Carpenter.'

'How could he be?'

'Why wouldn't he be?'

He consumed the last of the whipped cream, then lined up his cutlery, a collusive eyes-to-heaven, aren't-I-dreadful invitation meeting the resistance of my lack of expression.

Not my job; wives tell husbands not to eat fats, I thought. It is part of the concern they must show. In turn, that concern, repeated, makes them rejectable. Like English speakers talking extra loudly to foreigners who don't understand at any volume, wives emphasise the unacceptable again and again as if repetition would make it stick.

'OK,' he said, wiping his mouth with his napkin. 'Lemme describe him to you.'

Hearing Carpenter recreated in words added to, rather than subtracted from, the low-level excitement between Robert Allen and me. He enjoyed making me relinquish my conviction that I must know a different David Carpenter.

'He's heavier than you describe, if he's the same man.'

'Well, he stopped playing six or seven years ago; so he's probably put up a bit of weight.'

'Why isn't he managing a football team? I thought that's where all footballers ended up once they got too old or too injured for the game.'

'He did. That's what took him to France. But now I suspect he'll specialise in more general work. Management consultancy, probably. Team-building. Did people not recognise him when you were with him?'

'No. Although, now that you ask me—'

Now, the unusual friendliness of the Parisians was explained. The complicit nods I now understood to mean 'We know who you are, but we won't annoy you.' The initiation of conversations and his turning to them to exclude me also took on a new meaning: fans coming up and saying something flattering to him, or wanting an autograph. I didn't know whether to admire the panache of the deception (or perhaps it was concealment rather than deception) or kick myself for not having been more inquisitive at the time.

Robert seemed more interested in David Carpenter, past tense, than in David Carpenter, present tense. Carpenter had been a deadly combination, he told me, drawing on the tablecloth with his stubby forefinger. A great strategic brain. A sense of where each player was going to move to. Plus he moved so fluently. I laughed at the use of the word, and he smiled but repeated it. Fluent. That was the only way to describe Carpenter as a mover. I thought of the long shadow cast by street lamps in Paris and ached with an inexplicable nostalgia. I hadn't liked David Carpenter that much, and as he himself had put it, we shouldn't make more out of Paris than had been there. So why this blood-surge of sentimentality?

'If you're not into sport, what on earth did you and David Carpenter have in common? What did you talk about?'

'Due diligence and my sister,' I said truthfully.

'You never talked about his sporting past?'

'I told you, I didn't know about it.'

'What about your TV past?'

'He didn't know about it.'

'And you didn't tell him?'

I shook my head. He roared laughing.

'Jesus, the two of them have the most high-profile pasts anybody could have, and they let on to be anonymous.'

I thought about this. Not talking about the soap had given all of my relationships in Paris a freshness, as if I were new-minted. Never mentioning Richelle Governey had made her less real, less present. I wondered what she was doing now. Perhaps two and a half years had elapsed since I had last seen her.

'I'm sorry for reminding you of the relationship,' Robert Allen said very gently.

'Why? David Carpenter's a nice fella. I haven't a bad word to say about him. I was just thinking about a particular actress I used to know who really wasn't going to make it. In acting, I mean. I was wondering what she's doing, these days.'

'Don't all actors when they're "resting" wait on tables and serve behind bars?'

'Not any more. The majority of the women work as temps. Temping keeps half the businesses in this country going — you have good inputting speeds and familiarity with a couple of computer programmes, you can walk in and out of jobs easily. Literally, your show closes Saturday, you turn up at somebody's office on Monday next. I'm sure that's true of your company.'

'Particularly so since we started to grow. Helen keeps tight control of costs, and any time we need bodies above the number in the business plan, she says yeah as long as they're temps. No commitments on either side. No long-term overhead. You're telling me the plant is probably full of Kenneth Branaghs down on their luck?'

'Not necessarily down on their luck. Some of them might be like me: know they were good at a particular time in their life, but know too that they're not going to be great in their middle years. Shirley Temple was a great child actress, but once she hit her twenties — poof. It just didn't work. But she had the intelligence to go do something else. She was an American ambassador to somewhere. Acting is probably unique that way. Loads of people when they finish their real career take up writing — and make a good living out of it — but it's the other way with acting. People start acting and then go on to something else.'

'Like Ronald Reagan?'

'Or John Wilkes Booth.'

'Shakespeare.'

'Yeah – right! Oh, and Glenda Jackson.'

'Loads of TV and radio presenters. Melina Mercouri.'

'Who?'

'I forget how young you are. Her second career was in politics. What's your second career going to be?'

'I don't know. I don't want to rush into anything quickly. Remember, I've been working since my early teens.'

'And I presume, unlike the child stars in the tabloids, your parents invested your money for you?'

'I'd never have earned anything like the child stars, if you mean kids like the one out of *Different Strokes*, but yes, my parents took very good care of my salary for me.'

My poor father, I thought. Always – vainly – hoping there would come a day when I would be mathematically competent and eager for him to give me a full briefing about sliding scales, statutory and voluntary pension schemes, tax advantages and investment funds.

'You won't see me begging in the street this year, anyway, Robert,' I said, smiling and drawling the syllables of the name with an actor's sensuality. At the same time, I touched his arm gently.

'You're very good to care,' I added softly.

As we reached the front door of the restaurant, he was pulling his big belted camel coat around him, rattling car keys, offering a lift, accepting the return of his credit card and receipt.

I walked decidedly away from him before the door closed behind the two of us, hands deep in coat pockets, shoulders back. Watch me, my thoughts ordered him. Stand and watch me in the hope that I will glance back. But I'll not glance back, I thought, turning my face up to the wintry sun, following the icy-bright white lines etched by a tiny plane a mile high in the blue sky.

Sunshine on jet trails, I thought. I must use that phrase to him, sometime. It is the sort of thing he would like.

CHAPTER NINE

Proof Negative

———◆◇◆———

I wondered how, having told Robert Allen I would not serve as wardrobe consultant to his staff, he would find a way to stay in touch with me. There was no doubt in my mind that he would stay in contact. The only issue was how.

Within weeks, Robert rang to ask me to attend an international conference about image, grooming and self-presentation. His company would pay. It would ensure the service they eventually bought would match the best.

'We do a lot of benchmarking,' he said vaguely.

The conference would last two days in Greece. The Astir Palace hotel. Outside Athens. Towards the end of May. Only two days, he kept stressing.

'So I get to go to Greece and all I've got to do is listen and make a few notes?'

He laughed and told me that it was no free trip. I was reminded of something I had heard one of his sales guys say: that after a sales call, when Robert asked questions, he really asked questions and you felt like a wally if you didn't have your homework done.

'I've never been to Greece.'

'Spring – late spring – is a lovely time of the year to go there. Even for two nights.'

I promised I would do lots of homework, he promised to send me the tickets and the conference information, and a fortnight later I was on my way.

At the end of the first day, I went to my hotel room rather than join the conference attendees at a poolside candlelit dinner. I needed to record what I had heard during the day, and once that was out of the way, to work out how to turn myself into a serious one-woman business. I showered, then took the room-service menu out onto the balcony to consider what I might order for dinner.

The Astir Palace hotel, built into a cliff face, looked out over the bay towards Athens, each of hundreds of balconies so cleverly angled as to provide a sweeping view of the bay, the great swimming pool ten feet from the sandy water's edge, and the grounds, deserted now as dusk chilled the day's heat into a stillness that carried the sounds of waiters, setting the round poolside tables and lighting paper-sheltered lanterns at the rim of the dark foliage.

The sinking sun painted the lead-heavy polluted air over Athens in luminous shadowed brilliance, intensifying and changing with such imperceptible inevitability that to glance away became a decision, not a casual instinct. I was held in thrall, hugging the towelling robe as it absorbed the dying warmth of the day, the stone tiles under my feet already shaded, already cool.

As dusk became dark, the blue-filtered bright oblong of the swimming pool was shattered into running rolls of liquid light by a single swimmer, the sea became a sounding unseen presence, whispering to the shore, regular as a heartbeat, and, as if to wish away the primeval cold recurrence of its reminders, more people, miniaturised by distance, came into the grounds. Musicians arrived, leather-waistcoated in contrast to the waiters' white serving jackets, loosening their instruments from shoulder straps frayed with use.

Children danced in the frothing edge of the greater darkness, paddling and postponing parental summons until the older voices came in strident monosyllable. Now. No argument. This minute.

A long table was swept with unfurled white linen, the surface quickly subdivided again and again by serried ranks of stemmed glasses, transformed by poured wine into dark-red lozenges, the stems no longer visible.

I could hear laughter. The harsh-sweet exploratory laughter of women complimented by near-strangers — and the deeper bursts of men responding to one-line jokes. Sharp single notes cheeped for mates as the musicians tuned up. The lanterns burned brighter yellow as night drew in. The musicians stood together in a pool of light, shouting jocose abuse at waiters who stepped in the path of their spotlights, casting long shadows and briefly plunging the performers' faces into darkness. A sudden attack of music turned the party-dressed conference people around, away from their clustered groups to watch the musicians, united in a collective swagger of melody.

Then they began to drift, the guests, holding wine glasses with the care of the beginning of the night, gathering around tables, calling to each other, occasional faces lowered to red-bright light as one took a light for a cigarette from a hand-cupped lighter. Jackets were hung on the backs of chairs, the long chain-wrapped shoulder straps of dressy handbags looped aslant, as the guests opted for one table or another, the early sitters attracting little courts of three or four people, still standing but centred by the one choosing not to stand.

A ferryboat crossed the bay, orderly as a line drawn in the darkness, unnoticed by the diners, now applauding the end of the first set of songs as the musicians consulted among themselves on what should come next.

In the relative quiet before the next song, I was startled to hear the formally aggressive knock and call of 'Room Service'. For a second, I clutched the menu for reassurance that I was not imagining things. No. I had never read the menu, so could not have placed an order. Maybe I imagined the knock was nearer than it was? Even over the musicians starting up again, I could hear the second knock. There could be no doubt. The door being knocked on was mine.

Pulling the towelling robe's loose belt tighter at the waist, I re-entered the room (startlingly warm, now, in contrast to the unnoticed cool of the night) and, dodging around the circular table in my path, went to open the main door.

In the corridor outside was a waiter, a fully loaded, wheeled table in front of him, set for two. As I opened my mouth to direct him to another room, behind him I saw Robert Allen, laughing delightedly.

I retreated, acquiescing in the waiter's progress. The waiter gestured me into the chair he had pulled to one side of the round table, unfolding a vast square of stiffened shiny linen on my lap, making a presentation, in heavily accented English, of the virtues of the meal. Robert Allen, his thin hair softly damp from a recent shower, sat in kindly amusement until the monologue was over, then tipped him and saw him to the door, agreeing with whatever the waiter seemed to be proposing with a mixture of charm and dismissal the waiter evidently understood.

Door closed behind him, Robert Allen stood, delighted as a child with his coup.

'You going to do a translation of what the waiter was saying?'

'Not a chance. All I know in Greek is *kali mera*.'

'Fortunately that's the name of the starter.'

'No, it means . . .'

'Robert.'

'Yes?'

'I'll give you coaching in irony later.'

'Thank you.'

'Not at all. Sit down, for God's sake, and stop showing off your tux. I've seen it before, you know.'

'Everybody has,' he said comfortably, rubbing a

shiny part of the sleeve. 'Helen says I'll have to lose weight or get a bigger one.'

'Oh, the difficult choices of the rich.'

We ate the starter without talking, the music from the grounds clear through the half-open balcony door. Putting down my fork when I finished it, I made no move. I'll not play mother. Serve me. Awkward with lack of practice, he took away the small plates and replaced them, standing for a moment, irresolute, then pouring wine.

'You going to do that thing of lifting off the shiny covers simultaneously?' I asked.

'But of course, Madam,' he said, whisking the bulbous silver protectors off and putting them on the bed.

Then he launched into a promotional speech about the food, in nonsense-language. Startled by how good he was at it, I laughed, and he gestured wildly, the flow of talk out of him faster and more frantic, teasing with occasional syllables of sense, culminating in a passionate appeal of some kind, which brought him, sobbing, to his knees. Only when I had applauded him enough to justify his bowing in all directions from his kneeling position did he get back up and, sitting, take a swig of his wine.

'You've done that funny talk before,' I told him.

'The kids love it. I can't sing and I embarrass them if I try to dance, but they get a kick out of my funny talk.'

As he ate, he looked around the room, smiling a little at the conference folder, open on one of the two beds, highlighter pen brightly in evidence on some of the speeches.

'I was planning to write a summary for you of today. There's a lot of relevant stuff on transfer pricing. But if you're going to be here tomorrow, you'll be able to—'

'I won't be here tomorrow. Flying out at half six. And, with luck, getting home in time for at least some of my daughter's First Communion. I always knew I couldn't be here for the second day – Caoimhe would kill me if I wasn't there to see her in her white lace with pearl snowdrop headdress. Of course, I may fail to recognise her. I'm more used to her in jeans and mud. My youngest has a down-and-dirty approach to life. You must meet her sometime.'

'I must,' I said, and thought: you use your daughter like a talisman. Like a cop's badge, to be produced as an identifier, a free pass. You mention her to ward off any challenge to your status as a family man. You think it will protect you from betrayal by yourself, but that betrayal has now begun. Faithless already by virtue of making your journey here, you will be actively unfaithful whenever I choose to activate your yearning. But you have such a patent need to believe this is all an accident, unintended by either of us.

Because of your need to believe it is unmeant by either of us; right now, you are comforted by my lack of make-up, unglamorous dressing gown and lack of artifice. Had you encountered me in Victoria's Secret satin, that would have discomfited you. In snowy terrycloth, I seem natural as a sister.

But I watch us both as if from a camera held above, my every move is for effect. See me cup the wide bowl of coffee in my hands, the warmth seeping slowly through the thick white crockery. See me bend my face to the aroma, eyes closing in the pleasure of it, shutting you out. See me wander, preoccupied, onto the balcony, to watch the lessening number of dancers below, sensing you following me, knowing, without turning around, you have moved to stand three feet from me.

'God, isn't this beautiful?' he asked, turning his back, briefly, on the sea to examine the way the hotel had been chiselled into the wall of the cliff.

He had brought his glass of wine with him. His free hand he ran approvingly over the rough-hewn stone of the balcony wall. You are within your moment, I thought. Not a spectator at your own life, as I am. A witness at other lives. Tinkering for no reason other than that I can. Like a scientist testing. Without cruelty, although it may be felt as cruelty.

'So you have had one failure,' I said, turning to him with a sudden enveloping smile.

'I have?'

'You can't dance.' This said with a half-gesture towards the poolside dancers.

'Who says?'

'Your children.'

'Oh, no,' he said. 'Not so. I said my children think I'm *ridiculous* when I dance. They are embarrassed to see their bald, fat old father at that kind of thing. But I can dance all right.'

'You want to prove it?'

I set the cup and saucer down on the glass balcony table and moved to him in rhythm with the music from below. Smiling, not putting down the wineglass, he took me, one-armed, into a dancer's embrace and moved with me on the beat of the music, the sure maleness of this short, fat man overwhelming me with a surge of lust that stilled me in his hold. The wineglass was unsteadily set down and the freed hand was inside the shawl collar of the towelling robe, at my neck as he kissed me.

I must not let him hesitate, I thought, not knowing how I knew, but arching against him in a demanding surrender that heavied his breathing and turned urgency into imperative.

The last physical echoes of pleasure had not died away before I was pulling away from him, dragging the crumpled robe around me, stumbling through the strident light of the bedroom into the bathroom. The shower roared to life and I stood under it, heel of each hand to eyes, drowning thought in the noise, the heat and wetness of it. How ridiculous it is, I thought, when I felt with my fingers the imprint of the balcony tiling on the back of each thigh. How ridiculous, the noises and the awkward bumping of it, yet how potent the fleeting mirage of uniqueness it gives: the illusion that nobody else has ever felt such raucous abandonment, such risky rutting exultation.

Standing in the steamy sweating bathroom, the shower beginning to turn cold, I wondered at a pleasure that left no memory, neither the sated satisfaction left by a good meal nor the sweet spinning rapture left by a good wine. For me, it left only lack of need for what had seemed so necessary ten minutes earlier. A lack of need so aggressive, it reminded me of the old Garfield cartoon, where the fat cat is fending off the affectionate presence of the neighbouring dog.

Garfield's thought bubble reads 'Have a nice day —
someplace else.'

When I returned to the bedroom, tight-wrapped
in white towels, he was seated, fully dressed, on the
balcony. He turned and half-rose.

'Stay put,' I told him, uncapping a mineral water
bottle and drinking directly from it as I walked out
to the frank coldness of the night. Worshipful, you
fool, I thought, summing up the look of him. The
urge to actually say the Garfield line rose as urgently
as had the sex hunger earlier. I concentrated hard on
not saying it. On sounding grimly ashamed.

'This should never have happened.'

'No,' he said sadly. 'We are not that kind of
people.'

I *am* that kind of people, I thought. Not impul-
sively, irresponsibly sexual. I do not lurch from
affair to affair, driven by desire. It is mindful and
inquisitive, what I do, and I am not sustained, as
are you, by an ineradicable conviction of my essential
decency. I cannot pretend this night was anything
other than planned by me — to what end, I do
not know.

'Robert, you don't know what "kind of people"
you are. But I do. You are first of all a father, then
a husband, then a businessman.'

'It is possible to be all of those and to love someone else as well.'

There was a kind of dignity in his puzzlement. Is it always like this, I wondered. Is there always one who kisses and one who calculates?

'Go away, now,' I said. 'You need to get some sleep before your flight.'

Obediently, he rose and came to kiss me on the forehead. His hands on either side of my face unintentionally locked out all sound, leaving me with the pulsing echo a child hears within a great seashell. I realised he was crying. For a few minutes, he stood there awkwardly, unhelped by me, then, with an effort, straightened himself up and wiped his face with his hand.

'I am such a shit,' he muttered. 'I'm sorry. I'm really sorry.'

I held on to his upper arms, my own arms keeping him far enough away for there to be space between us.

'Does Helen know you're here?'

He shook his head, not looking at me.

'Does Myra?'

Myra had been his secretary since he started the company. She adored him and Helen with roughly equal fervour. Again, he shook his head.

'Who booked the tickets?'

Because, I thought, you did not. There are simple tasks like booking flights that a man like you always has done for him by someone else.

'A temp in for a few weeks.'

What a well-planned accident, I thought. There is innocence in you, Robert, and there is a small streak of sneaky cleverness you are now ashamed of. I must ensure you do not get ashamed enough to subvert that cleverness.

'Robert. Robert?'

He brought his blotched face up to look at me.

'If you keep your wits about you, Helen will never know. She should never know. Never. If she doesn't know harm's been done to her, no harm's been done to her. Just make sure this trip never surfaces where she can find out about it. She doesn't need that.'

He nodded and I turned him, back-patted him in dismissal. Only when the bedroom door closed behind him did I take the wineglass, the cup and the saucer into the room and close the door to the balcony, wondering, as I did, for whom his apology had been intended. For Helen, probably. The sheets were coolly welcoming as I slid into the nearest of the twin beds, turning out the lights at the console to my right.

Helen would never know. He would never tell her, lest telling her free a fierce strength in her that would wither and shrink him into the diminishing final phase of his own life, robbing him of the bumptious bolster that gave him bounce and gladness.

In a stark moment before sleep became total, a bleak view of self looked from skull-holes into my present time, possessing me with a primeval dread. I am, I thought, warming my hands at the fires I set with people. I am faking what comes naturally to everyone else, except in those minutes of sex when there are no names, no politeness, no thought. In those minutes reality takes me and tosses me in a mad honest jive.

But for the most part, I am at one remove, swinging in the ice-cold eternity between the stars, certain only of coldness and of death.

CHAPTER TEN

Accident

———◆———

Gavin's five o'clock colic was bad that evening. It took me a long time to walk the baby back to sleep, then cuddle him into the cot before telling a story to his older brother and getting Stephen, in turn, to sleep. Oliver was due back from concerts in France. The series of concerts had been more successful than even Oliver's chronic optimism had prepared him for. Papers back home had registered the impact he was having.

Now that he was on his way back, Gabrielle was project-managing the family celebration dinner. She had it timed and delegated so that she didn't even get into the car until Oliver rang her as he walked across the concrete apron to the plane at Beauvais.

No possibility of significant delay, so my sister set off first of all to pick up my mother at her apartment, then drive to the airport. Gabrielle, I thought, could run General Motors. She didn't tell me what time to get their kids to bed or start the dinner. Detailed, but not obsessive.

Even with Gavin's colic, I had the fire set and the elements for dinner neatly laid out in the kitchen when the phone rang. That's it, Oliver, I thought. Let us know when you're about to board, let us know when you're in the terminal building.

'Don't tell me,' I said, picking up the kitchen phone, 'you're just working up your courage to fight your way through a phalanx of fans?'

Not getting an answer to this unnerved me, and I apologetically helloed into the receiver again. Maybe some poor ordinary unrelated caller was being put off by being talked to about fans. Still no voice. But the line was manifestly open — there was ambient noise. At first I thought I had a heavy breather. Then the voices in the background became those of Gabrielle and Oliver. Faint, but clear. With a couple of comments, much louder, from my mother. She must be nearer to the phone, I thought, must have accidentally activated one of the speed dial buttons.

I whistled to attract their attention, without success. I could hear Gabrielle laughingly berate Oliver for a comment he had made before I started to listen. There was a dishonest pleasure in eavesdropping. I would be able to tease them later by quoting their real words back to them. They'd never work out how I knew what they had said.

'What was the food like?' Mam asked. Oliver's reply was muffled, but understandable a second later, like an aural double-take.

'Brilliant. They had this local goat's cheese to die for. I brought some of it home.'

'Lazy swine,' I heard Gabrielle say. 'Wouldn't do the decent thing and go shopping – just put a few extra lumps of cheese on the hotel bill.'

'Buckin' right,' Oliver said.

'You're very lucky,' said my mother. 'Lucky your wife has a sense of humour.'

'Unlike your other daughter, you mean?'

'Oliver!'

Gabrielle's voice sounded scandalised, hitting the first syllable in reproof.

'What a thing to say,' my mother said.

Oliver, I thought, you'd have got less of the shock-horrors if you'd said that to me rather than to them. I know damn well this character of me that

I play is missing some vital authenticators. Maybe one of them is a sense of humour.

'Dominique gets a great laugh out of things,' Gabrielle's voice said, her diction clearer with dissent.

'Absolutely,' Oliver's voice agreed. 'She just doesn't put a great laugh into things. Life is real, life is earnest and – whoo . . .'

All at the one time, his voice and the other two voices seemed to start something on a higher note. As I strained to distinguish between them, the mobile phone cut out, too quickly for me to catch words from any of them. I dialled the number. The electronic voice said the phone might be powered off and I should leave a message. That puzzled me. Unless the dismayed tone in their voices was an indicator that they had suddenly realised that they were 'on the air' and turned off the phone.

Funny they didn't check first to see there was someone at the other end. Not that I'd have let them know it was me. Too awkward for poor Oliver. I went back to food preparation.

Twenty minutes later, in an effort to get the timing of the meal quite right, I rang again. The same response. More likely, I thought, that the phone ran out of battery juice than that they had turned it off. Over the next fifteen minutes, I tried the line constantly. Definitely, the battery must have run out. I put the seafood casserole in the oven.

I turned the radio on, but selected talk rather than music. If the kids woke, talk downstairs might be a reassurance that the family was all present and correct. Not just Auntie. An arts show came on, with an academic eviscerating a new novel.

'The *deus ex machina* melodrama it degenerated into,' he said, as furious as if the author had done it on purpose to him personally, 'it's pure mack truck.'

For a moment, I thought I had misheard. Then the presenter indicated that he was as mystified as I was.

'Mack truck,' the academic repeated irritably. 'Mack truck. Oh, come on, you know the Mack Truck principle of bad fiction writing: you solve your plot problems by having a Mack Truck mow down characters you can't resolve the problems of.'

I wonder, I thought, would a Mack Truck, lightly applied, solve my sense of humour problem? I must ask Oliver. When he arrives. What the hell is keeping them? It's forty-five minutes since the phone cut out. Bloody hell, I'd better check the casserole.

When I took the lid off, it took me a while to work out what I was seeing. I had obviously put the two plastic salad servers down without looking and put the lid on top of the whole lot. The servers had taken on a Salvador Dali surrealism. Oliver, me oul' flower, I thought, let's see how funny you find seafood casserole garnished with bendy plastic. I fished them out and considered the possible impact on the seafood. It looked and smelled OK, so I put it back to stay warm in the turned-off cooker.

The arts programme had finished. A newsreader was talking about 'the delays caused by that horrific crash on the airport road'.

Ah, I thought with relief, that's what's held them up. Pity their phone has run out of power. If Oliver carried a spare battery, I could at least sympathise with them.

I sometimes thought, later, about pretending to have been worried from the moment the phone cut out. It would have established me as prescient. But the reality was that the bulletin about the traffic hold-ups gave me complete comfort. I was so unworried that when a knock came to the door, I rushed to it, ready to hear details of the hassle.

On the path outside stood two policemen, hats held to their chests. I had never before seen Gardaí stand like that. I half-closed the door before I could stop myself, as if by denying them entry I might deny entry to the horror they represented. They verified my name gravely, kindly. Identified themselves, hats covering up three silver chest buttons per uniform. Asked if they might step into the house.

They had a method, you could see that. I let them take their orderly way, holding back the scream, the one question I wanted answered. The senior man told about the wide-load truck, of how the prefabricated house it was carrying came adrift and cut through the top of their car. The driver and passenger died immediately, the passenger in the back seat had died in the hospital.

They paused to let me ask questions, then resumed in solemn order. When they seemed to have told it all, I looked at them and they told me more. They moved from reporting to advising. Far be it from them, they said, but they would suggest this and that. In these cases, they said, it can be recommended. At such a time, they added, it might be wise. I was holding up well, they said, but you could never underestimate shock.

The car would be towed here, they said, offering a card. It would have to be examined, they said. Forensics. If there was anything in the car – anything at all – it was safe enough. I started to ask them if they could retrieve the mobile phone.

'It's just – I think I heard them die,' I said, and saying it destroyed me.

Arms awkwardly around head like a peasant at a wake, roaring bursts of crying tore through me, racking me. Yet one distant observing part of me watched contemptuously as the policemen dragged the details of the phone call out of me, every syllable of remembered conversation now weighted with prophetic significance. One of them asked to use the phone in the hall. I could hear him telling someone, 'She probably heard the crash, too.'

That second of joined voices, high with fear. No word formed by any one of them. But each of the three reacting. Each aware. Each with that infinitesimal eternity of terror.

The Gardaí formally asked permission to release the names of the dead, and this made me telephone Oliver's parents' house. They were out, and in guilty relief, I told his brother and asked him to tell 'everyone'. The last news bulletin of the day carried their names, and the phone calls started. Immediately.

I sat in the sitting room, the two phones on my lap, and took one call after another. Reporters. They were sorry, but ... I spelled my sister's name again and again. Gave them Oliver's age. Told them how successful the French concerts had been. Read aloud the faxes Oliver had sent to Gabrielle of the French critics, endearments in his bad handwriting scribbled in the margins of the cuttings. Translated. Took the next call and the next. A couple rang back to check who I was, one of them, hurried into awkwardness, asking, 'Didn't you used to be?' Some friends heard it, too. School friends of Gabrielle. Pals of Oliver.

Around three in the morning, there was a lull. I went into the kitchen which still smelled of dried-out casserole, the two Dali spoons warped and distorted on the surface of the congealed seafood. I made coffee and tried to fix my sister in my head before her face and voice and essence were diluted to nothing by the banalities of those who remembered a lesser Gabrielle. I tried to remember my mother as she had been, before my father's death.

I thought of the man who had told me, when I was a little girl, that he was going to run away with my mother. His name was not in the phone book when I checked. I had not talked to her in years about him. Maybe he was dead. Fuck that for a haircut, my father had said.

'Well, fuck this whole thing for a haircut,' I said aloud, shovelling crusted casserole into the garbage and tossing the bent spoons after it.

I must get my act together, I thought. What time

now? Half-past four? No good going to bed; I would be afraid of nightmares and anyway, would have to get up again too quickly. I checked Stephen and Gavin. The children looked no more or less pathetic in the light of their new orphan status, of which they knew nothing.

I must press my mother's black suit, I thought. She will want to wear ... she was alive, my mother, at her own funeral in my head. But then, maybe I should press the suit anyway. No. There would be no open coffins, my mother's strong curly hair pretty against padded satin. The horrors chilled me in the dark house, my mouth obsessively shaping words like morgue.

When the first morning phone call came from the radio station, the researcher was relieved to find his intrusion almost welcomed. Aren't you great, he said, audibly appalled by my lack of hysteria. I listened to his bulletin, then to a DJ quickly reacting by playing one of Oliver's earliest recordings. Then the children woke, and I fed them between answering phones and listening to major figures from the world of music talking about Oliver and all he might have become. One commentator apologised for his crassness, yet still expressed the view that Oliver was better dead than left alive with his hands damaged.

Not so, I said over the baby's head. The essence of Oliver was not music, the essence of Oliver was delight. He would have survived anything as long as Gabrielle survived, too. Dead, he is a bounty unclaimed, and my sister is a prop. Something borrowed. O Jesus, Gabrielle, something borrowed, like my tears at your wedding. And my mother, not extinguished instantly, but left alive for an hour while they lifted the great weight off the car. I would never ask if Mam had been conscious from the time of the accident to the time of her death. They wouldn't know. They would lie out of kindness. They would lie badly and leave me worse off.

Anything we can do, the phone callers said, melting into one another. They followed each other so fast, said such similar things. Anything at all. I murmured and thanked, just once taking up the offer. When my old director from the soap opera telephoned from the TV station, I asked if he still had the same PA. He did, he said, puzzled. I asked to borrow her for two days. She was the sort of person who knew how to do funerals. An hour later, when she arrived, I had the children washed, fed and dressed.

'I've put a message into the telephone answering system,' I told her.

Stephen, the elder, was clutching me fiercely around the legs, making strange with this newcomer.

'It'll take care of incoming calls whenever you're on the other machine, but you'll need to change the tape, probably. There are so many people wanting to leave messages. I've left out any telephone numbers I can think of that might be relevant. I'll live with whatever choices you make of coffins or anything. Just please take care of it.'

'Where are you going?'

'For a long walk with the kids.'

I unpeeled Stephen's arms from around my legs and got the two of them into the twin buggy, wrapped up. I took them to the park nearby, and held the baby on my lap while the toddler played with sand. At one point, he came back, and rocking against my knees, asked, 'Where my Mammy?'

'All gone,' I said.

'All gone?'

'All gone.'

His eyes closed, his mouth contorted into an oblonged oval and he roared. Holding the sleeping baby one-armed, I slid a warm hand around the back of the little boy's head and rubbed it gently. After a while the first fury of the crying died away, and he put his head on the soft-skirted hammock between my knees, sobbing like a song, a lullaby. I slid the baby into the buggy and persuaded Stephen, now fat-eyed with upset and tiredness, in too. At home, I changed and fed the baby, first lifting the tired-out toddler onto his own bed and covering him up.

Three times that day, Stephen asked for his mother. Three times I told him his mother was all gone. Twice, relatives tried to intervene, to tell the boy his mother had gone to heaven, and with a slate-eyed cold fierceness I forbade them. One of them told me I was cruel, and left, never to speak to me again.

The church was so crowded, the night the coffins arrived, that not everybody could get in, and a clammy overheated smell compounded of sweat and incense came in waves. I sat, sickened, in the front row alongside Oliver's mother and father.

'Don't introduce me,' I whispered to the mother after about ten minutes.

Her natural politeness was leading her to introduce me to people who had known only Oliver, and who then had to offer condolences to a total stranger about the loss of her mother, sister and famous brother-in-law. Whenever this happened, many of them would then remember who I used to be, and tell me they used to love my programme. I used to love it, too, I thought. No real things happened in it.

When people got killed, they went off and joined the Royal Shakespeare Company or gave acting lessons. They didn't stay dead in three coffins in a church with an endless procession going up its aisle.

They shuffled past, heavily shifting from foot to foot, heads down, difficult to recognise, even when I knew them, half in silhouette, as they were, against the bright-lit altar behind them. Friends from school, solidified into adulthood, actors from the soap opera days, people from my mother's past, not met since my father's funeral, sweet-faced with shock. I endured their kindness and alternated my phrases of thanks, sometimes finding myself without a sympathiser because the next few people knew only Oliver's parents, not me. I would sit in the pew with a queue beside me, their eyes averted so as not to embarrass, their purpose to sympathise with the two people beside me. Don't worry, I wanted to tell them. Don't worry that you're bypassing me and offering me no specific sympathy. The peace of being ignored is the best gift you can bestow on me.

When you are the bereaved, you cannot look at your watch to find what hour of which day you are in. You embark on counting the people, then abandon the task after a few hundred, knowing that it will be said afterwards that nobody ever saw such a turnout. Such a tribute.

Long hours into the procession, one man breached the unspoken protocol that you never talk to the bereaved until you come around the corner at the front of their pew. He bent down to me, held my shoulders, turned me to face him.

'Well?' he asked, almost aggressively.

I was at ease with it before I recognised him as David Carpenter.

'That's not what you're supposed to say,' I whispered, smiling and beginning, for the first time, to cry.

'Move in there.'

The order came all of a piece with him pushing and sitting in beside me, his weight causing me to shove into Oliver's mother, who instinctively made space available. My face was warmed, smothered and tickled by his coat collar and loose scarf when he held me, more in protection than in affection or sympathy. If I was going to cry, he was there as policeman. Move along there, nothing to see, I'll tell her your message. It made me laugh, the idea of him as a policeman, and the concealment was welcome as the laughter plummeted into turbulent coarse grief, absorbed in the thick cloth smothering my face. When it subsided into discomfort and quiet shame, a big unfolded handkerchief was pushed into my hands. I mopped myself, assimilating his muttered instructions unquestioned.

'You've done enough of this. Keep the hankie against your face and your eyes closed. Just lean against me and walk the direction I take you. That's right. Keep walking. You're fine. Two steps down. Straight bit now. 'Nother step.'

In my hair I felt the cold outside air. He walked me, fiddling with keys. 'In you get,' he said, and I slid into the car seat, face embedded in the hankie.

Maybe it was lack of sleep that made his instruction, more appropriate for a child, sound quaintly comforting. I whispered it into the limp folds of the handkerchief as he got into the driver's seat and started the engine. In you get. In you get. For a few moments, the car was in tentative, low gear, then shifted as it reached an open road. I leaned back against the headrest, eyes closed, momentarily jarred by his activating some control that lowered the back of the seat a little. The new, gentler angle was soothing.

'Crazy,' he said after a few minutes.

Crazy, that procession of platitudes arriving in person to embarrass themselves and reinforce for the bereaved the awful unreachableness of anguished loss.

Knowing the full thought behind a lone word muttered by another, I thought, is more companionable than an embrace.

'I thought the paper said the house was private?' I opened my eyes to find him reversing the car past the front gate, seeking a parking place.

'What can you do?' I said, dully facing the prospect of a houseful of well-meaning relatives and neighbours.

'Plenty,' he said, and got out of the car.

I found the crumpled hankie and prepared to get out. When he almost folded me under his arm, I half-protested, then stumbled and acquiesced. Someone opened the door as the two of us walked up the path. I could feel, rather than see, the reaction to his apparently familiar face and to the gesture he used to fend off the people inside. Then I was climbing stairs and responding to the wakening cry of Stephen.

I had him in my arms, the little boy, and quieted, while the man fumbled through the drawers in the room. Like a burglar, I thought. It was only when he found them that I copped on he had been searching for nappies and baby wipes. Handing them to me,

he retreated to the baby's cot, out of the toddler's eye line.

'Want my mammy,' Stephen said, suddenly.

'Not now,' I replied, even-toned.

'Mammy!'

'Not here,' I said, with a tranquillity resulting from
exhaustion. 'You're OK. Now, *Teddy*'s not OK.'

I swivelled him so he could see the teddy bear,
hanging by the label, awkwardly, from the side of
the bed. He reached out and grabbed the teddy.

'You better give Teddy a big cuddle, 'cause he's
sore,' I told him, and as he enveloped the teddy in
a hug, matched the embrace, rocking on the edge
of the bed.

Rocking, rocking, rocking, speeding up again as
Stephen fought sleep, reviving every time the rocking
lost pace. Every time I tried to lay him down, he
stiffened and woke. The third time, I shook my head
at the man in the shadows, indicating, 'Go downstairs,
nothing you can do here.'

When he left the room, I was glad and disappointed, listening for his footfall on the stairs. Then he
was back, clutching two pillows from other bedrooms.
He replaced the child's pillow with the two, then
moved to slide my shoes off. Anchored by his hands,
I stood up and held the half-asleep child while the

man unzipped my skirt and stepped me out of it and the half-slip.

The movement as I lay down on the bed momentarily roused Stephen but I nestled him close and the man wrapped the two of us in a duvet, then put his big hand gently on my forehead as if to draw out the bruised headache behind it. Heavy-eyed, I watched the door close slowly, gently, slivering the broad light into a narrow outline pencilled in brightness.

Voices floated up from downstairs, louder as their owners came out into the hall and started to leave. Most of them would not have met this man, I thought, yet they would go along with whatever he wanted.

'A solid citizen, he sounds, Daisy,' Oliver had said, listening to me describe David Carpenter during a phone call from Paris. 'Don't know about making the earth move, but he'd always have the VHI paid up.'

Oliver, uninterested in sport, had never linked the name with football or fame. I would love to tell someone about that VHI comment, I thought. But now, there is nobody to tell. I have lived my days in a sweet conspiracy of quoted comment, sharing what Oliver said with my mother or father, trying out observations made by others on my sister. Now, the conspirators are all dead and there is nobody to tell. All gone, I thought. All gone.

The next day, when I woke, cramped from holding on to the little boy, the baby was making his exploratory noises. I slid out of the bed without waking his older brother, scooping the little one out of the cot, rewarded by Gavin's unqualified glee at the sight of me. So warming, and so indiscriminate.

'If Saddam Hussein arrived to get you up, you'd be equally thrilled, wouldn't you?' I asked him, tickling him. His eyes closed with the laughter.

'Or Hitler?'

He laughed again as I got him into the high chair and strapped him securely. The kettle had a label hanging on it.

'ILL BE HERE BY 8,' it announced, in the PA's firm printing.

When she arrived, the two children were clean and fed. Stephen's making strange had not lasted. He started to explain something to her, oblivious to the radio newscaster predicting that today would see the funeral of the three victims of the freak crash on the airport road. Flower deliveries began. The PA briefed me about the funeral as if it was another event to be managed. She had brought clothes for me to wear. There was a make-up artist ready. I protested, only to be told that the president would be there. The taoiseach would be there. She handed me a list of overseas VIPs, most from the world of music. This was how I should address the president. This was how I should address the archbishop if he turned up.

'I am lucky Oliver was famous,' I said to the PA.

If Oliver had been a music teacher in Mullingar, there would have been nothing to get between me and the raw agony of loss, whereas his fame gave me a series of formal scenes to play. I would call the dignitaries by their proper titles, I would listen, head slightly bowed, while they said their pieces, then I would vary the half-sentences of parting: 'How very good of you.' 'I am most grateful.' There would be no crying. In some roles, the actor must produce tears. In this role, I must not.

That is why I am lucky, I thought, stepping into the mourning car. Because out here where I am crafting a performance as chief mourner, the bloodied raggedness of grief does not reach. It lies in wait for me, but that's another day's work.

At the church, the car door was opened by Robert Allen, who almost lifted me out of the back seat into the arms of his wife. The two of them took me over, bringing me through the church, pulling me gently away from clumps of sympathisers threatening to stop my progress, getting me into the pew near the altar. Near the three coffins, side by side. Identical. The rustling, creaking, whispering hush of the church was cleaved by a soprano voice so perfect, so passionate that my breathing froze in my chest. As the pews behind filled to overflowing, as the black-coated undertakers' men carried wreaths and bouquets from one place to another, I was taken over by the singing, spellbound and awed by it. Oliver's father, the big vet, his voice hushed into bumblebee bass, told me the internationally famous name of the singer.

'Insisted,' he apologised, as if I were somehow bound to resent it. 'Says Oliver was the best accompanist she ever had.'

She sang for Oliver, but for me her voice celebrated my mother and my sister.

I joined the orderly disorder of the congregation rising to their feet, then kneeling in response to the priest's instructions, wondering, as I did so, if Oliver's Jewish friends from Israel and Vienna were in the church. Maybe they would find the crucifixes and the mosaic Stations of the Cross too offensive. Certainly, they would not associate them with Oliver, whose only link with religion was music. He had gone along with the baptism of his two sons in much the same way he had taken Vitamin C when he had a cold.

One of his brothers was on the altar now, talking about him. I had refused to talk on the altar. The priest could say what he knew of them. It mattered not, none of it. The only reality was that inside those coffins were cold, broken, waxy and yellowed parodies of the only people I loved. I recoiled at the thought.

Afterwards, in the wintry sunshine of the graveyard, I was politely proper to the VIPs, national and international, who came to offer sympathy. Nigel brought a tall blonde girl who stood behind him while he said a few kind sentences he had obviously thought about in advance. Robert and Helen Allen hovered within reach, unobtrusively helpful.

During the prayers at the graveside, I saw David Carpenter, black-coated and sombre, attracting worshipful glances, particularly from the sports fans, puzzling out where he fitted, who he belonged to, what connection they had missed. In response to a nod, he came over and shook my hand. As if he had not been there the previous night. You are peculiarly suited to funerals, I thought. Most people smile when they see a friend, and so, at a funeral, are constantly correcting their instinctive smiles. But you – you greet a friend, at any time, with an unsmiling nod of acknowledgement.

The Allens left me home afterwards. 'I'll be on to you about work,' Robert promised, embracing me.

'You'll need to get back to work quickly. Whether you want to or not.'

'Don't mind him,' Helen said. 'Taking care of two children under two will be plenty to keep your mind occupied for a while. We'll be in touch. You know where we are if we can be useful.'

CHAPTER ELEVEN

The Executor's Song

———❦———

The great thing about babies is that they have no precedents to go on. Gavin didn't know he was being shortchanged of both parents and one grandparent. A familiar face was there every morning when he woke up, his brother was there too, so as far as he was concerned, life was good.

Stephen, on the other hand, was used to his father being away for a few weeks at a time, but his mother was always there, so he kept looking for her in the house. Even though I had told him she was 'all gone' I had also, in the past, told him that the biscuits or the sweets were all gone, and they seemed to reappear after a while, if he was good. Therefore, he seemed to think, his mother would come back at some point. He nonetheless continued to ask questions.

'What's dead?'

This was asked at the top of his voice in the supermarket.

'Dead is like this,' I said, going floppy and letting my head hang down, eyes closed. Gavin, who was in the front bit of the trolley supported by a pillow, thought this was so funny he lost his soother over it.

'Can you talk if you're dead?'

Eyes still closed as I groped on the tiled floor for the soother, I shook my head.

'Can you eat if you're dead?'

By now I was moving again, soother in my coat pocket. I must remember to shove it in the steriliser before returning it to its barrel-bung job in Gavin's mouth.

'Well, can you?'

'Eat when you're dead? No. You don't need to.'

'But — ice cream.'

'Dead people don't like ice cream.'

'Why don't they?'

'I told you, they can't eat anything.'

'But—'

I know, I thought. You mightn't be able to eat

ice cream, but you might still like it. As a concept.

'Do they go to sleep?'

'When you're dead, you're always asleep.'

'Always?'

'Yes.'

'The whole time?'

'Yes.'

'Really always?'

'Yes.'

I took three packets from a shelf and tossed them into the trolley behind Gavin, who, at ten months, was possessed of a conviction that he could intercept and catch anything I could throw at him. He had never so far caught anything, but did a confident lunge every time.

'What's those?'

'These?'

'Yes.'

'Cous cous.'

'What's cous cous?'

'Sort of a pasta, I think.'

'What's pasta?'

'Well, you know spaghetti?'

'Yes?'

'That's pasta.'

'It is not. It is not!'

'OK.'

Long pause while I reached down a box of corn-flakes.

'Is it really?'

'Pasta? Yes.'

For some reason, this reached Stephen's inner wellspring of grief much more forcefully than the news that dead people couldn't eat ice cream. He stood in the middle of the cereals aisle and roared crying. Gavin strained to get upright enough to see him, beginning to grizzle in sympathy. I stood irresolute, debating whether I should take the soother out of my pocket and plug it into one of them, or if this would cause typhoid.

Other shoppers slowed down to watch the three of us, possibly thinking I had belted Stephen and he was punishing me. I stuck the soother in Gavin's mouth, but timed it badly. It went in just as he was about to gulp a couple of lungfuls of air into him and I was lucky he didn't breathe it in right down to the bottom of one of his lungs. Once he had gone back to breathing through his nose, he seemed to decide that there was little he could usefully do for a howling older brother, and went suddenly to sleep.

A couple of women, eager to show how good they

were at motherhood, stopped and tried to talk to Stephen. To get rid of them, he put his face into the muesli packets and howled through dozens of servings of Healthy Harvest.

'What's the matter?' one woman as old as my mother asked.

'I told him spaghetti was pasta,' I said.

She gave me a look of disbelieving contempt and walked away. I leaned on the trolley. It was as good a place to be as anywhere else. When there is nobody at home, there is nothing to rush home for. You might as well be in the supermarket comparing the fat content of one cereal with the fat content of another. After a long time, Stephen cried himself out and took his face out of the muesli packets.

'I think we should buy the ones you cried into,' I said, pointing out the packets I meant.

'Why?'

'You made them a bit wet.'

Convulsed from head to toe by late-breaking sobs, he lifted down the three packets decorated with his tears and dribble, and lofted them into the trolley. Then he came around to the front of it and, hands higher than his head to reach the handle, began to push it, looking up at his brother's feet.

'Is Gavin gone to sleep?'

'Yes.'

I bought marshmallows and popcorn, nudging the trolley gently in the general direction of the checkouts but leaving him with the illusion of total control. Another sob shook him, and he began to drive the trolley sideways, misdirected by incoming grief.

'It's all right,' I said hastily. 'He's not dead.'

'Are you sure?'

I lifted Stephen up. 'Give him a poke yourself to test.'

He gave the baby a poke. Gavin responded with a shuddering sigh and lost his soother again. I put Stephen on the floor beside it and he picked it up.

'My mammy doesn't like soothers.'

This was delivered with a fury which seemed to me inappropriate to an issue like soothers. Stephen was seething, looking at the thing, which had acquired a coating of miscellaneous debris during its visit to the floor.

'My mammy doesn't like soothers,' he said again.

Oh, boy, I thought. If you don't acknowledge, you get it again at a higher volume.

'I heard you the first time.'

'Well you didn't say anything.'

I was now at the checkout. The girl swiping my groceries past the gizmo that reads their price had that lobotomised look that says smiling and small talk belong to better-paid jobs than this. Sometimes, absence of good customer care is such a relief. Stephen began to shake the trolley so violently Gavin looked like a candidate for whiplash.

'Stephen, what are you at?'

'My mammy doesn't like soothers.'

I closed my eyes and breathed deeply. Back there again, were we?

'D'you think we should stop giving one to Gavin?' I asked, in that carefully respectful voice heard from mothers and mother-substitutes only when they know some other adult is listening.

'Yes. And I don't want a soother. They're just for babies.'

'OK. Put it in the rubbish container there as you pass.'

He tossed it with such venom that it bounced off the walls of the plastic container on its way down, but being feather-light and rubbery, made a less than satisfactory sound. If I had known grief would make you this raging, I thought, watching him stamp his way to the car, I'd have brought all the glass bottles and let you work it off smashing them into the recycling bin.

When we got home, a big grey Saab was at the kerb

outside. As I pulled into the driveway, the driver got out, a football in his hand. I released Stephen from the child's seat in the back and he stood watching the man dribbling the ball from foot to foot.

'You could do that,' I said.

He stared, silently.

I got back into my mother's car to get the baby out. I must, I thought, sort out the licence and insurance. Reversing carefully out of the car, I could see Stephen edging closer to where the ball was in play. I took the baby into the house and got him into his cot, then went back out. The two of them were passing the ball between them, not a word spoken, total concentration on both sides. I unloaded the car in three journeys, then got the kettle on. They came in when the tea was already on the table and the coffee grinder roaring.

'This is my ball,' Stephen announced.

'Show me.'

He brought it over and I turned it around and around.

'I've never seen this ball before,' I said, doubtfully.

'Him gave it to me.'

'David,' David Carpenter supplied, *sotto voce*.

'David gave it to me.'

'Why?'

'Because.'

'What did you say to him?' I asked, hoping Stephen might have expressed gratitude. Not a chance.

'I said we had to go in 'cause rain gives you moanie.'

I squinted slightly to concentrate on this one.

'It started raining,' David Carpenter said.

'And?'

'I think the theory is that rain gives pneumonia.'

'Nan says,' Stephen added, as a clincher, and my mother's voice echoed down the arches of the years to me. Come in out of the rain, do you want to get pneumonia?

I sat at the table, grief rasping my insides, my eyes sparking with tears.

'Put milk in your tea,' Stephen said. 'Or you'll burn the mouth off yourself.'

At that second reminder of my mother, I began to cry helplessly, which of course set Stephen off again. In what seemed to be the far distance, I could hear Carpenter's voice cutting Stephen's sobs short.

'Enough of that. You have to find a place in your room to keep the football safe. You go up and find a place and when you're sure it's the right place, shout for me and I'll carry it up to you. Take a biscuit with you to keep you going.'

The sobs came under control. Then there was the

thump of the little boy's sneakers hitting the floor as he was lifted down from his high chair. I sat, elbows on the table, face buried in my hands.

'G'wan, she'll be fine, don't pay any attention to her,' the deep voice said.

Then I heard Stephen's laboured climbing of the stairs and – at the same time – milk spurting from a container into my three-quarters-filled mug.

'Tea,' David Carpenter said, nudging the mug against my hand.

'I'm sorry,' I said eventually, drinking the tea. 'This is so pointless.'

There was no response. From upstairs, we could hear Stephen's voice calling for him. He lifted the football and disappeared into the hall. I could hear him take the stairs three at a time, then muffled voices. I drank the tea slowly, wondering idly if they would wake the baby. Half-hoping they would. Nothing to equal a newly-wakened baby as an exigent distraction. The metaphysical hasn't a prayer when an almost-one-year-old wants the physical.

You'd be proud of me, Ma, I thought. Gavin's never had nappy rash. Never had cradle-cap. All the little oul 'wans in the supermarket tell me he's a credit to me. If they only knew that he's a credit to only three weeks of me.

Three weeks. Not enough to dull the visceral conviction that it would somehow prove to have been a mistake. That they were alive. Or maybe my mother was alive. The awful thing was that I could summon up my father's laugh, my father's face, but of Gabrielle and my mother had only snapshot memories. Leaving the framed pictures of them on the various surfaces had probably been a mistake, I thought. But I had believed that Stephen needed to be reminded of his mother and of his father.

I was at the kitchen sink, dousing my aching hot face with cold water, when David Carpenter came back downstairs.

'Your nephew gave me a message for you.'

'Mmm?'

'I'm not sure I understood it well enough to do it justice.'

I looked questioningly at him and he shrugged.

'I think he said that spaghetti is his dinner, not a bastard.'

'Not a pasta.'

'Oh. That makes more sense. It *is* a pasta, though.'

'Don't go into it. He took the supermarket apart in fury over spaghetti being a pasta. God alone knows why.'

He sat down opposite me, hanging his jacket over

the back of the chair. His shirt had that squared-off crease at mid-chest level typical of laundry pressing.

'He showed me what dead people are like, too, did your little nephew.'

David Carpenter underwent a sudden bonelessness, terrifying in its totality, flopping in the chair, liquefied.

'Did he tell you they don't like ice cream?'

'No, he missed out on that bit.'

He got up and began to prowl.

'Don't go much for opening the post, do you?'

I shook my head. On the counter were hundreds of letters, some of them from overseas.

'I'd have to answer them if I opened them.'

'D' you want me to?'

'Why would you do them?'

'Why not?'

There were, I thought, a million sensible reasons why not. The least important of them came first to mind.

'The last time I met you, I told you to fuck off.'

'No, you told me to go to hell.'

'So why would you do my post?'

'You must remember that the first time I met you, you told me to piss off. In fact, you told me to piss off *before* I met you.'

I sat, fogged by the memory of Paris, of how the

homesickness was manageable because Gabrielle was always on the end of the phone, unchanging in her deadpan funniness and her understated concern for me. Gabrielle, now I am homesick at home. Home has become a place like one of those screensavers where no matter which way you turn, there's a wall to walk into. Everywhere I turn, Gabrielle, I spot something worth telling you, but there is no you any more.

'D'you want me to do your post?'

Gabrielle, the difference between him and Stephen is that when he has to repeat himself, he doesn't have to shout. How awful to be so small that you can't see when people are paying attention or not paying attention.

'I'm sorry,' I said, playing for time, playing for connection. 'How could you do them?'

'Draft a set of standard civilities. Personalise them. Bring you hard copy. Anything you don't like you don't sign.'

'That would be nice.'

Someone I know for a long time should do this, I thought. A friend of the family. Or I should. But it's as if the bones have been taken out of me, too. My eyes keep going out of focus.

He rooted in cupboards until he found where I had

stuffed the supermarket plastic bags and filled three of them with the unopened letters.

'Talk to you,' he said and let himself out.

When he came back, days later, with the draft responses, I decided to be brisk and unfogged, interrupting him taking folders out of his briefcase.

'Thanks for telling me you were a famous rugby player.'

'I couldn't tell you that,' he said evenly, laying out the folders on the table.

'Why not?'

'Because I was a famous soccer player.'

'Like there's a big difference,' I said.

For the first time since the funeral, someone laughed in the house. Not aloud. He had a peculiarly quiet laugh, but laughter took him over completely.

'You probably are the last great sporting illiterate,' he said admiringly.

'But why'd you keep it a secret?'

'Why would I tell you? Were you planning to start a football team? Would you have needed me as a coach?'

'You don't give information just because the other person has a practical need for it.'

He looked at me in genuine puzzlement. 'Why the hell else would you give someone information?'

'So they could get a better idea of what you're really like.'

'Tell me, Dominique, once you were told I'd played football, what major insight did it give you into what I'm really like?'

I thought about that and only when he had gone back to his paperwork could I come up with anything.

'It's probably why you have this – this self-satisfaction. I don't mean it negatively. You just don't want applause or praise or flattery. You're happy with your own self as defined by you.'

'I was happy with my own self as defined by me long before I played football. I would be just as happy with my own self if I had been a stonemason. Read these and see if they're OK.'

Because I had never been a letter-writer, I had no distinctive style these letters could have matched. At first, nevertheless, I resisted their formal politeness, some instinct in me wanting them to be the kind of letters Gabrielle would have written: naked in their honest response to the kindness of strangers. But then, I thought, I cannot take on her style in mourning her. So, having restlessly read and reread the first dozen, I relinquished the illusion of control and began to sign them, one after the other, automaton-fashion.

He sat at the other side of the table, taking them from me, folding them precisely, fitting them into already franked envelopes. He had brought red post office pouches with him. The stack of them fattened and grew beside him as we worked, silently.

'Didn't notice you falling over yourself to tell me about being a TV star,' he suddenly said. 'In spite of the insight it might have given me into the real you.'

'It would have given you an insight into the character I played, but how could it give an insight into me?'

He gave such a wide, knowing, silent smile in response to the question that I immediately began to trawl to find what personal weakness would have been explained by him knowing I had been an actor.

'There are other letters you need to make decisions on,' he said. 'Bills first.'

'How would it have helped if I'd told you?'

'I'd have understood why you want to be sure about everything.'

'Like?'

'Like an actor who knows what the other actors are going to do. How the scene's going to work out.'

He looked smug. I did a wide-eyed at him. Half-brought my hand to my mouth. Did a jolted half-gasp.

Started to say something, then stopped in such a way that he was forced to say 'Go on.'

'No, it's just I've realised – realised—' I let my voice rise a note or two, so I sounded like a twelve year old witnessing an apparition. 'How like God you are – God obviously didn't like me wanting to know the script in advance, so he hit those belonging to me with a mobile home.'

God can do accidents without advance planning, Gabrielle, I thought. Your natural law about a planned accident being as unlikely to succeed as a planned orgasm doesn't apply to God. God can just go, 'Why don't we put on a show? The *Great Accident Show*. We can do it right here – here on the road.'

I took out my cheque book.

'Unless you're a lot richer than I think you are, that's not going to cover everything,' he said.

I knew there was no hurry. The bank manager knew my mother's will left everything to Gabrielle and me. Equally divided. He wouldn't hassle me until probate or whatever it was called.

'Which brings us to this,' he said. 'Who is Mairead Houlihan?'

'Oliver's aunt.'

'Did you know she was the executor of his will? And Gabrielle's?'

'I'm amazed they had wills, never mind executors. But if you were doing a will, his Aunt Mairead would be first choice for executor. Talk about a sense of duty.'

Mairead Houlihan's sense of duty led her to notify all sorts of people about the unexpected deaths of the two people whose will she was responsible for. She did not quite suggest, in the letters, copies of which she had punctiliously forwarded to me, that I was now sitting pretty as the prospective guardian of two small offspring of a musical genius who had laid down enough tracks in his short recording career to ensure royalties for decades to come, but between the lines, the message was clear.

'What does she want?' I asked. 'To adopt them?'

'No, I don't think she wants to adopt them. I think she wants everything done properly — as she would define—'

The doorbell rang. The anoraked woman on the doorstep gave me a curiously conditional half-smile. I had the feeling if I played my cards right, I might get a full ear-to-ear version. She was a social worker. From the health authority. She believed my sister and her husband . . . ? And my mother, I said, standing back in surrender and letting her in.

'This is David Carpenter,' I said. 'My business

adviser. We were just discussing a letter from the executor. She says she's letting you people know about the deaths.'

From upstairs came a roar.

'David! David!'

The social worker and I sat, silently listening to the three-steps-at-a-time response to this. Your business adviser, her expression said, is sufficiently familiar with your nephew that he runs upstairs unsupervised? We could hear talk, clearly led by Stephen, laughter, then a bumpier, slower descent of the stairs, the little boy obviously accompanying the man. They came in together. David plugged in the kettle. Stephen looked at the social worker.

'D'you want drinking chocolate, too?' he asked with uneasy generosity.

'No thank you. I don't like drinking chocolate.'

Before he opened his mouth, I knew what was going to come out of it. I could have said it in unison with him.

'Dead people don't like ice cream.'

A mantle of counselling attentiveness almost visibly dropped on her bundly jumpered shoulders.

'Who told you that?'

'Daisy did,' he said, pointing at me. 'Auntie Daisy,' he added, as if this in some way improved me.

David Carpenter made an attempt to deflect his attention by offering him the chance to mix the chocolate powder and milk, but Stephen didn't often have a completely new audience so evidently riveted by what, to him, were fairly mundane ideas.

'They look like this,' he told her, going boneless and rolling his eyes up.

'Who do?'

He gazed at her, mystified. The two words sounded like a bird hooting. He watched her, half-expecting a joke. Or maybe a lesson, along the lines of, 'And what do we say when someone gives us a sweet?'

'She wants to know who looks like—' I said, doing his invertebrate mime.

'Dead people. My mammy looks like that now,' he told her.

She looked at him in solemn silence. He took a slurp of his chocolate.

'I'n sorry,' he told her. 'I'n sorry for making a big noise. And my daddy. And my nan as well.'

One for everybody in the audience, I thought. All gone.

'They got deaded in a clamity, and they'll never come back ever ever.'

By way of emotional punctuation, his brother started to cry upstairs. I went to sort out Gavin's problem. Gavin's middle name should have been Niagara Falls. No nappy could hold him. I stripped him of Babygro, stripped the cot of sheets and protectors, removed his nappy and listened to his observations on the state of the world. Gavin seemed destined for politics or showbiz. Devoid of data his discourse might be, but he could keep on message for ten minutes at a time without repeating a syllable, or needing much of a response.

'You going to come downstairs and show the social worker what a poifect specimen of well-cared-for orphan you are?'

He gurgled and the weight of his big head unbalanced him towards me.

'This won't do, kid,' I said, poking him back into a sitting position with an index finger in his solar plexus. 'Ya gotta show da social woiker ya can sit up. All on ya owniers, ya got me?'

He began to laugh and fall forward again. I fingered him back into position and dropped to my knees, so the next time gravity dragged him towards me I could let him drop off the surface into my arms. This decided him he was the cleverest thing going, and he pulled on my hair as I carried him downstairs, apparently convinced that he could ring bells of celebration somewhere by tugging at my locks.

I put him in the bounce seat. Stephen came over and nuzzled him. Gavin told his older brother several chapters of the story of his life. A comedy, if his chortles were anything to go by. The social worker watched me while I puréed food for him.

'I have explained to Mr Carpenter that I cannot give him details, even if he does act for you,' she said, as if there were only the two of us and the two kids in the room. I glanced at David Carpenter, now explaining to Stephen that no, he couldn't go out to kick ball at the moment, even though it wasn't raining.

'Details of what?'

'Like inheritance.'

'That's to do with lawyers,' I said. 'What else?'

'What will be the arrangements for the children. When you're overseas, for example.'

'When I'm over — I'm never overseas. Except when I'm on holiday. I was an au pair once, but only for—'

'Tell me,' David Carpenter said, over the head of my nephew, now sitting on his lap. 'What immediate steps do you have to take?'

For a moment, she looked self-conscious, then gathered her anorak up and started to shove her arms into it. She smiled carefully at him, then answered his question to me. If she had put up a sign reading, 'This man may be present, but he has no rights,' she could not have made her position more clear.

'Miss Dempsey, I don't want to take up any more of your time. There is no intervention necessary at this time. We're concerned only with the well-being of the children, and they're getting good care. I will leave you my card so you can contact me if you should need to.'

As I led the way to the front door, both of us could hear Stephen's question.

'Will she die in a clamity?'

Her eyes met mine. Reprovingly. 'Such a heavy burden, that knowledge, for a pre-schooler,' she observed.

I opened the door for her, allowing myself to look puzzled.

'For a – oh, right. You mean a little boy?'

She lowered her head and looked at me in total silence from under her brows. Oh, what big eyebrows you have, Grandma. All the better to scare you with, my dear. But Grandma, I don't scare easy. In fact, I could give you lessons in how to do a scare performance better than you do.

She was off down the path to her stubby Renault, and I stood, an object lesson in politeness, until she drove away. Trouble, I thought.

CHAPTER TWELVE

Sending the Right Message

<hr />

They are there in hordes on the day of the funeral. But once the ceremonies are over, you're on your own. Avoid the recently bereaved. Maybe death is catching. Or maybe what keeps them away is embarrassment, dressed up as sensitivity.

So there we were, the three of us. (Or, to be mathematically accurate, the one and three-fifths of us. Being forced to spend so much time studying figures about Oliver's royalties and my mother's estate, I found myself dividing even the kids up numerically.) Gavin walking, plunging, running and falling. Stephen minding him when the older boy wasn't, himself, being shaken by tornadoes of alarming rage, related only tenuously to the apparent subject of his fury. Me, newly fearful of all social workers, reading up anything I could find about bereaved children to make sure they could not catch me doing things wrong. All this at a time in my life when I should be out partying on all the nights except the few devoted to dyeing my eyelashes or waxing my legs.

Once the three-fifths were asleep in the evenings, I would try to figure out what to do about the threat that they might be taken from me. Examining my own conscience. Did I want to 'own' them? Honest answer? Yes. Not a politically correct answer, of course. Dangerously indicative of possessiveness. Was I thinking first of the children's needs? Yes. But I was also thinking first of Gabrielle's needs. And of my own. Not of Oliver's, curiously. Because Oliver was always throwaway, ironic, humorous, after death he seemed written on air. Insubstantial. Not to be considered. Not to be disregarded, either: Gabrielle would speak for him in my mind.

I had a handful of certainties. That I must hold on to the boys was the most important of them. I sat, night after night, in a house dark except for warm-eye cyclops lights plugged into every socket, bought by me to fill up the spaces so that Gavin would not thrust whatever came to his hand into the three-pin holes and also to help Stephen be braver than darkness inclined him to be. I sat, asking questions of myself. In a whisper, lest Stephen wake and think me a ghost.

'What's the biggest threat to me holding on to the boys?'

'That social worker.'

'No stereotyping, here. Good bunch, social workers. Awful job. Must see so much abuse of children.'

'Then why doesn't she bugger off – go catch the real criminals – not hassle me?'

'In fairness, now, she appeared once only. Plus she offered to be of assistance.'

'She sent out vibes.'

'Like? Specifically?'

'That she'd take them from me quick as look at me.'

'Never said anything of the sort.'

'She would, though.'

'Unless?'

'Unless I prove I am the perfect mother – ersatz mother – for the next year.'

'Prove? How?'

'Not put them in crèches. Not take a job. Maybe not even freelance. Not go overseas. Be here. Smell of home baking welcoming Stephen home from school. Jesus, maybe I should keep Stephen out of school for another year.'

'How's the social worker gonna know all that? You going to send her daily e-mails?'

'Christ, no. Don't need a meaningful with her.'

'So how's she going to know you're Surrogate Mother of the Year?'

'I could invite her for tea. Free viewing. Open house. God, I'd rather be dead.'

'Alternatives? An anonymous letter saying, "Dominique Dempsey grows veggies for the orphans to eat"?'

The back-of-the-mind interrogations were muted during daylight hours by the routines of motherhood, and by trying to deal with agents, lawyers, car insurance brokers and the police. Everything from someone seeking permission to use one of Oliver's solos as a counterpoint to the words in a new song, to Gardaí updating me on what their forensic people had to say about the scene of the accident.

The worst task was having to take my mother's possessions — some of them still in tea chests — from her new apartment in order to sell it. I brought the children with me, involving Stephen in packaging clothes for the charity bin at the supermarket car park. The job had limited appeal to him.

As his interest waned, I began to make decisions more ruthlessly, less sentimentally, so when I was finally down to those things I could not bring myself to throw out or give away, the pile was smaller than it might have been. The detritus of my childhood in clumsy piles on a shining hardwood floor. Traces of my parents' marriage: a photograph in black-and-white of the two of them, laughing lovingly into each other's young faces, her in a white tailored blouse, black straight skirt, him tweed-jacketed with a moustache. Traces, too, of my torn-away sister: funny letters written to my parents from continental holidays and even one — riotous in its lack of religiosity — from a school retreat.

I left my mother's apartment without regret. There was no flavour of her there. No 'there' there. But then, there had been little trace of my mother in my mother for a while. To truly understand the loss meant reaching back to what she had been before my father's death numbed her, and it is difficult to re-establish old realities through the lens of the recent.

Back in our home, I played back the messages left on the telephone, noting names, numbers and requests into the computer beside it. Dutifully. Social worker, you watching? I get a brownie point for this? No? Oh, it doesn't have a direct enough connection with motherhood? Shit, you're right. I should be out there in the back garden watching Gavin come to terms with his world. Not letting Stephen do my job for me. I can do this message-taking later, you're right. You're absolutely right. Of course you are. It's all that training makes you so wise. Not to mention your natural sensitivity, too, of course.

'He's all right,' Stephen said the moment I stepped onto the patio. 'He's just washing worms.'

Which was true. Having harvested about twenty fat earth-worms from the flower bed soil, Gavin had them all lined up for washing.

'I filled his bucket from the hose,' Stephen said. A little worriedly.

Kid, I know where you're at, I thought. Under-fives never know when the designated grown-up will find monstrous something you did with the best of intentions.

'I put in a mug of hot,' he added. 'So they wouldn't get shivery from the cold water.'

Work study in action, Gavin was immersing the worms one by one in the plastic bucket, gently easing off any dirt stuck to them, then laying them out on the warm, sundrenched cement slabs on the other side of the bucket. One side clean, one side dirty. Like those signs good mothers stuck on their dishwashers. Must get one of those, I thought. It would be one of the million tiny authenticities that would testify to me being a good mother.

Apart from a slight tendency to stretch each worm before laying it down (a physical echo of what I tended to do with my handwashed tights) Gavin's bathhouse of the vermicelli seemed reasonably humane. Sustainable development in child's play, too: after a few moments' stunned recuperation on the warm cement, each worm took off back towards the flower bed, so as soon as Gavin's first instalment was fully laundered, half the clean ones were dirty again, ready for another good washing.

'Did I do that?'

'No, Stephen, you never went near a worm at Gavin's age.'

'Why's he doing it?'

A social worker might find the behaviour suggestive of – of what? Maternal obsessive over-cleanliness? No. I could not be accused of that, I decided. I kept the boys clean, but not so clean you could eat your dinner off them.

'Why do you think Gavin's doing it?'

See, Ms Social Worker? See me stimulating Stephen's speculative capacity?

'Because he's stupid,' Stephen said.

'Oh, Stephen, how could you think that?'

Oops, there's a mistake. Making a pre-schooler feel guilty when he should be surrounded by a non-judgemental warmth.

'They're going back the minute he's finished with them to get dirty again. That's stupid. He should leave them dirty. They probly like muck. They probly hate being washed. *He* hates being washed.'

In deference to Stephen's concern, I told Gavin no worm should ever be washed more than once in a day, and that way, got him out of the garden and into his own bath, which, as Stephen rightly pointed out, he loathed.

In a misguided effort to get him to like it, I had used neon-pink bubble bath in it the week before. Because he bawled his eyes shut in advance of any bath, it wasn't until he was fully into it that he registered the colour. Convinced, I think, that the puce water was caused by something leaking out of his person, he screamed the place down and now approached a bath as ritual torture inflicted on him by me. He fought it all the way, which meant I needed to take a shower and change every stitch I was wearing immediately afterwards.

Later that night I went back to listening to the telephone messages. One was from a journalist saying, in a hushed, rushed way, that she knew I had been through a really awful time and was really sorry to bother me, but her editor really wanted an interview with me about taking on the responsibility for two little boys – my late sister's two sons, she added, lest I be confused as to which boys I was caring for – and thought it would be a great way of getting people to really remember my late sister and would I please ring her back, these were her numbers, at any time, and even if I couldn't do it now, would I please keep her in mind, because she could really assure me that she would handle it the way I would want it handled and not do anything that wouldn't be in the interests of the two – of my two nephews. Little nephews, she added, self-consciously.

I sat looking at my shortened version of her message and considered it.

'Hey, you know what? This could work.'

'How?'

'Send an anonymous message to the social worker, via a newspaper.'

'Megaphone diplomacy by media?'

'Right.'

'You're not serious.'

'Why not?'

Decision made, I planned it meticulously. I let a number of weeks pass. Then I rang her (she nearly fell out of her car with surprised gratitude) and postponed it a few more weeks, but allowed as how her nice message had been very persuasive. Then rang her again, laying down all sorts of conditions. No pictures showing the children's faces. No picture of the accident site. No quotes from friends. (The enhanced memories of a Nigel would not, I figured, greatly serve my desired image as the mother of all stepmothers.)

The night before she came to the house I wrote down everything I wanted to get into the feature. It would be good if she understood I didn't use TV as an electronic babyminder, so I unplugged the set and left the flex where she could see it, giving, I hoped, the impression that it had been unconnected for weeks. It would be helpful if she wrote about me cooking or baking, so I lined up a week's tasks beside the cooker. A positive portrayal would show me as an earnest student, so I left the books and printouts about bereaved children on visible surfaces. The visit was also timed to ensure Gavin was tiring, almost ready for a nap. Which meant that when I had bedded him down, we could talk and I could concentrate on getting into the feature what I needed to.

After she left, I checked the notes made in advance

and was pleased to find how little was missing. The feature, when it appeared, reflected the preparation faithfully, delivering a portrait of a woman in her early twenties almost totally devoting her life to two orphans, learning everything she could in order to meet their needs.

There were lots of phone calls after it appeared. It seemed to serve a delousing process. People who had been at the funeral resurfaced, confident they could cope with me on the phone, now the bereavement was in the middle distance. One of the calls came just as David Carpenter arrived with the latest paperwork related to Oliver's recordings. I let him in and wound up the phone call as quickly as possible.

'Hate that kind of crap,' I said, coming into the kitchen where he was making tea.

'What kind of crap?'

'"Read about you in the paper, aren't you wonderful" kind of crap.'

'Who forced you to talk to the paper?'

'Nobody. But I didn't do it to get praised by gobshites.'

As he handed me the mug of tea, I could see my preparatory notes on the surface beside the kettle. He could not have missed them.

'Strategic planning?' he said dryly, nudging the notes.

A wash of warmth came up the back of my neck. First wave, embarrassment: what will he think of me? Second wave, defiance: what do I care?

'Fair dues to you, Daisy, you never surrender to the randomness of life.'

'You're saying I'm manipulative.'

'Didn't know I needed instantaneous translation.'

'I didn't say one solitary word to her that wasn't true.'

He looked at me, silent.

'I didn't behave in any way that wasn't what I would do in real life.'

The silence whipped me into more and more words.

'I just — just — concentrated things, selected things so she wouldn't get distracted from the truth.'

'That's a very good definition.'

'Of what?'

'Propaganda.'

'Propaganda isn't — look, are you saying I should just leave all this to chance?'

'Are you saying the end justifies the means?'

'Oh, fuck off, would you?'

'Some other time. Right now, we have to get you

sorted, and I bring you three options for how you can make sense of the insurance money, your mother's estate, trusts for the boys, the whole lot.'

One of the options was to set up a limited company with a sufficiently flexible description to allow me to use it, later, as a base for a career, whether in theatrical direction or consultancy work. David Carpenter wanted me to pick a name for it. Any name.

'I can't think of anything that sums up the box of allsorts I'm dealing with,' I said. 'In fact, I can't think of any name. I'm sorry. This must be very irritating to you.'

Shut up, I thought. What's wrong with you, trying to coax this man into denying the small emotional reactions you know he does not have. Trying to ease the knotted self-contempt you feel over the newspaper feature.

'Not easy to invent a good company name,' he said. 'I once had a bunch of guys who ended up calling their company Sweet Effay because of the same problem.'

I kept wondering what Gabrielle would want. Anything to stay in contact with my sister, preserve her presence by conserving her contribution. Of course, it was ineffective. I was sliding down the face of a glass mountain, kidding myself that digging in with my fingernails would halt the descent. Every day brought some choice, some decision, some idea to remind me that I was on my own. Not only that I was on my own, but that trying to play the 'What would Gabrielle want me to do?' game was counter-productive. I was just freezing her in the limitations of the past.

I slid my hands up the sleeves of my cardigan, looking out the window at jet trails fattening in the sky as the wind dispersed them from the two narrow lines of brightness left immediately behind the plane. Sunshine on jet trails. Who had said that and why?

Three sheets from an internet site were put in front of me. Colour pictures, poorly reproduced in black and white, of planes creating messages by releasing puffs of smoke at planned points in the sky. It was headed Mort Arken and the Skytypers. I read it, fascinated. This Mort, after his military service, bought old fighter planes, using them to do 'sky-typing'. This seemed to be a variation on the old, single-plane system where, as 'smoke oil' streamed out from the plane's exhaust, the pilot looped the plane through the air to write characters. That, the handout indicated, was OK if what a client wanted written in the sky was something as simple as a heart with an arrow through it. For longer messages, sky-typing was the solution.

For sky-typing, five planes flew in tight formation

at 10,000 feet, each letting out smoke puffs in a pattern read from a perforated tape.

'The result,' said the text, 'is a message eight miles long with dot-matrix style letters twice as tall as the Empire State Building. It can be seen for thirty miles in any direction, which means a message of up to thirty characters reaches an area of nearly four hundred square miles.'

People used it to make marriage proposals, and one client hired the Skytypers to send a rude message to a former colleague.

'Wouldn't you love to do that?' I asked, momentarily consumed by the idea of it.

'Pay a fortune to have planes write 'Fuck Off' in the sky, rather than say it personally?'

'No. Be one of the planes. One of the pilots, I mean. Write messages in the sky for a living.'

David Carpenter shook his head. 'No. You're the one hooked on jet trails. Why don't you call your company The Skywriter? Covers anything and everything.'

I went back to the window. The trails in the sky were huge now, puffing into the shape of the tubed cotton wool that comes out of the top of pill bottles. Soon, they would be as softly shapeless as any other cloud. As any other memory.

'The Skywriter,' I repeated, trying out the sound of it.

'Novelettish,' my mother's voice said in my head.

I nodded at David Carpenter, silently.

'Yes? The Skywriter OK?'

'It's fine, it's fine.'

Mam, if you're going to be a talking memory, would you ever be a real and present memory, instead of a bloody one-word pruning shears?

David Carpenter was making notes on his laptop. Those notes meant that business cards for The Skywriter would duly arrive, as would letterheads and envelopes. When I asked about being invoiced for the work, he looked furious and said it was out of the question.

'Tell me something.'

He looked up from his notes, poised to resume.

'Why? Why do you do all this stuff for me?'

'Why do you need a why?'

'People don't do things for other people like this. You've been running me since the accident. I would have been lost.'

'Haven't been running you. Just getting some of the obstacles out of your way so you can run yourself.'

I was silent, still bothered by how much he was doing for me. It would be OK if he was a partner.

Or a lover. But since the accident, we had never gone out together. We saw more of each other than many married couples, but without physical intimacy. The odd pat on the back was about the limit to what he offered. Nor did he create in me the need for anything more than that.

Idly, I wondered if, now he had his own home in the city, he had a partner. There had been a wife a long time ago, I knew. A household-name model who, after the divorce, had remarried. I hoped he had someone who would appreciate his understatedness for what it was, not mistake it for dullness as I once had in telling Gabrielle about him. At a time when everybody said 'I love you' to everybody else, he was the exception, never expressing affection, never articulating sympathy, never giving the 'why' behind him arriving, doing something useful and going away again.

He had become the necessary infrastructure of my life. I was minding two small boys, running a career and coping with the ragged edges left by the accident. For the first time in my life, everything was real. Nor had I any need to create situations like the one I had created with Robert Allen.

'If I wasn't so sad, I'd be happy,' I said. 'You're sort of like plumbing,' I added.

'Thank your lucky stars that social worker isn't

hearing this stream of consciousness,' he said. 'She'd have you in a straitjacket. Fecking plumbing.'

I could see, rather than hear, him laugh.

'Did you know that Dostoevsky said you couldn't judge people until you'd heard them laugh?' I asked. 'He said it didn't matter what people said, only how they laughed. I wonder what he would have made of a soundless laugh like you have.'

He started to pat his pockets, obviously looking for something. Found it eventually in the plastic file holder in front of him.

'The only letter I couldn't make a stab at answering was this,' he said. 'It came several weeks ago, very quickly after the accident, but you had much more important things to be doing, so I kept it.'

He pushed it across the table at me. There was no address on it, although it was neatly typed.

Dear Dominique Dempsey,

Having seen the pictures of you at your family's funeral, I know you may be really affected by their deaths, although how an actor would not be able to produce a few tears is beyond me.

I have been watching you a long time and I know you will be basking in it right now. Well, you may fool some of the people but you don't fool me. You would need to have a lot

*worse happen to you before I would believe you had feelings
except for yourself.*

Yours faithfully,

(The signature was a wild scribble, deliberately unread-
able as any name.)

I held it, chills spreading across my shoulders
and down my arms. I know who wrote this, I
thought. There is only one person could write
it. She had grown small and distant in my mind,
but even the passing of years has not made her
go away. Or dimmed her hatred of me. Dad, you
said there would come a time when I would not
remember Richelle Governey's name. You promised me.

I pushed the letter back across the table to David
Carpenter.

'Peaches and cream, fame and fruitcakes,' I said,
trying to sound casually dismissive.

'You've had a few of these, down the years.'

I wasn't sure whether this was a question or a factual
statement.

'I checked with the people who worked with your
mother on your fan mail.'

'The ones who called her The Wrath of God?'

He nodded, discarding the possibility of finding
this interesting.

'They have a file. All following the same layout. All with the same phrases. All with variants on the same non-signature.'

'David, do you remember the time in Paris you told me to stop thinking?'

'No,' he said, indicating that I should concentrate on the issue at hand.

'You got so ratty with me. You made "thinking" sound like the greatest waste of time. Now that everything's so immediate and urgent and one bloody thing on top of another, I think I have stopped the kind of thinking you were giving out about. I'm certainly not going to do any thinking about some poor sad sod who is so eaten away by contemplating my fifteen minutes of piffling fame that they'd puke up a letter like that to send.'

He didn't react to this. Unlooked-for giving and unexpected withholding could be the two snaked chains of his DNA helix, I thought. After a moment, he slid the letter back into its place in the file.

'We may discuss this again,' he said.

And we may not, I thought.

'When will we be seeing the next newspaper instalment of Portrait of the Artist as a Young Mother?' he asked, lightly, turning off the computer and inserting it into its black canvas case.

'If and when I think it's necessary,' I said, the initial smile frozen and fading on my face.

'Necessary for the social workers of the world or to give you a vital signs check?'

I had no idea what he meant, and said so.

'Oh, Dominique, I'd have thought you'd know about that addiction. Afflicts people who've been famous. In fact, afflicts *only* those who've been famous. Even pifflingly famous. They need to read about themselves or see themselves on TV now and then to be sure they're still alive. Real life is insufficient evidence.'

'Why are you being so cruel?'

He seemed genuinely taken aback. 'Come on, Dominique, don't tell me you weren't just a little relieved to see that reminder of yourself in the paper.'

'The sort of shallow shite who'd be relieved by reading about herself in the paper would also be upset by reading nasty anonymous letters.'

He wiped his face with his hand twice, forehead to chin, then stood silently, eyes closed, hand over his mouth as if he had forgotten to complete the movement. Finally, shaking his head, he opened his eyes, smiled, picked up the computer case and left the house without answering.

CHAPTER THIRTEEN

The News of the Screws

Handing two children under five into the care of someone else, on their premises, for just one day requires more planning, preparation and ingenuity than Scott needed to set out for the South Pole or wherever he was looking for. Especially when one of the children makes like the day is going to be his last in civilisation.

'For Jesus sake, Stephen,' I ended up saying, 'you don't have to pack pemmican and water-purifying tablets. They only live in Drumcondra.'

Abashed, he put the proposed inclusions back in place and sat down in the hall. On the bag of Gavin's stuff. Which resulted in me doing a fast silent assessment of whether or not there were items in the bag his weight could damage. If there were, I could not call them to mind. Then I realised that my considered stare was making him uncomfortable and he was rising, guiltily, off the bag.

'Honey, do us a favour.' I handed him the car keys. 'Get the car open and put your bag and Gavin's bag into the back seat while I get him up.'

I opened the front door for him. He was not quite tall enough to reach the catch, yet. Halfway up the stairs, I added, '—and don't forget the car alarm.'

In a sitcom, it would have been great timing. The alarm screamed the neighbourhood awake before I could get to him and snatch the remote control out of his hand to stifle it. We stood in the dawn-dark garden, him shaking with fear, me surveying the neighbour's second-storey windows to catch if curtains were pulled aside to reveal faces filled with (justified) bile and venom.

'Now you can get the bags in,' I said to Stephen, quietly. Very quietly, all the while wanting to shriek, 'Don't look at me with that panic in your face, when have I ever lifted a hand to you, for Chrissake?'

I raced up the stairs and got Gavin up, washed, dressed and strapped into the car in about eight minutes. He was untypically silent as I started the car. Normally, first thing in the morning, he was in high good humour. The early start and the speed of dressing seemed to have headed his good humour off at the pass, leaving him neutrally silent. Which was just as well, because Stephen's insecurities were in full voice. How long exactly would I be gone for? Would I be home before they went to bed? Would I telephone? Was I going on the airport road? Was there any way I might miss the plane?

'Going there or coming back?' I asked, getting to the outskirts of Drumcondra as a church clock struck seven.

'I don't know,' Stephen said, so sadly I wanted to stop the car and hug him.

At a red light, I leaned back over the back of the passenger seat and gave him a kiss.

'There's police,' he observed and I sprang back into my proper place and ground the gears.

There were two Garda motorcycles and a squad car.

'Will they come after us?'

'No. They're escorting a government person.'

'What's pemmican?'

'I don't know.'

'But you said it.'

I drove down the avenue to the McDermott house. Oliver's mother was at the open door. Gavin began to strain against the tethers of the child safety seat to get to her. Stephen expertly unclipped him and she lifted him out, looking ridiculously small and frail compared to her youngest grandson. Oliver's father shook hands with Stephen, looking ridiculously vast and powerful compared to the boy.

'Ask your grandfather that after breakfast,' I said, turfing the two bags into the hall and muttering *sotto voce* to Mr McDermott that he'd better find out what pemmican was. He said he knew what pemmican was, but was curious as to what had put it into Stephen's mind first thing in the morning.

'Who knows?' I shrugged and, giving Stephen a quick hug, was back in the car.

Mr McDermott did a gesture asking me to halt.

'Don't do this to me, please,' I begged, getting the words out like a ventriloquist so he could not read the desperation in my lips: 'Don't do this to gnee thlease. I'n late. Don't delay nee any nore. Don't keet nee any later.'

'I see in the paper that your friend Mr Carpenter has been made a partner in his firm,' he said. 'Please convey my congratulations.'

I beamed, gave the thumbs up, and was heading for the airport road as fast as I could do it without drawing the police on me. Thanks for telling nee, Dathid, I muttered, still not letting my lips move. Keet it a secret, thy all neans, you getting a thartnershit.

Inventing the word 'thartnershit' put me in good humour. I was going to be well paid for this programme and I could afford, out of the proceeds, to give David Carpenter a present to mark his promotion. I could write a card and use the new word. Or, I thought, running across the airbridge towards Departures, I could ignore it, since he was being so shagging secretive. Or (halted, now, while the security guy ran his geiger counter over my briefcase), maybe I could buy something and have Stephen give it to him. Nobody meant more to Stephen than 'Uncle' David. Some of the older boys had told him David had been something of a soccer star, but this, to Stephen, was beside the point. To him, David Carpenter was a beloved uncle who knew everything but never told on you.

On the flight, instead of working out what I was going to say in the interview, I was back to thinking about Stephen. He was so impressed by David refusing to change my rules, even under heavy persuasion from him and Gavin. I overheard David saying, one day, to the child, 'Stephen, if your aunt makes a decision about something, it's because she knows all the bits and pieces. I don't know the bits and pieces, because I'm here maybe once a week. She's here all the time. That's why she gets to make the rules, and I get to obey them.'

The interview was easy enough to allow me to be back at Heathrow well in advance of scheduled check-in.

'You know what that means, don't you?' my mother's voice asked in my head.

Mam, I thought, you know what happened to Cassandra. Not that what happened to Cassandra is any worse than what happened to you. And not that anything else can happen to you, now you're dead in a clamity and can't eat ice cream any more.

The guy at check-in was looking at me with such astonishment, for a moment I feared I had said all this out loud.

'Sorry?' I twittered.

'That flight is delayed and we will not be checking passengers for another ninety minutes,' he said, in that monotone that manifests mannered restraint at having to repeat oneself.

I found a phone and rang the McDermotts. Oliver's father came on the line.

'They're gone,' he said.

'Gone?'

'They weren't well. Marina took them to our doctor.'

Who the hell, I wondered, was Marina? Then it struck me it must be Oliver's mother. From the very first time I met her, I thought of her either as Mrs McDermott or as Oliver's mum, but she had not always been Mrs someone.

'He says it's a forty-eight-hour virus that's on the go. Quite a high fever and you have to watch them for complications. But they're OK. He gave her a prescription for antibiotics in case it goes into their chest, but you know antibiotics. She filled it out though and sent it home with them.'

'Sent it home with them?'

'Your friend David Carpenter rang and offered to pick them up. Well, he actually rang in the afternoon to talk to Stephen. They've probably got there by now.'

I asked him to thank Marina and rang off. Swipe-carded the phone again before dialling my own number.

It was answered formally by Stephen, who told me with great dignity that it was really Gavin who was sick. He, Stephen, was fine. This in the understated tone of the hero going out of the tent into the blizzard and announcing, 'I may be some time.' The effect was somewhat spoiled when it struck him that me ringing was a sure sign I wasn't halfway between London and Dublin on a jet.

'I knew you wouldn't be home,' he said accusingly, and burst into tears.

There were confused noises, including much tired crying, before David Carpenter's inappropriately amused voice came on the line.

'Just delay a plane out of spite any time, don't you, Daisy?'

For some reason, this question brought me close to a version of Stephen's febrile grief.

'How bad are they?'

'Interesting.'

I shrank forward into the kiosk, speechless. Oh, God, if there is a God, be a good God and don't let my kids have an interesting headache like my poor father. I'll believe in you and everything if you just hold off this time.

'Dominique?'

'Mmmm.'

'It's a forty-eight-hour virus.'

'I know.'

'Not bubonic plague. They'll live. I guarantee it. Hold on.'

I could hear muttered negotiations going on, and

then Stephen came on the line, all Robin to David Carpenter's Batman. I would be home in no time and I was not to worry, so I wasn't. There was another background prompt.

'You go and have a cup of chino,' he finished.

I promised I would.

'A big cup of chino,' he added, lest I underestimate the offer.

When I got home, both boys were awake, reacting to their fevers in quite different ways. Gavin, normally the sunniest and chattiest of toddlers, was like a fat, red stuffed cat. The fever seemed to have almost swollen him. He was silent and languid. Stephen, on the other hand, was frenetic, inattentive and shrill.

David suggested I cook something while he put them to bed. Rather you than me, I thought, as Stephen burst into tears, claiming improbably not to be sick at all. Somehow, David got both of them settled down and the two of us ate in the kitchen. I told him about the programme and the comments the presenter showed me, already on tape, from international music celebrities.

We were drinking coffee when from overhead came piercing screams. The two of us took off up the stairs, David taking them three at a time, to find Stephen awash in tears and ashake with panic.

'You were dreaming, pet,' I said. 'It wasn't real.'

'It's over. Gone,' David offered. Stephen shuddered in relief.

'Tell me what was the bad thing,' I said, rocking him. 'Tell me what you were dreaming about.'

'Crocodiles and alligators,' he choked, miserably.

I was a little disappointed. From the screams, I had expected something more spectacular. A little more wide-screen Technicolor.

'Was that all?' I asked.

'They weren't cooked enough,' he wept. 'They were still moving!'

David thought this was desperately funny, and moved away from the bed to have a quiet laugh, not wanting the child to think his horrors were not being taken seriously.

'Don't go 'way, Uncle David. Please. Don't go 'way.'

'But I'm here,' I offered, only to be favoured with the kind of ruthless kid's stare that says a) you couldn't cope with a half-cooked alligator to save your life, and b) I'd be ashamed to be rescued by a girl. David tried to get him into bed, but Stephen had a seriously real dread of being left with his fever-induced (or perhaps medication-induced) horrors and would not be reassured unless David was in the bed with him.

David pulled off jacket, tie, shirt and trousers and slid in beside him, giving me the eyes-roll-to-heaven look of total surrender to the child.

'Go to bed yourself,' he told me. 'This could take ages.'

'You'll let yourself out?'

He nodded again, his chin tipping off the top of Stephen's head. A couple of times, before I went to sleep in my own room, I could hear gentle talking, indicative of Stephen coming up to the surface of wakefulness and being soothed. When next I woke, it was to David's unmistakable footfall on the stairs. I looked at the clock. Six in the morning. Slipping into a robe, I went downstairs, to find the front door open and David coming back in to collect something he had forgotten.

'Wake you, did I? Sorry. Kettle's boiled, though, if you want a cuppa.'

He headed out the door. I stood in the cold dawn light, wondering about waving to him. Then it struck me — bloody hell, this friend has screwed up his entire week minding kids with whom he has no blood relationship at all. I padded across the red-paved front garden to where his car was parked. He turned and noted my bare feet.

'You'll freeze.'

'Only for a second. I just wanted to say thank you. I mean, really, really, thank you.'

I reached up to put my arms around his neck. He automatically bent to allow me to kiss him.

'Now, g'wan back in before you get whatever the kids have,' he said, patting my rear to speed me on my way.

'You know something? You have damn all understanding of how bacteria and viruses are spread, if you blame the paving on front gardens for it,' I said, then ran for the front door to wave at him as he drove the big Saab away.

That was Thursday morning. Mistake Number One, had I but known. On Friday morning, I got a peculiar phone call asking me how long I had been dating David Carpenter. The call was from an English journalist, who obviously knew David as a former soccer star, and knew me not at all. I just laughed at him.

'None of your business,' I said.

'But wot I'm giving you's the opportunity to pu' yo soid of the story,' he whined.

'There is no story. I have no side of a story. But I do have two sick kids, so forgive me, I'm cutting you off.'

Mistake Number Two. But so minor, it seemed

at the time, that I never even mentioned it when David rang during the day to check how the kids were doing.

Next thing it was Sunday morning, with the phone ringing before either child woke. I leaped across the bed like a panther to shut it up.

'Yes, yes, *yes!*' I hissed.

'What an old charmer you are,' David's voice said. 'What an old seductress. Voice like warmed maple syrup flowing over—'

'Jasus, it's effing six in the morning on effing Sunday and I have two convalescent kids still asleep – OK,' I said, remembering his care of those kids earlier in the week and damping down the impatience in my voice. Or trying to. 'Whattya want?'

'Words with you – now. Don't ask. I'll explain when I get there.'

Of course a chill should have run up my spine. A warning *frisson* at the edges of my consciousness. But – as proven earlier – I have little prophetic sense of advancing threat. As my mother used to, I had bustled myself into good humour by the time he arrived, and was taken aback by his closed expression. Not as taken aback, however, as I was by the front page of the tabloid newspaper he threw on the table.

It was the *News of the World*. Three-quarters of the

front page was a picture of the two of us. David Carpenter and me. An angled shot, showing just enough of his face to identify him, but catching me in three-quarter face to the camera, my eyes alight, smiling as I kissed him, my arms linked behind his head, pulling his face down to me. I looked tiny without high heels on. The photograph included my bare feet, pale against the reddish paving. Plus, of course, my towelling robe, looking pretty skimpy for visits to a front garden.

DAVE CARPENTER'S LOVE NEST WITH CRASH TRAGEDY STAR, the headline screamed. There was little space for anything much over and above the picture and headline, but a single paragraph trumpeted that former soccer star David Carpenter had healed the heartbreak of his first failed marriage and found new love with an Irish soap opera star whose family had been wiped out in a freak car crash. See pages 6, 7 and 8, invited the tag line at the bottom.

On the inside pages, there I was again. This time the photographs showed David leaving the house ('after a night of passion'). David returning to the open doorway. Leaving again. Me standing in the doorway. Me running across the garden ('for one last kiss'). The hug. Then us laughing, his patting me on the rear. The latter detail they had in one of those circular enlargements with an arrow pointing back to its smaller version.

The story took a heavily sympathetic line for the first few paragraphs. David Carpenter, whose first marriage to a superstar model (inset picture of superstar model) had sadly failed, was now going through happier times with Dominique Dempsey (pet name Daisy), once a star of soap opera, whose family had been wiped out in a freak accident on Dublin's Airport Road (inset picture of accident). The house owned by the dead couple, star pianist Oliver McDermott and his wife Gabrielle, had been turned into a love nest by the besotted pair, determined to keep their passionate relationship a secret.

'I don't believe this shit,' I said, turning the page.

'Believe it,' David said.

The last page had a vague piece about David Carpenter's first journey down the aisle failing after three years. Neither he nor his ex had ever publicly said why. Indeed, the paper said admiringly, his ex, reached last night by the *News of the World*, had only good things to say about Carpenter. Said they were still the best of friends and he was good to the children of her second marriage.

'You obviously belong in the *Guinness Book of Records* as the guy who pays most attention to other people's kids,' I said bitterly, going back to the previous page.

'There something wrong in being nice to kids other than one's own?'

'No. But.'

'But what?'

'Oh, I don't know. Belt up and let me read this again.'

He was still and silent while I read, then threw it from me.

'Implications,' he said, flatly.

'For you or for me?'

'For the kids, first.'

'The kids won't know. But the partners in your place will. The partners in your place are the kind of people who buy the *News of the Screws* and let on it's for the sport.'

'So?'

'So it'll do you career damage.'

'On the contrary, it will raise my reputation several notches. I'll move from being a soccer star whose wife left him and who turned into a dull accountant into being a hell of a dog – screwing a TV star on the sly. I mean look at her—' he said, gesturing at the photographs. 'Mad for it, even after a night's sleepless continuous seamless screw.'

'That's not the phrase,' I said, trying to remember. 'It's zipless fuck,' I told him.

'None of my partners would have rated me as a zipless fuck up to now,' he said. 'I can tell you without fear of contradiction.'

Noises from upstairs. The two of us — me in the robe made infamous by the newspaper — climbed the stairs and got the two boys up. Carrying Gavin downstairs, David, one-handed, swept the newspaper on the table into a fold. As the boys ate cereal and delivered their views on whatever struck them, Stephen seemed to have forgotten the ghoulish goulash of his nightmare.

I wondered how much damage the story might do me and what I could do about it. I could sue, on the basis that David Carpenter and I had not been in a 'love nest', but non-sexually minding two sick children. It might be difficult to prove reputation damage, though. Association with a sporting legend might be considered advantageous to me.

The other half of the story took the boys into the garden. It would never have occurred to me to observe of a man that he was graceful, but, watching him, I understood the caption under one of the old pictures of him in the middle of a match: 'Dancing David Carpenter at his peak.'

'Why did Dancing David Carpenter's wife leave him, anyway?' I asked when he came back into the kitchen and went to wash garden soil off his hands.

'He wasn't much of a stud,' he said, pulling kitchen paper off a roll.

'Meaning?' I asked relentlessly.

'Hallie's previous experience was marathon, all-night lovers. Me, I'm good for the hundred-yard sprint. Once. She might have lived with that, but when she found I've a sperm count so low as not to be worth counting, forget it. She always wanted kids.'

His ex-wife, reading this report, would have to wonder how this Irish girl in the tatty robe had turned her ex into a sex machine.

'See what I mean about it improving my reputation?' he said ruefully.

'Can you imagine,' I asked, 'if we decided to set the record straight?'

'Press conference,' he improvised. 'GP confirms I brought the kids to him.'

'Then tell how I came home and when one of the kids had a nightmare that could only have come from some form of abuse, went to bed and left my accountant to get the kid to sleep. Wonderful, that alternative, from my point of view. Wouldn't even comfort the child herself, the rotten bike.'

'Bike?'

'You don't make the front page of the *News of the Screws* half-dressed unless you're a bike.'

The Allens would be disturbed, I thought. They had always seen David Carpenter as closer to the children than to me and certainly not as my lover. A few other people might take it amiss. The hell with them. However, part of me was glad that my mother would not see the pictures, each telling a story which was exciting, albeit without foundation.

'Tits,' I said in disgust.

'Not so,' David said, laughing. 'That's the real injustice of it. There you are, on the front page, small but perfectly formed, untouched. Untouched by me, anyway.'

'Double tits,' I commented.

'There is one serious problem, however,' David said gravely.

'It being?'

'Adoption.'

My skin was iced at the word.

'I thought when they asked adoptive parents about sex or stuff like that it was to find out if they were child molesters.'

'They're not supposed to ask adoptive parents about sex at all,' he said. 'But we're not talking about adoptive parents. We're talking about adoptive parent. One. Female. Young. Unmarried. If there's a doubt about the suitability of that one female parent, it'll be added to by this. No respect for kids; bonking divorced men in the next room.'

'Man. Singular.'

As I looked at the pictures, the random thought came that I should probably burn all terrycloth dressing gowns. They apparently fulfilled a bad-penny function in my life.

'You might also take into consideration, although I know you won't want to, your anonymous friend who sends you letters of glee when your family gets wiped out.'

'What could she do?'

'Why do you think it's a she?'

'What does it matter?'

'I think you're right, by the way, but that's a side issue. All I'm saying is that this bitch may be provoked into writing to the Health Authority.'

'Writing what?'

'Nasty stuff.'

'There is no nasty stuff. I don't have offshore accounts stuffed with money I didn't pay tax on. I don't have perverted relationships with budgies. What the hell could she say?'

'Don't ask me. I have no imagination.'

But I have, I thought, and I know what she would write. If she knew about Robert Allen, for example, she would write plenty about how I would put at risk a family with children nearly as small as the ones I wanted to adopt.

'What am I going to do?'

I imagined the social worker, all her worst suspicions confirmed, arriving on the doorstep to take Gavin and Stephen away. Into care. Into *care*. Confused, I found myself wondering how I would tell Gabrielle. Then realised this would be the ultimate razing of a family. My family. A wasteland, it would be. A wasteland without Stephen, his broad thoughtful face lighting up with mischief. A wasteland without Gavin, at that wonderful age when cuddles are sought and relished without pretence.

Suddenly, my machinations to achieve the newspaper interview of a few weeks earlier looked pathetic, in that this six-page exposé certainly outweighed any positive aura cast around me by the previous piece. Not only that, I thought, but cynics would now theorise that the interview piece was a PR exercise, a planted story designed as damage-limitation in the event that some probing journalist revealed all about the love nest.

'Did you ever see anything less like a frigging love nest?' I said, gesturing at the corkboard with its crayon drawing with Stephen's printed message: DIR DAVD I LUV U.

'None of this may happen,' David Carpenter said.

'Thanks,' I said bitterly and wept, putting my head down on the hard table.

After a while, his hands were on my shoulders, massaging away the pain of crying. I sat up and tried to pull myself together.

'I'm sorry. I just thought I had the handle on the adoption thing. I really did.'

'Why don't we get married?' he asked.

'Oh, for fuck's sake, David.'

'I figured I'd get an answer along those lines. But why not?'

'Be serious.'

'I am being very serious.'

'What would we get married for?'

'The kids, first of all,' he said. 'Then for — what was it? "Sex, love, intellectual growth and companionship."'

It sounded like a reference to something, but I wasn't going to be distracted.

'What the hell would getting married achieve for the kids?'

'Make a family out of a love nest.'

'You can't change things just—' I snapped my fingers. Or tried to.

'Dominique, don't forget, this isn't a love nest.'

'No, but they think it is.'

'They being the *News of the World*.'

'And the social worker. She wouldn't think it was OK for us to be married. Anyway, nobody gets married for someone else's kids. Most people can't be arsed getting married at all any more, but if they do – they certainly don't get married unless they really fancy each other. Nobody gets married without being in love.'

'People get married for all sorts of reasons,' he said calmly. 'Not all of them known to the couple at the time.'

I was still trying to figure out if anyone other than me and Robert Allen could possibly know about the Hotel Astir Palace. That was the one thing that could add to this mess. I tried to rate the danger posed by someone who might know about my one-night stand with Robert Allen writing an anonymous letter to the Adoption Board. David Carpenter was watching me. I flailed at him to indicate that I was not giving deep consideration to his proposal. Although it struck me that I had no right to be so churlish, given that he had so little to gain out of what he was suggesting. After all, he could do what he wanted with his life, and needed like a hole in the head to tie himself up with a ready-made family. Especially having already had a bad outing. Not only should I not be churlish, I should probably be grateful. Even a registry-office wedding could establish us, in the eyes of the state, as respectable and suitable for adoptive parenthood. Consequently, it might remove the awful spectre of losing the children. No doubt all of these considerations were playing across my countenance, which he was regarding with some amusement.

'You have a horse-buyer's look to you,' he laughed. 'Want to examine my teeth?'

He passed me on his way to put his cup in the dishwasher, and on impulse I grabbed his hand and pulled him back so he was sitting down beside me. He hugged me for a long time, warm against the somewhat threadbare robe. There was the fleeting fantasy that a solution had been found, peace had descended.

'You don't wheeze under stress the way you used to,' he observed after a while.

'David, you know what the funny thing is?'

'Nope.'

'The funny thing is that we know each other far too well to get married to each other.'

'Dominique, you know what the — the sad thing is?'

'No. What?'

'The sad thing is — oh, never mind.'

'C'mon,' was the next thing he said, over my head.

I pulled away from him to see Stephen hesitating in the doorway. The boy took a mad run and landed between us.

'Got us into trouble, this week, Stephen did,' David said, apparently in grave reflective mode. Stephen immediately became more alert.

'Remember the night he had the bad nightmare?' David asked me. 'He made me stay with him, and the next day, a newspaper took pictures of me leaving the house.'

One-handed, he unfolded the paper. Stephen could not yet read, but followed the sequence of the pictures avidly.

'You'll get you moanie,' he warned me. 'Going out with no shoes on.'

He wanted to know the precise degree and location of the problem. Would Auntie Daisy get into trouble over not wearing shoes, was that it? No, David told him. The real problem was readers thinking Auntie Daisy and Uncle David were letting on to be mammies and daddies when they actually were not. Stephen considered this.

He then delivered himself of the opinion that Auntie Daisy and Uncle David should be mammies and daddies. It would, he opined, make Gavin's life much easier. Gavin couldn't say 'Uncle David' but he could play a blinder if David was just Daddy.

'So you think Daisy and I should get married?' David prompted.

'You are,' I whispered venomously, 'the most self-serving, twisted human being I have ever met. Trying to get an innocent child to advance your plans.'

'Don't I do it well, though?'

'If you got married, we'd be a fambly,' Stephen observed. 'And Uncle David wouldn't ever have to go to his own old place. 'Cept when you had a fight.'

David muttered that he wasn't sure a luxury apartment in the Financial Services Centre would be justified as an occasional refuge when he and I had a row. Not that we would have rows, he assured Stephen, who agreed that when we were married there would be no need to have rows.

'We haven't had many rows up to now,' I yelled from the garden on my way to rescue Gavin, who was suffering loudly from his abandonment by Stephen.

'No, but imagine how few we'd have if we were married,' David called after me.

'Oh, for feck's sake,' I said. 'I mean, for Jesus' own sweet sake.'

Which last utterance was breathed in by Stephen and repeated verbatim one week later in the middle of his playgroup when another kid knocked over his almost completed jigsaw. The playgroup leader was so manifestly shocked by his reaction that he repeated it for her benefit. When I picked him up, he was under suspension and the nursery school teacher implied that his suspension extended to me. A week away might allow him to forget bad words like that, she suggested.

It also allowed him to get involved in David's half-joking, whole-in-earnest campaign for us to get married. David drew my attention to every comment made to him about the newspaper story, constantly pushing the logic of a quiet, even silent, wedding. It's not the *logic* I have a problem with, I thought. It's the feelings. Or the lack of them. You might quench a great grief by drowning it in the details of child-rearing, but to marry in numbness, in anaesthetised acquiescence to the perceived needs of an administration, seemed close to welcoming the drowsing duplicity of carbon monoxide sleep. You might wake up dead. Legal, but dead.

'Not only dead, but very pink,' David said when I raised this with him. 'Exhaust gas poisoning turns suicides a deep puce. There, you see. You wouldn't have expected me to know that.'

'You're a secret student of suicidology?'

He nodded, quite seriously. Every time he told me something of interest about himself, it was always when I was en route to something more important, so it tended not to register with me permanently or get elaborated on.

I decided the only way to squelch it was to go along with the hypothesis and use it as a way of pointing out that this man never claimed to love me, could not deceive himself that I loved him, but must therefore face up to the inevitability that one of us would at some point in our lives experience an ardour beyond mutually appreciative affection.

'Say if we were to go through a ceremony,' I said to David Carpenter one evening. 'And a few years pass with us as man and wife, and then some day I fall really in love with someone? You know the kind of passion that takes you over — "forsaking all others"? Someday, I have the feeling that kind of experience might happen to me.'

'Say if it does.'

'What would happen then, if we were married?'

'The kids would have a few years of tranquillity and stability under their belts. Every year would give them a bit more resilience. Bit more natural resistance to the trials of life.'

'Can you really do that? Build up that resistance?'

'Very definitely. If you'd had a normal child-hood—'

'I beg your pardon?'

'If you'd had a normal adolescence,' he corrected without flurry, 'you wouldn't find life so . . .'

He seemed more interested in locating the precise word he was looking for than finishing his point.

'What was abnormal about my adolescence?'

'No real contact with your peers, no pals, no crushes, no mitching, no games hence no teams, no leisure, no skiving off, no rebellion, no posters on your bedroom wall, no mad changes of make up and hairdo, no social life, no boyfriends. Plus your own faithful hate-mailer. Other than that, I suppose it was fairly normal.'

Not only could I now imagine my mother's voice, saying contemptuously that I hardly needed the major-ity of the things he had mentioned, but I could imag-ine my sister's voice fairmindedly contradicting her. Voices in my head. Plural. Having arguments. Next step, I thought, will be believing I'm Napoleon.

'Do mad people still believe they're Napoleon or do they think they're the head of NATO?' I asked aloud. 'And don't tell me *non sequiturs* come from a troubled adolescence.'

'I never said you had a troubled adolescence. I said you had an abnormal one.'

'So I'm damaged goods.'

I should know by now, I thought, that he never rises to one of those pleas for denial and reassurance. True to form, he ignored it.

'You can see without effort the end result of that abnormal adolescence,' he said. 'Think about it. What friends do you have? Mostly, you have Gabrielle's friends.'

'Saves me going to bloody barbeques and gin and tonickaries. Anyway, who are you to talk? You didn't have exactly a normal adolescence, getting talent-spotted and uprooted and put in a boot camp with a bunch of other brainwashed sports freaks bingeing on steroids and Creatine, all trying to grow up to be David Beckham.'

He seemed quite impressed that I knew the name of another soccer player, and agreed, very equably, that he, too, had experienced a peculiar passage to adulthood. He would hope, he added, that Stephen wouldn't be quite good enough at sport to put him in danger of anything remotely near that experience, because it too often turned out great players who were also profoundly damaged or inadequate human beings. His smile dared me to postulate that he was one of the latter. All he wanted to say, he summed up, was that five, ten, or — with luck — fifteen years in a stable family situation would do wonders for the boys, including giving them the bounce-back capacity to survive a later divorce if and when the hold-the-front-page passion of my life appeared.

'So the boys would survive it,' I said, logic driving me beyond sense. 'But what about you?'

He looked at me coolly. 'Don't flatter yourself, Dominique,' he said. 'I would survive.'

'That's not what I meant.'

'It doesn't matter what you meant. Leave it. Just — leave it.'

It was as sudden as a power cut, the slicing finality of the instruction. Nobody had hammered the heel of a hand on a table to indicate that the negotiation was over, but that was the reality of it.

'Make my mind up time?' I said, trying to be light, trying to laugh or make him laugh. Falling at all fences.

'Precisely,' he said with neither inflection nor expression.

'Right now?'

'Whenever.'

I went off and read up about the psychological effects of spending key formative years away from a peer group and the possibility of natural friendships.

'Bottom line,' I told Gavin, trying for the nth time to sneak mushrooms into him, 'bottom line is that I'm probably lucky to only have remembered voices in my head. I could just as easily have real voices. I could, in fact, just as easily be a serial killer.'

The mushroom purée, cleverly coloured pink, to fool him, by the addition of some tomato purée, betrayed its true identity to Gavin's taste buds and he sprayed the whole lot back into my face instantly. I stepped back from his high chair, on the basis that it's difficult to be a child murderer at five paces unless you have a gun or a bow and arrow or a long two by four. He examined me with quiet rapture. In the little mirror over the cork board I could see why. Dark grey and red spots were evenly distributed in my hair, on my face and all over my T-shirt.

'Gavin, you win,' I said. 'I surrender. Mushrooms? Never heard of them. Probably filthy things that grow in the dark somewhere. Funguses or worse. No decent toddler should be expected to stomach them, you're right. How about I never, ever try to get a mushroom into you again? Not a straight mushroom, not a bent mushroom, not an outed mushroom, not a disguised mushroom still in the closet.'

I opened a jar of commercial baby banana pudding, starting to spoon it into him while I talked. 'Why will I be so amenable to your wishes in future, Gavin? I'll tell you why. Because I have to foster your self-esteem. Your sense of security. Your concept of yourself as being surrounded on every side by unconditional love. I have to do all this for fear Stalin the Social Worker comes around to take a sample and finds your self-esteem has a leak in it. I have to do it because Snitch of the Week, my very own anonymous shit-stirrer, might inform the powers that be. But let me tell you something, kid. The minute I get signed off on this adoption thing, the powers that be can stick their opinions where the monkey stuck his whatsit, and the shit-stirrer can stick her missives where the sun don't shine and the powers that be can stick their powers on the highest rafter of the roof of their arse. And when that blessed day comes, what, I ask myself, am I going to feed you? Bloody right. An unremitting diet of wall-to-wall mushrooms.'

Gavin, liking the banana purée, and possibly also tapping into some genetic link with his father, Oliver the Great Accompanist, began to hum loudly on in and out-breaths while continuing to eat with delight. The two of us got quite a good rhythm going.

'You'll have mushroom porridge for breakfast,' I crooned as I spooned. 'Mushroom kebabs for lunch. Mushroom milkshakes for mid-afternoon, with just a tablespoon of mustard added for the taste. Mushrooms with a dusting of horse manure for dinner.'

With the edge of the spoon, I harvested the dribbles of banana from around his mouth and inserted them between his lips. Too late, I remembered that David Carpenter now had a key. He was standing behind me, with Stephen, the two of them listening to the mushroom monologue with rapt attention. I ground to a halt at both word and pudding delivery. Gavin yelled for resumption of supply, and, automaton-fashion, I obliged. Silently.

'Dusting of horse manure,' Stephen repeated prayerfully.

'In practical terms, it would have to be a dusting of dried horse manure,' David offered helpfully.

'They dry everything these days,' I said. 'Look at sun-dried tomatoes.'

'Sun-dried tomatoes are everywhere,' he agreed. 'You can't get away from them. They get into everything.'

'Them and basil.'

'Another ubiquitous hoor,' he solemnly concurred.

I could see Stephen trying to get his mouth around that one and failing. Oh, Gabrielle, remember me doing that at the meeting you were at? I upchuck Chip. When I lifted Gavin down out of the chair, Stephen hustled him out of the room, possibly in the belief that he was thereby protecting his brother from being force-fed mushroom afters. I swiped with a tea towel at the pinkish stains on my once-white top.

'That T-shirt looks better with dots on it. It was dullish, before,' David said.

'Shag off sideways.'

'Sideways?'

'Frontways, backways. I don't care.'

I pulled the T-shirt over my head and sat there. I had a sports bra on underneath. More than half the spots had come through the cotton on to my skin. I looked as if I had upper-body measles and spotty gangrene.

'You'll stop at nothing to seduce a man, Dominique,' David said, admiring my underwear and handing me a dampened kitchen towel to wipe the speckles off.

'If you're setting out to seduce someone,' I said wearily, 'you wear a Wonderbra, not a sports bra.'

'I'll keep that constantly in mind,' he promised.

I thought about mushrooms and why it seemed so

important to get them into Gavin. They had some vital trace element in them, but I could not remember what it was.

'Although, for what it's worth, my personal view is that Wonderbras make boobs look like buttocks,' David said, taking back the towel with my imitation measles transferred onto it.

'You're right,' I said. 'I've always felt they have the same effect as you did. Do you remember the time when you held my face like so—' I pressed my hands hard against my cheeks so my features were pushed into the bulging middle.

He pulled over a stool and sat down opposite me, close enough so his knees were on the outside of mine. When I let my hands fall into my lap, he examined them carefully, perhaps in case they'd caught any of the mushroom spray, and then held them firmly.

'Dominique, if I ever had any doubts about the rightness of marriage, today has banished them,' he said, his voice so low I had to strain to hear him. I tried to remember the key events of the day, but nothing stood out that would justify marriage.

'I could not leave an innocent child,' he said, 'in danger of being fed mushroom milkshakes with mustard and horse manure.'

'Only one. Not both. Mustard or horse manure. They don't go together.'

'But quite apart from that, how could I let slip a woman of such sensibility? My God, if I had a recording of the Mushroom Monologue, it would have the same emotional impact as Perlman playing the *Schindler's List* theme. The theme song from *Titanic* would be wiped out by it.'

I sat there, half-hoping the humour would edge into passion. But he simply held my hands for a while.

'I think I should give up fighting you on everything,' I said.

'So we get married?'

'I'm too tired to fight you but I'm too tired to get married either.'

'That's because you are not physically fit,' he said. 'Certainly not physically fit enough to be in charge of two small kids.'

I must remember, he added, that I was now a lot older than my heyday as an au pair and I really needed an in-house personal coach to get me motivated and properly toned. Once he was in-house, he said, he would have me doing cross-training before dawn. I shrugged. See, he said, even shrugging was a chore to me, I was so unfit. No matter what he said, I gave back no answer.

Because I gave up arguing with him, a lot of things happened almost immediately without me making any very positive decisions. Most notably, we did get married the following month, with Stephen (dressed up with a little bow tie and shirt) in charge of the decorative pillow with the rings on it.

What I had not anticipated, not having been to a registry-office wedding, was that although the atmosphere was lovely, the carpet was threadbare. So when Stephen was called to present the rings, his new shoes caught in one of the ragged places and he went flying, losing cushion and rings in the process.

He got to his feet, surveyed his now dusty front and askew bow tie, and spoke.

'For feck's sake,' he said to the registrar. 'I mean, for Jesus' own sweet sake.'

As David put it later, being told 'you may kiss the bride' by the registrar is in the ha'penny place to that outburst, when it comes to quotations, memorable, from our wedding day.

CHAPTER FOURTEEN

Earwigs and Ladybirds

———◆◆◆———

It seemed as if every possible obstacle to my adopting the children was flattened in the aftermath of our marriage. The only disadvantage was that I needed some humour in order to survive the parties we were invited to in the months after the wedding. Every heavy-handed wit who announced us as The Secret Lovers, Ho, Ho, Ho seemed convinced they were the first to do so. Every woman who told me how really warm and ordinary David was, in spite of being a sporting star, seemed to be sure I was way too dumb to notice his warmth and the ordinariness.

David, on the other hand, had to sit through the often inaccurate recollections people claimed to retain of particularly moving episodes in my soap opera.

'She was so beautiful,' a dinner guest said to him, fervently, one night. 'So innocent.'

'Aged badly, didn't she?' David asked, knowing that even at ten paces and while ostensibly embedded in a quite different conversation, I was earwigging on his.

It was a game we frequently played. So when, at another party, a woman told me she had spent her teens dreaming about dressing David Carpenter up and dancing with him, I could see, out of the corner of my eye, him shifting about, very slightly, but enough to send the message to me that he was dancing.

'Why did you start your dreams with him naked?' I asked, in an earnest way.

'I didn't,' she said, giving me an air-smack of reproof. 'Just, whenever I saw him, he was playing football.'

'Oh, only partially naked.'

'If I was a sculptor, I would have wanted to sculpt his legs,' the woman said, and David put a protective hand against his thigh as if to fend her off.

'D'you get jealous?' she asked. 'Knowing that he was the love object of a generation?'

I shook my head and she nodded, the nod saying sure didn't you beat off all opposition and take him home across the pommel of your saddle?

Other female acquaintances were turned on by

hearing that David and I had met in Paris. *Paris*, they said. Must have been so romantic, they said. I tended to do enigmatic smiles when this came up. One night at a dinner party in Robert and Helen Allen's house, one of the guests wanted to know precisely where in the city we had encountered.

'Near the fountains at Place de la Concorde,' David said.

'And did a spark fly between you that first time?'

'Bloody difficult for a spark to fly between us given the condition she was in,' David said, choosing cheese.

There was a moment's silence.

'Everybody around this table now believes I was pregnant in Paris, David,' I said, receiving the cheeseboard from him.

'Pregnant would have been no bother,' he assured the questioner. 'She was purple in the face, blue in the fingers and sounded like a hoover having sex. You haven't seen Daisy in one of her asthma attacks? Anything less romantic would be hard to imagine. Pregnancy would have been major-league erotic by comparison.'

He told the story, making it funnier than it was by emphasising my rude greeting to him. At the end, he rooted in his pocket, producing a Ventolin inhaler.

'I have these stashed all over the place for prevention purposes,' he said, tossing it into the air and catching it backhanded. 'That's how romantic that Parisian encounter was; I avoid any possibility of a repetition.'

'Why doesn't Daisy carry her own?' Robert asked.

'She does. But she has a lot to worry about,' David said solemnly.

'Like what?'

'If I come out the front door in the morning and there's a snail in my path, I step over him.'

'Or her,' I offered.

'Or her,' he conceded. 'Or I might pick him or her up and feck him or her into the grass so whoever comes down the garden after me doesn't squelch him or her. But if Daisy encounters the same snail, it's very different. She wonders about her own motivation in wanting to shift the little bugger. Maybe it's not in the snail's interest to be kept alive. Maybe evolution will be best served if the more stupid snails, the dopey ones that line up on people's front paths, get mushed out of the population. Or, if she fecks him into the garden (or her), will the poor bastard spend the rest of the day as traumatised as a human swept thirty feet in the air by a tornado. Or maybe she's afraid that if Stephen steps on the snail, Stephen will just scrape him off the sole of his shoe and be undisturbed, which would indicate a serious sensitivity deficit in Stephen and if she wasn't there when the incident transpired, how would she know she had to help Stephen with the moral failing thus revealed?'

The other guests were looking at me as if I was half mad. Helen Allen winked at me. She said that if Robert encountered a snail on his way out their front door, he would telephone her from his cellphone in the car to suggest she might come out of the house to take care of it. Robert admitted he was a little challenged by crawling things.

'Snails and slugs I can just about live with because they don't have much of a turn of speed, but anything with a lot of legs bothers me. And I don't think much of the way ladybirds open up their backs, either.'

I could hear David asking the passionate gardener beside him what was the name of those insects ladybirds hunted. Aphids, she said. She had been looking into the possibility of setting up a mail order business in ladybirds. In the United States, it was possible to phone a company, order two thousand 'ladybugs', as they called them over there, give them a credit card number and within days, a safe container would arrive in the mail, alive with little red coats ready to go eat aphids. He gave her some advice on structuring such a venture. As she thanked him, I could feel her looking across the table at me. Through the other conversations, I could hear her returning to him and me and romance in Paris. How soon had we known we were in love? Go for it, David, I thought. Let me hear the spin. Realising, at the same moment, that Robert Allen was just as tuned into the other conversation as was I.

'Daisy, rescue me here,' David said, raising his voice slightly. 'I'm telling Audrey that we got married only for the sake of the children. She doesn't believe me.'

'Absolutely true,' I told her, deadpan. 'We've nothing in common except the kids.'

'When Daisy heard I played football, she thought it was rugby I played,' he said, and some of the men looked at me as if I had recently arrived from another planet.

'Plus he never saw any of my touching performances in the TV soap,' I said.

'I did look at them later on videotape, though, three weeks after we met. Does that count?'

I looked across the table at him in genuine astonishment.

'See?' he said to Audrey. 'Didn't even know that about me. Told her very early on I was doing due diligence on her, but it never struck her to credit me with the wit to find out who she was before she was an au pair.'

Audrey, who was perhaps one glass of wine too far for her own social good, became insistent. When had he told me he loved me? Ah, go on, David, tell us that anyway.

'Never,' he said, looking so grave everybody assumed he was joking. 'Now, go on, ask me when she told me she loved me. Ask me was it at the top of the Arc de Triomphe? Or after a Monday poetry reading at Rue de la Bucherie? Or drinking espresso on a *bateau mouche*?'

It was like the hand-hiding game he played with Stephen and Gavin, moving so fast that the secret gift he had brought home for them was never in the hand they captured and forced open. He was teasing the dinner guests with apparently random place names, yet sending small shared jokes, little resonant references, to me. They waited for the punch line.

'None of the above,' he said, and a few of them made a noise between a moan and a boo. 'If I remember rightly, in the Arc de Triomphe, halfway up the two hundred plus stairs, she told me I had a goddam nerve—'

There were ribald suggestions as to what he might

have been attempting halfway up the stairs of the monument.

'On a *bateau mouche* she told me I was an over-confident pain in the arse, and in several different locations she told me to eff off. Not to mention refusing to make me coffee. Ever. In the face of abject pleadings. If she snuck in an assertion about loving me in the middle of all that abuse, I must have missed it.'

'Was he that abusive to you?' Audrey asked me.

'No, he was never abusive. That wasn't the problem. He was just an over-confident pain in the arse, always looking for free coffee.'

Robert Allen wanted to know when was this, exactly, and I ignored him, knowing he needed to pin his Greek encounter to it somewhere.

'I just realised at a certain point,' David said, 'that I would have to marry this woman if Stephen and Gavin were to be protected from her. Makes rules for everything, you know,' he said, in a loud whisper, to Audrey, who flowered in his attention.

'Even for worm-washing.'

He swept the table with a glance.

'You wouldn't believe that, would you? Worms, according to Dominique, should be washed only twice a day. Not once, not three times. Twice.'

'Who the hell washes worms?'

'Gavin. Our son.'

'Why?'

A few of them glanced at me, expecting me to be responsible. I shrugged and opened my hands at them, indicating total ignorance.

'How often?'

'How often does Gavin wash worms?' David thought about this for a moment, then said I was the record-keeper, so I probably knew best.

'On a clear day,' I said, 'on a good, sunny day, he'd do it from morning until night.'

'This kid needs help.'

'Jesus, I would have thought it was the worm population that needs help.'

'That's why I set down the rule: two washings maximum.'

'How does he know it's the same worm twice?'

'Daisy counts and tags them.'

'I don't tag them.'

'But you count them?'

'I keep an eye on them. Wouldn't you?'

'On worms? No.'

'But you wouldn't like it if every time you got into your own place, someone hauled you out and washed you. Again and again. All day long. Someone has to protect them from that.'

Other young parents chimed in with accounts of the embarrassing habits of their offspring, and the interrogation of the two of us drifted. Not without its lesson, though. Watching David it came to me, like a revelation, how easy it is to deflect people from the truth simply by telling it. When people were told we never declared love for each other, they believed they were being invited into a deliciously duplicitous game. That our mutual declarations of love must be so momentous as to be above public discussion.

The guests in the Allen home went away happy, if unenlightened, at the end of the dinner party.

'If you and David want to get away for a weekend at some stage, Helen and I would be chuffed if you'd dump the kids with us,' Robert said to me as he left us to the car.

Just as you once used your daughter's name as a talisman against sin, now, I thought, you use the children in my home. It is almost as if old married parents – even if adoptive – are moved by parenthood beyond sexual recklessness.

David Carpenter (who I still tended to think of with surname attached) was so natural a father that people who didn't know about the adoption frequently commented on features one or other of the young lads seemed to share with him. As a result, I often wondered whether the resemblances people claim to see between parents and offspring are genuinely observed genetic inheritances or wishful thinking. Not that all the links were in traits like eye colour. When Stephen was observed to have footballing talent, onlookers would reflect aloud on the marvels that could be handed down from father to son. To correct them caused pointless confusion and curiosity. As time went on, we nodded and let it pass, the children doing it naturally because they saw no contradiction at all. To them, he was the ultimate insider in their lives and they had as much difficulty addressing the concept of him being their stepfather as if they had been told they were not natural brothers.

But I would watch him, this laid-back man I had married without loving. I would watch him letting them in on athletic secrets. I would watch him withdraw from them, silently, unobtrusively, the moment they became fully engaged in something. I would watch him listen to them, prodding them with prompts to discover, sometimes, what they didn't want to take into consideration in the story they were telling, or the complaint they were making. I would watch other people identifying him and whispering about his past fame. Now and again, he would catch me at it and whisper 'Stop thinking', in my ear.

The Skywriter, meanwhile, barely got off the runway. It traded, stayed in profit and paid me a token salary. I learned enough about royalties and percentages of royalties to take over managing Oliver's estate. It took a few hours a week.

'You don't have to keep driving your mother's car,' David observed on one occasion, as he was clipping back on a hubcap scraped off against the gatepost. 'We can afford to get you a much better car.'

'Like what?'

'I don't know. A convertible. A sports car. Something appropriate to your age and earning power.'

I laughed. 'Only problem is that half the time I'm transporting two small kids, and I'm not sure a sports car would suit that. I may have to postpone the sexy car entitlement until a bit later. Anyway, I'm earning damn all at the moment.'

I kept thinking I should be worried about this gap in my career path, without being able to muster a real worry.

'I should be making progress,' I said to David the following day.

''Course you should,' he said, in the tone used for a doting nonagenarian.

'I should have a five-year-plan.'

'Definitely.'

'If you were a proper feminist, you'd be pushing me to achieve my full potential,' I said, beginning to get seriously shirty.

'I'm not any kind of a feminist, proper or otherwise. Anyway, your dead mother does all the pushing you need,' was the response.

Since I rarely if ever talked to him about the recurring voices in my head, this puzzled me, but I would not ask him how he knew.

'Why do you want pushing when you haven't decided where you want to go?'

'I'm just marking time. I'm not achieving any-thing.'

He looked over the top of his book at me and pointed silently to the boys.

'Any half-competent child-minder could do what I do.'

'Still worth doing.'

'Easy for you to say that.'

He bookmarked his page carefully and put the book down. 'Would you like to do a swap? Me take time away from the partnership to take care of the boys, you to get into fulltime career-building?'

I had the sensation of walking into a smooth wall. He would do it if I acquiesced. Furthermore, it would work. I shook my head. Waited for him to do an

Aesop on me: the moral lesson is. No moral lesson came, and when I looked at him, he was watching me with both amusement and pity.

'What's so frigging funny?'

'You have such a need to define yourself. You're like someone swimming in the Atlantic ocean and demanding they put walls around this swimming pool because it's too bloody shapeless.'

'You have a definition you take everywhere. Dancing David Carpenter.'

'My arse,' he said, making to pick up the book again.

'But it's true. You achieved something early on.'

'So did you.'

'A sodding soap opera, for Chrissake.'

'A fucking football field, for the love of Jaysus. In a thousand years' time, if some archaeologists dig up the trace evidence of the two of us, Dominique, you think they're going to say, "this guy played in the World Cup team and so is more important, in the run of history, than this woman who was on TV"? You think there's a God somewhere with a score sheet, marking you down because you're not appearing on the business pages as a mover and shaker?'

'I would be happier if I were using my capacities – making full use of—'

'You're not a bloody red onion,' he said, his voice rising. 'You're not a bloody onion waiting for a hamburger to enliven. You're a human with a huge bundle of capacities.'

'I don't get the significance of the onion?'

'If you're an onion,' he said, lowering his voice to a humouring-the-irrational tone which made what he was saying sound even crazier, 'if you're an onion, there's a limited number of things you can do with your life, a limited number of ways you can express your inborn talent, a limited number of achievements you can notch up before you go to the great landfill in the sky. You can lie on a hamburger or go in a stew. You can't decorate the top of a – a – lemon meringue pie or join in a tiramasu or add to the *je ne sais quoi* of a lemon soufflé, you're just an onion. You get on with being an onion. But if you're a human being, you've got limitless possibilities right up to the moment you snuff it.'

The boys and me were all paying him full attention by now. He drew a deep breath and closed his eyes for a moment.

'I have no idea what point I was going to make,' he concluded, then got started again out of annoyance. 'The difference between you and an onion is that an onion is just an onion, gets one go and has a short shelf life. You're anything you want to be, whenever you want to be it, you get dozens of goes and with luck you'll live to be ninety. If you think you're going to be made more happy by being able to point to one particular hamburger and say, "I lay on that one", you're clueless about happiness and you'll hang around the wrong airports for the rest of your life waiting for it to land. Just *be*, would you? Just stop trying to shape every shagging thing out of a need to justify yourself. Nobody's looking. Nobody cares. Us three don't need any proofs.' (The two boys, not following any of this, nonetheless evinced a vivid need to support whatever meaning they could draw from it. Gavin nodded solemnly and Stephen shook his head. Both meant 'You're right, Dad.') 'We buy you, Daisy. We accept the offer. We don't need any end result. We'll give you the trophy right now. I'll give you a personal citation inscribed on a shagging sheepskin that without your neverending angst I would probably be even duller than what I was when I met you, instead of needing to go for a walk to cool down from – from—'

'Telling her about onions,' Stephen supplied.

David laughed and lifted Stephen high in the air, lowering him so their foreheads bumped gently off each other, then swung him down under one arm.

Gavin, hands up, wanted to be part of this, and a general rough-housing began. When the two of them drifted off, exhausted, to their original game, David, forgetting his promise to go for a walk, sat down again.

'I'm taking them to Mosney tomorrow,' I whispered, not wanting them to know in advance and get excited. Stephen just asked a lot of questions when excited, but Gavin was intolerable.

'Good,' David said. 'That's exactly what you should be doing at this stage of your life.'

'Going to a holiday camp?'

'Having the adolescence you never had.'

Before I could work up to a fight on this one, Stephen asked from the other end of the room what a holiday camp was, so I had to concentrate on being vague until the following morning, when we set out. Gavin, now red-headed after a long period of committed baldness, brightened the trip with random observations.

'Iss rainink,' was the first. True.

'This car is wrecked,' was the second.

Messy might be a kinder way of putting it, but hell hath no fury like an honest toddler.

'Stevie is sick,' was the third observation.

It took me but a moment to work out that his

pointing finger was directed towards his older brother. Car sickness had undone Stephen's insides. Now a solid small boy, he tended to long silences and the odd pronouncement about the dental endowment of dinosaurs. We parked on the hard shoulder to let things settle.

Stephen's insides might be settling beautifully as a result of the pause, but Gavin quickly got panicky that if we didn't go immediately, Mosney would be over. After a while, we moved off again, at four-and-a-half miles an hour. Halfway there, they both decided I was probably going the wrong way. Even when we arrived, they managed to imply that if they hadn't kept an eye on me, we'd be in Cork.

Then, they saw it all. Stunned, they gazed at swings, roundabouts and mountain slides, until Gavin waved an arm, and said, with an air of summing the whole thing up, 'Things!'

Thirty seconds later, they were buffeting around in little cars painted to look like ladybirds, and I was standing at the railing, joining in the mothers' chorus:

'Sit down! Hold on! DON'T DO THAT!'

They had six goes on the ladybirds before the man in charge said fairness demanded others be allowed their chance. Stephen gave in, more because he was queasy again than because of his sense of fair play. Gavin went into a paroxysm of persuasion, ending with the statement that he had a new T-shirt, too. Impressed, the man let him on again.

Stephen and I stood together until this seventh ride was complete, then Stephen boarded the Puffin' Billy express for a tour around the camp. I dragged Gavin off to the loo, believing prevention better than disaster any time. We discussed his T-shirt, the weather, my boots and anything else that seemed relevant, but no good came of it.

Eventually, we gave it up and went back to meet Stephen off the Puffin' Billy, only to find it had been and gone and he wasn't there. Gavin improved the shining hour by making friends with a glamorous blonde who asked him what he did last. He told her he visited the loo, confiding solemnly that he Couldn't Go.

Stephen arrived back, casting me the sort of look the Princes in the Tower must have thrown at Richard III, and wanted to know where was I when he came back the first time? I could see I was for impeachment if he wasn't quickly distracted, so I dragged them into the children's playground, where they got up on a see-saw. Gavin was a good two stone lighter than Stephen, so any action on the see-saw led to being powered by me. When I tired, Stephen climbed off his end of the contraption. Which would have been fine if I had had the wit to hold on to Gavin's end. I didn't, so he suddenly dropped six feet to whap off the ground with a report like gun-shot. I expected to see his spine standing up three inches north of his head, but he only clasped both hands to the back of his neck, walking away with a curious shocked waddle.

'Now we will have some sweets,' Stephen said determinedly.

He ate half a million Jelly Tots while losing £1.50 on the one-armed bandits. I made a note to take him to Gamblers' Anonymous before he got any older or I got any poorer. Gavin, meanwhile, discovered a curling trail of ants on the ground, going through the hyperactive workaholism ants always go through.

When I hauled Stephen away from the one-armed bandits, he in turn hauled Gavin off nature study, announcing loudly, 'You can look at creepy crawlies at home anytime,' which I'm sure convinced all the other adults that I ran a home infested with insects.

Three rides on the chairplanes left Gavin beatific and Stephen putty-coloured. He tottered off, sat down and said with great precision and a small shiver that he didn't feel well at all. Gavin, whose capacity for empathy was minimal, wandered off to explore the children's scrambling tunnel, coming back shaking with terror because he met a Dalmatian in it.

When I announced it was time to set out for home, both broke into lamentations and refused to budge without cast-iron guarantees of return visits very soon. That night, Stephen gave David an expurgated version of the trip, without mention of nausea.

'You've great patience with them,' David said, after Stephen had gone to bed.

'It's easy, when you're their aunt,' I said, half asleep.

'Easier than being their natural mother?'

'Much easier.'

'Why?'

'You give them back. They belong to someone else. Well, that's the illusion, anyway. I wouldn't be as patient if they were my own.'

CHAPTER FIFTEEN

Curtains

———◆◇◆———

Being patient the following morning was not easy. When I woke, David was up on one elbow, looking fixedly at the wall. I followed his gaze, but the wall seemed pretty much as it always did.

'Shhh,' he said. From the boys' room next door came odd noises. Odd, untypical noises. Untypical in volume, for one thing. Hissing whispers.

The two of us looked at each other in the unvoiced instinctive forensics of child-minders: if they're whispering, it's a secret. If it's a secret, it's probably a bad secret. If it's a bad secret, it should be nipped before it flowers into a suppurating, festering efflorescence. Which of us? You – you move more quietly. Don't frighten them, now . . .

David opened the door to the boys' room quietly but so suddenly that Stephen, who was standing on a chair at the window, turned and fell off it down on top of Gavin. Survival instincts to the fore, Gavin scrambled out from under him, belted him, then ran past David to embed his face in my nightshirt. It's hard to conditionally stroke a child's hair, but knowing Gavin only too well at this point, it was fair to assume that any sudden onset of toddler insecurity on his part was designed to distract from something else.

So as my hand smoothed the silky hair, my eyes did a quick check, starting with the window, where Gavin had been. Window intact. Curtains in place. Curtains – whoa ... Carrying Gavin with me by the force of my urgency, I rushed to the window. The curtain was punctured by about thirty V-shaped cuts. It looked as if it had been folded and then snipped along the folds with a scissors, but the purpose was unclear.

I peeled him off my leg and looked at him. Purple from trying to cry, he had his eyes squeezed tightly closed. The sound effects were impressive. Stephen, on the other hand, now that he had been righted and patted over by David, was white as a sheet and looking from one of us to the other in a frantic repeating sequence. Gavin snuck an eye open to check how his performance was going down with the audience.

'No more of that out of you,' David instructed, index finger wagging from a fisted hand.

Gavin's eyes snapped closed again and he opened his mouth, sucking in half a roomful of air, ready for a roar.

'You heard me,' David said, so quietly implacable that Gavin let the air out of himself and began to genuinely whimper.

'Which of ye?'

'You shouldn't be making them informers,' I said and was ignored.

'Which of ye?'

Gavin's head went lower and lower, while his lower lip fattened and fattened. David seemed to take this as a tacit confession and turned his attention to the older brother.

'What were you at?'

Stephen mutely held out a straight pin.

'Trying to fix it?'

A silent nod. David reached out and hauled my stolid little nephew into a hug.

'I wouldn't want you to fall out the window,' he said. 'Please don't stand up on things near the window.'

Then David addressed me over Stephen's head as if his younger brother wasn't in the room with us.

'I'm sure Gavin didn't know it was wrong to cut up curtains,' he said reasonably.

'And he won't do it again,' I responded. (Gavin, without letting on he had heard a word, nodded vigorously.)

'So he should get dressed and we could all have breakfast,' David concluded, provoking Gavin to an orgy of relief and over-compensation that caused him to fall down the stairs. We could hear Stephen calling that his brother was OK, no harm done. I looked at the curtains.

'And have you worked out what Gabrielle would do in this situation?'

The question, casually asked as he shrugged out of the T-shirt he slept in, rocked me, because I had been trying to work out precisely that.

'Well, she would——'

He shook his head.

'No, no, Dominique,' he said evenly. 'I don't need to know what Gabrielle would have done. *I* don't have to live up to the myth of a dead sister. That's *your* problem.'

A moment later, the shower was thundering behind the closed bathroom door. Later that morning, I took

Gavin to a playgroup, not dropping him but staying with him, mainly because he had been fired from the first one he had attended and I was trying him out in this new one. The nursery furniture was so covered in multicoloured daisies, I expected to have a psychosomatic asthma attack. But if there's one thing to be said for chipboard, it is that it doesn't give off much in the way of pollen.

'Today is Thursday, the weather is wet,' said a notice on the wall.

I did a quick calculation. Today was definitely Friday and at the last count was dry and relatively sunny. I pointed this out to the playgroup leader.

'Oh, that gets changed later on, as part of the morning's work,' she said briskly.

I subsided into the corner near the Wendy house, asking for the fifth time if she was sure I wouldn't be in the way. Not at all, she said, the children would be far too absorbed in their work to take a blind bit of notice of me. The kids all around me seemed to be playing rather than working, but who's going to argue with a playgroup leader?

I had already got on the wrong side of her by trying to help a child I thought was going to strangle himself getting out of his anorak. He had got the cord of the hood around his neck in the cleverest way, which ensured that every time he pulled off one of the sleeves, the noose tightened around his jugular, but the playgroup leader told me that what he was doing was problem-solving and 'We mustn't prevent that, now, must we?' The anorak kid seemed to me to be problem-causing rather than problem-solving, but when your kid is one down in the playgroup stakes, you don't get into an argument on semantics with his potential keeper on the day of the try-out.

Another of the children, on arrival, removed his outerwear, encouraging himself with a little commentary in song. 'Now my hat,' he warbled gently to himself. 'And now my coat,' continued his personal song, 'and gloves into my pockets.' I had an instant picture of his mother.

Gavin at first wanted to stay in his coat and then tried to take it off by brute force. I ducked to dodge the flying buttons, wary, following my earlier experience, of helping him.

'It's better to push buttons through the holes,' the playgroup leader told him cheerfully. 'Easier than pulling, you know.'

Gavin presented her with his chest and she did a demonstration. At the end of it, of course, he was out of the coat and was no further along in button-pushing than before, but the playgroup leader felt pretty good about the transaction.

'I told you I had a hook in my coat,' Gavin told another little boy, who looked crushed.

'What would we like to do first?' the playgroup leader carolled.

'Cutouts!' yelled one little girl, echoed by Gavin, who had no clue as to what cutouts were, but who bought into the excitement she showed.

'Well, then,' the playgroup leader said, approaching Gavin, 'we'll need to take off the mittens, won't we?'

Gavin was not used to this determined collectivism and made it clear that if he was the plural she was talking about, he wasn't having any. These mittens were staying.

'We're not going to wear mittens all morning, are we?' she asked.

We sure were, he indicated, getting a lip on him that suggested he might make her wear her mittens all morning, too, if she didn't stop banging on about the ones he had on. As Gavin tried to make a scissors work, somewhat hampered by having all his fingers jammed together in a woollen mitten slightly too small for him, another child piped up.

'Teacher, Teacher, my balloon burst yesterday.'

'Oh, did it make a big bang?'

There was a small silence. Then the child responded, reprovingly, 'No, it made a loud noise.'

At this point the playgroup leader's son, who was somewhat younger than the general run of children attending, departed the room, playing peek-a-boo with me using the door. Having decided that he had brightened my day, he disappeared, returning a few minutes later eating a piece of cake. The playgroup leader, busy handing out every kind of materials other than cake, was too busy to notice. Some of the children opted to paint at the painting board and were neatly overalled for that purpose. Some began cutting meaningless shapes out of paper with Einsteinian concentration. (Gavin, meanwhile, was slicing his left mitten into a filigree of fractured wool, casting me a triumphant blackmailer's smile: 'Let's see you yell at me here in the middle of all this child-centred stuff.' Don't blame me if you cut your finger off, I thought vengefully.)

The little boy who had sung his way through the disrobing procedure was now doing a jigsaw. I decided it would be more calming to watch him than to keep an eye on Gavin, who now had the scissors in his left hand and was shredding his right mitten. The little singer had put enough jigsaw pieces together to get a picture of a little cottage. He then put a piece featuring a sparrow upside down on the roof, the sparrow's legs pointing happily skywards, and beat it into place with his elbow. The playgroup leader arrived and they had an amicable discussion as to why the sparrow would be footless on the roof.

Over in one corner, a little girl who had been silent and withdrawn for some time began to cry quietly. Seeing that this got her no attention, she cried noisily for a while.

'The'th upthet,' the playgroup leader's son said, around the cake in his mouth.

This kid has the makings of a great reporter, I thought. He gets to the nub of the news. The leader comforted the little girl, and the young reporter left the room in search of more cake.

Along with several other children, Gavin, meanwhile, had moved into the Wendy house, from which snatches of conversation emerged, the first a major negotiation on who should be mother. It was obvious that mother was the star of the domestic show, and it rapidly emerged why. Mother, as portrayed by three year olds, is a cross between an SAS man and Hitler. And that's on a good day. Do this. Go there. Take that.

'You make the dinner,' Gavin's voice said.

He wasn't in the place an hour, and already had

achieved a leadership role, I thought, gathering up the shards of his mittens and secreting them in my pocket.

'No,' another voice in the Wendy house said. 'I'm the granny. Grannies never make the dinner.'

'I want to be the granny too,' a third voice said, obviously liking these job specifications.

'A-a-all right,' Gavin's voice said, in a bizarre parody of my own whenever I was trying to soothe him. 'We'll have a cup of tea, then.'

I wasn't sure whether this was to avoid propagation of grannies or to obviate strife over who would make the dinner, but this course of action seemed to meet with general approval, since realistic slurping sounds broke out within the Wendy house.

'You have a broke collarbone,' one of the grannies said, apparently tiring of the tea.

'I do not,' Gavin's voice responded, insulted.

'Well, betend,' the granny voice said, impatiently.

'Won't,' Gavin said.

'You have to, you're the mammy,' said the second granny.

'I don't want to be the mammy any more,' Gavin said. 'I'll be the granny.'

Such competition for the role of granny I had never come upon before. I can't wait to be a granny myself, if it gets you out of having broken bones and making dinners.

At this point, the playgroup leader's son, eating a third piece of cake, reversed in a red plastic truck over her foot. A spasm of pain crossed her face, but she only said in a strangled way, as she crashed a hand, outflung for balance, into a set of mobiles, 'We should look where we're going, shouldn't we?'

Her son considered this, then pointed to the still agitated mobiles.

'That nearly falled,' he stated. 'You nearly broke it down.'

At eleven o'clock, the little desks and chairs were arranged into a horseshoe shape and we all had orange and biscuits. It was then that the weather and day chart was brought up to date, it being agreed democratically that today was Friday and that the weather was cold. Then we identified colours and shapes for a while, one of the children yelling triumphantly when an egg outline was produced: 'I know, it's a yoval.'

After elevenses, I approached the playgroup leader humbly.

'Would you mind if I went now and collected him later,' I asked. 'I have a headache.'

'Oh, do you find it noisy?'

Beside her, a child was hammering play-dough with

a spoon, connecting more often with the desk than with the dough. Noisy? A foundry would be eerily silent by comparison.

'They get great aggression out in banging,' she said happily. 'It's a pity you have to go, though. There's good things coming up. I'll be reading *Three Billy Goats Gruff* to them, which is terrific, because it gives me great scope for acting and funny voices and they love it. Then we'll be doing Movement to Music. That's interesting too, because you see how the communication interaction works.'

Gavin suddenly erupted from the Wendy house on hands and knees, doing so good an imitation of an enraged Rottweiler that three of the children burst into tears and said they wanted their mammy. I scooped up the Rottweiler and said maybe I'd better, on second thoughts, take him with me, because it was only his first visit and perhaps two hours was enough, this time. Gavin, under my right arm, indicated severe disagreement with this course of action.

I gently pressed his face into my jumper to stifle his protest and he bit a lump out of the jumper. However, he did it on the side the playgroup leader couldn't see, which was fortunate, because I'm sure jumper-biters are not welcomed by child-oriented services.

I grabbed his coat off the hook and got out of there.

Later that evening, when my husband asked Gavin about his experiences, all Gavin could remember was that some kid other than him had eaten three pieces of cake and all he, Gavin, had been offered was orange juice and a Marietta biscuit. He gave the biscuit its full title, as if to sum up the outrage. Not a Ginger Nut. Not a Toffee Pop. But a Marietta Biscuit.

Since he was beginning to retrospectively upset himself about this, I had to help him look on the bright side.

'You got to be the mammy,' I pointed out.

'Why didn't you ask to be the daddy?' my husband wanted to know.

'There was no daddies,' Gavin told him, beginning to nod off.

David looked questioningly at me.

'We don't need daddies,' I explained, in proper playgroup collective terms. 'We get all our aggression out by banging.'

David's mouth twitched. 'I would have thought daddies were handy for that, too,' he observed.

I told him if he was going to talk dirty in front of the children, I'd let Gavin make bits out of his socks the way he had made bits out of his own mittens. He looked at me long and consideringly over Gavin's red-gold curls, standing up so fluidly the child did

not waken. Gestured at me one-handed. A flick of
the fingers, no more. Summoning. Come here. Now.
Stand close to me.

I moved nearer. The summoning hand sketched
my breasts while he watched me try to pretend to
be unaffected. Until the ache was a grinding desire
that hoarsened my voice when I spoke.

'Stephen must be tired after today, too.'

'Probably.'

My speech and thoughts were slowed by the
urgency of my need.

'Ready for bed, really,' I said, still standing there.

'Aren't we all?' David asked.

CHAPTER SIXTEEN

At the Water's Edge

——————⋙◦⋘——————

'Would you sleep with me again?'

The two of us – Robert Allen and I – had walked perhaps a mile without conversation. Barefoot, along that cool sea-smoothed sand between water's edge and shingle, that darker strip where one wave in a series will wash over your feet before retreating, rolling miniature rounded stones and shells with it. In front of us, all the time, scurried sandpipers, constantly trying to keep one foot dry, never believing that the waves will always come back to catch them as soon as they put down that second claw.

Now and then came the soft-sand thump of sneakered feet as serious walkers outpaced us, elbows angular in effortful statement, black wiring connecting earphones to a player at the waist. The bad-tempered wasp-noise of the jet-skis had died away as the sun went down into a unity of sea-sky warm coral, wattling sheen. It was all of a piece and perfect, so perfect that even his question seemed minor, an irritant pin pricking the wide-skied eternity in which we walked. It hung and waited while we walked, the sun sliding so quickly behind the horizon that the round of its reflection flattened, narrowed and was an echo before we reached the darkening pine at the end of the beach and turned to go back.

Had we been a couple, we'd have made the turn like formation swimmers, knowing each other's movements as we know our own, but as it was, he turned to his left, I to my right, colliding us and bringing our hands up to steady each other, then pull each other closer. Laughing and at ease with the accident. An undergirding there of the need that pushes laughter out in its harsher drive. We stood, pleasured by the closeness, tempted by the nearness. All it would take would be one push of the hips, reaching for an answering push. One hand slip-sliding away from the safe upper-arm embrace to add to the arousal. One face raised blindly for the deep kiss that would let loose the sequence, inveitable as time.

I raised my arms as if to suggest restraint and

he raised his, open-handed in mock surrender. We turned to go back, me now walking above the shingle line, in the softer, whiter sand, him at the edges of the waves, kicking them so that from a distance, his would have been a sputtering, splashing child-like progress.

'Well?' he asked, impatient as if the question had been put thirty seconds before.

'Would I sleep with you again?'

'Would you?'

'Would you ask me?'

Colour gone from the sky, great lowering livid clouds banked in threat. I felt no-see-ems starting to bite, so let go the fold of skirt I had held up to keep the hem dry. Cold water-weight would hold it low and make it cling to my ankles: a damp barrier against the insects.

'I didn't ask you the last time.'

'The only time.'

'As if I didn't know.'

'Well, then,' I said, as if summing up the whole issue.

He stood in the rollicking little waves, hands jammed deep into Dockers' pockets, and laughed out loud.

'Anyway,' I added, by way of a clincher, 'you said

yourself we're not the types. And that was before I was up to my armpits in children.'

We were walking again, darkness coiling, folding in on us like a fog, the heat of the day sweating into cold condensation on the face of my watch.

'I thought that would make it go away,' he said after a while.

'What would make what go away?' I asked, knowing the answer, knowing he needed the question.

'Motherhood. Would make the attraction go away. Your being a mother would make me want you less.'

'I'm an aunt, really.'

'You're a really good mother, you shouldn't discount yourself.'

'I don't. I come across like a good mother because I don't do motherhood at all. I know how to be an aunt. For a while there, I thought I had to be a mother, but time has made me more realistic. I find that if I just behave all the time as if I had the kids on loan – as if I were just an aunt and they were going back at the end of the day – I'm much easier and more relaxed.'

Oh, Robert, I thought, you believe you are listening to me with all your attention, but, like a camera, I can catch every flicker of your boredom. You do not want me to talk about the kids. You want me to talk about you, so that you can circle the possibility of another

— what? Another sexual episode with me? My parents would call it a roll in the hay. You would not like to hear it so described. But then, you couldn't cope with it being described at all. You are stumping along there on the damp, cooling sand, stuffed with the possibility that I might slide sideways the eighteen inches that would bring me into hip-bumping embrace with you, for us to walk the rest of the way back to the hotel tilted towards each other in pre-sex flaccid dawdle.

He looks like an enlargement of Gavin sulking, I thought, seeing him silhouetted, tubby tummy thrust out, head down, unrelieved of his feelings of guilt in spite of confessing them, knowing the admission to be a greater betrayal than its consummation. Perhaps, having married a man without first sharing that heart-racing, swing-lowing abandoned hunger with him, there was less guilt for me in imagining sex with someone else.

We are two different species, I thought. You do not want to fail in your fidelity, but have an unconscious, even innocent, hope that circumstances will propel you into the pleasured guilt of it and at the same time excuse you; no malice aforethought. I, on the other hand, am a spectator at my life and yours, blocking the scenes, juxtaposing the possibilities. No malice aforethought, either — because none of this is real to me.

I wondered how many of the people on this beach faced each day, not as a participant but as a kind of script consultant. Less than human, I am, trying out models like shape-gridded computer simulations. Bothered by my grim-faced silence, Robert was looking at me.

'If I was busy, I wouldn't get into this shit,' I told him and he looked hurt. 'My mother would say you don't get migraine or insomnia or introspection if you have enough to do.'

'My mother would say the devil finds work for idle hands,' he offered, and the two of us laughed. Unhappily.

None of which stopped the errant inevitable thought, sounding in my head like a bell-clapper against the insides of my skull: Gabrielle would never do this. Gabrielle would never think this.

'Go on up. Order me tea or something,' I told him, suddenly sickened and chilled.

'Hot tea?'

I nodded in the dusk and he, retrieving his boat shoes from where he had thrown them under the boardwalk to the hotel, set off up the boards, hesitating in unspoken question.

'Five minutes and I'll be after you.'

I pulled a frond of sea-grass to fan myself with

and sat in the singing stillness of the tropical night. Gabrielle, I thought, I talk to you in my head, but is it for you or for me? Do I talk to what you were to fight off knowing that what you were is dead and gone? Do I talk to what you were because you are more forgiving than the voice of my own conscience?

It would be merciful if our dead left us without memories of them, without the choice of veneration or betrayal. Because there is no other option. They define us by our veneration of them, the beloved dead, as we imitate and emulate, as we quote the creepy axioms of another time and croon to ourselves the comfort songs of their brutalities, harmonised by time and distance and the shallow sad assertion that they never did us any harm, those brutalities. Or they define us by our betrayal of them, the dead, because we are the little living that could and does forget them.

'Oh, God, I am so frightened,' I said aloud, the evening breeze turning my tears cold against my cheeks, my knuckles grinding them away.

For the first time, I realised the fractal truth of what had happened to me. It was not that I had lost those I loved, though that was part of it. It was not that the loss was a sudden, rough-torn totality, though that, too, was part of it. The accident had robbed me of the surrounds that surely shaped me and which constrained the worst of me. Against the sweet certainties of Gabrielle, of my mother, I could rattle without damage. Against the funny provocations of Oliver, I could react and find a synthesis. Without them, I was a malicious meddler, an observer with a need to tinker, a commentator without an integrated worth. I was dangerous and dislikable, except when absorbed in the children, and perhaps even that absorption was self-serving.

I flung away the crushed frond and got upright. Focus on those boats. Those boats out there on the horizon line. They are there, they are now. See the bright swinging lights arcing in the black to attract the fish into the nets? Time the swing of the lights. Listen for the echo of the sounds carried by the stilly surface of the water. Stay with now and fill the arcing void with thin-sliced scheduled slots of time and toil. Let David look, unfrightened, into middle distance for hours at a time, but you get your head down, your eyes on the detail of other lives so you do not have to look at your own. Run for cover, run for cover, one book to the next, one task to the next, like the walkers wired to a Walkman, fleeing the unpatterned sounds of nature.

Gabrielle, teach me how to become a 'natural' at real life. You knew how to do it. I don't. I start from a point of distance, of observation, of planning to be who I am, and it isn't working. I keep hoping that one day I will wake up and for that whole day, simply react. Do things without rating them. Say things without critiquing them. For a long time, I thought that this instinctive self-criticism, this constant crafting of the self, would result in a more perfect me. Now I know it results in a 'me' who is more imperfect by the day, less acceptable by the minute.

Because self-absorption, diagnosed, is no less noxious than unaware self-absorption. But how to fix faults without scrutiny of the flawed self? Or can they be fixed? Perhaps each of us is a continuum of pre-allocated traits. You, an absolute angel from the beginning, me a screamer without cause. Oh, Gabrielle, David says I am living up to a myth of you. He is hatefully right. I must not refer any more to you. I am older now than you ever grew to be. I do you a disservice by dragging your name and unreality into the lives of two little boys who no longer know you or need you or want you or love you and who can be made only regretful and remorseful to a non-memory that they will covertly hate.

But if I let you go, I have no carapace to shape me, to give me certainty, to tell me what I do and who I am. Without you as that carapace, I am lost, shapeless, raw. I do not know what I think about anything but the simple superficialities of white next the face and bran flakes give you heartburn. I have joined my life to a man of deep-rooted quiet certainties, but he will not lend them to me nor let me hide behind them. Nor can he. They are integral to him.

Ahead of me now was the brightness of the Boca Raton hotel and the cyclical sounds of laughter and of music. A promise of bright busyness.

'I've had enough of this crap,' I muttered to myself behind a cupped hand, pushing the whisper back into my own face and ears. 'You're too old to keep waiting for reality to knock on your door and announce itself. It has. This is it. This is all there is. There's nothing better to wait for. There's nothing worse to look forward to. There's only now.'

When I walked into the hotel, the curling tendrils of conversations pulled me in. I concentrated on making people laugh, looking at the unpretending realness of faces glossy with alcohol and social warmth. Reality, I thought, is what you decide it is. Now I will decide for myself: this is reality. Tasks and the children and being a wife.

The next day reinforced the decision. It was a day filled with such warmth, such shared triumph, that it was as if everything up to this had been tuning, and now all the instruments were on the same single note.

At this AGM of their parent company, Robert Allen's people were presenting some of the innovations they had come up with. I had been invited as one of the people who had been helpful to their growth in the past year. So Robert said. My own belief was that it was a four-day freebie trip to a warm exotic location, offered in the hope of renewing what happened in Greece and in the confidence that I would not let it be renewed. On that final evening, everybody received presents. I didn't open the flat package left at my place, but admired everybody else's. Particularly what the group presented to Robert. I had helped a little with the preparation of his gift. It was a coffee-table account of some World Cup or other, signed on the title page by all of the players. The staff had come to me months in advance to ask me to involve David in getting all the famous names in place. Including his own.

When I got back to my room after the dinner, the phone was ringing.

'So. Was it enjoyable?'

'David, it's the middle of the night, your time. Why aren't you asleep?'

'Woke, peed, checked on the boys, rang you. That OK?'

'You shouldn't be waking yourself up.'

'Dominique, you may not have noticed, but I can sleep anywhere, any time. And I can go back to sleep anywhere, any time. When we finish this, I will toss and turn for at least thirty seconds.'

I described the dinner.

'We all got gifts, too,' I said, tearing the paper off the big rectangular package I had been given.

'Well-wrapped, anyway, by the sounds, whatever they gave you. What is it?'

'You.'

'Mmm?'

'Yeah. It's a huge silver-framed picture of you with two other guys. You look a lot younger, and you have a football jersey on you.'

'Colours?'

'Of what?'

'The jersey, for Chrissake.'

'Oh. Dark red and blue. The guy on your left also has a jersey on him. Same colours. The third guy is much older with those glasses that have no sides to them.'

'Pince-nez?'

'Yeah.'

'I know the picture.'

'When's it from?'

'1989.'

'Who owns the dark red and blue?'

'Claret.'

'Claret and blue.'

'Aston Villa.'

I waited, looking at the pictures. There was improvident laughter in the two young faces, the trusting triumphalism that says, 'Rejoice with us, we're the best.'

'Don't bother your arse telling me anything about the picture, I've a long tradition of being pig-ignorant about your past.'

'The other lad is Richard Davey. Dubliner. One of the best ever. The guy with the glasses was his father. That was the year we won the UEFA cup. I see Robert Allen's hand in this — I mentioned Richie to him a while back. Does it bother you that you gave Robert something connected with football, in the light of this?'

'No. He was thrilled with it. Are you pleased about this picture?'

'I'm neither pleased nor displeased. If it gives you pleasure, great. I'm going back to sleep. Congratulations again.'

I sat, holding the big picture in its expensive frame, trying to work out where in the house I would hang it. Not in any of the general rooms. It would look like showing off. The kids' room, maybe. Stephen would like that. I propped it on top of the chest of drawers while I got ready for bed.

'It's not the picture you don't like,' I told David's laughing younger face. 'It's that you don't want anyone using a relic to get close to you. They never succeed in getting close to you but the attempt irritates you. I wonder why?'

The face, ignorant of all future concerns, laughed out at me.

'And another thing,' I said. 'Don't think for a moment I will allow you to age into a prickly pedant who corrects someone when they say "dark red". Claret my arse.'

CHAPTER SEVENTEEN

Thing and Other Thing

❧

I was planning to make that point to him the following night, while the boys were occupied with the airport junk toys I'd bought for them. The big pink plastic Slinky spring that walked down the stairs was a big hit. I was launched on my account of the final day of the trip when the doorbell rang.

'That'll be Ralph,' David said. 'One of our partners. Dropping in for a minute.'

I had made some inroads on the table chaos when the door from the hall opened and elegance itself walked in. I half-heard the name as the man swept off his hat and, taking my hand, kissed it while gazing at me in consumed admiration with huge brandy-brown eyes. Emerging fluidly from the bow, he presented me with a single long-stemmed rose and in almost the same movement confided his coat, silk scarf and kid gloves to David, who took them from him with as much deference as if he had been rehearsing to be his footman. I found a narrow vase for the long-stemmed rose and doused the kitchen trying to fill it from the tap.

'My dear lady,' the elegant man said, controlling the tap with one hand, and taking the vase from me with the other, 'perhaps if we—'

I had forgotten the vase had a kind of cap on it. Removed, it was quite easy to fill. He returned it to me with a flourish that cried out for swords at dawn.

'D'you want to play with my Slinky?'

Gavin had arrived and, as was his wont, gone straight to the point. The man fingered his silk cravat, in the folds of which nestled a diamond stick-pin.

'Could you trust me with something so valuable?' he asked solemnly.

'I'll teach you first,' Gavin said, extending a small dirty hand.

The man took it without hesitation and followed him into the hall for a concentrated lesson in making a pink spring perform. When he turned his back, I could see he had a long queue of greying hair, tied with a black velvet ribbon.

'This is an accountant?' I hissed at David.

'Chartered secretary, actually,' David said, grinning.

'And he drives a Bentley,' Stephen added, jumping a mile when the man's hand grasped his shoulder. He turned guiltily.

'Stephen, might I impose on you for a favour?'

Struck dumb, Stephen nodded. The man handed him his car keys.

'I should be so appreciative if you would correct the balance of the speakers. I have the impression of minor distortion somewhere within the system.'

Stephen waited for instructions, realised he had been briefed and took off like a bullet.

'Never fear,' the man murmured. 'A clever little device will obstruct your brilliant son should he consider turning the engine on.'

'I asked Ralph to deliver something in person—' David began.

'Couriers must remove their helmets,' quoted Ralph unexpectedly, doffing a phantom helmet and tossing it to David.

'—because I knew you wouldn't be able to refuse him anything.'

Ralph stooped and lifted from the floor a hard plastic container, flipping it open to reveal two tiny kitten faces, one white, one black. The black kitten probed the air outside with a tentative paw. Ralph advanced the pet carrier towards me and placed it on the floor. The black kitten promptly made a dash for the decorations on my shoes. The white one came to the edge of the carrier, but when I bent to have a look, retreated into its darkness. It was at this point that Gavin, pink Slinky dangling from his still-dirty hand, came into the kitchen. The black kitten moved from my shoes, advancing slowly towards the new arrival, watching the up-and-down motion of the Slinky. Gavin halted in the doorway and gestured with the toy.

'Thing!' he said triumphantly.

'What a very splendid, all-purpose name,' Ralph said.

'Is it a him?' I asked.

'Both are. Brothers.'

The white one sidled out and aligned itself with Thing. I thought Gavin might have a seizure with delight.

'Other Thing!' he crowed.

'That takes care of the christenings,' David observed, handing Ralph his scarf and holding the grey tweed coat for him. Bowing over my hand, Ralph managed to establish, without words, that meeting me had transformed his life into unparalleled bliss and that he would live in hope of a return engagement. In the interim, he would ensure my elder was returned to me post haste. As he proceeded down the hall, carrying the pet container, both kittens half-followed him, the sinuous grace of their progress giving an odd impression that they were imitating his gait.

'Do we get Things for keeps?' Gavin wanted to know.

'Hmm,' I said, and the white kitten turned on me a look of such pathos I went straight to the fridge for milk. Stephen, face red as a fire-engine from the thrills of the Bentley, came in at what for him was an untypically fast pace. The kittens scrambled behind a chair in terror. Gavin whacked him with Slinky.

'You frickened Things,' he told him.

'They ours?' Stephen asked.

'Yeah, so I believe,' I said, setting down the saucer.

'What's their names?'

'Things,' Gavin said impatiently.

'The black one is Thing, the white one is Other Thing,' David said.

'Can we have them in bed?'

'No.'

Gavin opened his mouth so wide, preparatory to crying, that both kittens instinctively cringed.

'Don'tcryyou'llfrightenthem,' Stephen said. Gavin's mouth closed.

Gavin had the makings of a *Guinness Book of Records* crier. He could cry for Europe. He was a triathlon crier. To have stopped him with a one-word sentence was some achievement.

'Feel the little bones of them,' David said, guiding Gavin's fingers. 'See how delicate they are? If you rolled over on them at night, you might break them.'

He got launched on a tutorial about litter boxes. The two boys followed him, one carrying an oblong plastic box, the other a package of cat litter.

The kittens watched them depart. Other Thing was almost split in two by a pointed triangular yawn that revealed the tiniest teeth in the world. I picked up the two and set them on my lap, herding them gently back whenever Thing would lead the exploratory charge. When the two boys came back, the kittens were like a yin-yang sign in my lap, curled in sleep.

David agreed the boys could give the kittens a kiss goodnight. Gavin did his level best to kiss them with enough sound effects to wake them up, but the kittens slept as heavily as he did himself. Stephen kissed the white one on the darker fur between its ears.

'What was the Bentley like?' I asked.

Stephen tended to spend a little time with me

each evening before following his smaller brother upstairs. I asked him questions. Some nights I got single word answers. Other nights I got free-flowing philosophy. In this particular case, he seemed to be having difficulty reaching a word to match the wonder of it.

'Brill,' he said eventually.

Stroking the sleeping kitten, his hand already carried a hint of the squared strength it would have when he became a man. He went down on his knees so as to be only inches away from the white kitten.

'It has fuel injection,' he said, with the hushed piety of one announcing the Second Coming. For a split second, I thought he meant the kitten. Then he started to explain fuel injection – again, as quietly as if he was giving Other Thing a subliminal lesson in motor mechanics. This is a bright boy, I thought, curbing the desire to stroke the back of his neck while he talked. I wonder what we should point him towards? Then, like snapping a rubber band against my wrist, I reminded myself: No future tense. Just concentrate on the here-and-now.

'You are a manipulative sonofa—' I said to David when he came back from bedding down the two of them. 'You knew bloody well I wouldn't have wanted kittens.'

'Why wouldn't you?'

I tried to think.

'They'll make me wheezy.'

'That's the device your mother used to prevent you having pets.'

'Maybe, but still.'

'Your asthma has eased back quite a bit. If the kittens get it going again, we'll get rid of them.'

'After they've bonded with us?'

'Bonded my arse. Cats?'

'What about fleas?' I asked eventually.

'No cat from Ralph's house would ever be landed on by a flea, never mind give one house-room,' David said.

'I still can't believe Ralph,' I said. 'Is he always like that?'

'Always.'

'How the hell does he fit with all your ex-rugby accountants?'

David laughed. 'The more decorative part of their portfolio. Shows diversity in their investments.'

'You're the sporting bit, he's the Edwardian Eccentric bit?'

He shrugged and simultaneously lifted the kittens off my lap into a basket padded with an old towel. You brush me off, I thought, when it comes to looking at you or how you are seen by your colleagues. You do not believe there is anything you can learn by self-examination. You will, next, make mugs of tea for the two of us. We are completely incompatible, you and I, but have a comfortable groove of shared responsibilities and mutual kindnesses. No struck-by-lightning moments of happiness. But maybe a flat baseline of content is enough.

Thing and Other Thing got so much tough love from Gavin, they were lucky to survive it. If either of them snuggled down for a nap, he would arrive to wake them up, yelling affection and caressing them with such force they got flattened to the floor like dachshunds at the end of each stroke. When they tried to escape, he would pick them up and tuck one under each arm. Stephen ran interference for them.

'They're getting squished,' he would say.

'Not fall on the ground, I careful,' Gavin would protest.

'Look how squished they are.'

The kittens were squeezed so tightly under Gavin's arms that Thing's little mouth was forced open. Other Thing was held the other way around, so only his tail was visible. It had the look of a flag of surrender.

I held out my hands. A kitten fell into each and

was lowered to the floor. They fled. I hugged Gavin, tightening my arms so he squawked.

'That's how they feel if you hold them too tight, but they can't tell you.'

He nodded wisely.

'Can't talk yet.'

'They'll never talk,' his brother told him. 'Cats don't talk. They just miaow and purr.'

Gavin went prowling in the direction the kittens had gone. I hoped they had hidden themselves efficiently. Otherwise they were in for a hard time, explaining to him why they had given him the impression that within months they'd be hosting debates and running table quizzes. Keeping his eye on him, Stephen stayed put.

'Why do they just miaow and purr?'

'What did you want them to do, moo like cows?'

'But budgies talk as well as do their own noises,' he objected reasonably.

'I think this may be an "ask your father" situation,' I said, and went to tidy up the kitchen. I must, I thought, ring someone about the water pressure. Filling a kettle shouldn't take twenty minutes. As I plugged it in, I noticed the red light on the phone and picked it up, assuming a call was just about to come through.

'. . . speak to David Carpenter, please?' I could hear Stephen's voice asking.

Then David was on the line, being asked about budgies and their linguistic superiority to cats.

'Bloody good question,' I could hear him say. 'Hold on a sec.'

His voice went smaller because he was talking to someone in the room with him.

'Anybody know why a budgie can be taught to speak but a cat can't? My son wants to know.'

I could hear muffled laughter in the distance. God, I thought, he must be at a meeting. I'll kill Stephen for disturbing him. People at the meeting made various suggestions and he relayed them back, eventually telling Stephen he'd bring him home a book with answers. With the huge formality of a child, Stephen asked him to thank everybody at the meeting, and the phone clicked off.

There is no blood connection between this man and this boy, yet they are father and son, I thought.

CHAPTER EIGHTEEN

One Perfect Summer

———◆———

Never was there a summer like it. The warmth came in April, trailing unseasonal queues at the bus-stops near the beaches. In May, the boys chased each other in the thickets of trees in St Anne's Park while I sat, absorbed by the quiet bluebells clustered at the tree roots, shaded yet bright. In June and July, there were great swatches of sunshiny days, trailing slowly into short, cool nights.

I bought rollerblades for me and Stephen. Padded at knee and elbow, braced at wrist, our heads sweaty in helmets, we fumbled our way to proficiency. In the evenings, David would hoist Gavin on his shoulders and follow us along the cycle path at the sea's edge, answering Gavin's endless questions. I would warn

Stephen not to do dramatic leaps or circles in the path of an oncoming bicycle, and, letting him speed off ahead, I would skate back to the tall joined figure of man and child, one of them asking an endless series of questions, the other answering.

Once, as I joined them, Gavin pointed to a man just coming level with them and asked in bell-like tones why he was black. Red blush rose like a tide over my face. David had no such reaction.

'Why don't you ask him yourself?' was his response.

'Why are you black colour?' Gavin asked, elaborating in case the man wasn't as clever as David.

'Because my father came from Nigeria,' the man said.

'Where's Nigeria?' Stephen asked, coming up behind me.

The man obliged with a short geographical outline.

'Did you have no mammy?'

The man looked up at Gavin, laughing. 'I did have a mammy.'

'Well, why didn't she make you get clean again?'

'He's not dirty,' Stephen hissed.

The man looked down at him. Stephen retreated behind me, very nearly knocking me off the rollerblades in the process.

'This will probably take more time than you have,' David said to him.

'David Carpenter, isn't it?' the man said.

'That's right.'

'I was in New York for the match against Italy,' the man said, and reached up to pat Gavin on the leg. Gavin immediately checked to see if he had left a black mark on him. 'Hope you got the footballing genes,' he smiled, and was off.

A few days later, when we shared a bus with what seemed an infinitely extended black family, I expected Gavin to embark on interrogation, but apart from a few sneaked covert glances, he evinced no interest in them. After we got off the bus near Christchurch, our tourist venue of the day, Stephen whispered to me, 'Daddy told Gavin he wasn't to ask anybody else why they were black,' he said. 'He said some black people might be upset and Gavin should just be the same with them as he would be with anybody else. Isn't Gavin good?'

You are your mother's son, I thought, watching him catch up with Gavin and steer him gently away from the edge of the pavement. Always looking out for the younger one. Wanting your junior to get full credit.

Not that Gavin earned any credits in Christchurch. Far too young for the history-laden trip, he was quieted only by the odd exhibit of a cat and mouse, suffocated unexpectedly several hundred years ago when the organist in the cathedral began to play. The cat had – as its mummified shape demonstrated – been about to pounce on the cowering mouse when both had the life sucked out of them by the activation of the bellows within the great organ, leaving them to be preserved by the dry atmosphere, permanently frozen, predator and victim. Gavin had to be dragged away from the two of them, and looked at Thing and Other Thing with new eyes when we got home.

Thing and Other Thing looked at all of us with new eyes a few weeks later, having been spayed. Instead of regarding every other cat alive as a sworn enemy, they both now took a much more live-and-let-live approach. To other cats. Further than cats they did not go with their new tolerance, as David found out. Having developed a gastric infection that made him throw up for hours during the night, he called in sick and went back to bed. The two boys reverently patted his cold clammy forehead and asked if he wouldn't like the sheet pulled up. No, he muttered, the cool air was pleasant on his skin.

We left him and set off for the beach, assuming that he would sleep all day. In fact, three hours later, he was startled into sudden wakefulness by Thing standing squarely on his naked chest. Eyes closed,

David stroked the cat. The cat complained. David unwillingly opened his eyes to find Thing poking a paw at something he had deposited on David's chest. One oversized, very dead magpie.

'I barely made it to the loo before I threw up again,' he said later. 'And when I got back out, Thing was standing on the bed looking at the magpie, upset that I hadn't given him a round of applause for it.'

He explained to the boys that cats bring their kill by way of tribute to those they like, and that the right reaction is not shock-horror (or even throwing up) but affirmation. Which explained why Gavin and Stephen stroked Other Thing almost bald when, a few weeks later, he deposited a dead mouse on Stephen's duvet. They didn't even want to throw out the dead rodent, for fear it might damage Other Thing's sense of self-worth. I got it on a newspaper and tossed it as far as I could into the back garden. Not a good move, as it turned out. Other Thing lovingly retrieved it and brought it back to me, which meant I had to follow instructions, praising and stroking the cat for bringing me this disgusting cadaver.

'Put it in the wheelie bin,' David said when I rang him.

'But Other Thing should eat it, shouldn't he?'

'He's probably not hungry enough.'

'If I throw it into the rubbish, he'll surely feel cheated.'

'Cats have no memory. Put the bloody thing in the bin and forget about it.'

'Is that what you did with the magpie?'

'Of course.'

'God, I hope the bin men don't look at the contents of the wheelie bins as they unload them. They'll be convinced that our family is engaged in hand-to-hand combat with Mother Nature. Trying to wipe out whole species.'

'Somebody should long ago have wiped out magpies as a species.'

'Oh, I don't know. They dress well.'

'Poncing predators eating other harmless smaller birds,' he said with unexpected venom. 'Wouldn't give them daylight.'

There was something else he wouldn't give daylight to, but I couldn't remember what it was. Some insect of which he took the dimmest of dim views. David rarely criticised people other than by silence, but occasionally let loose a jet of intensely personal dislike, either at an inanimate object, a sport ('bugger racing,' he would say whenever a commentator would announce that they were loading horses into boxes) or an animal. The boys picked up his dislikes unquestioningly, no doubt because they were so rare. I probably held forth on so many behaviours, books, TV programmes or friends worth condemning for any one of a dozen reasons that they no doubt decided my dislikes were too indiscriminate to be copied, whereas their father's not only had the appeal of rarity, but were easier to remember for the same reason.

Because David was run off his feet that summer, I ended up organising our day trips on my own. Whenever I took the two boys to the beach in the early weeks, I had first to fight Gavin's belief that the cats yearned to travel with us. Just as he was convinced that the two of them ached to share his bubble bath with him, he was also convinced that Thing and Other Thing couldn't wait to go swimming in the sea. In addition, he would point out, as I strapped him into the car, the two cats could eat pinkeens if he and Stephen caught them in a bucket. Which would, in turn, save cat food.

Once we arrived at whatever beach we chose on a particular day, he would forget about the cats. Even on days when the tide was so far out that darkened hillocks of damp sand seemed to stretch for miles, he would want to get into the distant water immediately. Not far into the water — unlike Stephen, he did not like swimming *per se*. His preference was to get good and wet, to splash sea water as high and far as humanly possible, and then to pick shells and catch pinkeens at the water's edge.

Stephen would hover near him like a small sturdy guardian, and I would watch from the dry sand, ready to race to them the moment anything untypical happened. Thus I was on the run, over the hard sand, the moment I saw Gavin apparently beating the water with his spade.

'Leave it, leave it, leave it,' I yelled, dragging him away from the jellyfish he was chastising.

'I told you,' Stephen said in the resentful tone of the child-minder unminded by the child in his care.

'I killing it,' Gavin protested, struggling in my arms in his endeavour to get back to the fray. Real fray, I noticed. He seemed to have flattened and marginally fragmented the jellyfish, now trailing threads of threat as it washed in and out with the waves.

'You can't kill a jellyfish,' I said, noting how solid and heavy he was getting.

'Can you not?' Stephen's voice asked, his delivery impeded by chattering teeth. 'Ever?'

'Well, maybe a jellyfish can be killed,' I conceded. 'But there's no way Gavin could do it.'

We got back to the rug where I wrapped Gavin in

a bathtowel, rubbing him dry and warm again while Stephen went off to check on his bucket of pinkeens. He came back with his teeth still chattering, but the rest of him suddenly still, mutely holding out the bucket. The pinkeens lay inert at the bottom of the water, eddying to and fro as the bucket moved.

'Take them and throw them into the sea,' I said. 'If anything will make them revive, that will.'

Stephen ran to the water's edge and tipped them in. I could see his figure in the distance, bent over surveying the tiny fish he had let out of the bucket. After a moment, he trailed disconsolately back to us.

'They didn't revive.'

He sat down in total defeat.

'At all. None of them.'

I put a towel around his shoulders and he pulled it tight for comfort. Pinkeens, for God's sake, I wanted to say. There's six thousand million billion pinkeens in the bloody ocean, why are you getting suicidal over twelve or thirteen of them? Why don't you catch yourself another dozen? I turned his cold-skinned face around. His cold-skinned, tear-stained face. He looked at me in total despair and buried his face in my side. I rocked him, speechlessly.

For the luvva Jaysus, a voice in my head said.

Pinkeens are not the Einsteins of the goddam deep.
They don't suffer.

'Pinkeens get eaten by other fish,' I offered, eventually.
'Maybe the fact that they were already dead would make
it easier for a tired old fish to get his meal.'

Stephen looked at me with such withering silent
contempt at this anthropomorphic morsel of comfort
that I could only laugh. Eventually, he began to
laugh too. Gavin had fallen asleep on my lap in a
bundle of bathtowel. His brother helped me slide
the little boy onto the rug, and pushed sand underneath to form a pillow beneath Gavin's head. I
opened our plastic food box and laid out a few
sandwiches for the two of us. The tea from the
thermos was slightly tarry. Someone nearby had a
boombox playing.

'That's the teacher song,' Stephen murmured, half
to himself.

'The teacher's song? What teacher?'

'I don't know. Just.'

'Just what?'

'He's like the teacher in school saying things.'

I listened. Against a melodic background, a deep
solemn voice seemed to be giving a list of unrelated
bits of good advice. Not to read beauty magazines
because they would make you feel ugly. Not to hang

around with depressing people. To do something every day that scares you.

'Is it a song or an ad?'

'It's a song. The man doesn't sing at all, but it's a song. I've heard it before. Listen to the end of it.'

The deep voice gave a few more bits of advice, then said, by way of a summary, 'Trust me on the sunscreen.'

'It starts by saying you should wear sunscreen,' Stephen said, and I realised why he had been so amenable to having SPF 15 thickly plastered on his shoulders. I now reached out to check. Warm, but not that dry heat that bespeaks sunburn. He took a Club Milk biscuit from the pack.

'This is my favourite,' he said, showing it to me. 'Did you and my mother come here when you were small?'

'Yes.'

'What did you do?'

'Your mother used to make perfect sandcastles with shells for the windows and I used to get the sand wet in a bucket and make chocolate-cake castles.'

I smiled out at the sea, remembering the pre-school Gaudi I had been.

'Did you ever get stung by a wasp or did my mother?'

'No. Never.'

'Tell me stuff,' he said with sudden impatience.

'Well, my dad, when he was a student, was making a sandwich when a wasp landed on one bit of the bread when he had it all buttered and ready for the egg, so he smacked down the other side of the sandwich.'

'The other slice of bread?'

'Yep.'

'Buttered bit—'

'—to buttered bit.'

'And then?'

'And then he gave it to his best friend to eat.'

'His best friend?'

'His best friend.'

'He could have had his tongue stinged.'

'He could.'

'He could have had his insides stinged all the way down.'

Stephen considered this with relish for some time. When he had drained all the excitement from it, he demanded that I tell him more stuff.

I told him about Gabrielle taking me to the Laytown races, where the horses raced along the long strand, thundering loud, the echoes of their beating hooves captured by the rising bank of the land so that, as a child, I experienced it as a thrilling assault.

About fishing for mackerel off Howth with our father. About picking raspberries with our mother, white hankies around our necks to protect us from the sun. When I ran out of memories, he sat silent, tilted against me, his head heavy with sleep, and I stroked his hair, ignoring the initial token resistance, until his head heavied more and a shift of my hip brought him sliding in sleep alongside me, cheek on my thigh.

Even when the sitting made my back ache, I wanted the time to last forever, the sea sheeting thinly over the hard sand as the tide came in, the sandflies hopping at our feet, the breathing of the two boys just audible, occasionally competed with by the sunscreen song on its nth repetition. 'Enjoy the power and beauty of your youth. Oh, never mind. You will not understand the power and beauty of your youth until they've faded.'

I shooed a fly away from Stephen's face and he sighed in sleep. These are my children, I thought. I could not love them more if I had given birth to them. An ache came to the back of my throat at the thought of their mother. In the distance, the infinitely sad call of a wood pigeon. For the first time, I thought, I am observing what I do, not pretending. No person living recognises their own happiness at the time, I thought, but I do. This is my summer, and the burnished comfort of its half life will last me a long, long time.

CHAPTER NINETEEN

Blindsided

The sunscreen song had become both a motif and an irritant by the time David took to watching sports programmes on TV with a stopwatch in his hand and a notebook computer on his lap. The first time I became aware of this was in September, when he came in from the garden, where he had been building what Stephen somewhat formally told me would be A Water Feature. Stephen loved to have a transistor with him and, from the garden, I could hear the now-familiar words.

'The real troubles in your life are apt to be things that never crossed your worried mind, the kind that blindside you at 4pm on some idle Tuesday.'

David had obviously stashed a clean pair of tailored

khaki shorts and a polo shirt in the utility room, so he came into the house looking more presentable than I expected.

'You know, you're better looking now than when I first met you,' I said, surprised.

'Positively traffic-stopping,' he said, about to go to the room where the TV was, but halting to check if the phone call was for him. I shook my head, mouthing 'Robert Allen'.

'You don't sound as cheery as I'd expect at the end of a great summer,' Robert said. 'What's up?'

'Oh, Robert, it's obvious what ails me,' I said. 'I haven't seen you for so long, the spark has gone out of my life.'

'You need me to take you to dinner before the week is over,' he said. Playfully. Half-joking, whole in earnest.

'No, Robert, I don't,' I said, smiling into the phone to soften the rejection.

'Is that a refusal, then?'

'What part of no don't you understand, Robert?'

Why am I doing this, I wondered? Why do I need to rub the idea against his mind until the swelling starts, the heavy-eyed need, the knowledge that one extra step forward and there would be no steps back? I have had a great summer without any of this games-playing. I've promised not to do it any more, and I'm not going to. You are a sweet man. I screwed once and that's it. You were grown up when we did it and you're grown up now and stop trying to pull me back into something that makes you feel near the edge, gets the adrenalin bounding through your veins. You need that, go do bungee-jumping or wind-surfing.

Hell, I thought, now I've let a long silence fall, he will take it as meaning something it doesn't mean.

'I will always love you a little,' Robert said lightly.

'Yeah, well you'll have to keep the flame burning without dinner,' I said tartly. 'Was there something?'

'We have a pony.'

So? I thought, but did not say.

'My daughter Caoimhe is the proud owner of this pony. She would regard herself as promoted to cloud nine if at some stage, when you wanted to get rid of your two, you lent them to us and allowed her — under appropriate supervision — to teach them how to ride it.'

I asked warm questions about the pony, although ponies rank right up there along with other people's dreams as a route to homicidal boredom to me. I thanked him, asked after Helen, asked how the business was going, and parted from him as unemotionally as if he was a plumber or a civil engineer being dealt with as part of business. It was no kindness to this man to leave him the illusory glow of a faintly surviving love.

The truth of it was, I thought, I would *not* always love him a little. There was none of the 'torn between two lovers' myth about whatever tenuous relationship existed between us. Liking, no more than that. Affection. Affinity. Admiration for his talent and hard work. Worth perhaps twenty minutes of conversation, after which his company would be effortful, any flirting on my part muscle-bound, not fan-flick fluent.

'What was the name of that guy from the ad agency I dated before I went to Paris?' I asked David, putting a cup of coffee in front of him.

'Nigel,' he supplied. 'Thank you.'

'Nigel,' I said. 'Right.'

'What put him into your mind? You haven't mentioned him in years.'

'I was just thinking how completely turned on I was by him while at the same time I thought he was the most God-awful bore. Men feel like that a lot, I know, but women don't. Or maybe they . . .'

I trailed off, losing the idea.

'Maybe they have a more calibrated sense of guilt.'

'Calibrated?'

'Men either admired Bill Clinton or condemned him. For what he did with Monica Lewinsky. Women who admired him did it secretly. Women who condemned him felt that carrying on with her was bad enough but giving her *Leaves of Grass* was ghastly. Physical adultery bad, intellectual adultery worse.'

'But isn't it? Worse?'

He looked at me as if I was failing a not very difficult oral exam.

'If you're screwing Robert Allen,' he said, patient as a teacher, 'it doesn't make it better that he fails to quote Ovid to you at the same time. It is sophistry to believe that the position of your brain cells elevates the act. All that matters is the position of your private parts.'

'Why on earth did you use Robert Allen as an example?'

'Oh, Dominique,' he said. 'Please.'

'What do you mean, "please"? It was a strange thing to say.'

'Was it?'

'Yes, it was. I mean Robert Allen, of all people.'

I laughed slightly to underline how silly the idea was. Something in my laugh seemed to provoke him.

'Robert Allen and Dominique Dempsey, of all people. In room 137, Hotel Astir Palace, Athens.'

I gaped at him, and he finished off by giving me day and date for the encounter. At which precise moment, Gavin arrived indoors, a front tooth in his hand, blood all over his T-shirt, bellowing with panic and personal affront. David dropped on his knees in front of him and began to talk so quietly into his ear that Gavin had to reduce his volume just to hear him. I went for TCP and towels. Children are God's way of giving you time to think.

I took the child off to bed on the premise that I needed to explain the financial, i.e., tooth fairy, implications of the lost tooth. Gavin, as always, responded to shock by going almost immediately to sleep. When I came back down, David, untypically, did no more than give me a preoccupied nod. His attention seemed totally focused on the television.

Leave it alone, a voice said in my head. What the hell would you want to open it up again for? Watch the telly and keep your mouth shut. Yes, of course, you can tell him it was only the once, and long before his time, but it's no bloody business of his one way or the other and you're likely to tell him that. Anyway, he probably thinks Robert and I were at it during that later trip. Maybe that's why he rang late at night.

To check up on me. No, he actually wouldn't check up on me. But if he wouldn't check up on me, how the hell does he know about the Hotel Astir Palace?' Who knew? Robert wouldn't ever tell him ...

I forced myself to watch the screen. The programme was an international soccer match, commented on by a panel of three, chaired by a well-known TV presenter. One was a journalist who specialised in verbal attacks so personal and inflammatory that the public was evenly divided between believing he had no control whatever over his feelings and those who believed he was doing it all to add to the emotional temperature of whatever show he was on. The second was a tiny ex-footballer with a voice like a child sucking helium out of a balloon. The third was a big handsome man who seemed always on the verge of being struck dumb by the vituperation coming from the journalist.

'He's the guy with the tune, isn't he?' I asked.

David looked at me.

'Oh yes,' he said. 'Ooh, ah, Paul McGrath.'

'D'you know him?'

For a long moment, he looked at the ceiling, rather than the TV.

'You could say that.'

'Oh, you know him well?'

'Daisy, I played for Ireland for three years with Paul McGrath. Him and me were the centre-halfs. Defence.'

'What's he like?'

'Lovely fella. His wife's a great centre-half, too.'

'Sorry?'

He laughed.

'Keeps the parasites away from him. Rock of sense, Carol is. Adores him and adored him right through the bad times.'

'What bad times?'

'The bad times in any relationship. When you wonder about everything. Shh.'

I sat, dumbfounded, trying to work out if the reference had wider currency than its relevance to the man on the screen. There was no clue from the way David sat, listening with his wristwatch pulled forward on to the back of his hand, so he could judge how long each man spoke for. The duration of the comments got shorter suddenly, as the little helium balloon man tried to defend his viewpoint against the journalist, who repeatedly interrupted him and eventually erupted, yelling, 'You wouldn't know a sliding tackle if it bit you in the arse, you malignant midget from Middlesbrough.'

I laughed because I thought I should. David didn't.

Oh, God, another mistake. The TV station cut to an ad break.

'Why are you timing that programme?'

'Got an invitation to do a bit on it. Want to get the parameters.'

'Making comments about a match?'

'Mmm.'

'You going to do it?'

'Haven't decided yet.'

'Do you want to do it?'

'Not particularly.'

'But you might?'

'Mmm.'

'Why?'

'Why not?'

'You don't like to be reminded of your past.'

His head cocked to one side, he gave me a curiously amused yet angered look. 'I won't be talking about my past, I'll be talking about the matches, the players.'

'If you do it.'

'Do you want me to do it?'

I sat down, floored by the question, and thought about it. The ad break came to an end, and battle resumed among the panel.

'To be perfectly honest——' I started, only to find myself being gestured to silence.

The two of us sat, gazing at the television in a way we had never done up to that point. He kept clicking the stopwatch after each guest on the show made a comment noting in his computer how long the input had been. I just watched, in much the same way as I watched people in Paris the first two months I was there: aren't they clever, being able to talk this incomprehensible stuff which means very little to me, but obviously means something to them. When the signature tune came on and the credits rolled past the sports personalities while they did that pretence of continuing to have an animated discussion, David doused the sound and turned to me.

'Yeah?'

'Yeah what?' I asked, confused.

'You were going to tell me if you wanted me to appear on the programme.'

'I would only want you to be on it if you were very good,' I said.

'No other consideration?'

'What other consideration should I have?'

'Effect on the boys of me being revived as what we'll laughingly call a celeb.'

I considered this. It was unlikely to do either of them much harm, I thought. Gavin would turn it in some way to his personal advantage, and Stephen, already shaping up to become a quiet, thoughtful boy, would be reached only if he heard critics saying David Carpenter was useless.

'Does your partnership want you to do it?' I asked.

'I didn't ask them. Probably yes. Your kind of conditional yes. Yes if I'm good at it.'

'Do you think you would be good at it?'

'I won't do it unless I'm sure I'm good at it.'

You cocky sonofabitch, I thought, watching him. Except that there was no cockiness in the way he was now checking off the timings he had taken. He was attending a one-person course in television, delivered by himself. At the end of the course, he would put the student through some kind of exam, and once satisfied that the right standard had been reached, would submit himself to the real thing. Satisfied with himself was how I had described him, at first meeting, to Gabrielle. Not smug. But satisfied.

'Matter of interest, sez who that I don't want to be reminded of my past?'

'If we're in a pub or at a party, you always switch the conversation.'

He looked amused. Amused in the same way he looked when Stephen or Gavin misunderstood something by applying the logic of childhood to the complete illogicality of the English language.

'Don't patronise me.'

He looked at me, deliberately expressionless.

'Don't frigging patronise me with your glances that say you see way beyond what I see, because I'm only a poor gobshite and you're the king of insight and sensitivity. I said you shut people up in a pub or a dinner party when they talk about your past. Ergo, I assumed that meant you didn't want to talk about your past. I humbly apologise for misreading the runes, O Master of the Inexplicable. What was I supposed to deduce from you not talking to people socially about your fucking footballing past?'

'That people with a visible level of alcohol flowing through them who ask you about your past just want to tell you their half-remembered version of your past. I don't need to spend the rest of my life listening to people describing the piss-up they had with their mates the night we won the final.'

'What final?'

'Any final.'

'You weren't turned on by the picture the Robert Allen people gave me. The one of you and your friend.'

'No.'

How the hell did I allow myself to get to this point, I wondered desperately, but knew I was long past the point of no return.

'I suppose that was because you thought it had something to say about *my* past.'

'That never occurred to me,' he said.

In that case, you must not have known about the Hotel Astir Palace when I went on that trip to Boca Raton. You found out since. Somebody told you since. But why would someone tell you? And who would the someone be?

For quite a while, he wrote figures down on the pad in front of him. Then he put down the Parker and began to transfer them into the computer. That done, he turned to me.

'The picture you brought back from the trip?'

I nodded.

'The lad in the photograph with me is dead. He was one of my closest friends, and he dropped dead in my path in the middle of a training session. I remember him in my own way, in my own time. I do not want a picture of him wished on me to show the giver – givers – have gone to the bother of finding out about my past friendships.'

After a moment, as if it had just occurred to him, he came back to it.

'And I particularly don't want it given indirectly through my wife by someone who thinks they can get closer to my wife by poking about in my past.'

Not true, David, I thought, but could not say. Robert Allen is more innocent than that. He wouldn't think like that. In your anger at me, you do him a disservice. David gathered all his belongings up and headed for the door. Just short of it, he stopped.

'Just one more thing,' he said, and turned. 'Daisy, do not kid yourself that my amusement at your quite false reading of the realities of my life, past and present, is patronising you. You are bloody lucky that I choose to interpret your continued ignorance about me as an endearing foible. Some day, I may get tired of that interpretation.'

He left the room. When, about ten minutes later, I encountered him in the kitchen, he talked as if he had never given me that conditional ultimatum. You do that with the boys, I thought. You tick them off good and proper, but then you move on to something else without carrying the rage in your voice or your body. See? I do not have continued ignorance about you.

However straightforwardly he answered any of

my questions, I nonetheless felt excluded, during those preparation weeks. He doggedly tracked dozens of sports programmes, watching the clothes, the background, the mannerisms, the clichés but not making them a subject for discussion with me or with the boys, any more than he would have made any of his business projects a subject for such discussion. I am from the world of television, I thought resentfully. You might gain from some of my experience. Except that with a sinking feeling, I realised just how much of a difference is made by five or six years' absence from TV. The pace, the pauses, the immediacy of presentation change utterly.

Watching – silently – with him one Saturday, I was about to offer a suggestion. So near to the offering was I that his head came up in response to my audibly indrawn breath and he looked questioningly at me.

'No,' I said. 'Nothing.'

'You're not wheezy?' he asked, considering another possible reason for me to gasp.

I laughed and shook my head.

'I was just realising that I'm sitting on a diminishing asset,' I said. 'TV changes so fast, not only am I going to be forgotten – probably am forgotten already – but the skills I used to have are very soon going to be too dated to sell.'

'Nonsense,' he said briskly. 'Acting doesn't change that much. You could teach it. You could teach people how to be confident. You could teach people how to dress. There's a big feature in that thing about women making a million doing personal coaching by phone.'

'That thing' was the *Guardian*. His favourite paper.

'Lots of people would find it incongruous, a soccer player reading the *Guardian*,' I said.

He gave me a peculiar look.

'What have I said now?'

'Nothing.'

'Well, why'd you look at me as if you thought I meant something more than I did mean?'

'Dominique.'

Oh, God, I thought. Moving from Daisy to Dominique is bad enough. Dominique with an audible full stop after it means I'm in deep shit.

'A soccer player named Graeme Le Saux has been all over the papers in the past year being called queer because he confessed to being a reader of the *Guardian*. For just a moment, I thought you might know about that and be referring to it. You weren't.'

'No, I was insulting soccer players on a narrower basis. "Isn't it amazing they can read the big words."'

'Fans of the *Guardian* would say it's amazing anybody can read the big words,' he muttered. 'Because the proofing is a bit iffy.'

His attention went right back to the screen. I had wanted him to ask me to help him. I now wondered why. His judgement - that I would be of no value to this task — was probably well taken. Because my skills were all in the emotion business. In letting a camera see you think. In helping it, without words or movement, deliver a truth to the viewer that made the viewer's throat contract around tears. He would be in the content and reality business. No emotion. No exposure of his vulnerabilities, no nakedness with borrowed feelings. I stood up and he glanced at me questioningly.

I smiled, a big vague, general-purpose smile to cover a multitude of messages. No, I've nothing to offer. No, I don't need you to do anything. No, I've other things to do. And no, I don't mind that you don't need me to help you be good. You will decide to be good. You will, by observation, identify the specifications, you will do all the work on your own to meet those specifications. I'll just go fill in the time doing something useful. It will be something useful to me, because I am not minded to be a whimpering leftover.

What surprised me, the day before his first appearance, was him mentioning a flight to London.

'I thought you were doing the programme tomorrow night?'

'I am.'

'Are you sure you'll get back in time for it?'

'Back from where?'

'London.'

'The programme's being done in London.'

'Why?'

'The programme comes from London. The programme always comes from London. The programme is a British programme, made by the BBC.'

'Oh, I thought it was RTÉ.'

So it was, forty minutes before air-time, we had a brief conversation with him, me and the boys. He told Stephen how to make sure the TV was on the right station and how to get the videotape to record it so he, David, could look at it later. When all the instructions had been absorbed, I got on the line to say a quick goodbye.

'Are you nervous?'

'Yes.'

'Don't be. You'll be good.'

He turned out to be better than good.

I watched him that first night, sick and dry-mouthed as the introductions were made, viciously silencing Gavin's questions. He came onscreen with such understated authority that the cameras went closer to him, lingered longer on him. Even when not speaking, he exuded a presence, a promise, a secret indication to the viewer that the next truly interesting thing said on the programme would undoubtedly come from him.

'Is he being good?' Stephen asked worriedly.

I nodded. Then nodded more vigorously, because I could not speak. Like an old impresario leaning forward to demand a rerun of a camera test, I had no doubts that what I was seeing was more than the old chestnut of a star being born. I was seeing a new era in sports broadcasting being born.

When the phone rang a couple of minutes after the end of the programme, I told Gavin it probably wasn't his dad, because he would have all sorts of things to do before he could ring us.

'Is so Dad,' Gavin told me triumphantly.

He and Stephen enthused, then agreed that they were way past their bedtime and would go quietly. Stephen handed the phone over.

'You were superb,' I said.

'It went fine,' he acknowledged.

'I'm not talking about "it". You, personally, on your own, were superb.'

'Oh,' he said, sounding surprised. 'I thought I was OK.'

Someone talked to him and he promised to join them for the post-mortem, then came back to me.

'Anything I need for the post-mortem?'

'No. No. You don't want to be telling them a list of things you did superbly.'

He laughed softly, then told me he'd see me the next day, and rang off. I sat there, puzzled by the small pause before the goodbyes and by the idea that I had failed him in some way. The phone rang again and I had it lifted, hoping it was him, before the first ring was finished.

'God, that was quick,' Robert Allen said.

I laughed and explained I had just put it down after talking to David in London.

'Oh, I thought I'd get you before he did,' Robert said deflatedly. 'I wanted you to tell him how fantastic he was. Helen and I just couldn't get over it. Talk about hitting the ground running.'

'I'll tell him.'

'You must have been pleased, yourself?'

'I thought he was breathtakingly good.'

'Yeah,' Robert said, pleased to be in such total agreement.

'Robert?'

'Yeah?'

'While I have you — c'n I ask you something?'

'Like?'

'Like, d'you remember the temp you had working for you the time we went to Greece?'

There was a long silence.

'Ribena-head? Yeah.'

'Ribena-head?'

'Had her hair dyed maroon colour. She had lipstick and fingernail stuff — enamel? polish? varnish? — to match.'

'She booked your flight, right?'

'Jesus, Daisy, do we have to?'

'I'm not going to ask you anything you'd have difficulty answering even if Helen is sitting beside you. Just bear with me for a split second, OK?'

'She did.'

'Book your flight?'

'Affirmative.'

'And mine?'

'Ditto.'

'She would also have booked your hotel room?'

'I'd have no argument with that.'

'And mine.'

'Nor that. Care to expand on that point?'

'David knows.'

'Sorry, I think I misheard you.'

'David told me a few days ago he knows we were, the two of us, in room 137 in the Hotel Astir Palace, Athens, and he has the date right, too.'

'Holy shit.'

'Yup.'

'But how?'

'You tell me. Nobody in my life knows.'

'Nor mine.'

'The only one outside the two of us who'd know the room and everything would be Ribena-head. Is she still with you?'

'If she was with us three weeks, that's as long as it was. I got uncomfortable with her because she was always asking me questions about you. Said she was your greatest fan.'

'What was her name?'

'Don't remember. Could find out from HR. Something like Pearl.'

'Would you, please?'

'Would I what?'

'Would you find out from Human Resources what—'

'I know. It wasn't Pearl. It was Shell.'

'Shell?'

'Yeah. Shell. It was short for some longer name she didn't like. Michelle?'

'Richelle.'

'That's the one. Yeah, that's it. Definitely.'

'Great. Look, don't worry about it. David's not going to do anything.'

There was a silence so long I was just about to do a check to see that he was still on the line, when his voice came again.

'David Carpenter goes up in my estimation even further. To do a job like he did tonight with that on his mind, fair dues to him. Listen, I'll ring you. Goodnight.'

I checked on the two boys, then went back to the room where the TV was still on. About to unplug it, I remembered the VCR. Usually Stephen worked it, but after a little trial and error (facilitated by leaving the phone on the answering machine so I would not be disturbed) I got the tape back to the start and watched it again. Talking to him.

OK, first thing is that you're better-looking on TV than – no, not better-looking than reality. Maybe TV just makes me look at you again. Like the time my father shaved off his moustache, having worn it from the time he met my mother, and she never noticed until *her* mother met the two of them and let a scream of surprise out of her. Maybe I am so used to the way you look that framing you on a small screen makes me see you afresh. Or maybe looks were never an issue. We had a relationship before I noticed whether or not you were good-looking.

You are very handsome. You have great hair and plenty of it. Deep dark eyes so toffee brandy brown they could be black, hooded so they have to put a pup light on you, from the floor. The papers won't say you are like someone, because you will never remind any viewer of another commentator or player. They will say *other* people are like *you*.

In your playing days, you were sinewy like a runner. A lesser level of activity has softened the outline of you, but you are a big, fit man who moves like a dancer. Even sitting down, that fluidity of movement is there, that ease of intervention signalled by a sorting shift in your chair. You said to someone once, not to me, that men who have played sports intensively when they were young are better communicators, more confident public speakers and better movers than non-athletes. I heard you and meant to ask you more.

The tape played on. His every input was confident.

He matched the mood of the programme – no, I realised, he instinctively matched the mood of where the programme was going to be. So when the others would be engaged in a bit of banter, perhaps even a bit of banter initiated by him, he would be the one to cut through the humour to the next serious point.

Once or twice I pressed the pause button in a sly secret subversion; let's catch you in an unfortunate freeze-frame. But there were none. At the end, I ran it back and was about to look at it again, stunned by the impact of him.

The room was dark now, darker still when I used the remote to turn off the VCR. Sitting on my own in the darkness, it was clear to me what distinguished him from all the others on that programme and on so many other programmes. He was unneedy. He didn't need popularity. He didn't need audience approval. He didn't need comradeship with the other presenters. He didn't need a particular chunk of airtime. He didn't need to be likeable.

He was self-defined. Once he met his own standards, there was nothing else for him to seek, and so onscreen, he was completely present, completely at ease, at play. One minute he would showcase another panellist's ideas, another he would rescue a presenter who had missed a cue. But he didn't do any of it for approval.

I watched that tape again and again, that night and later. Once, freezing a shot, I noticed something that pushed me to go to the desk drawer where he kept the stopwatch. I went through the footage until I had the confirmation; except when he was talking, being called to talk, or making the moves that would create the space in which he could talk, he was still. Absolutely still. A couple of the reaction shots showed the instinct of the director. The camera would catch him in midshot. Hands as relaxed as in sleep. No twitching, no fidgeting, none of the fast blinks that say, 'I wish you'd finish what you're on about, I want to get my bit in.' Yet, two seconds into the shot, this subtle expression on the face that made a comment as understandable as a verbalised announcement. In one of the reaction shots, the comment was amused agreement. In another, courteous scepticism.

I was wrong, I thought. It's the same skill he has that I had. He is not unaware of the cameras, but he is not playing to the cameras. He is just being and the cameras know that and pick it up. I will not tell him this, I thought, going slowly up to bed, and I do not know why I will not tell him. Because I do not know the reason.

All I know is that a seeping sense of dread has come back into my life. That sense of dread has been missing for a while. I am moved by the genius you have for television and rocked by how little I know you. The terror is that in playing with Robert Allen's life to find out who I was, I may have created something that will steal you from me before I cease to learn you.

Within weeks, every conversation with everybody I met started with what a find David was for the TV station. Stephen's bedroom wall was soon covered with profiles of him, decorated with old photographs of him in action, including one where, tackling a man at speed, he had managed to drive the two of them into a pack of photographers on the back line of the football pitch, smashing cameras, spectacles, two fingers (not his own) and a set of false teeth (also not his own).

'He is such a lovely unaffected man,' women began to tell me. 'Always mentions you and the boys in interviews.'

The third time someone said something like that to me, I mentioned it to him.

'It irritates me,' I confessed. 'I have this urge to say "for Jaysus' sake, who do you want him to mention, Yassir Arafat?" I find it annoying, the way people assume someone would have married you without appreciating you.'

He made a neutral noise. The odd contradiction was that there was nothing neutral about him when he was on TV. On the box, it was as if he was lit from within. The camera tended to go to him, even when he wasn't speaking, more often than it went to anyone else. Even in silence, he was alive under his skin, watching the other talkers with an air of latent threat. Once or twice, when an aggressive journalist attacked him personally, he came through with a cut so fast and surgical the deep wound closed up before it was registered. Football, talked about by him, became as intricate and strategic as a ballet or a battle, peopled with flawed geniuses.

'You make it sound very interesting,' I said, meaning it as a compliment.

'It *is* interesting,' he said crisply, and took the boys from Stephen's class off to meet the newly selected Irish team.

Stephen had a black eye, earned when he discovered one of the more mercenary of his peers was planning to flog the autographs from the team and had beaten out of him a promise that any autographs he got he would keep until he was seventy. Stephen muttered to me that if he ever again found the classmate trying to make money by selling autographs of David Carpenter, he personally would make bloody sure the classmate didn't live to be seventy. Or even seven.

CHAPTER TWENTY

A Voice from the Past

———◆———

'Mrs Carpenter?'

'Yes.'

'Myfanwy Sterling here. I'm production assistant—'

'Oh, I know, on David's programme. He's talked
about you. I gather you could give tutorials in quiet
efficiency.'

'Ooh, I'll slip him a few quid for that one. I was
just asked to let you know we got the filming done
ahead of schedule, he'll get the earlier flight. They
just thought you'd like to know.'

'How kind of you.'

The boys were delighted. This way, they could
lark about in their pyjamas a little after their official

bedtime, whereas when he caught the last flight, they would be fast asleep by the time he arrived.

'You can surprise him,' I said, when we heard his car pulling in. 'Go into the sitting room and be very quiet until he is sure you're gone to sleep, then pile in on top of him.'

Snuffling and snorting with the excitement of it, they went off to hide. When they flung themselves on him, he was adequately taken aback and delighted, played with them for a while, then sent them off to bed. His face, when he came back to me, was unexpectedly serious.

'How was that little lot set up?'

'Sorry?'

'How'd you know. I was going to be early?'

'The production assistant rang to tell me.'

'Who?'

'Myfanwy.'

'Myfanwy?'

'Yes.'

'You sure?'

'How the hell could I be sure? I've never talked to Myfanwy before. She sounded like she would be Welsh, though. What's wrong with her ringing me, anyway?'

'Dominique, any information I want you or the boys to have, I will communicate to you.'

'You didn't ask her to?'

He looked at me in irritated astonishment. How could I ask a question so dumb?

'She said you did.'

He now looked as if he thought I was making things up.

'No, now that I think about it, she didn't say you'd asked her. She said someone had asked her to make the call. They . . .'

Maybe, I thought, he was planning a surprise early arrival and she had accidentally spoiled it on him.

'What harm did it do?'

'None.'

'They'll get used to you. They probably thought they were doing you a favour. They'll learn.'

'They will.'

Two days later, his arrival home was even less joyful. Stephen and I were in the kitchen when the car pulled in. David hardly greeted me as he arrived.

'Stephen, why is your teacher stammering and blithering instead of talking to me the way he usually does when I meet him?' he asked.

Stephen got very red. Gavin was suddenly between us, in full voice. Certainly meant for showbusiness, Gavin was possessed of twin convictions. One was that any group of people trapped in any area he could dominate became, *ipso facto*, an audience. The other was that as an audience, they would be delighted with his presence. David silenced him with a glance.

'Stephen?'

'He was asking me questions about you and you being on the telly with that other man.'

'And?'

'I just didn't think it was really his business.'

'And?'

'I sort of . . . I made like it was upsetting right now to be asked questions about my parents.'

'Your parents?' I asked, startled.

Stephen shrugged as if that was the end of the story. David was relentless.

'What happened then?'

'He immediately thought I was like Lawrence.'

'What's wrong with Lawrence?'

Stephen began to squirm.

'His father has a second relationship.'

Our silence unnerved him.

'I didn't actually tell him you and Dad were having a second relationship.'

David looked at him so grimly, it kick-started Stephen into more speech.

'Lawrence has been weird. He hit Mikey Laker so hard—'

'Unacceptable, Stephen. Unacceptable. You don't tell lies and you don't put people in the position where they tell themselves lies. You certainly don't sell Dominique and me down the river to get a gossipy teacher off your back.'

Stephen stood transfixed by the distant unemotional condemnation. Gavin, confused, slid his hand into David's and the two of them disappeared upstairs. After a long time, I went over to Stephen and put my hand on his shoulder. He tolerated it. We could hear the other two coming downstairs, Gavin now in conversational overdrive. When they came back into the kitchen, David never glanced at the two of us, just started to pull food out of cupboards. I began to help.

'You want a week in Paris?' he asked.

'What? When? Why?'

'Big match in Parc des Princes two weeks from now, and someone in French TV discovered I've respectable French. Offering me indecent sums of money to go over and do a commentary. Well, not a commentary. Inputs, whenever called for, on the Brits. You on?'

A wave of nostalgia for Paris swept over me. But what about the boys, I thought. Of course, I could have them minded.

'Don't worry about it,' David said, interrupting my

thought process. 'I'll be too busy to notice, anyway. You'll probably achieve more while I'm away. I'll bring you back something from Prisunic.'

He was taking the stairs three at a time before I had absorbed that the invitation had been withdrawn as quickly as offered. Why on earth, I wondered, had he been so eager not to have me join him? Although in practical terms it made everything simpler for me to stay in Ireland, there was a part of me that wanted to up stakes and go, to walk with him in Place de la Concorde, to sit with him in cafés beside the Seine, to listen to his French cranking up from memory to fluency as he used it.

For Stephen to use the device of a failed step-parental relationship bothered me even more, although it was not until I was on the verge of sleep that night that the reason became clear to me. It had the ring of aversion therapy. We will give you a little taste of what you are afraid of, and then when the real thing comes along, you will be half-used to it. I did not like the idea of Stephen giving himself advance inoculation against the possibility of David and myself failing as a couple.

I lay on my back, looking at the darkening ceiling. There had been a time when David and I, unplanned, turned in tandem in the bed at night, fitting like spoons to each other, instinctively reaching for each other's warmth. Now, we lay companionably but distantly, almost apologising if bodies went bump in the night. It had been months since he made love to me. There was no grief in it, no fury of resentment at the loss of a great love. If there was a loss, it was the loss of a hoped-for half-dream. A half-dream of a great love burning like a brand its ownership on me and mine, a passionate possessiveness, an unspoken understanding so instinctive it distanced an unimportant world. A race memory of bodies so attuned a glance would induce animal abandon, a hand gently placed become a primeval imperative. There is something infinitely sad, I thought, about nostalgia for what never was, about wishfully seeking to recreate what never existed.

I looked at him, shadowed and sinister in the semi-darkness. When I married you, I thought, you were a refuge, a minder, a solution to the problem of two little boys orphaned. I never pretended to more than the love of a friend and I never realised how dependent I would become, not on your love, but on your friendship.

There is distance now between us, there are glances; quick decisions I cannot understand. I need to talk with you as I have always talked with you, so that confusion settles like the snow in a waterglobe. But I cannot talk to you as my best friend when the talking would be about the sudden withdrawals you have visited upon me through fast-finished sentences, curtailed opportunities, dropped glances. You talk to your best friend about a lover, a partner, even a husband, but when the best friend is your husband, and your husband is on the run from you while ever-present in your shared lives, then you are without confidant.

A journalist from the *Independent* had rung me a couple of weeks earlier, wanting a quote on foot of new research, just released, which indicated that the magical, chemical 'in love' aspect of a relationship lasts at most fifteen months. After that, she explained, the researchers had proven the body chemistry was different, so you could not expect that lift in the heart when you saw your beloved. What did I think about that? I laughed and, as always, taking refuge in the truth, was saddened to learn it.

'I've obviously got something wrong with my chemical works,' I told her. 'Because if I turn on the TV and there's a promo for David's programme, I'm stuck to the floor by watching him. When I come off a plane and – you know that moment when you scan the crowd to see if someone has met you? I do that and then spot him, and I have this idiotic adolescent urge to run to him. I get this naked smile on my face and I can't wait to be tucked in under his arm and push the luggage trolley the awkward way you do as a twosome, you know? There's no book I read, no song I hear and like without wanting him to read the book or hear the CD.'

She laughed, did the journalist, and said I was lucky. How long was I married now? I had well passed that time the scientists had divined. I apologised for screwing up her story and she told me it was nice to hear someone who was so obviously in love.

David sighed deeply in his sleep. Me too, I thought. Me, too. What was that song? It's the wrong time. And the wrong place.

One of the cats, the white one, Other Thing, came padding into the bedroom and leaped onto our bed as if he owned it, stalking across both of us before settling alongside David and giving his characteristic squeaky miaow. David's hand rose instinctively, half-cupped, finding the cat fur and stroking slowly, from forehead to tail. When his hand dropped, the cat would shove its head under the hand and almost butt it back into action, the purr becoming continuous.

It was now so dark that only Other Thing's white

fur made a lighter than black shape on the bed. David was breathing gently, the cat's purr softening as sleep took it over. There is something so grimly appropriate, I thought, in all those old-wives phrases they used to use. You have made your bed, now you lie on it. Here I lie. Bed made. Like a thirty-ish Alice, doors to right and left of me getting smaller and smaller and smaller.

I had once thought I could keep Gabrielle alive if no night passed without my dreaming of her, no day passed without my thinking of her. Gabrielle, I thought, maybe it applies to me, too. Maybe the two boys in the next rooms are already old enough to be facing a life that fills not only their every waking moment, but their sleeping moments, too, so that I have become a small familiar thing in their lives. A small familiar receding thing of diminishing value, like a hit song from a year ago. Like the sunscreen song, its advice consciously clichéd as a mother's litany, yet sweetly reminiscent of some ideal, some functional childhood none of us ever had.

This is the proper role of mothers, I thought. To move from crucial to essential to necessary to useful. The proper function of wives? To move, perhaps, from passion to comfort to companionship. I can play the part, but not quite yet. Not now.

I do not, I thought sleepily, I do not yet know my lines.

'You didn't even know the lines.'

I struggled up in the bed so suddenly that the cat yowled and leaped defensively away. Now I knew who the new production assistant on David's programme was. The surname was different. She must have married someone in the meantime. But Richelle was the name of the dark, dark girl who had hated me so much for getting the part she wanted, who had loathed me even more when I had said my character, as delineated in the soap opera, could not credibly be revealed to have a secret half-sister.

I shrank back down into the warmth of the bed. Strange, I thought, wakefully, that there is so little pleasure in saying 'I told you so' to oneself. I told you there was a reason for the heavy dread you have been feeling. It now has a name.

Richelle.

CHAPTER TWENTY-ONE

Lift-Off

<hr />

'You're the only woman I ever got lent to,' the voice said. 'You may not remember. I was working for—'

'You rescued me the day of the funeral,' I said. 'Rita, isn't it?'

'You're fast, I have to hand it to you,' she said. 'Although your husband-to-be didn't call it rescuing. Anyway, can I drop out to you — I want to put a proposition to you?'

She arrived within the hour, looking much as she had looked when her boss, the director of the soap opera, had lent her to me to see me through the two days after what Stephen until recently had continued to call 'the Clamity'.

'What did you mean by the crack about my husband-to-be?' I asked, pouring coffee.

She was looking around the house, nodding recognition. It hadn't changed that much since the day of the funeral, partly because I was almost superstitiously unwilling to remove anything Gabrielle had chosen.

'Well, I arrive out here, get you out to the church, allow in half the neighbourhood with food for a wake you've sworn to me is not gonna happen, get Gavin and Stephen to sleep – howya, Gavin, I'd know you anywhere – put on some of the food to heat just in case some of the wankers come back in spite of the house private notices, cope with a few dozen of them, each one of them saying they've some special relationship with you or your sister and want to leave a message or whatever, hear Stephen yelling the place down for his mother or his aunt, ask one of the neighbours to look after the front door while I cope with Stephen, arrive back down to see this bloke who looks vaguely familiar but no more than vaguely steering you up the stairs, follow you when I hear Gavin giving tongue, find this bloke undressing you for bed, go back downstairs because he seems to be pretty practised at it, get barracked by half the neighbourhood who want to know who this total stranger is and by the other half who say he's the famous footballer David Carpenter but what's he doing upstairs with Dominique because he's never been in the house before they're certain sure. I am trying to cope with all of this when he comes down, works out that I am in some way loco parentis, tells me to go into the kitchen, throws the rest of them out, comes back and gives me a chewing out for letting them in and says I'm to be there no later than eight the following morning. I'll tell you, having survived that, I went back to the day job with some relief.'

'I knew David got ratty at all the mourners in the house, but it never struck me he blamed you for them.'

'Now, let me make it clear, he does a good chewing out. Never raises the voice. No swearing. It's only afterwards, when you wonder what you keep tripping over, you realise it's long strips of your own skin that he peeled off.'

During all of this, she had lifted Gavin onto her lap, charmed him to death by inviting him to investigate her pendant, which looked like a small bottle, largely because it was a small bottle filled with detergent. The little bottle had its own screw cap, which came with a tiny wand for blowing bubbles through. Gavin had bubbles everywhere and the two cats thought these new toys were wonderful.

'You just must have kids, Rita,' I laughed. 'You're an old hand at this.'

She raised one hand, splayed.

'Five?'

'Why does everybody look so scandalised when I say how many kids I have? Is there a law somewhere that says you don't exceed a decent three?'

Gavin had got some of the soap into his mouth and didn't think much of the taste of it, so I gave him a chocolate biscuit and permission to see a TV programme.

'My five kids are behind my proposition to you,' Rita said when I got back. 'I don't want an eighty-hour-a-week job like I've had on the soap. I've researched this new software and bought the franchise for this territory for it.'

The software would allow any customer with access to the Internet to e-mail Rita digital photographs of themselves. She would then analyse their appearance and develop a complete grooming, make-up and ward-robe plan for them, e-mailing it back to them with the new make-up, hairdo and clothes electronically positioned over their own photographs so, without committing themselves to anything, they could get a very good concept of what a new look might mean for them.

'That all sounds wonderful,' I said, when she had finished showing me the business plan. 'What's it to do with me?'

From the time the software was first piloted, she explained, it had emerged that while as much as 60 per cent of the market was made up of people who loved the convenience and fun of seeing an electronic makeover of themselves, roughly 40 per cent was made up of people suffering from social anxiety of one kind or another. Some were painfully shy. Some had physical defects which robbed them of confidence. Some were obsessed by some particular feature which, they were convinced, turned them into figures of fun. This group's problems were not solved by buying a software make-over package. They needed coaching in social and self-presentation skills.

'I can do that. Gissa job,' I said.

'That's why I'm here.'

We kicked it around a little more, agreed a day for me to do a viewing of the software's capabilities, and I said I would talk to David about the best corporate structure for the venture. The major investment would be time. Virtually no capital would be at risk.

'Your fella's doing OK for himself,' Rita said, preparing to leave. 'Is he full-time in TV now?'

'No, nor ever likely to be, if he can avoid it,' I said.

'If he could do TV with a mask on, so nobody would know him out of the studio, he'd do it. No need to be admired. Tolerates fans, but that's about it.'

Did I remember, she asked, the actor on the soap who couldn't *even* tolerate his fans? The one who was always so desperately, wittily cruel to people who recognised him and asked for autographs? Stung by the reference to the young actor I always tried to forget, I nodded, silently. Conor was drying out for the third time this year, she said. Frantic to change the subject, I asked her about Richelle Governey. She looked blank.

'The name rings no bells,' she said and we let it drop.

However, in the middle of the software demonstration a few days later, the name recurred.

'You remember your pal Richelle?'

'Pal is overstating it a bit,' I said mildly. 'But yes?'

'I looked up the files and talked around the office a bit.'

'When do you actually leave the programme?'

'Two weeks from now. One of the guys says she belongs in the Fornicator's Follies.'

The 'Fornicator's Follies' was the collective term covertly given to the fast-changing sequence of girl-friends of the series producer who followed Call-me-

Chip. Chip's successor was better known for his sexual than his TV output.

'They also said she was walking wounded before he ever got to her. Had a father that made Frederick West look like Father of the Year. His daughter was gonna be a star and earn him big bucks right now or he was gonna beat the shit out of her, and maybe he'd beat the shit out of her anyway, just to keep his hand in. She doesn't seem to have made it. She's not even an Equity member any more.'

'No,' I said, adding mischievously, 'In fact, she's doing your job or something like it on my husband's programme in London.'

'There you go,' Rita said easily. 'Walking wounded probably make great PAs. As long as she doesn't have five kids.'

David arrived shortly afterwards, as did Rita's lawyer, and the partnership was quickly and cleanly set up. The 60 per cent of the market which needed only the electronic makeover would be dealt with by Rita. Anybody needing any kind of coaching would be referred 'to our associate company, The Skywriter'. I would then take over and meet the client either in a hotel or in my own home, provide them with whatever they needed, and bill directly. If a client came to me directly who I thought would benefit from a new look,

I could refer them to Rita's company in exactly the same way.

'Hey, I believe you've got a reject from your wife's soap working for you,' Rita said to David as she prepared to leave. 'Richelle Governey.'

He stopped so still it unnerved even Rita, who sent me a 'Was I not supposed to know?' look. I shook my head, indicating it had not been a secret.

'My wife's greatest fan,' he said carefully. 'Chelle Brueck. Spent her childhood watching my wife develop her wonderful, her unique talents. Learned everything she needed to know about life from my wife.'

I didn't know whether he was mocking me or seriously reporting what the refreshed, renamed Richelle was saying to him, and I wasn't sure which was worst. My distress obviously showed, because he relented.

'Forget it, Daisy,' David said. 'She didn't survive her trial period.'

'See,' Rita said to me. 'Didn't have five kids. What can I tell ya?'

'Didn't have any kids that I know of,' David said easily, and I knew the topic was being tied up, closed off, sealed and shelved. 'Very intense young woman with the most improbably purple hair I've ever seen. Wasn't working directly for me. But she'll have no problems getting another job. No problems.'

We both looked at him with unconcealed curiosity, which he chose neither to see nor to meet. Rita gave me a heavy wink. You've got a right one 'ere, went the wink. Cor blimey, ain't 'e discreet, though, Guv?

I thought he might refer to it later, when the two of us were alone, but he didn't. So I cleared out the spare room we had picked as my consulting room, and chose furniture out of a catalogue.

Within weeks, word-of-mouth had Rita and me busier than we could ever have imagined we would be. Her side of the business had her working longer hours than when she was on the TV crew, and my side, The Skywriter, boomed more than I wanted it to, that winter. Someone, somewhere, seemed to have made a decision that appearance came before reality, shadow before substance. It didn't matter how talented, committed or expert you were, if you didn't look impressive, your career path had speed bumps all over it.

So I had a succession of brilliant surly fat girls in my sitting-room, purple with self-hatred and resenting every inch of me. Sent by their mothers. Or their bosses. Or, occasionally, their fathers. I had a notion that there was a Masonic league of parents out there, exchanging secret handshakes, exchanging my business card and giving their daughters a birthday present of a makeover with The Skywriter.

They came up the red-bricked front garden, these girls, swinging their handbags to an internal song of desperation, most of them garbed in draped knit black like Muslims or ancient Spanish widows, their eyes bright in the encroaching padding of their boneless faces, kohl-circled because someone had told them their eyes were their best feature: Many of them had lovely hands, lovingly tended, plump, pale, unwilling investments in an unwrinkled, un-liver-spotted future: these girls would never sunbathe.

Whenever I could, I met them when Gavin had come home from school. Constant interruptions by a demanding, highly verbal youngster seemed to make it easier for them to relax with me. If he wasn't around, I would make sure to be noticeably maladroit. Oh, God, I would say, you wanted coffee and I've made tea. What kind of fool am I? Or I would spill something. Or find no biscuits in the tin and worry aloud if Gavin had fed them to Thing or Other Thing.

I would dress for the occasion, too, in something with a bleach stain or in a jumper covered in unshaven fabric pills. Then feed them an implicit comparison.

'Very daunting for a midget, to see someone so strikingly tall coming up one's path,' I would say.

I learned never to try a direct compliment, knowing they bat a direct compliment away and run from it, lest they be seen as fooling themselves: lest they miss their chance to get first to the jeer about their weight. No fool I, they almost say, as they rush to judgement, hurry to hear themselves make the jokey reference or include the mention of weight on the way to some other topic.

They're all suckers, though, for an indirect compliment. Lay it down in no-man's-land, and they're over the barricades and running to grab it before someone else does.

'Crucial to wear crisp cuffs with such pretty, expressive hands,' I would say.

See? went the sub-plot. I didn't compliment you on your pretty hands. For heaven's sake, you have so much going for you, I hardly noticed them. Just a casual reference. They could have belonged to anyone.

They would try to talk about me. The Masonic ring of fat girls' mothers probably, I figured, hand around a card with that advice on it: 'If you're fat, you have to be a good listener and make people talk about themselves.' Plus a card saying, 'If you're fat, never eat in front of anyone else.' And one reading, 'Be everybody's best friend. Be there for them.'

Every now and then, I'd meet a girl who had failed to get the last card, or if it had been delivered, she had rejected it. Instead, she stayed home and read books. The best-read females in the business, fat girls are. You don't have to diet or dress up to join people in books. One enormous twenty-two-year-old told me she had the perfect life for someone weighing 190 pounds. She worked in a call centre, where her soft-voiced helpfulness and speed on the computer made her the most successful operative, and lived alone in a book-lined apartment. Her problem was that her success on the phone was prompting her employer to use her to train other operatives, and he felt her appearance would rob her of credibility.

'Do you want to train people?' I asked her.

'No. It's a promotion, though. I get a title.'

'Corporal, rather than Private?'

'Something like that.'

'More money?'

'Probably less money. I can always pull an extra shift where I am, and get whatever extra money I want.'

'So what's in it for you?'

She was so fat that even in quite a high-necked blouse, cleavage showed.

'You can't refuse to make progress,' she said.

I showed her the methods to give her fatness a

businesslike acceptability, and she went away happy. They all did.

'That's the effing problem with this business,' I said to David in February, when he was going through the books for me. 'In order to be trusted by them, I have to invest such an amount of time making myself no threat to them. You can almost see them going through a list. First, I'm not as stuck up as they expect a TV has been to be. Second, I'm a messer and my house isn't that clean or sophisticated. Third, I have a kid that gives me lip. Fourth – I forget what fourth is.'

'You let them know you know what it's like to be fat.'

'You mean I act?'

He put his Parker carefully parallel to the line on which he was working, to free himself to look over at me.

'I thought that's what you were, an actor?'

'Yes, but acting isn't telling lies, acting is – is getting into the skin of a truth and making everybody see it – feel it.'

His brow wrinkled, then he picked up the pen and went back to the figures. He did that frequently. It was not quite questioning what I had said, as making *me* question what I had said.

'Half the time, I don't know what I think until you force me to work it out,' I said.

'Most of the time,' he responded.

'Jesus, you really fancy yourself, don't you?'

He looked surprised. 'No,' he said, after a moment's thought.

'I do a good job making – helping – people to get other people to take them seriously.'

'Very true.'

'I just wish they'd frig off afterwards.'

'You're like a Chinese rescuing someone from drowning. They own them from then on.'

'In order to get to where they can let down their guard and trust me, I have to reveal so much of myself and my own vulnerabilities that they end up not just trusting me, but feeling close to me.'

'Women and men alike?'

'No, much more women.'

'All you have to do with men is flirt with them.'

What flummoxed me most about that one was that it was said in the detached observational way you'd use to give street directions. He slid the accounts back into their folder and handed them over.

'You're doing well. You should consider codifying what you do so that you could employ other people, maybe have a separate premises.'

'It was Richelle Governey – Chelle Brueck – who gave you the information about Robert Allen and me at the Astir Palace.'

He refused to be drawn. I blundered on.

'I'm amazed you listened to her. So amazed, I presume she showed you ticket counterfoils and everything. Anything, to do damage to me.'

'Damage?'

'In your eyes.'

'No damage.'

'Then why did you throw it at me?'

'I didn't. You asked me why I picked Robert Allen's name as someone you might have an affair with. Association of ideas, no more than that.'

'She's not my greatest fan or she wouldn't have shown you stuff like that.'

'What's it matter? She's gone. *Finito*.'

I did not believe this. Ireland is a very small country, and so for someone I know to turn up working for Robert Allen would not be a great surprise. But for that same somebody to turn up in London, working close to David Carpenter, could not be a coincidence. The enmity that possessed her as a kid, that was exacerbated by Gabrielle's removal of her from the regular team, inflamed by a series of failures, during her teens, to match me in fame, was still there, except now it was in sharper focus than ever, leaving me daily heavy-bellied dread to be dragged about.

David was standing with a bored, have-we-finished air to him.

'Well, at least she can't think I had anything to do with her not keeping the job in London,' I said wearily.

For a moment, it looked as if he was going to disagree with me, but he had second thoughts and said nothing.

CHAPTER TWENTY-TWO

A Pocketful of Misery

––––––>●<––––––

If it could have happened in a new or different way, it might have been easier to bear. It was the formulaic nature of it that made it unbearable. Picture this: wife decides to have husband's suits cleaned so that he can be sure of a wardrobe of freshly pressed choices. In tidying out the pockets of the suits – ah, yes. Two small pages, folded. Victorian cursive handwriting. So easy to read. So easy to read that a phrase selected itself for presentation, much as TV programmes showing documents highlight relevant lines and darken the rest.

'I will never tell our son why I named him David, so you need not fear that he will make contact with you in the future.'

You must not read this, I thought, as I read it. You must not play into a soap-opera script. Of course, if you do read it, you will laugh when you discover how innocent it is. Victoria was the sender's name. Somewhere in Berkshire the address. End-of-the-affair the tone.

This would be the only such letter she would ever write, she promised. In the future, if they met, there would be no references to this past year, to the happiness he had given her. As he wanted, they would be simply acquaintances, no more. But it was important to put on record how much she owed him, how lucky she was to have met him. How there would be so many occasions in the future when she would look at their growing son and be reminded of the older David. Other people who had known him as a sports figure or who now learned of him as a TV pundit might find him attractive because of his looks or his cool presence or his wit, but she had been lucky to experience a David Carpenter who was much more than attractive. Who could change someone's life with his generosity, his understanding.

I sat at the end of the bed, reading and rereading the letter long after I had committed every word of it to memory. There was no date on it, so I could not work out what age their son, their David, would now be. There were no references to his stepchildren, no references to me. It was a letter of quiet dignity. I hated the writer more because I liked her so much. Eventually, I put it, folded, in among the MasterCard slips, the Post-It notes, the plastic hotel card-keys accidentally brought home in his pockets, closed the wardrobe and took the suits to the cleaners. Yes, I told the squat little girl in the cleaners, I had cleaned out the pockets. Great, she said, thumping the cash register, her eyes at its level, looking as if she had been meant to be five foot six or seven but that a heavy weight had brought her down to less than five feet and given her a spraddle-legged waddle. Tuesday OK? Tuesday fine. I curled the long row of yellow tickets around my fingers as I walked back to the car. The ten o'clock Mass-goers, the little old ladies with the black hats and the widowers with the courtliness and the walking sticks, were clustered here and there on the footpaths, talking of slips of this and the possibility of titrox moth on the roses.

Throughout the day, there were moments when I would stand, transfixed by the need to locate and name the pain. It was not that I had forgotten it. But the name of it, the knowledge of it, would slide away, so I would stand there, dragged almost to my knees by the period-cramp tumescent hot ache of it, knowing it to be awful before remembering why. All my life I had worried about being at a distance from reality, reaching for a role half-remembered, easily played. Offering antithesis to every thesis. How little comfort there now was in absolute synthesis. The inescapable truth finds me without a line.

'Pathetic, isn't it?' I said to Thing, who followed me into the house on my return. 'It's not as if this situation was unprecedented. It's old hat. Any fool could handle it.'

The cat padded ahead of me through the house. In Stephen's room, I found myself, bundled clothing bulking out my arms, reading, one after another, the framed, glassed-in features about his hero, finally staring at the laughing face in the picture given by Robert Allen's people. The other footballer was laughing towards the camera, an instinct to serve his public showing. David Carpenter was just laughing. Disengaged. Powerful as only those without need are powerful. Arrogant?

'No, arrogance requires an object,' I told the cat. 'Arrogance requires a victim. Someone to be impressed. To be put down. He has never needed that.'

The cat looked at me expressionlessly, then rolled over, inviting my hand. I tickled and scratched it until its purr could have belonged to a small motorbike. A habit learned from David. Until I had seen him with the cats, I had believed felines should be stroked softly, sensuous gliding along the glossy surface of the coat. But then, my every day was now filled with unacknowledged imitations of him, with application of his attitudes to issues – what would David think of this – without direct reference to him.

The need to discover a vicious element to those behaviours yielded little more than wonder that I felt such need. The man chose to give the boys and me an aspect of himself at a time when it was needed. Without pretence. I had taken what I needed and shared with him what I perceived he needed at the time. Without pretence. So if nothing had died, for what was I grieving? For my self-esteem, perhaps. For the fact that I could work up no hatred. For my wonder at why he had lied to me about his fertility. For the fact that a boy in Berkshire named David had, all unknowing, set in train a sequence of sad inevitabilities.

Stephen and Gavin had a hold on David that would never weaken. But why use a word like 'hold'? This was a decent, other-directed man, not amenable to moral blackmail. He had become their father out of choice, and he would stay their father out of the same choice. For me, there would always be friendship. The friendship the reporters constantly commented upon. 'Daisy my best friend, says Carpenter,' a tabloid had reported, quoting an unnamed close contact of his. Since I had led the charge when it came to refusing to falsify what we have by prating about love, it must betoken some recessive gene in me that I now experienced reflex resentment at the absence of such prating.

The mother of the younger David, according to her own letter, was signing off on a relationship with gratitude and without bitterness. So he did not have plans to have an overseas relationship. Surprising, I thought, that he could become so attached to two boys not related to him by blood, yet not seek visitation rights to this younger child. Essentially, though, if I put the folded letter back in the pocket whence it came as soon as the suit returned from the cleaners, there was nothing to fear. No discrete threat.

'We're not talking collapsing bridge, here,' I said to the cats, curled sleepy on the hardwood floor. 'We're talking beach erosion. Little grains of sand. It can be slowed, buttressed.'

Gavin was silent that evening after homework. The lack of prattle was unusual, but not unwelcome. He tended to be in constant transmit mode. At one point, however, preparations for the evening meal in full swing, I tossed a question over my shoulder to him and got a mumble in response.

'For Chrissake, would you speak distinctly?' I yelled.

'What would you like me to say?' David's voice asked, right behind me. I leaped the way Other Thing leaped when a crow buzzed him in the backyard.

'I didn't know you had arrived. Gavin was mumbling some bloody thing.'

'Gavin?'

'Mmmf.'

The sound was a bit like you expect from a hippo surfacing from a mud bath. I turned around. David had dropped to his hunkers in front of our younger.

'What the hell is it?'

He was asking so gently that Gavin began to cry, pointing to his mouth, which didn't seem to move.

'Oh, God,' I said. 'Bell's palsy.'

'Hmmf mmm mmna,' Gavin said. He wasn't great on the syllables, but the tone had a passionate argumentative urgency to it. I had the impression that he was disputing my diagnosis.

'What the frig is Bell's palsy?' David asked me over his head.

'Oh, never mind, I'm probably wrong. Think horses before zebras.'

Both of them stared at me with something akin to fear in their faces.

'Shmmrm?'

'Zebras?'

'It's a thing they teach student doctors,' I said apologetically. 'When you hear hoofbeats, think horses before zebras. In other words, go for the more obvious, simple explanation.'

'So what,' David speculated, 'what is the obvious simple explanation for Gavin being struck dumb?'

Gavin started to go purple with the effort of explaining his speechlessness. David, still on his hunkers, was looking desperately into the purple face as if the clue could be found there. I located a pencil and a bit of paper.

'Write it down,' I ordered.

Gavin began to write, then turned it around so we might read it.

'What the frig is that?' David asked, straightening up and looking at the incomprehensible squiggle.

Gavin began to bounce up and down, weeping more vehemently.

'You stop that right now, or I will deck you,' David said coldly.

He never threatened them with physical violence. Gavin snorted into submission.

'Superglue,' I offered.

Gavin nodded frantically, but David had his back turned to him.

'What do you want Superglue for?' he asked me, wearily.

'I don't. I'm just telling you that's what's wrong with Gavin. He's glued together.'

David looked at Gavin, but since Gavin was now hanging his head in shame, had to chuck him under the chin to get a good look at him.

'Try to part your lips,' he ordered.

Gavin whimpered.

'Do it.'

Gavin strained, and his mouth pulled pointlessly at itself. He looked from one to the other of us in frank terror.

'Keep breathing, Gavin,' I advised. 'You can panic later.'

However he had managed it, Gavin's fingers were glued together and stuck to the thumbs on each hand. Stephen, arriving from training with friends, brought this to our attention.

'Stephen, ring the GP and ask him what we do in this situation,' David said.

Stephen disappeared. I applied ice to the child's mouth, on the basis that ice hardens chewing gum and allows its removal when it has become attached to hair. It made no difference to the Superglue, although Gavin was pathetically grateful, half-sucking, half-breathing in some of the water. I found the syringe for injecting melted butter into the skin of a turkey, filled it with water and poked the needle end through the tiny gap between his gummed lips, depressing the plunger very slowly so he had time to swallow.

'Dad?'

'What did he say, Stephen?'

'Could you come here for a minute?'

David followed him into the utility room, where Other Thing was standing, glued to the floor by his left front paw, purring.

'Well, at least he's happy with his situation,' I observed.

'He's not,' Stephen said in a shaky voice. 'Cats sometimes purr when they're in a panic. He's frightened.'

I stroked the cat. His sibling came and rubbed a black head against his snowy fur.

'What did the doctor say?'

'He said we could spend the night in Casualty, or we could make sure Gavin could breathe through his nose and leave him alone. It wears off in a day or so.'

'Go take the pillow off Gavin's bed and pin the duvet so it only comes to his waist.'

'David, he'll freeze,' I said mildly.

'Good enough for him,' David said, rummaging through his tools until he found a Stanley knife.

For one moment, both Stephen and I thought he was going to cut lumps off Gavin with it, but he got down on hands and knees beside the frantically purring Other Thing and with infinite care began to cut away at the vinyl flooring to which the paw was stuck. It struck me that I had never noticed, up to then, what graceful, strong hands he had. It took him ten minutes, but suddenly, Other Thing was free, to the extent that he was no longer stuck to the structure of the house, but merely to a detached, paw-shaped piece of vinyl. The latter puzzled him enormously, not least because, compared to his own paw, it was quite slippery, and so he found himself skating drunkenly across the kitchen. Thing assumed that this was some kind of game, and began leaping on Other Thing playfully, until Other Thing's attempts to defend himself with his armoured front paw dealt Thing a sledgehammer blow that sent him under our bed to sulk. I fed Other Thing, having instructed Gavin to get into bed with two T-shirts on him.

Twice during the night David got up and went to check on him. He was gone so long the second time I got worried, and went in after him. He was lying alongside Gavin, hugging him. He got up somewhat sheepishly and followed me back to our room. I snapped off the light.

'Did you ever do anything like that when you were growing up?' he asked in the dark.

'I cut a worm up to make small worms. It never struck me to glue myself dumb.'

The two of us lay there, parallel, in silence.

'I wish it had, though,' I admitted.

'Me too,' he said.

'Do you think Gavin's going to be a delinquent?'

'What do you mean, going to be? He is one.'

'Oh, that's OK then.'

If Gavin had just taken an emery board to his mouth and filed his way to freedom, it would not have been so bad. But waking at dawn the next morning he had gotten creative with the sandpaper and then decided to overcompensate by bringing us all breakfast in bed.

I was so horror-struck to be woken by an apparition bleeding from mouth and fingers, and asked to sit up for breakfast, that I got David into a sitting position without saying anything. So he was coming out of the depths of the deepest sleep when from the next room came screams of shock and panic. The two of us bolted out of bed, crashing into Gavin on the way, so that David and Gavin ended up on the floor of the landing, bleeding freely in a kind of family way, while I rushed in to find Stephen standing where his pillow should have been, trembling with rage and outrage.

Interrogation established that, arriving with a laden tray for his brother, Gavin had tripped over the bedside rug, so that Stephen's first notification of incoming breakfast was a facial peppering of vastly undercooked pink sausages. These he assumed to be some kind of infestation and was fending them off when the contents of the teapot reached his feet through the duvet. The scalding heat propelled him to where I found him making a speech promising a variety of particularly disgusting revenge mechanisms against Gavin.

David and Gavin came in as Stephen was running out of steam although his duvet was doing pretty well in the steam department. Other Thing, who seemed to have adapted to the vinyl paw-accessory, was leading a search for the pale pink sausages.

'And don't think you can get away with it by bleeding at me,' Stephen finished up, which folded

David in two and made Gavin cry. He did a curious two-phase cry. It started quietly enough, then escalated into a squeal of protest as the salt in his tears hit the raw parts of his filed lips. I wiped the tender area gently with the duvet where it was wet with warm tea. A curious parody of every illustration you have ever seen of mother-and-child, we were, this child bleeding gently into a dampened duvet held by a small blonde in an oversized T-shirt.

David and Stephen between them made a second breakfast for us all, and the atmosphere softened somewhat, although Stephen did look somewhat askance at me when I announced that I was keeping Gavin home from school. His older brother seemed to see this as a reward for evildoing, although I pointed out that even opening his mouth to answer a teacher's question was going to be difficult for him, while inadvertent laughter would split the tenuous healing around his mouth and render him liable to infection. Not to mention pain, I added, since Stephen quite obviously would have welcomed any chance of Gavin suffering punishment pain. David seemed at one with him on this after Other Thing, replete with under-cooked sausages, sat down on the suit David had laid out on the bed while he showered – and threw up on it.

Other Thing, having recovered from his sausage-induced upchucking, decided that Gavin needed heavy-duty minding, and draped himself across the youngster's thighs, the vinyl snowshoe attached to his paw acting as a constant mute reproof. I made spaghetti for Gavin's lunch and he managed to eat it without mishap. He was regaining his devilry, too, I noted, telling me a series of appallingly bad jokes and slapping his hand over his own mouth to keep it from widening in laughter when I winced and complained at the quality of his humour. Later, I listened to him rhyming off his tables, less distinct than usual because of his need to keep his mouth undisturbed while it healed.

I turned away and fell over Thing, which had a knack of standing broadside-on to whatever direction you were likely to take, especially if you were in a hurry.

'You stupid cat,' I told it.

'Shouldn't call him stupid.'

'He doesn't understand English.'

'You won't let me call Seamus stupid. And he is.'

In the past, in this kind of situation, I would have got David to talk to him about people disadvantaged by life, the universe and everything. About the differences in self-esteem between felines and humans.

But the knowledge of David's namesake toddling around Berkshire made me less willing to invoke his expertise in human relations, or even his advice for the kids. Half the time, after the two boys were gone to bed, my mouth was pursed around aborted conversation-openers; ideas I wanted to hear David's views on, yet never articulated because of the inherent falsity of any views against the background of that letter. Because I had always been the initiator of conversations, arguments – even laughter – there was more silence now. With nobody eager to hook and pull him out of quietness, he became even more quiet.

It is not hard to unlearn the little gestures, the small habits of affection. We retrain ourselves effortlessly not to slide a hand into a waiting hand, not to touch a shoulder in passing, not to stand at the window and blow a kiss to mark a routine departure.

Like the padded handrail on escalators. You step onto the moving staircase, put your hand on the rail, theoretically should be decanted off on arrival at the next floor, hand in the same position for the journey. Instead, your hand begins to pull ahead of the rest of you so if you stay clutching the point of the rail you grasped at the start, you finish the journey being dragged at arm's length by your own hand. Even in parallel, run from the same motor and self-evidently the same length, looped stairs and looped handrail seem to obey different time rules.

Similarly, just as my own life seemed to have moved into a cruising lassitude, a casual crawling towards joylessness, David's seemed to be moving faster. No frenetic flavour to the speed; just enough to make me feel that my arm was at a stretch to reach him. Just enough to make me develop, if not a self-censorship process, at least a selection process, so that I presented him with the minimum of time-absorbing tasks.

I administered The Skywriter's business myself, taking care of correspondence first thing every morning.

When the anonymous letter arrived, it did not evoke the upset it might have, earlier. It fitted into a general low-level misery, paradoxical in its infuriated insisted assumption that I was nakedly, ostentatiously, unfairly happy. My come-uppance was on the way, it assured me. It was a matter of time before the world discovered what I was really like.

In the past, I would have given it to David straight away. Now, however, I put it away, peeling off the layers of contradiction implicit in the action. You want and need to show it to him, but you won't, because you cannot afford to show him that you are more dependent on him at a time when he is withdrawing. But not showing it to him cuts one of the contact lines between us. Well, if that's what has to happen, that's what has to happen. You do think, though, don't you, that Richelle Governey is writing them? Of course I do, but what can he do about it? She doesn't even work for the programme any more. She could be anywhere.

That possibility loomed larger in my mind as the days went on. I found myself glancing behind me as I walked, looking more than was my habit into the rear-view mirror of the car. If there was a positive end result of all of this, it was that I became a marginally better driver. The negative end result was that I was edgy with the children, panic-stricken if they were later than they had promised to be in getting back to the house. Stephen began to humour me with elaborate patience, as if I was a frail, fussy old age pensioner like Oliver's mother. When I spotted him smoothing me down, I would laugh and regard myself as a fool.

Until the phone calls started. We were ex-directory, but there is always a fan, somewhere, related to someone in the phone company who gets access to the ex-directory number of a famous person. So now and again, we'd experience a rash of annoying but harmless calls. Invariably, just as we were about to change numbers, they would die away.

Not these, though. Not these. They started in a way

SWINGING ON A STAR

that caught me completely off-guard. It was David's habit – still – to telephone within five minutes of the ending of any live programme to hear my verdict on it. The phone calls came at precisely that time. When I would pick up the receiver, expecting his downbeat 'Well?' there would be nothing but silence. In the beginning, I guessed he had misdialled or been distracted, or that someone had come into the dressing room just as the phone call started, so he had put the receiver down and would come back to it. The pattern quickly established itself, however.

In a kind of second-wave response, for a few weeks, when the silent calls came, I would bang down the receiver within seconds. Then I got the letter that said, 'You'd better get another line. You can't cut me off.'

'David, have you been having difficulty getting through here on the phone after your programme?' I asked him after this letter.

'Mmm.'

'What difficulty?'

'Engaged tone.'

'Why didn't you tell me?'

He smiled at me with a knowing coldness that baffled me.

'You choose who you want to talk to and when you want to talk to them. I don't own your time.'

'But you always ring me after the programme.'

'Indeed.'

I stopped what I was doing and tried to make sense of the cold anger obvious in the non-answers he was giving.

'What does that mean?'

'Leave it.'

Ah, the ritual dance of the marital fight, the surefooted mutual timing of cues, the linked voices of disharmony.

'No I won't bloody leave it and don't give me that arrogant wave of the hand.'

He put both his hands flat on the surface in front of him.

'What precisely is the significance of this abstruse stuff about your phone calls? You obviously understand it. It's a mystery to me.'

'Dominique. You may choose to talk to someone at that time in the evening, on a particular evening each week for a particular reason. It may suit the two of you, because children may be in bed. Or there might be an information objective.'

'Now I'm going to get accountant-speak as well, am I?'

'Dominique. A scenario. Let us assume you had not watched my programme on any given Tuesday. But let us further assume that you did not wish me to know this. You might require a method which would allow you, in advance of my phone call – my predictable phone call – to get the highlights of the programme, the items worth commenting on.'

Rage transmuted into sadness. I sat down in the nearest chair, watching his shape alter and slide as tears obscured my vision.

After a moment, he came over and went down on his hunkers in front of me. I looked at him, my blood thundering through my ears with an audible heavy heated sound. Even then, I longed to put my face against the soft cotton of his sweater, be held, encompassed, silenced into calm by the confident easy breathing of him and the firm, double-hit heartbeat. He rocked, silently.

'Daisy?'

The gentleness in his use of my pet name made the sadness absolute.

'We always knew this might happen. I've always been braced for it. You're entitled to be happy. You don't need to do this – this – performance.'

The word moved me from yearning to a frenzy of shrewish wrath.

'Don't Daisy me, you duplicitous bastard,' I yelled into his face. 'The *idea* that you should pontificate about someone else *performing* while you're lying and pretending and fooling people up to the two eyes, while you're living a double life dropping offspring in bloody Berkshire.'

The rocking stopped. He was still, so still it seemed he had stopped breathing.

'. . . dropping offspring – precisely what are you talking about?'

'You know bloody well what I'm talking about. Victoria and her son and how you changed her life and how she'll never knock on your door looking for child support, just raise little David all on her saintly own.'

Almost casual in his movements, he rose and went upstairs. I could hear his footsteps, track their direction. He went to the wardrobe. Stood for long enough to try a few pockets and locate the folded sheets. He came downstairs very slowly, stopping with both feet on each step. He came back into the room with the letter in his hand.

'You read my private correspondence,' he said, so softly I had to strain to hear him.

'Don't think you can—' I began and was frightened into silence by the look and the gesture.

'That is beneath contempt,' he said as quietly as before, and left the room.

CHAPTER TWENTY-THREE

This Is a Recorded Announcement

From then on, everything seemed to speed up, so that I was spiralling, spinning towards something without any capacity to slow the spin or change the direction. On the one hand, I was doing more and more business, the boys were a joy and David was so successful as a TV performer that he could call his own tune, which for the moment included demanding that he fly in to London at midday on a Tuesday and get out that evening, thus allowing him to continue his 'day job'. Because he was saying so little to me about anything, I was unclear as to why he felt it so important to hang on to the 'day job'. I just knew he did.

I got on with work, and whenever someone like Robert Allen telephoned, I did my sunny success performance. As it happens, that was wasted on the one occasion Robert rang after a gap of a few weeks.

'I told Helen about us,' he said, cutting through the chit-chat.

'What did you tell her about us?'

'Greece.'

'And?'

'And nothing. There hasn't been anything else, remember?'

'No, but did you tell her you wanted anything else?'

'No, I didn't. I ring-fenced the Athens disaster.'

'And?'

'And she took her car keys and walked out of the house and I didn't see her for three days. I got a message on my mobile telling me not to be idiotic and have the guards looking for her, that she didn't need that shit as well.'

That, I thought, was typical of Helen. Practical and kindly. Waste nobody's time, yet ensure she could not be reached.

'She came back to me,' he said, and if I had said one word, he would have cried. 'She said I was a complete fool but that making herself feel good wasn't enough to make her leave me. She didn't blame you. She said you were just trying things out. That you were lucky to have met David, because he wouldn't let you try things out with him. But she came back.'

'What possessed you to tell her?'

'That temp knew.'

'But after all these years — she wouldn't tell her.'

'She told David.'

'But that was to get at me.'

'So she might decide at any moment that getting to Helen would get at you; how do I know the workings of a mad mind? I'm never going to be in anybody's power, even if I have to do what I did. There's nothing she can do to me now.'

'You're right. I think she's insane and there's nothing she wouldn't do to me. Tough on Helen, though.'

'We'll be OK,' he said and rang off.

Like an animal caught in a trap, I thought, you would rather chew off half your own leg than be owned by something else. You would rather create the worst possible situation than have it created for you. Now, for you, it's over and you can rebuild something with Helen.

For me, it was far from over. My anonymous caller's use of the telephone became more and more methodical. Directly after the programme ended, the call would come. A couple of weeks, I tried to fool it by ignoring the first call and picking up the second or third, but when that approach meant ignoring David's call without meaning to, it complicated an already bad situation. Anyway, after a couple of weeks of it, the caller added other times of the day, so that when I would have completely forgotten about her, when I would have got cheerful as a result of a very good session with a client, I would pick up an incoming call and encounter that deadly chilly silence.

Then, one night, when I picked up the phone after David's programme, it was his voice I heard, greeting me in such an upbeat positive way, my heart lifted. I made a comment about the programme which he cut through, saying something so unrelated to it that I was silenced. At the end of the statement, he cheerily bade me goodbye and rang off. I was still sitting by the phone, baffled, when it rang again and David was there, asking me courteously, evenly, for my verdict on that week's show. I began to think I was losing it.

The following week, it happened again. He came on, all upbeat, saying something general and pausing for me to answer. When his pick-up from my answer was grossly unrelated to it, it hit me. This was a recording of him, taken off air. I slammed down the phone. This wasn't just heavy breathing. This was a pre-planned, infinitely effortful cruelty. This was stalking. I thought about going to the guards, but half-remembered something about the law being inadequate at handling stalking.

Anyway, I could not see myself explaining to the guards without them wanting to hear it from David, and his reaction would be that this was layering another untruth on in order to distract from whatever affair I was having. If I told him first, before telling the police, I would have to convince him without evidence, because, of necessity, he was never there when it happened. I could not involve Stephen as a witness. Of course I could make a recording as it happened, but since someone had already tinkered with off-air tapes of him, what was to prevent me doing a more elaborate and confusing version of the same thing? If I met the police and himself at the same time, he would be sure I was up to something complicated or would believe I was just embarrassing him for no purpose.

I could go to the British police, I thought. But then, when the calls escalated, a number of things transpired. One was that they could not be coming from anywhere but Ireland. Or so I convinced myself. Nobody could afford to make so many, long-distance. Not just to annoy another person. The other was that they were made by someone who could often see me as well as hear me. I started to get faxes and e-mails, too. The e-mails were bad enough, because there, in the middle of a list of calls from prospective clients, would be one calculated to arouse no suspicions, because there were no attachments. It was just a brief note from a client or acquaintance, I would think, then click on it.

'He never liked that burnt-orange coat,' one of them read. 'Why do you insist on wearing it?'

Other observations about what I was wearing followed, including comments about what I was wearing when I was *inside* the house. When the phone rang, I found myself looking out of the window, seeing if I could spot someone out there observing me while I took the call. I even shifted the phone out to the hall, on the basis that nobody could see me through the frosted glass of the front door.

Then I began to get e-mails telling me she knew I had opened the other e-mails. As if that wasn't bad enough, my fax machine would give its sudden bleat and when I would go to it, there would be a single page, often with a drawing of me in that day's clothes. Every time I went out, on my return, I would hear the fax bleat as I walked through the front door. There, on the machine, would be a single page telling me everywhere I had gone, in town.

A couple of weeks after the confrontation about his son in England, I realised David was no longer calling me after the programme. The first week it happened, I didn't notice, because it was one of the weeks when the stalker was playing me recordings of him. The second week, I noticed but asked no questions. We had not quite got to the 'Ask your father' stage, or perhaps we had passed it. We had very few questions for each other. We each asked the boys lots of questions and answered the ones coming from them, but between us there was a neutrality as uninflammable as asbestos. Whatever about the kindness of strangers, the courtesies of strangers are grim indeed when applied within a family.

I often wondered if Richelle Governey knew I could not tell David what she was doing to me. Once, when she was doing one of her heavy breathing calls, I cried on the phone. Like a fool, I asked her what she thought she was achieving, did she have any idea of the misery she was causing me, why was she making my life so ghastly when I had never done anything to her? Over the following few days, in bits and pieces, on e-mails and by fax, I got my answer. I had stunted her career by cheating to get the job she would have got. I had stood in her way again for no good reason when she had the chance to play my sister. I had put my husband up to having her sacked by the programme. I was reading this last one when the phone rang and there was nobody at the other end.

'I never told him to sack you,' I screamed. 'I never knew you had been sacked until afterwards. I didn't even know it was a sacking. You're blaming things on me that I had nothing whatever to do with, you mad twisted bitch, you crazy, crazy cruel loony. It's not my fault your life is in shit, it may not even be your fault, but fuck off, would you, just go away, drop dead, slit your wrists, take an overdose, for Jesus' sake please do anything but leave me alone, leave me alone, please, please, please, what can I give you, what can I offer you to make you please just go away and leave me alone?'

At the end of the phone call, I was kneeling on the floor, my forehead against the wall, crying in great gobbets of hatred, grief and fear. I reached up over my head with the receiver, groping for its place, and someone guided my hand. I opened my eyes to find Gavin looking at me with a mixture of pity, horror and disgust as he helped the phone find its home. I stumbled to my feet. He backed away. I pulled squares off the kitchen roll and mopped my face, my nose, jolted by sobs I could not seem to quell, trying at the same time to explain that everything was OK, that he had done nothing wrong.

'But you are afraid of that person,' he said.

I tried to think of some reason I might have been crying, some audition, perhaps, for a grief-stricken character, but could not.

'Dad will stop that person,' he said. 'Tell Dad about him.'

'Her,' I said without thinking.

'He'll definitely stop a girl,' Gavin said, with such happily biased contempt that laughter fought with my grief.

'It's OK. I don't want your dad to know at the moment. Later, maybe, but first I need some time to think this through.'

'I think you should tell him.'

'Why don't you just give me a hug? I need a hug.'

The blotchy look of me might have given him reservations about hugs, but he braced himself and gave me a hug to end all hugs, even staying with it when it made me cry all over again.

'What does she want to do to you?'

I pushed him gently away and told him we weren't going to waste our good time talking about this silly woman who didn't like his mother. The hell with her.

'To hell with her,' he corrected.

'Some people say "the" hell with her.'

'All right, then, the hell with her,' he agreed.

After he had gone out to play, I pondered the answer to his question. What did she want to do to me? Maybe, came the answer, maybe she wants to do precisely what she has already succeeded in doing: make me crazy. Make me suicidal. Make me fearful of being seen, being followed. I had not gone for a walk in months. I had taken to dropping into garage convenience stores in order to grab food, rather than walk around a large supermarket where she could follow me and then send me a message about the items I had purchased. People must now think I have a nervous twitch, I thought, because the moment I go out the front door, I am skimming suddenly to my left and right, to see if I can catch and meet the eyes of whoever it is I am sure is following me.

David had to take an extended trip to Britain the following week, and so I got many more phone calls and faxes. She seemed to know whenever he was away that I would be instantly reachable in location and in psyche. Even phone calls from David himself became jerky and irrational, with me trying to maintain a calm monotone, trying to keep a handle on the subject of the conversation while the background bleep indicating a call waiting would happen again and again and again. David sometimes pretended not to notice it, but after it happened a few times got brusque about it.

'I hear another caller trying to get you. Goodbye,' he would say.

I dropped Stephen and Gavin off at a birthday party on the first night David was away, promising to be back for them around nine. When I reached the turn for home, I flipped the indicator back up after a couple of seconds, bypassed the turn and drove north. Out along the sea. Howth. Donabate. Broadmeadows. Waiting all the while for the old sensation of wind in my hair, peace in my heart. Convinced that another car was following me, but unable to catch or identify a particular car. I stopped at Broadmeadows and walked out along the slob lands, alive with bird noises. David and I had often come here in the months after the car crash. We would sit on the broken sea wall and I would talk about Gabrielle. If I closed my eyes, I could see him there. See him better, perhaps, than I had seen him at the time. Because at the time, I had never registered the look of him. I had just leaned into the strength of him. This was what a good friend would do, I thought, accepting it as my due. Not because of any personal worth, but because of grief.

Now I wondered what had been behind his constant presence in those months. Was he just a helper, or did he love me a little? Or – given the son in Berkshire – was he attracted to women who would believe he had rescued them? What startled me was my unwillingness to believe that possibility. Like a fool, I thought, you need to believe he loved you, even if he no longer does.

The evening was chilly, and I turned my coat collar up. Out of the side of my eye, I spotted movement, and turned precipitately, almost coming off the sea wall in the process, but there was nobody there.

I walked back to the car, hands deep in pockets, wondering why sea birds all have a mourning cry, whereas most land birds have cries filled with expectation and busy delight. The car started and I put lights on, perhaps a little ahead of the legally required time. I was driving badly, I knew. Dithering in and out of lanes and sometimes even driving on the hard shoulder. But this veering in and out made me sure of what I had suspected. There was a car trailing me. A big, dark car. Dark green, perhaps. Hunter green. How appropriate, I thought, then realised I had said it aloud. Predator and prey. Or predator and pray, if you're religious.

Better not change the pattern of your driving now, no matter how erratic it has been, I thought, crossing back towards the hard shoulder. The dark green car dropped back, because we were on a long straight stretch of road with no other cars in sight. But because the night was drawing in, and perhaps because, not having switched on any lights, she believed the car to be virtually invisible, it began to catch up on me, little by little. What do you want? I thought. You don't want me to see you, so what is the purpose of this?

Out of nowhere came the memory of a conversation between two people in Robert Allen's home one night. Something about a practical joke. As I accelerated, I checked the details through in my mind until I was clear. My speedometer was climbing quickly. 60. 70. 80. Probably believing that I was trying to get away, the big dark car speeded up too. 90. Still with me. 100. I had never driven so fast and was running out of straight road. I could not continue to drive at this pace once the bends came up. I horsed the car down through the gears and as it jolted, stood on the brakes. The car screeched, held to its line and stuck. The big green hulk behind me reacted – a couple of seconds too late – screamed as brakes went on and ploughed into the back of my car. I was out on the road, running. Running along the broken white line, back towards her. She was scrabbling to get the green car going again, glancing up, confused to see me running purposefully past her. Out of range as she got it into reverse, I memorised the number plate.

She yanked the car back away from mine, spun the wheel and screeched out onto the wrong side of the road to pass my stalled car and speed towards Dublin. Other cars stopped. A red-faced, porter-bellied man with a Louth accent told me to get into my car, I was shaking. Not to move it. He had called the Gardaí on his cellphone. He parked carefully on the hard shoulder, then came up to where I was.

'Miss, I was behind the green car.'

I nodded, teeth clenched to keep them from chattering. He smelled of sweat and cigarettes.

'I'm going to tell the guards she was going twice too fast and that she left the scene of the accident. I have a bit of the registration.'

I held out my hand, where I had biro'd the full reg. The numbers he had written down matched mine, although mine was complete.

'That's all I'm going to tell them. Because I don't want to get involved in any family shite, and this looks like family shite to me. She was going awful fast. But you started it. It was like playing Chicken. I don't know what the fuck you were at, Miss, but I want you to know I think you were bloody lucky you didn't kill some innocent person with shag all to do with you or her.'

With enormous dignity, he left my car just as the cops arrived. They made notes of my smashed brake lights and the panel she had pulled loose. Took the half-reg from the Louth man and the full registration from me.

'Let me get this right, Mrs Carpenter,' one of the guards said. 'The green car rear-ended yours, and you got out of the car and went – you didn't go to the passenger window or the front of the car behind you, you went to the rear of the car to get the number.'

I nodded. He went off and had words with his colleague, then went to the hard shoulder and spoke with the Louth man.

'Mrs Carpenter, why didn't you look at the front number plate?'

'Because it was hidden in the rear of my own car.'

'Why didn't you talk to the driver?'

'She was trying to get her car started again.'

'But she might have been just checking to see was the engine still on.'

'Yes, Guard, she might.'

'You didn't think she was, though?'

I hugged myself and tried not to cry.

'I thought it was important to get the number plate.'

'Quite so, Mrs Carpenter, but it still seems strange that you didn't talk to her. Did you know the driver?'

I opened my mouth to lie, and couldn't do it. I nodded, dumbly.

'Is she a relative, Mrs Carpenter?'

'No.'

'A friend?'

'Oh, no, no.'

'How do you know her, Mrs Carpenter?'

Oh, Jesus, I thought. Of all the cops in all the world, I have to get one with the potential to be promoted straight to Commissioner. The other guard came over to say he had all the road measurements and to check if it was OK to let the Louth witness go. They had his phone numbers, he assured his persistent colleague. They could always reach him if needs be.

'How do you know the other driver, Mrs Carpenter?'

'I only think I know her. There is a woman who I believe has been stalking me, sort of. She was fired off – off—'

Suddenly the spectre of headlines saying 'David Carpenter's wife victim of stalker' rose in front of me, and I panicked.

'I can't tell you. I was the one run into. Why am I – I probably shouldn't talk without a lawyer.'

'That's certainly your right, Mrs Carpenter.'

'What time is it?'

'Twenty five to nine,' he said, without looking at his watch.

'Guard, please. I have two small children expecting me to pick them up in Clontarf at nine. Could I drive and you follow me and I'll give you a statement then? Or tomorrow?'

The two of them conferred and he said they would leave it for tonight. They had got a lot of information and would be taking action. If I believed I was being stalked, I should get legal advice immediately, or talk to the unit that dealt with stalkers. Their unit. Very expert. Very experienced.

I could expect to hear from them very soon. I drove off sedately. Long after I was out of their sight, I continued to drive with extreme caution. It's difficult to speed if you are checking every lay-by, every intersection, every off-street parking lot, for a dark green car with a damaged front.

When the car pulled up outside the house where

the birthday party was, most of the child guests were already being loaded into people carriers and runabouts. Stephen firmly shepherded Gavin to the back door of the car. Just as Gavin was about to get in, he spotted the damage.

'Look, there was a crash. Mum, your whole car is wrecked!'

The party parents came to twitter questions and sympathy. I got the kids into the car and home without sharing much information with anybody and begged the two to undress themselves and get themselves into bed without any delays because I was a bit shook. I slipped into my own bed, half-dressed, listening to them until they both came to kiss me goodnight.

'It's all right,' Stephen told me, stroking my arm. 'It's all right. If the radiator was gone, you'd have overheated long before you got here.'

I held on to him for a long time, this expert in motor mechanics, as a means of consolation.

'Will I ring Dad?' he offered.

Oh, yes, please, Stephen. Tell him. Beg him to come home. Right now. As if he had never gone away from me. To come home and take care of me as if he had never fathered a son. Come home and pretend everything is the way it used to be. *Don't it always seem to be that you don't know what you have till it's gone . . .*

'No, I wouldn't want your dad to have to deal with this when he's on a business trip. He'll be home the day after tomorrow.'

'And then it's half-term and we're on a break.'

I had forgotten. I must pack their things. David had some kind of surprise lined up for them.

'Mum?'

Gavin had climbed up on the bed beside me and was kneeling to look down at me.

'Why are you so upset?'

I waffled about damage to the car, shock, the police. He listened solemnly.

'Did the girl you're afraid of hit you?'

The long silence was ended by him sliding off the bed.

'The girl she's afraid of hit her,' he told Stephen. 'I'm going to get Dad to kill her.'

'Mam said we weren't to ring him.'

'Not tonight. He can kill her next week,' Gavin said with sleepy assurance and padded off to bed.

CHAPTER TWENTY-FOUR

On Message

The car looked bad but drove perfectly the following morning. I dropped Stephen at school and Gavin at junior school without much checking in the rear-view mirror. Now that her registration number was in the hands of the guards – and she must have worked out that this was the reason I had run to the back of her car – she was in danger of being pulled over by any observant cop, so I figured she might lie low.

In fact, it was me who had to deal first with the Gardaí. A white car was parked in the paved front garden when I got home. I parked and headed for the front door, nodding a greeting. One of them was on the car phone. The other gestured a 'give us five minutes,' I nodded and went in, leaving the door slightly ajar. When good police knuckles rapped on it extra hard to indicate they wanted in, I pulled the front door open and there they were, the two of them. Not caps to chest, but so like the two in build, in uniform, that I was staggered. They gazed at me – I was visibly struggling with tears – and followed me into the sitting room.

'I'm sorry. My family were killed in a road accident and for a second there, you both looked like the officers who came the night of the crash to tell me.'

They nodded. Asked if I was up to it. I said I was up to it. Whatever 'it' was, I wasn't sure. The information had been passed on to them, they said, at the local station. It had been brought to their attention (last night's particulars not giving this level of detail) that I was Mrs David Carpenter. That changed things.

'What things?'

Well, Mr Carpenter would be a well-known name. A star. Not to mention being a millionaire.

'I have no idea,' I said honestly. 'I never took that much interest in how rich he was.'

They absorbed this in polite disbelief. Lads, I thought, did ye but know the number of things about David Carpenter I never took that much interest in until it was too late. His money was the least of the things I managed to ignore about him.

'That kind of person would attract a very serious stalker,' one of them observed. I wondered if the inference to be taken was that half-remembered old hacks from soap operas would only attract a minor mucky kind of stalker. A stalker who had a day job and just did a little stalking by way of a nixer. Bit of overtime.

'It's not David who's being stalked,' I offered. 'It's me.'

But there would be a connection between Mr Carpenter and the stalker, now, would there not? They would need to have a word with Mr Carpenter. Oh, he was away at the moment? But that was only for his programme — oh, right. This time he was away for longer. He would be back when, exactly? And what had been Mr Carpenter's reaction to the accident of last night? Oh, he hadn't been told. Because it wouldn't do to worry him while he was on a business trip. Of course. Of course.

I ended up giving them several of the faxes. The e-mails I had always destroyed. Pity, they said. But they would take the PC away with them, if that was all right with me. Their electronic forensics people would surely be able to get them back up and readable. Nothing really went permanently off a hard disk, you know yourself.

I thought about fighting the removal of the computer, but its absence would at least mean I could get no e-mails from her. I thought, too, about explaining Richelle Governey from the brief moment I first met her, but I had the feeling they were convinced David was having an affair with her and would take the truth as the sadly self-serving confection of a wronged wife. I saw them to the door, one of them carrying the notebook computer under his arm, although it would have fitted comfortably in his big hand.

Half an hour after they left, the fax whimpered, then disgorged a single sheet of paper with six words hand-scrawled across it.

Now, I HAVE NOTHING TO LOSE.

I have to get away, I thought, shrinking against the wall, away from the windows, as I passed. I found myself packing, not just for Gavin and Stephen's trip, but pushing items into a bag for myself, although I was not planning to travel with the boys. It was something to do with horses, I thought, they were going to be involved in.

The fax bleeped again. I went downstairs. Expecting another single-sheet scrawl. Nothing, with a surge of dread, a transmission of several pages waiting to be read.

When I turned it face upward, however, it was in

David's classic, legible handwriting. In the clinical tones of a complete stranger, the letter on the front page indicated that since I had invaded his privacy and read his personal correspondence, I might as well get the full story and be in possession of all the facts. That was the purpose of his current, extended trip to Britain. His full signature, surname and all, ended the note. The next page was a photocopy from some tabloid.

'A Little Kicker for Sammy' read the headline. Beneath the headline was a picture of a man in a wheelchair, beaming up at a woman standing beside him holding a swaddled and obviously new baby. The story said that former place-kicker Sammy Talbott had just become the proud father of a son, his first. Thanks to the high-tech assisted fertility services at some private clinic, Sammy (a quadriplegic since his cycling accident ten years earlier) and his wife Vicki (a physiotherapist who had met and married him when working in a rehabilitation hospital in York) were now parents of eight-pound two-ounce David.

Vicki. Victoria. The woman in the picture looked more a Vicki than a Victoria, puffed as she was with pre-birth padding and grinning unselfconsciously down at her husband.

The third page was a fax from her:

Dear Dominique

David tells me that something has convinced you that my son is also David's.

He is not, and I am sorry someone gave you this upsetting impression.

Your David did play a part in the arrival of my David. For many years after we were married, Sammy and I assumed we would never be able to have children, although we wanted to. A home centring on a quadriplegic tends to be a bit short of the readies, and we knew we would never be able to get together enough money to go for assisted fertility treatment. However, your David, who kept in touch with Sammy since they played together, picked up on our longing for a baby, and staked us.

Our son is now nearly two and is a daily joy to us both.

I hope this clears up what must have been a shattering possibility for you.

Sincerely,

Victoria Talbott

The last item was a photocopy of an 8 x 10 studio

shot of the little boy. He looked not a bit like David Carpenter. But he looked very like the man in the wheelchair.

I spread out, then tidied the sheets time after time. Imagining David's contempt. Imagining his distaste at having to revisit the issue and get the letter from her. Wondering how he had explained it to her. She made no reference to my reading his correspondence.

I wandered the house like a stranger, stopping at the framed photographs. 'In happier times' is how the tabloids would caption each of them. I did not feel bereaved so much as stood up. I had a sense that I had come near to something infinitely precious with David and that I had scored the face of the possibility with deep scarring lines.

The fax was silently pushing out another page. It was one of those messages from a clamshell phone with a keyboard in it. From Richelle Governey.

'When I sent this,' it said, 'I was outside the house on your road with the new fence around it. By the time you get it I'll be somewhere else.'

It was possible to call the police, of course, but they were already on the lookout for her. I looked at the two zippered bags belonging to the boys and rang Oliver's dad. Was there any chance he would pick them up from school and keep them overnight? David would pick them up tomorrow. An extraordinary thing had come up, he knew I would never normally ask but—

Like all the McDermotts, Oliver's father made it sound like he had been living kind of a dull life until I had brightened it by this generously bestowed task. I dropped the bags around to his house and Mrs McDermott asked me if I'd like tea, coffee or a steak. It was tempting to reply, 'No, but how about asylum until they catch my friendly local stalker?' but I restrained myself, got back in the car and went home.

The brightness of the early morning had drifted into cold overcast. My own house glowered around me, dank with loneliness and threat. I must think things out, I thought. Standing at the kitchen table, I noticed one of the budget airlines was launching a new service with an amazingly low price. Paris, £29 return, it said. I telephoned for a ticket for the following morning. Done. I did not need to book hotels. Paris I knew like the back of my hand. I would find somewhere to stay when I got there.

When the phone rang, it startled me. I snatched it up quickly, forgetting I had nobody in the house to be annoyed by the noise or roused from sleep by it. Half-hoping it might be David, yet knowing that I had nothing to say to him. Nobody answered my greeting, but there was no doubt that someone was there. The call was not coming from a land line, but from a mobile phone in a car, because in the background it was possible to hear the engine.

For the next couple of hours, I let the phone ring, unanswered. But, after darkness had fallen, the phone calls were paced by the fax. Every fifteen minutes, a single sheet would issue, telling me the woman was in such a Grove (ten minutes away) or such an Avenue (eight minutes away). She was circling, circling. She was probably sending e-mails from that phone, too, not knowing that they were probably popping up on the PC in the local Garda station. But those e-mails would probably not be read until morning. Electronic forensic work was not the kind of thing they kept guys up all night to work on.

Occasionally, just in case, I would answer the phone, hoping it would be someone else. Once, it was my business partner, Rita. When she asked me why I was so tense, I told her a little about the phone calls and faxes, leaving out the car crash.

'You should ring those guards and ask them to come around. They probably have ways of tracking calls that you don't even know about. Also you wouldn't have to answer the calls yourself.'

I said I would think about it. Shortly afterwards, I picked up the receiver and this time, even though the call was certainly from the same mobile phone, there was no car noise. Whoever was driving had parked. When I put down the phone, I went upstairs and into one of the rooms at the front of the house. Without turning on the light, I went to the window. About seven doors down, under a lamppost, was the dark green car.

It was now ten o'clock. I could ring the police and they would come to arrest her immediately. Well, not immediately, I thought. A local station doesn't send out a fleet of cars at the drop of a complaint. As I watched, the car started and moved away. The lights over its number plates were broken, so they were impossible to read at any distance.

The fax machine bleeped. When I got to it, the single page message said: 'I know where the kids are.'

Maybe she was alternating between the McDermotts' house and mine, I thought. But what harm could she do them? She could not go up that long drive to the McDermotts' house without a good reason. And at least three of Oliver's brothers still lived at home and could take care of her, individually or severally, if she posed a threat to their nephews. The phone rang. I could hear the car engine, then silence. Silently, I went upstairs. She was back. Even if I called the guards, and even if they succeeded in a car chase over the speed bumps of the traffic-calming suburbs, I would then end up in arrests, in trials and in publicity.

Putting down the phone, sitting in the dark, I began to grope on the surface next to me for my car keys. The gates were open, I knew. I fingered the car-door key out from among the others. When it rang again, I let it ring as I ran down the stairs and grabbed the transistor radio, turning it on and putting it on the floor, a female voice coming out of it, but faintly. Then I quietly opened the front door, lifted the phone off the hook, put it on the carpet and slid out the door, closing it softly behind me. Into the car. Engine on and car moving, no lights on, out on to the road, hard left, roaring up through the gears like a rally driver, past her, hard right into the next avenue, quick spin to the right again into a cul-de-sac, all the time praying not to meet another car.

Third entry down. Sigginses' house – into the entryway, pulling right as soon as half-way in, so I was turning off the engine with the car hidden directly behind the front hedge. I could hear the big quiet engine of her car hesitating at the entrance to the cul-de-sac – could imagine her thought-process: Dominique'd never go into a cul-de-sac, no way out. The big car revved and moved.

I slid out of my car, locked it and ran to the little

laneway connecting the back gardens of the cul-de-sac with the lane running behind our own house. Lack of lighting made me slow down, for fear of falling. I could still hear the big car engine. The back garden gate was easily opened. Through the back garden, along the side of the house, pause. No sign of her. I ran around the front of the house, got the door open and was in the hall pulling it closed when through the frosted glass came the cold fractured circles of headlights as her car came back into the road. I dropped on to the floor and began crawling away from the growing brightness. Faster as the hall became brighter than daylight and the noise filled the garden – she had driven into the driveway. I had managed to slide into the sitting room when I heard her footsteps and saw the shadow she made against her own headlights, peering through the door glass, trying the front door to see if it would open.

The front door would yield no clue, I realised – not like a car, where a warm bonnet will reveal recent movement. After a moment, she ran back to the car and reversed it out of the gateway, roaring off to search the neighbourhood. I went upstairs and positioned myself at the window where I could see any car coming into the street. In three hours, five other cars arrived, either to park or drop people and depart again. Her car returned twice. The lack of a car in my driveway seemed to convince her that I could not be in the house, and she finally drove away.

She might sit somewhere close by, I thought, but as long as I couldn't hear her or see her, I could live with that. The phone rang intermittently throughout the night. I never answered. When I telephoned for a taxi, I used the fax phone. Would they send the car at five? Never mind what time my flight was, I wanted the car at five, OK? OK. That would give me an hour to spare in the airport, but better in the airport than in this prison with a motorised enemy circling.

I rang David's mobile phone, confident he would have turned it off for the night. It invited me to leave a message. I told it that I had left the boys at the McDermotts' with their cases for him to pick up. I thanked David for the material he had sent me on the fax, saying I needed a few days to think and would they look after themselves for those few days.

I thought about making coffee, but worried that opening the fridge door for milk would flood the kitchen with light which might be visible from outside. When the taxi came at dawn, I asked him to meet me at the roundabout — it would be easier than finding the house, I said, talking down the dispatcher's puzzled observation that they often picked me or Mr Carpenter up at the house. I could do with the walk, I laughed, and I had little or no luggage to carry. I'd see him at the roundabout. I got to the roundabout through back lanes. Drive a convoluted route to the airport, I told the driver, and, mystified, he agreed. Bobbing up and down to look out the back window, I could not see anyone following us. At the departure gates, I waited until everybody else was on the plane before I came forward to board. Once seated, I fell instantly asleep.

I slept in the coach taking me from the airport to the hotel. I slept, immediately and at length, in the hotel. Every time I woke up, I checked my watch. Purposelessly, because I never did anything as a result, just turned over and went back to sleep. Once, I went to the window and looked out at a grey, drizzling afternoon in Paris. I should really get up, I thought, climbing back into the tall single bed. I should really get up and shower and start to think out my future, I thought, as sleep claimed me again. That night, although I assumed I would become wakeful, more sleep came, settling over me like a snowdrift, isolating me in dreamless oblivion.

When sunshine poked in through the window on my second day, I decided to get cleaned up and dressed. Every choice seemed weighted with exigent implications. If I chose the black bra, I would have to wear the grey jumper. I made my decisions in a leaden way, picking up and then rejecting a waterproof trenchcoat about eight times. That final rejection was probably a mistake, I thought, picking up a paper and heading for a café.

But so what if I got drenched? Who would see me or know me or care?

I drank thick white bowl-cups of coffee one after another, sitting outdoors in a patch of watery sunlight. I must be dehydrated, I thought, trying to recall if there had been a drink beside my bed during the previous thirty-six hours. As the caffeine kicked in, my headache lifted. Now I would be able to think. To assess my options.

An hour later, I was back in my hotel room, trying to rationalise what had brought me there. It ceased to matter. There was the bed, freshly made up. I got in and slept until breakfast time the following morning. However, this time I did not buy a newspaper, but brought some paper and a pen with me to map out what I should do.

First of all, Richelle Governey. At long distance, the threat she posed seemed much more manageable. The police would talk to David today or tomorrow. They would catch her, particularly if she kept driving that car, identifiable because of the damage at the front, even if she obscured the number plates. Of course, she might decide to cool it by getting out of the country for a few weeks. She probably would not take the car onto a ferry. Did the cops have routine checks on the number plates of cars as they embarked?

That was where, even at long distance, it became less manageable. I could see that the ideal, from her point of view, would be to lie low for a few weeks, then start on me all over again. If I had her arrested, I would be in court, as would David, and the ensuing publicity would attract others to do the same. The boys would learn about it and it would give them nightmares. Even Gavin, the most resilient of them, had been disturbed by how frantic I was on the phone to her. If an adult could be that terrified, they would reason, there must be truly awful things lurking out there waiting to get at them. A court case would not, as the TV counsellors put it, 'bring closure'. It would worsen everything.

Since it was my perceived happiness and success that provoked her, arguably the simplest solution, I thought bitterly, would be to get stories into the papers to the effect that David and I were no longer the perfect couple. They would be true enough, God knows. The papers would love rerunning the pictures of me in my terry robe embracing David in the front garden.

Stories like that might even ensure that The Skywriter business took a nosedive. Would this madwoman go away if her target ended up as a single mother, temping for a living? It seemed that, robbed of a career and of fame, she had chosen to establish a presence in reaction to mine. If mine ceased to exist, would she cease to be a stalker? Or should I simply adapt to this factor in my life, the way people adapted to losing their hair or having a post-accident limp? Should I say, 'Howya, Richelle, you again? How's the old stalking going? Tell us, have you scared the shit out of any celebs recently?'

There had to be a downside attached to that. The fierce, harsh pleasure of jeering the unseen presence might be paid for. Growing up, we were told that if a man ever flashed at us, exposed himself to us, we should stay calm. If we spoke at all, it would be to say something cutting like, 'Put it away, I've seen bigger and better.' Nowadays, they said that was the worst thing you could do, that if you didn't shiver and squeal satisfactorily, the flasher might turn nasty and bolster his self-esteem by stabbing you to death. Maybe the same applied to stalkers. Maybe they need to believe you to be terrified of them, and if you get smart with them, perhaps they will be tipped into more damaging action.

What was maddening about this woman was that she was so peripheral. If life was made up of concentric circles, with the loved ones in the inner circle, then immediate and current friends, then past friendships, Richelle Governey belonged in the outermost circle. Her capacity to frighten allowed her to jump every queue, to become more central to my life than my own children. No, I thought, desperate to retain something. That wasn't true. It was as if I had put the children behind me to protect them. Or was that, too, just another self-serving construct? Stepmother Courage?

A tall, thin, bearded American asked if he might share my table. I nodded. Brown-rice academic, I thought, rather than tourist. When the waiter came, he got into a tangle trying to explain what he wanted. I helped him. He complimented me on my French.

'Where are you from?' he asked.

'Dublin, Ireland,' I said, bracing myself for small talk. Oh, I'm Irish too, my greatgrandmother on my father's side was from County Donnygal.

Instead, he reached into his haversack. After a moment's rustling, he produced a thin tall paperback from a university press. *The Psychology of Mass Migration* was the title.

'Yours?'

He nodded. I turned it over to read the blurb, which

said that a major theme running through the book was the 19th century exodus from Ireland occasioned by the potato famine.

'Are you a psychologist or a historian?'

'Psychologist. My colleague brought the historical perspective to the book. But I got to visit your country on a number of occasions.'

How verbally formal are educated Americans, I thought. Irish people would say 'a few times' rather than 'a number of occasions'. We talked long enough to need more coffee.

'Do you know anything about modern psychology?' I asked.

He looked puzzled. I laughed and explained that while I knew the nature of people and their mindsets didn't change from century to century, I was being harassed by a very modern phenomenon: the stalker.

'They didn't have them in past centuries, did they?'

He leaned back to think about this one, eventually suggesting that since there was a pattern in American history of assassination requiring the assassin to travel in pursuit of the victim, there might be some basis for suggesting that stalking did not originate in this century. Some of the presidential assassins and would-be assassins engaged in stalking before they got to the point. And of course, some of them did not get to the point of actually making an attempt on the life of a president. It could, he also suggested, be postulated that perhaps Lady Caroline Lamb had been something of a stalker to Byron.

'It's like an extra taking centre stage in the final ten minutes of a play,' I said. 'No dramatist would get away with it. It's like a chair taking over. I never had a relationship with this person, never set out to be anything but acquaintance-civil to her, and yet she has, on several occasions, forced herself to the centre of the stage – in a sense, taken over the central role in my life from me, taken the initiative, redefined me. Put me in the audience, helplessly watching what is happening to me. I keep thinking there must be some complex motivation involved, something to justify this quantum leap in positioning.'

'That is rather the essence of the stalker,' he said mildly. 'Because their profile is one of social and sexual inadequacy, they are rarely intrinsically interesting. They are made interesting in a transient way only by their actions, as students of psychology frequently discover when they visit stalkers and would-be assassins after conviction. The more florid the delusion of connection with a famous person, the more interesting the stalker, but once the delusion has been set aside, the stalker is frequently of no interest at all.'

'That makes it worse,' I said. 'I'm looking over my shoulder, waiting for the stab of a knife – no.'

I had forgotten he was there, and sat, lost in thought. It would, in fact, be easier if I expected something as imaginable as a blow from a weapon or the pain of a knife going in. It was the unimaginable, unshaped expectation that could not be coped with. He was now looking at me as if trying to judge how delusional I might be.

'If I have a stalker,' I said, sitting up and trying to sound academically interested in a concept, rather than frantically frightened of a reality, 'they seem forty feet high and backlit. They've got total power over me. They can decide where I go, how I live, what bodyguards I must have – everything. Yet, you say, if I were taken away from them – they wouldn't even be a nonentity, they would be less than a nonentity.'

He shrugged. 'It would appear that without a host, they lack focus.'

'Or they change host.'

'It is not always easy to locate a host who matches the perceived connections. A stalker who develops an elaborate internal network of supports for the delusion that, say, he must stalk or kill a president will not easily shift that framework to focus on somebody other than the president. By their nature, such persons are not flexible in their management of their lives.'

'If I stopped living in Ireland, though, wouldn't that serve? Although it might tip her into . . .'

I was suddenly tired again, yearning for the coarse-woven white linen of the hotel bed. I asked if I might purchase the book. It was a gift, he told me. I scribbled my name and address for him, offering to be of assistance if he ever came back to Ireland.

'By the time you visit my country again,' I said, smiling, 'I'll be shook of my stalker, I promise.'

He expressed the hope that I was proven right, and strode off, humping his back a few times to settle into the broad canvas straps of the haversack. A curious loping bounce to his step took the grace out of him. Increasingly, I found myself watching strangers and near-strangers, instinctively comparing the way they moved to the way David Carpenter moved. It was as if he had become some kind of definition, with everybody else a deviation fromthe norm. Even though his tendency to walk with his head down and shoulders slightly hunched was not calculated to attract the eye to him, indeed had probably been developed with the opposite effect in mind, people nonetheless registered the self-contained presence. Whenever I spotted some man walking, head up, shoulders back, I would find something in that posture to criticise — it was showy or conceited.

This is the thinking of someone newly fallen in love, I accepted, grimly. The thinking belonging to that period when the magical chemistry creates an aura around the beloved, attaches a set of significances to every move made by the loved one. Only those recently bereaved or those recently in love imagine constantly — as I was doing these last several months — that they see the loved one in a crowd, follow the imagined friend for a moment, then realise they are tracking a stranger. Even as they relinquish the imagined relationship, they nonetheless admire, in the stranger, the physical trait the stranger has in common — but crucially diminished — with the loved one. Lovely easy stride to that man, I would think. Not quite as rhythmic as the way David moves, but I bet he was a sportsman, too.

When you are newly in love, nothing exists except insofar as it relates to the person loved. Every clothes shop has a coat designed, unbeknown to the designer, to be worn by the loved one and only the loved one. Nobody else will quite do it justice. Every book carries a subtext understandable only by the reader and the reader's loved one. While to all others, the loved one may be no more than a good example of a given trait or talent, to the lover, they become the quintessence of that talent or trait, the measure by which all others may be found wanting. It seems self-abnegation to the lover: see how selflessly I worship and appreciate this unique person. In reality, though, it is a clever covert self-love, too; in admiring, we enable the other to be more than they are, so they owe to us their empowerment. We are rendered special by our capacity to see them as special.

A few years back, in this city, I had not seen David Carpenter as special. On the contrary, I had seen him as so normal that, back in Dublin and based on my depiction, Gabrielle had thought him dull. In those early meetings, he had been at such pains to barely dole out data, to eschew sweeping brush strokes of brilliant colour, not because he lacked those sweeps of vividness, and not because he believed he lacked them. Rather, because he was a refugee from recognition.

A man fulfilled at that point in his life, seeking to serve as quiet background to other lives.

CHAPTER TWENTY-FIVE

No Surrender

━━━━━►◆◄━━━━━

'Don't come into the bathroom. We have to take the film out of the camera,' Stephen instructed me, David winking over his head. I could hear a lesson in how to safely unwind a film going on in the dark bathroom. Then they came out and opened curtains everywhere, so that Gavin stirred and woke, as did the cats. Thing banged his head off the door, then nuzzled it.

'I think Stephen is right about you,' I told him. 'You're thick as a plank. The door hurt you, not you the door.'

My own voice woke me up. Narrow single bed. Chilly slivered dawn light. Paris. The dream was gone, leaving a black hole of recognised loneliness. I sat up, noting, absently, that I had been sleeping on a feather pillow. Without repercussions.

My asthma had virtually disappeared, although I had no idea why.

'There's a good thing,' I said aloud. 'There's something to be happy about.'

(Going through Dublin Airport, picking up a newspaper in Hughes & Hughes, I had noticed a tiny book with a title like *1,000 Things to be Happy About.*)

'How am I happy? Let me count the ways,' I told the Vermeer housewife in the print at the other end of the room. 'I've no asthma any more. Don't need rescuers. Stand on my own two lungs, I can. Good business, ready to grow. If I pushed myself – if I spent more time planning with Rita, we might win that Businesswoman of the Year award. Get champagne for life. I even own a house with no mortgage on it.'

And you own a car with no back bumper on it.

I sighed, attempting to climb back onto the mood I had been trying to create.

The car which is sitting in the Sigginses' front garden.

'The Sigginses won't mind. Nice people. Now, what else have I to be happy about? Two smashing boys. Stephen is witty and thoughtful. Gavin is fun. Plus, he's going to make money. Legally or illegally.'

Keeping him out of jail is the priority.

David, I knew, occasionally worried about Gavin's desire to sell items associated with David's fame. He might not know about the concept of sponsorship, but he had copped on that jumpers owned by famous people were saleable. David had caught him closing a sale and intervened. He had been very seriously concerned about it, too.

'I don't see what's the big issue,' I remembered saying to him. 'They sold Marilyn Monroe's dress from *Some Like it Hot.*'

'That was congruent with her life. She ate out the inside of herself until there was nothing left to sell except her clothes. And it was *The Seven Year Itch.*'

'Oh, yes, whatshisname the footballer she was married to at the time took a dim view of her showing her knickers in the scene over the grating.'

'Baseballer.'

'You'd have thought he'd be bloody glad to see she had knickers. According to everything I've read about her, knickers and Monroe were not synonymous.'

'Di Maggio.'

'"Where have you gone, Joe Di Maggio—"' I sang.

'He hated that song,' David said. 'Using his name as a sales point.'

'I thought it was very romantic, the way he used to send roses to her grave every week,' I said.

'Even though she had left him because he was so dull,' David said.

I wondered, now, if his comment had carried references to us that I had missed at the time.

The sliver of light from the window was brightening. No way was I going to get back to sleep. Because it was an old-fashioned hotel, there was no coffee-making equipment in the bedroom. I prowled the room, hungry. I could not remember eating anything the previous day. There was a plastic bottle of Evian water and I remembered a bar of chocolate bought in the airport. When I took it off the wardrobe shelf, one end of it was frayed.

'*Les souris*,' I muttered. 'I have one miserable bar of chocolate, and they eat it.'

I ate squares off the un-nibbled end, drinking water. Everything I touched, everything I did evoked some recollection. It struck me now that I had been surprised, some time previously, hearing David say to someone, 'Whenever I go to the States, I take a box of teabags with me. Hate the American teabags.'

'But what do I know?' I said aloud. 'He likes espresso, I know that. If he's going to drink coffee, that's what he likes. Does he prefer dark or milk chocolate? I don't know. If I was doing a school report on myself, I'd have to write Must Try Harder. Of course, school reports always assume there's going to be another year, another chance.'

Leaden-legged, I dressed and left the hotel, walking along the Seine until I found myself close to the Louvre. Might as well go in and see if the original of my window-lit Vermeer woman is here, I thought, but could not find her. The first time I had ever enjoyed being at the Louvre was when he had brought me to an exhibition of paintings by his namesake David. The great action-filled naturalistic canvases one after another. Then the dead man, arm hanging, stiffening in the chilling bath water that had soothed his inflamed scaly skin. I had wanted to be unmoved by the unsubtly overt intent of the works, but ended up gaping, enthralled as a child.

Wandering now without further purpose, I found myself beside a sculpture of six monks in mourning. Pall-bearers. Hooded. Robed. Faceless. Anonymous. Subservient to an infinite sadness. The tourists rushed to the best-known attractions in the great museum, ignoring my six mourning monks because they did not appear in their popular guide books, therefore could not be of importance. In a quiet corner of a room the monks stood, poised to move to the side of a fresh-dug grave, their sorrowful dignity more moving than any display of grief. Early on, David, I thought, you showed me your namesake's Sabine Women, arms outflung in frenzied woe. Now, at the end of it, I would so wish to show you the ultimate contrast: this tableau of hushed affliction.

It was only when I noticed the respectful glances I was getting from tourists that I realised I had been weeping. Angry at the pointless sentimentality of it, I rubbed my sleeve across my eyes and headed back out to the sunshine, walking with one group of tourists, then trailing another, following wherever they led, so that I found myself in the wooded walk parallel to the Champs Élysées, resting a few moments on one of the wooden seats, looking at a gilded statue of an Egyptian Pharaoh.

Suddenly, the statue uncurled and stretched. I screamed. Other people in the shady walkway laughed. The Pharaoh bowed to me, turned its back and went back to being utterly still, facing the other way.

'Bloody street theatre,' I imagined David saying. 'Hate the shagging thing.'

He would probably hate this kind of street theatre most of all, I thought, walking again, passing another 'statue', this one white. They seemed to be tightly wrapped in some kind of stretch material, which probably helped them stay absolutely still. The purpose — if the exhibits had a purpose — seemed to be to attract viewers and then move, so the visitors laughed and put coins in the bowls at the foot of the pedestal on which each 'statue' stood. A terrified over-reaction like mine must be a bonus.

David would hate it because it would make him think of his friend Sammy Talbott, the former place-kicker frozen into a wheelchair by injury. Because of that connection, he would find nothing charming or witty about able-bodied people pretending to be so frozen. The only time he had been furious with Stephen was when the child imitated a mentally handicapped kid he had seen in the supermarket.

It was probably the sudden coming to life of the 'statue' that recreated the awful sense of being followed, observed, watched. I could not get away from the street theatre statues quickly enough, but even sitting at a café drinking coffee, I could not shake the dread Richelle Governey had induced in me, nor stop myself taking sudden glances around me to see if I could catch whoever I was convinced was watching me.

Some American visitor had left a *USA Today* on the chair beside me, turned to a page with a Sprint ad on it. Around the central slogan was a quarter page of white space. To distract myself, I wrote messages to myself on the white section.

Now she has realised I'm not in Dublin, what will Richelle Governey do? Will she go after the boys? I don't think so, but am I sure? Why am I not more afraid of that possibility? Is it because I believe she has found me here? Is that why I was so frightened of the moving statue? Because it seemed the shadowy dread following me had come to life? How mad is she? Will she go after David? No — if she was going to go after him, she could have done it — would have done it — before now. Why was she fired from his programme, anyway? Oh, Jesus, if the guards arrest her, that means a court case with me giving evidence. It will come out that David and I are separated because we will be by then. She will probably believe she did it. When she comes out of prison, if she gets a prison sentence, she will come after me again because now she knows it works. Probably there aren't long prison sentences, so she will come out quickly and be even angrier.

EARN FREQUENT FLYER MILES WITH THESE SPRING AIRLINE PARTNERS said the line at the bottom of the advertisement. I had run out of space. I folded the paper into a stick and twisted it, using it to give a poke to a ruby-footed pigeon who was scavenging around the legs of the café chairs. It fell near him, flurrying him into brief knee-high flight, but the attraction of the fallen food outweighed any threat it might hold for him. He came tittuping back.

By now, the sense of being watched was so oppressive I wanted to run, ideally into the traffic, away from people, out into the bright hot moving metal machines. It took real control to walk down towards Place de la Concorde instead. Now and again, I dodged around trees, standing on the circle of filigreed iron at their base to see if I could spot a pursuer. Once, I slid into a perfume store laid out like the old New York Automat, 'browsing' by walking along the displays, using their mirrors to observe the people around me. Nobody seemed to be taking much of an interest in me, yet I was sure — sure as I was that I would have a shadow in the bright sunlight — that someone was walking in pace with me, stopping when I did, sliding into anonymity in the crowded street.

Helen, I thought, I am sorry. You were not real to me when I did what I did to you. You were a cut-out when I was trying to find out what real life was like. I am sorry, and I am being punished, Helen. Punished by this pursuing presence that withers the fun and the hope out of me.

Coming out from the shadow of the perfume

store awning into the eye-closing hot sunshine, I had a sudden flash of memory: a piece of footage showing David Carpenter in his younger days. It was taken on the field by one of those early video cameras which adjusted too slowly to radical changes in light saturation. Carpenter had run from summer sunshine into the black shade cast by a stand, and for moments had (visually) ceased to exist, only the results of his actions seen in the bright section of the field. I had met him at a point in his life which mirrored that video extinction, happening on him as he ran into darkness. Later, the lens would adjust and he would be seen again, but back then he was content to watch from the shadows, to effect but be uncredited. The human contradiction to the old PR axiom about doing good and getting credit for it.

At fifteen, I'd learned how easy it is to deflect people from taking an interest in oneself. Yet I had never noticed this man using that same skill on me. Here in this city.

It was not that he was secretive. There was no concealment. No question, asked, that went unanswered. Each question had been honestly answered, but none had made him do more than share small aspects of himself. Like a pointillist painter, he had laid down the tiny spots, one by one, until they had cumulatively become the portrait which I had zealously ignored. Like a bag lady who paints a Cupid's-bow mouth on her half a century after the lips the Cupid's-bow once fitted have shrivelled, shrunk and corrugated, I kept to my first impression of him.

Kept to it. Even valued and appreciated it. Except that I had poured appreciation into only two discrete scan-sliced aspects of the man. Had found him kind. Generous. Loving to the boys. Admirable and admired, his good deeds had been remembered and mentioned to others in much the same tone as one uses when recounting the kindness of strangers. The friendship was valued, too. Cherished as the kind of casual alliance more typical of two men who journey from boarding school through college to careers and companionship. The friendship that served as catalyst, the listening so casually given that as I talked to him, without comment from him, I sorted priorities and learned what it was I really believed.

That friendship, dead, would be the worst loss.

Passion lost would be a fading bruise, an occasional aching hunger. On the face of it, we were sexually mismatched, my appetite greater than his. And yet — until the recent months — that mismatch had served us well, my need building so that when he would stand back from me with that frankly considering look to him, then quietly begin to finger the buttons of my dress or cup my breast through a T-shirt, my breathing would be a noisy giveaway. Just thinking about it, in a distant city, walking among the backpackers, passing the map-scrutineers on every corner, brought on a lust so exigent I was minded to lean against a tree, eyes closed, to imagine what it had been like with him. And afterwards, the quiet shared wakefulness, the cooling skin, the touches of comfort and belonging.

An end to that would take me a long time to learn. But nobody has ever died from loss of passion. Loss of friendship, on the other hand, would drain and dry out the spirit, carve hard bright smiles into my face to conceal the privation.

I am making myself into an expert commentator on loss, I thought, trying to drum up an alternative course of action. None seemed credible. How does one apologise for failure to notice the best of a man, for assuming the worst of a man, for bringing on him the humiliation of asking someone to whom he has given an intensely private gift to – in effect – send an acknowledgement of that gift to a total stranger? I must, I thought, write to Victoria. She should know that David would never have put her through writing that letter to me unless ... For a moment, I wondered hopefully:

why would he have got the letter from her unless he loved me?

Too quickly came the realisation that it was more likely to have been done because he left nothing unfinished. He rarely talked about his parents, but I knew that after the death of his mother, he barely kept in touch with his father, and then only to provide an almost formal support system.

I have already relinquished the relationship, I thought. These days are a watershed between what I had and will have. Like Esmé, I am in mourning for my life. I am sitting shiva for the hundreds of tendrils linking me to a man I did not know I loved, tendrils curled like sweet pea growing to a trellis. I grieve for the diminutive daily reassurances. Significant only in retrospect are those half-winks delivered deadpan as my car drives up, him standing at the kitchen window, hand reaching out of sight, automatically, to turn on the switch so that when I gather my belongings, lock the car, alarm it and arrive in the kitchen, the kettle would already be snoring into action.

And at night, when he would first turn out the light, then sit on the edge of the bed. In the sudden darkness, I would hear the staccato wasp noise of him winding the watch his parents had given him for a twenty-first birthday present. It was a ritual with him, this watch-winding. Always in the dark. Always sitting on the edge of the bed, before the balance of the bed would shift as he got in beside me, letting out a small wordless sound of satisfaction when all the bedclothes were circled warm around him.

I could not remember being haunted thus by evocative minutiae after the death of my family, but perhaps I had too little time after the tragedy to observe the traces, absorbed as I was with the boys. Now I had the poisonous luxury of walking through my virtual life and finding that at every point, in every room, in each of the most mundane tasks, this almost invisible man had left a mark as unique as fingerprints on glass. None of them grandiose. Some of them merely idiosyncratic. Cranky. He would never, for example, use the dishwasher, so there would always be three or four bits of crockery handwashed when he came home before me, and he would dry them, tossing the teatowel on to his shoulder while he did other tasks.

It was strange, I thought, that, having failed to notice so much about him, I had nevertheless developed a mental directory of his every distinctive move, whether it was putting three spoons of sugar in his tea, stirred as if he had found sugar to be resistant and needing to be bullied into assimilation, or forcing lumpy butter onto bread in unspreadable lumps rather than give the butter twenty seconds in the microwave.

His sneezes frightening, like a deliberate shout. His big hands gentling the ears of the cats so they sat, eyes closed in the pleasure of his caresses, then when he released them, shaking their heads until the ears flicked back to normal position. The muscular legs of him in summer, tanned so that the old football injury scars stood out in pale relief, each carrying a story. Stephen and Gavin knew each and every one of the stories, yet nagged him to repeat them, the way you long to hear a favourite song replayed.

I had been walking faster and faster, so I was almost breathless. Strange, I thought, how habit takes us back, unthinking, to the same places. I was now opposite the statue of the lion atop the pillar at one side of Place de la Concorde. Where I had first met David.

Once, in school, Stephen had been asked what animal his father would be, were David to be an animal. Without hesitation, he had instantly said a lion.

'Lazy but vicious,' was his explanation.

At the time, I had rejected the description. Now, I knew its truth. A master of easy inaction, David Carpenter never made a redundant move, never wasted even a gesture. If action was not called for, he would languish in slow-blinking torpor. But always, within that inertia, the threat of instant swift wakefulness, fleet of foot, fierce in lacerating efficacy. Lazy but vicious.

I walked more carefully across the cobbles fanning out in semi-circles; stony lace patterns repeated right across the great square. In this open place, I thought, I might catch sight of the presence I believed was following me. I circled one of the black pillars, pretending to examine its gilded detail, always giving the impression of having been painted just minutes before. At the same time, I glanced covertly to either side. Purposeful Parisians, purposeless tourists. No familiar or threatening face, no figure shrugging away from being seen, ducking a face into an upturned collar.

Weary of the fruitless search, weary too from the walking, I moved to one of the white cement bollards marking off the parking area, sitting down on one of the row of them as if it was a stool, arms on knees, forehead on forearms, circling traffic noise loud in my ears.

How appropriate, came the bitter thought. A place of execution, where they had dragged the aristocrats, one tumbril after another delivering its consignment of prison-pale nobles to the foot of the guillotine. Beneath the fanned cobbles, to this day, might be a deep layered stripe of blood-red soil, like the band of black beneath modern London left by the Great Fire when it raged through that city.

In a sense, I was in the aftermath of an execution, having willed the death of a relationship without understanding it. The bleak truth was that what bound me to this man was not one great rope, but a thousand unnoticed ties, feather-fragile. I had severed them on impulse, not fully aware of them. Here I am, I thought, among the frayed fragments. Loose threads a-flap in the leftovers from something undervalued.

Empty-handed.

I pushed my hands out in front of me, wide open. Unadorned except for the broad flat wedding band: one of the two that had gone flying off the cushion in the registry office when Stephen tripped. I wondered if David still wore his, and the realisation that I didn't know, had not noticed, crushed me down into a weeping crouch, hands hanging at the end of straightened arms, head bowed so the tears dropped navy blots on the blue cloth of my trousers. The blots seeped and spread, joined circles of darkened, chilling misery.

For a second, I thought a dog was nuzzling my right hand, then realised that my hand was being closed around the cold glass of a bottle.

I lifted my head, dazed. He was on his hunkers in front, looking up at me. Expressionless.

'If you drop that Coke bottle, when I've carried it around Paris for two days, you're in serious trouble.'

He straightened up, rubbing the small of his back with his knuckles, automatically altering his stance in order to block the sun from my face.

'You were following me. It was you who was following me.'

It came out so low and shaky I did not think he would hear it, but could see his head nodding, silhouetted against the sky. Pulling something out of a back pocket, he sat down on the bollard next to me, turning me to face him, my knees almost touching his. The thing he had pulled out of the pocket was a twisted roll of newsprint. The newspaper I had left with the fat rosy-footed pigeon.

'I knew someone was following me. I was frightened. I was so frightened.'

It came out of me in a near-scream of relief.

'Ah, Daisy,' he said softly, his hand to my cheek. 'Ah, Daisy, I'm sorry.'

I turned into the hand, boiling tears wetting the palm, clutching it with my own.

'Never meant to frighten you, Daisy,' he said.

Over the sound of my own snuffling, I could hear

him root in a pocket, then flap a hanky loose from its ironed folds before pushing it into my grasp – first taking the bottle out of my hand and setting it on the ground.

'Clean hankies on demand. Bottles of Coke. Your every need catered for,' he said. 'What would you do without me?'

What I have been doing for the last few days, I thought, rattling around a dark cold tin-rattling cage. Dry-mouthed, I reached for the bottle and drank before speaking.

'I apologise for reading your letter.'

'So you shagging well ought to.'

He patted my hand in an oddly contradictory way. 'Carried its own punishment, I imagine.'

I nodded, dumbly, trying to keep my chin from wobbling like that of a chastened child. He reached across the gap between us to bump the wet away from under my eyes with the arch of his wrist.

'You said I was beneath contempt,' I protested, lest I was being forgiven under false pretences.

'No, I said reading the letter was beneath contempt,' he said. 'And it was.'

Miserably confused, I sat on the chilly stone, revisiting despair.

'Daisy?'

'Mmm?'

'Very few of us get through life without doing a few things that are beneath contempt. I figure you're not planning to do one a day for the rest of your life?'

I shook my head.

'Good. Because two's enough.'

'Two?'

His gesture at himself drew attention to the fact that he was wearing unfamiliar clothes.

'I forgive you,' he said formally. 'For locking two cats for at least twenty-four hours in my side of the wardrobe.'

'Oh, Jesus, you're not serious? I didn't know they were there. They must have been asleep—'

'Well, when they woke up, they must have been hellish rested, because you wouldn't think any two cats could claw and crap and chew as much as Thing and Other Thing did. The time Gavin peed in the wardrobe had nothing on this. I'll never forget it. Had to burn almost everything and buy new stuff.'

'Where are they? Now? The cats, I mean?'

'The two of them are in corrective detention in Oliver's father's boarding kennels. The two boys are learning horse-riding from Robert Allen's daughter Caoimhe, God help her.'

It was as if we were locked in the eye of a hurricane.

The traffic was approaching rush hour, the frequency of beeps increasing, the time individual cars were held stationary getting longer, their drivers looking at the two of us for nothing better to look at.

'What did you tell the boys?'

'That their mother had gone ahead of me to get settled in to Paris for our second honeymoon.'

'*What?*'

He shrugged, palms out: what else could he have said? The move reminded him of something and he flipped the left arm to see his wristwatch.

'Got to make a phone call in about ten minutes.'

He scoped the area until he found a public phone within sight.

'How did you know I would have gone to Paris?'

'Rang Blue Cabs. Correction. Rang Blue Cabs after coping with Mrs McDermott's broken hip, Robert Allen's private detective, a marathon session with the cops, a fumigation and destruction exercise resulting from Thing and Other Thing's incarceration, a phone call from your business partner and a visit from a mystified Ger Siggins who was mildly curious as to why you should have abandoned your car in his front garden. Thanks for marking my card on all these things.'

He went on to reassure me that the boys had neither

caused nor been frightened by Mrs McDermott's fall downstairs, and that their grandmother was in better shape than might be expected. The fall had happened after he had collected them to take them to Robert Allen's house, where they were due to spend a few days learning to ride the pony.

'Very shortly after I arrived at the Allens' house, I indicated I wanted a private word with Robert. Told him my wife was missing, no forwarding address, and that since he had a special relationship with her, if he knew where she was and if he knew what was good for him, he'd tell me awful fast.'

I didn't know whether to laugh or cry at the image this evoked.

'He told me to get fucked.'

'Robert did?'

'Robert did. Said I was a self-righteous shit that had colluded with a sick bimbo who'd been stalking my wife since my wife was a little girl. Colluded by accepting crap I'd been peddled about his wife's relationship with him. Allowed the bimbo to do damage, not just to his wife – my wife – you, I mean,' David said, '––but to do damage also to Helen, who was a complete frigging innocent bystander. He further said if I was worth a shite it would be me, not him, that had my house ringed with private detectives and because he had ringed my house with private detectives, he at least could tell me the bimbo hadn't attacked or kidnapped my wife, that my wife had got out of the house under her own steam before dawn.

'The night you donated your car to Ger Siggins, Allen's detectives were watching. They couldn't make head nor tail of what you were doing, but they didn't have to. She was the one they were watching, gathering stuff on. And by Jesus did they know about her. They knew her every move. They knew what she'd eaten, when she'd eaten it, where she'd eaten it. Where she'd slept and for how long. So, when I got back to our house, I had a—'

'Hang on. Go back. When did you first encounter Richelle?'

'Production meeting. Three, four months back? She's filling in for one of the PAs who's on maternity leave. Competent. Eager. Eager to tell me she's been a fan of my wife since they were both so high. Watched my wife grow in beauty and ability down through the years. Learned so much from my wife.'

I closed my eyes and let my head sink down again, sickened.

'Then she gets hyper-helpful. Messages to you from me, messages to me from you. I never lock my dressing room door. Notice a couple of minor things missing. Not necessarily expensive, but personal – very identifiable as mine. Then this letter with a photocopy of air tickets gets left on my dressing-room worktop. You and Robert in Greece. Yeah, I threw that one at you. Why? Why'd I go along with that crap? (Jesus, I must watch the time. I have to make that phone call.) I go along with it because I can see we're drifting. Maybe this is an explanation. Easier than acknowledging I'm in another Hallie situation.'

I shook my head frantically.

'OK. Not an excuse. Shouldn't have. Except when I did, oh, Daisy, the reaction.'

'Of course you got a reaction, you thick. You got a reaction because I knew nobody in the world but me, Robert and the temp who'd bought the tickets knew details like the hotel room. I was immediately trying to figure out why a temp would set out to do me such damage—'

He was standing in front of me again, tipping my head up to look at him.

'Daisy.'

'Yeah?'

'If I go over there to make that phone call, will you stay here?'

'Where would I go?'

'Will you stay here?'

'Yes.'

He ran the hundred yards to the phone, one hand pulling his jacket closed in front. Throughout the call, he was mostly silent. Nodding a number of times. Asking a few questions. Fiercely concentrated. Business, I thought. You can't just drop everything and head off to Paris if you're David Carpenter. The devil is in the details.

When the call finished, he stood for a long time where he had been during the conversation. Then turned to come back towards the line of bollards. Walking very slowly this time. Head down, hands deep in trouser pockets, bunching the tweed jacket.

'Is everything OK?'

He sat down and did his characteristic thing of wiping his face with his open hand.

'OK might be putting it a tad strongly.'

'Oh, Jesus, what's happened now?'

'Nothing you have to worry about. I'll get to it. I'll get to it.'

A few days after he had thrown the dates of the visit to Greece at me, he went on, Chelle (as she now called herself) had made some comment which made it inescapably clear that she was the person who had left the information for him.

'She always over-reached herself,' I nodded. 'In

a sense, she has never been bright enough for her own evil.'

'The producer asked her, before that night's show, if she'd meet him and me afterwards in my dressing room. He wanted to have a word with her about joining the team permanently. And to cover another matter. She was ecstatic. Came around to the dressing room just after I've removed my make-up. There's a bottle of champagne in a cooler, three glasses. Producer says we want her help. That she's a lot younger than many people on the programme, shown that she wants to give 110 per cent, gone out of her way, blah, blah. We want her view on something. Anything, she says. I slide two letters in front of her and ask her if she sees any stylistic giveaways to the fact that they were written by the same author. One of the letters is the Greek trip letter. The other is one you received three days after your family was wiped out on the airport road.'

'Where did that come from?'

'My files,' he said flatly.

The PA was shocked into overreaction by the realisation that any talk that was going to happen about permanent membership of the production team was going to be negative. David talked quietly about the need whoever wrote these letters had for psychiatric care. She screamed at the two men. A security guard arrived at a run. She took off and that was the last time they saw her.

It was only when the police were later questioning David about the possibility of something or someone ratcheting up Richelle Governey's hatred for me that he realised producing the letters might not have been a good idea.

'She undoubtedly assumed the old letter had been given to me by you, probably saved by you down through the years and produced by you when it could be useful against her,' he said. 'So now – given her mad logic – you've lost her another great career possibility. Time to come home to Dublin and do some dedicated, one to one, personalised, no-messing stalking.'

I shuddered.

'Robert came back to the house with me, called in the guys he had hired. They were briefing me when the cops arrived and added their twopenceworth.'

'*Allez vite, les flics,*' I said, trying to laugh.

'You'll be charmed to know you don't have to *allez vite*. I scotched their suspicions of you.'

'Of me as what?' I asked, reaching down for the Coke bottle, warm, now, against the cobbles.

'As *agent provocateur*. Accident-causer.'

The sounds of traffic welled up into the lengthy silence.

'This is a "no comment" situation, is it? Hmm. They believe you drove the long straight stretch of the dual carriageway after the turnoff for Skerries at about a hundred miles an hour in order to get Richelle Governey to go equally fast, and then slammed on your brakes to make her run into the back of your car. I asked them would a mother of two little boys do anything so brainlessly reckless? I also speculated aloud as to whether that wasn't more the kind of thing a fella would do, rather than a girl. Bit of sexism always helps. Then I asked innocently if they had a witness or something concrete that would help them. Bottom line: you're safe to return to your country of domicile without fear of being charged with what I have no doubt you actually did.'

I told him the story of the phone calls and the silent car, parked four doors away. It gave him the final links. The Gardaí had told him the outline of it, he explained, and he had filled them in on what he knew.

'Daisy, this sounds like we're playing a new board game: Apology. I'm sorry I didn't tell you how Governey got fired. It would have helped if you'd known more.'

I finished the Coke. He consigned the bottle to the garbage container. I balled up the damp hanky and poked it into his pocket.

'They hadn't caught up with her the night I came home. But they were very confident they would. I was telling them about your missing car when Ger Siggins arrived, and we had a sort of round table guessing game as to why you'd left it in his garden. Figured it had something to do with Governey. The cops had a look at it before they went off (not that they could judge, it was dark by that stage) then I drove it back to our place. Which was when the calls started.'

He had picked up the phone but said nothing.

'Why didn't you say anything?'

'I was hoping she'd seen the car driving back into our garden and figured you, rather than me, were the driver, and so thought you were back in the house. I didn't want her to know it was me. I very gently put the receiver down. Told Robert to let the local cop shop know where she was. Got into my black tracksuit and went out the back gate. Circled so I came into our street from the other end and there she was, sitting in the car parked away from the street lamp, holding the mobile phone.'

Before she had time to see more than a moving shadow, David was in the car with her, taking the keys out of the ignition and central-locking the car. The windows were half-rolled down, but not far enough for her to get out through.

'I wouldn't move if I was you, Chelle,' he said, very softly. 'This is what's called a citizen's arrest. The Gardaí are on their way to charge you with stalking. They already have a full statement from Dominique, from Robert Allen and from me. Plus witnesses who saw you leaving the scene of an accident. In the few seconds before they get here, I just wanted to make one thing clear to you. My wife is beside herself with fear of you. She's had that fear for more than ten years. Too long, Chelle. Too long. I've woken her from a lot of nightmares. Those nightmares can be traced right back to you. Fear like that won't go away easily. My wife will be waiting for when you come out of prison. When you do get out, Chelle, if I were you I wouldn't think – not even for a minute – of frightening her again. Because if you do frighten or hurt her again, I will kill you. Simple as that.'

'That's enough of that, Mr Carpenter,' a voice said behind him as a hand came down on his shoulder. The guards had arrived. Richelle Governey screamed, crying to the police officers that David had attacked her.

'Bit difficult to attack you with his hands in his pockets,' the female one muttered.

'I'll tell in court that you threatened my life!' Governey screamed at David as he unlocked the car and slid backwards out on to the pavement. 'The media will know!'

'Good,' David said.

'For God's sake,' one of the cops said to David. 'What's wrong with you, threatening her like that? If she calls on any of us as witnesses, we have to confirm that you did it.'

'Good,' David said.

'You don't want OTT stuff like that appearing in the media,' the policeman said, reasonably.

David stood with the guard and watched as Richelle Governey was led towards the squad car, then favoured him with a huge smile.

'Please tell the guys in both cars how much I appreciate their speed in responding to my call,' he said, taking the keys to her car out of his pocket and tossing them so they landed noisily on the bonnet of her car, skittering across its surface to the officer standing beside it.

'What will you say if you're in the court case and they ask you about threatening her?' I asked when he went silent at the end of the account. He looked surprised.

'That I did it.'

'Threatened to kill her?'

'Yeah.'

'David, the damage that would do to your career.'

'Dominique, I'm not sure you understand. I don't give a flying fuck about my career. Never did. If I have to make a living tomorrow digging roads, I'll dig roads and be just as happy as I am consulting or commentating. If the papers pick up and repeat my threat – great. Because maybe seeing it in print will make her realise I mean it. Us, the kids – that's all there is. All that matters. She comes near you again, or near the boys, I will kill her.'

'You don't really mean tha—'

'Dominique.'

'Yes.'

'Let me tell you something. Remember I said I talked to Blue Cabs? Right. They locate the guy who drove you and he rings me back. Yes, he knew your final destination – not only did you tell the guy, because he asked you, where you were going, but you asked him to drive the oddest route to the airport ever. He said it was like a bad spy movie, no offence. "Lookin' out the back window she was, the whole time, checkin' were we bein' followed, you know? She all right, Dave? No offence, I thought she was a bit dawny lookin'." No taxi driver is ever going to see you again in that kind of panic. Nobody is. And if the administration of justice doesn't prevent it, I will.'

He pulled me to my feet and stuffed my hand into his pocket along with his. Walking brought us to the pavement surrounding one of the fountains. It was quite difficult to get close to the fountain because of banked sets of metal barricades nested on their sides, waiting to be set up around the Place to control the crowds on Bastille Day the following week. I sat down on the rim of the fountain. He looked at the figures of mermaids and fishes in its bowl. Not seeing them.

'When I was a very small kid, my father now and then would stop being the good bank manager and beat the living crap out of my mother. Not often. Once, twice a year. At one point he was based in Cork, which is where my ma is from. At some point in the Cork sojourn, he knocked hell out of her. It was just his bad luck that one of her six brothers dropped in the next day and reacted to the visible bruises by interrogating her. It was just his bad luck that the brother didn't believe her story. It was just his very bad luck that the brother brought the other five around that night and established beyond any possibility of doubt that they would break every bone in his body if he did it again. In all the years we were there, he never did. Later, in Britain, he began to regress. Beat her, then tell her he loved her.'

It had begun to drizzle, very lightly. He turned his face up to the soft damp, eyes closed, the fountain noise flowing into the silence between us. He lowered his head and looked into the dirty darkness of the water at its base, smiling a humourless smile and enjoying the memory that evoked it.

'Wasn't too long before he was more afraid of me than he ever had been afraid of her brothers,' he said. 'Long as he was afraid, the mad bad side of him stayed dormant.'

I watched him, silently.

'Not going to arise, anyway,' he said grimly. 'She's dying.'

'Dying? Does she have a brain tumour or something?'

'No. According to Robert—' he gestured at the phone where he had made his call '—the guards got her into court. Charged her. She was released on own recognisances, went back to her apartment, took a shit-load of paracetamol tablets and ended up in Beaumont Hospital. Didn't take quite enough to kill her straight away. But she will not survive the week. Organ damage.'

'Oh, Jesus.'

The two of us stood in silence, my hands, for balance, on his shoulders. After quite a while, he looked up at me.

'You're sorry.'

'Well, of course.'

'I'm not.'

'You wouldn't wish a painful death—'

'On anyone. But I'm not sorry she's dying. She was no good to herself or anybody else.'

I started to argue.

'Daisy. Let's agree to differ on this one. I'm for taking out the ones who are dangerous, venomous bastards without a good bone in them. Always had a great admiration for Stauffenberg.'

'Who—'

'Guy who brought the bomb in the briefcase to take out Hitler. Anyway, I'm not going to have to kill her, but if we're going to stay married, Daisy, you'd better factor into your understanding of me that I would. Never told you a lie, never going to.'

'David, I'm surprised to hear you talking about us in the future tense. I kind of felt "us" was past tense.'

'Did you want it to be past tense?'

'No. But there was that kind of drift. Even – you haven't made love to me in months. Although if you

never made love to me at all, it could still be "us".
I just thought, OK, we're both changing and us as a
couple was really a device same as you'd use to get a
passport, so there shouldn't be any recriminations if
at a later stage it turns into something different.'

I gestured that I was finished. He narrowed his
eyes, head cocked sideways, going through what I had
just said.

'We got married to get a passport?'

'No, but you know the way people do.'

'Yes, but what was the equivalent for us?'

'You made sure the kids would be adopted and
have stability and stuff.'

'Oh, my arse,' he said impatiently.

'Mine is wet,' I said without thinking.

'What?'

'My arse. There's too much water in this fountain.
Waves have been lapping at my rear.'

Without warning, he lifted me so I was standing
above him on the flat rim of the fountain and turned
me round to inspect the sodden patch at the back of
my trousers and jacket. The bowl of the fountain
was filled with sea gods carrying fishes, each fish
spewing a column of water into the air. Except for
the fish nearest me, whose open mouth wasn't spewing
anything. One silent, screaming fish. I turned on the

smooth, wet edge of the pool and steadied myself with hands on his shoulders, looking down at him. Meeting the same unwavering gaze as when he had told me, in this same city, not to make more of reality than was in it.

I tried to explain that, in wanting to make more of reality than was in it, I had missed the point of what we had been. I had missed the minutiae of affection, mislaid the significance of actions bespeaking attachment. Anticipative of a lightning stroke of passion, I had not known for what it was the steady-pulsed daily devotion that, withdrawn, left a neutral darkness of infinite loneliness.

He waited until he was sure I had nothing more to say. Then he walked away, rubbing the back of his neck. Maybe looking up at me had given him a crick.

'D'you remember when Gavin glued himself shut?'

The question came at me, almost thrown over his shoulder from where he stood at the edge of the pavement, hands jammed into trouser pockets.

'Yes.'

'You said a thing about zebras.'

'When you hear hoofbeats, think horses before zebras.'

'Might be useful if you learned it.'

He walked back around the fountain slowly, hands playing with small change in his pockets. Stopped in front of me.

'I meet you here—' He gestured towards the pavilion where the asthma attack had struck me down. 'Take you home. Write to you. Ring you. Date you in spite of constantly being told to eff off or get stuffed. Follow you back to Ireland, marry you – and you think all of this was to give stability to orphans? Daisy, my beloved, not only are you full of shit, you're full of zebra shit. If you can't come to terms with the obvious explanation, we should have called your company The Headbanger, not The Skywriter.'

He lifted me down and began to move quickly towards the intersection, conscious of a surge of traffic about to be unleashed by the traffic lights.

'David. Do you love me?'

He halted, right there in the middle of the road, turned to me, folded his arms. A wasp-yellow Renault screeched to a halt, stopping a line of cars behind it.

'Daisy, hear this and hear it well, because I'll not say it again. I will not make love to you to prove anything to you or about me. I'll make love, same as anything else I do with you, when the context is right, not to order. I will not ever act as you want me to act or as your sister would have liked me to act. But above all, I will not be blackmailed into articulating any particular formula of words. At any time. By you or by anybody else. The answer to your question is to be found in every day of our lives since the day I met you here. Not writ large in the sky. Not skywriting. Writ small. In my handwriting. It's there. In every day of every week of every month. If you can't read it, that's your problem.'

The cars began to beep. In his own time, he got us to the pavement, starting towards an outdoor café which had been a favourite of ours, years before. The coffee-drinkers seated in the steel chairs on the pavement watched this encounter avidly.

'I want to say something to you,' I said.

'You can say it sitting down.'

'No, I can't. It's important.'

He halted and saluted extravagantly, indicating total attention.

'I just never appreciated how essential you have become to me,' I said haltingly. 'How lost I am without you, how complete I felt the moment you were beside me back there.'

'I grow on people,' he said lightly, and it enraged me.

'I *love* you, for Chrissake,' I yelled at him. 'I loved

you then and I love you now. I didn't tell you before, Jaysus alone knows why, and you may not want to be jumpstarted into telling me you love me, but I *do* love you. I'll probably regret telling you now, but I love you. That's all there is to it and if you want to get cool and ironic and smartarse about it you can just shag off sideways.'

There was a stir of laughter and approval from the gathered audience. He bowed to them, then bent to put his face so close to mine that they could not hear him.

'Took you frigging long enough to realise it,' he said quietly. 'For a bright woman, you're an awful slow learner. Now, what are the chances we could move down from this high level of drama and just get on with it?'

'Get on with what?' I asked, not quite whispering in response. But nearly.

'Our second honeymoon.'

'Are we talking a quick bonk, here?'

'Well, you know me. A quick one is all I'm good for.'